The Manor on Orchid Lane

Aubrey Taylor, Rowan Stone

Book Cover by Catarina Cruz

Editing and Proof Reading by Becky Clapham

Illustrations by Aubrey Taylor

First Edition 2024

Contents

To all the oldest daughters

Family don't end with blood.

Green Eyes – JOSEPH
The Matrix - Mother Mother
Bruises – Lewis Capaldi
This Must Be The Place - Kishi Bashi
Young and Beautiful (Violin) - Dramatic Violin
LABOUR (the cacophony) - Paris Paloma
What Kind Of Man - Florence + The Machine
Dangerous Indeed - Rare Creatures
Who's Afraid of Little Old Me? - Taylor Swift
Famous Last Words – My Chemical Romance
The Fire – Vincent Lima
I'm On Your Side – The Glorious Sons

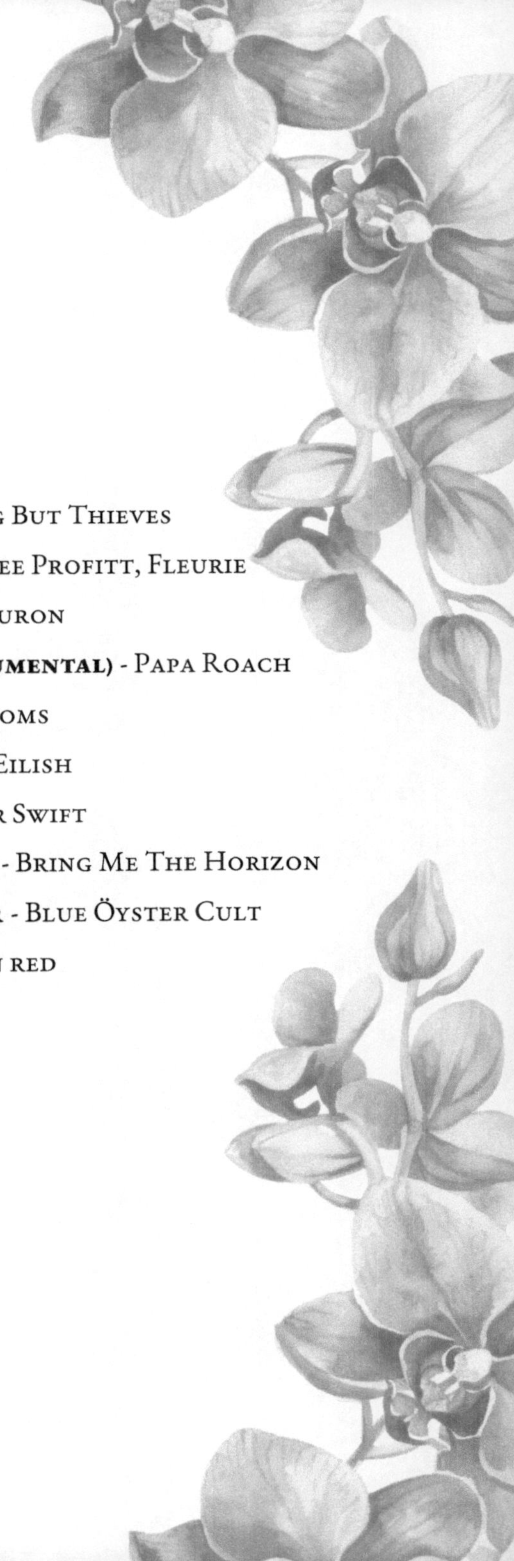

Neon Brother - Nothing But Thieves

Hurts Like Hell – Tommee Profitt, Fleurie

Way Out There - Lord Huron

Leave a Light on (Instrumental) - Papa Roach

Bad Things – The Phantoms

THE GREATEST – Billie Eilish

Don't Blame Me - Taylor Swift

Can You Feel My Heart - Bring Me The Horizon

(Don't Fear) The Reaper - Blue Öyster Cult

Body And Mind – girl in red

All – Snow Patrol

Blood/Gore

Self Harm/Suicide (talks of suicide and assisted death)

Violence

Supernatural/Paranormal conversations and monsters

Domestic Violence

Abortion (In conversation only)

Open-door Sex (with multiple partners)

Crude language

Take breaks, get some water, snuggle your loved ones and pets.

Be kind to yourself, being a human being is tough.

Orchid Lane lay dormant under a thick cloak of fog that outstretched like fingers grasping for purchase along the expansive grounds. Unlike in many other parts of rural Ireland, where the mist ebbed and flowed and rolled along the countryside, there it hung heavy and suffocating. It felt almost as if the mist itself was leaking from the Manor, its sole purpose to conceal and misdirect.

The estate was large and imposing, a three-story stone masterpiece so thickly covered in ivy that, at a glance, most would believe it to be derelict; though beneath the vines, the stones remained stubbornly in place. The surrounding gardens were extensive, twisting in labyrinths that enticed visitors to wander in with the heady scents of white clover and foxglove, along with many other wildflowers that grew abundantly throughout the untended gardens.

An ornate wrought iron gate hung slightly off-kilter as it peeked out from overgrown and unruly shrubs that concealed the rest of the fence that barricaded the Manor and its plentiful acreages; until it disappeared beneath the heavy fog that surrounded the house. The gravel road leading up to the house ended at an oversized porch with columns that held an open terrace above the extravagant wooden door.

Even on clear days light never seemed to fully permeate its walls. It was always somewhat in shadow, always slightly too cold. There was a sense of *other* here. Of wrong. The countryside Manor stood along the outskirts of a bustling city of high society. Ever present and foreboding for generations. So old, no one ever really wondered when or how the house came to be in the first place. It just always was.

So it remained.

PART ONE

It had been too long since brightness and wonder had filled the halls. The woman grew listless and fatigued, complacent to remain in one room for weeks, months at a time, barely moving. Becoming another fixture in the space she inhabited. While everything around her was restless, shifting and changing to no avail.

So it began. Her youth, once vibrant and ever preserved, began to leach from her being, leaving spoiled wit and blemished skin behind—no longer even an echo of who she had been. Almost as if in retaliation for no longer being interesting, the sickness crept in, both of body and mind. She was not something to be enthralled with, not something worth holding and keeping. She was not enough.

The air felt suffocating, gravity pulling harder and making every movement that much more difficult than it had ever been. Her twisted fingers, bent with untold age, shook as she completed the letter. She took her time to fold the parchment in half and then in half again, giving her final words as much care as she could muster. One last time she lifted the quill to address the front of the note:

Florence.

FLORENCE

I forced myself not to fall into a daydream as my husband, Lord Cabot, continued to yell at our new dining staff about the apples added to his porridge. The poor girl was shaking, clearly trying not to cry, and flinched with each hand gesture that waved too closely by her. *Good instinct.*

At this rate, she would quit before our Cook even decided what to make for lunch. I both pitied and envied her. *At least you can leave.* The bitter thought bubbled to the surface before I could control myself.

The only saving grace to the ostentatious dining table was that I was not within grabbing distance when he began his trivial fits of rage. The slightest inconveniences triggered his temper, and he would spend all of breakfast berating the innocent, mousey girl for doing her job and delivering the food. I forcibly swallowed a sigh and looked out of the window. The city's busy streets were bustling, and I ached for the rolling hills upon which I had been raised.

With a slow inhale, I could close my eyes and picture in detail the farmland in the countryside outside of a small county—my childhood home, so near yet so far. The smell of blooming trees and the tall wheat waving in the breeze. I yearned for the simple days of being nothing more than a farm girl.

Despite what others believed was a homely upbringing, I had always been a voracious reader and thinker. I was the pride of my Father who, at every opportunity, taught me about the goings-on of the wildlife on our farm. I could birth a foal alone by the age of twelve. I spent most days waking early, helping with the daily chores, problem-solving missing sheep, engineering fences, and nursing sick animals back to health. Most evenings I spent content, reading by lamplight. But my Father had always wanted bigger things for me. When my mother passed in the childbirth of a sibling I was never to meet, she had made him promise not to keep me at the farm all my life. So, when I turned eighteen, regardless of my contempt for the idea, he began to take me into the county for social visits and salons to keep his promise.

It was there that I was introduced to Lord Cabot. When we first met, he had always referred to himself as Matthew and had appeared to be a sweet, pragmatic man. He arrived in the county briefly and impressed my Father with his title and seemingly strong morals. He charmed me with his smile and what I believed then to be shyness. Somehow, he had hidden his true self from us both. What I mistook for shyness was aloofness, and morals were always strongly inflated in his favor. I had fallen in love with the idea of him, his dark brown eyes and curly hair but, over the five years since we wed, I came to understand how foolish I had been to put my faith in a man. Especially this man.

During the first year of our marriage, I tried to learn to love him. Desperately seeking his approval and love in return. I was naïve and wouldn't allow myself to believe the man I had married was actually a monster in disguise. He uprooted me from everything I had known and loved, promising that high society would be a new adventure. Little did I know

I was merely being primed for a cage so suffocating it almost rivaled that of my marriage. I hated the pleasantries and the expectations. I could not stand the etiquette of always having to be prim and proper. I yearned to get my fingers dirty and help something blossom, not just stand around and make tedious observations that no one actually bothered to listen to. My wild heart wept for the countryside. I tried to find solace in my garden, happy there for days at a time.

Matthew quickly became exasperated, constantly finding me with my fingers in the soil. Jealous and irate, he insisted we be moved into a grander estate further into the city.

"Groundskeeping is for the help, Florence. Really, don't any of those books you insisted on bringing with you from the country have any examples of Lady-like behavior? You are Lady Cabot, and how you act reflects directly on me," he shouted at me when I expressed my disappointment at moving further into the city and away from the garden I had spent a year cultivating. I could still feel the fear and disappointment that bubbled like nausea as he stepped onto the medicinal herb I had been coaxing to bloom and yanked me up by the scruff of my neck like an animal.

"Maybe if you spent less time on your knees fiddling with plants and more time on your back producing an heir, you'd have more appropriate ways to fill your time." That was four years ago, but the memory still made me bristle, and I returned to the scene playing before me in the dining room.

The maid was in the midst of making unintelligible apologies and reaching out for the bowl in an effort to take it back to the kitchen, but Matthew grabbed her wrist and twisted it painfully to pull her closer to him.

"Darling," I said through gritted teeth, in the closest approximation to sweetness I could muster. Matthew dropped his attention and grip on the maid to look at me.

"I suggested that Cook add the apples to the porridge this morning. We've been eating so decadently lately that my stomach has been out of sorts. Fruit is good for you, and apples are in season. The girl knew nothing about it. Can we let it rest, please?" I turned to the maid and gave her a small smile, nodding in dismissal.

Her eyes widened gratefully, and she curtsied quickly with a breathy "Ma'am" before she ran from the room without sparing one backward glance at the Lord, who was sitting red-faced at the end of the table.

Matthew sat there and stared at me, eyes narrowed and lips pursed, turning a shade of crimson that I have long since given up hope were the early signs of angina. I knew what I had done. I had just taken away his favorite toy. Even more outrageous, I had done it in front of the staff. The other waitstaff shifted uncomfortably in the corners of the room where they loomed until they were called upon. I knew I would pay for my *outburst* later, behind the privacy of closed doors. But undoubtedly, I would have regardless- at least now I could feel relief that yet another young girl was not in his grasp.

"Thank you, *wife*." It came out staccato, each word short and clipped but with a significant emphasis on the last. "Perhaps I need to remind our staff who approves those suggestions in the future."

"Yes, my *Lord,*" I hummed, sliding back into the uncomfortable yet familiar shape of *'obedient wife'* to make the rest of our spoiled meal go by quicker. We ate in silence. His eyes were always on me, never relaxing. I shifted in my chair uncomfortably; the laces of my corset pulled so tightly it made it difficult to breathe, let alone eat.

Never missing a moment to enjoy my contrived discomfort, my cruel husband smiled. Cold and prideful. "Not hungry this morning, dear wife? We don't want the fruit to go to waste now, do we?" He reminded me mockingly, picking up his spoon and bringing it to his mouth, his lips twisted into a snicker. "I noticed your clothing has appeared a bit tight as of late, so I suggested your Lady's Maid may not be tying your laces correctly. I am glad to see that the issue seems to have been remedied."

I had questioned Aisling this morning as to why she was pulling me in so tightly. She had mumbled something noncommittal under her breath in apology—I should have guessed it would have been at his insistence.

"God forbid I actually do get pregnant if this is what awaits me," I scoffed, then froze, my blood turning to ice.

It had left my mouth before I had even finished forming the thought. I cursed myself—it had been so long since I had accidentally thought out loud, and to have mocked him in such a way... in front of him? His spoon clattered to the table, and I barely had the chance to register the sound of his chair screeching across the floor before his hand was at my throat, lifting me out of my seat.

His hair was disheveled, and his eyes were dark with rage as he spat at me, "God forbid? Yes, God does seem to forbid, doesn't he, Florence?" Lord Cabot hissed out my name less like a question and more like an accusation.

With my heart in my throat, I did everything I could to keep the panic from showing in my eyes. His fingers squeezed tightly around my neck, forcing me on tiptoe to meet his glare. He pushed me backward until my shoulders grazed the wall, and he leaned in so closely that I could feel his hot breath in my ear.

"God knows I have enough bastards in Ireland so we both know I am not the problem don't we, wife?" His voice was pitched low so only I could hear. Nausea rolled in the pit of my stomach. "If I find out you are somehow keeping yourself from bearing me my rightful heirs, not even God Himself will be able to help you." He squeezed tightly until I saw black spots and what little breath I had left my lips in a high whine.

Over his shoulder, I saw the waitstaff looking at each other nervously, no doubt wondering the same thing I was; if this was the time he took it too far... My vision darkened as my lungs burned, his fingers flexing deeper when a throat was cleared. Kingsley, our doorman, arrived. His eyes widened upon realizing what he had interrupted as he announced himself formally and waited. Lord Cabot's grip relaxed slightly, and I could touch my heels back on the floor.

"Do not fret, dear wife. I have set up a meeting with the physician for this week. I do so know how the lack of your fertility troubles you," he said this loud enough for the trapped spectators to hear, but his eyes were daggers and clearly conveyed a different message.

I was on borrowed time.

Lord Cabot's hand snaked around my head and gripped the hair at the nape of my neck, using it to force my gaze to meet his. Leaning in, he pushed his lips against mine, forcing them open with his tongue in a sick pantomime of romantic gesture, with bitterness and hatred behind it. It fooled no one, least of all me. He returned to the table where the doorman stood, waiting at attention.

I stifled a harsh breath of air and blinked away painful tears that prickled at the corners of my eyes. I would never shed them for him but his grip burned against my skin and pulled them from me. I readjusted myself as he moved across the room like a cold shadow.

"Kingsley! What have you there?" He spoke jovially, as if he hadn't just threatened me in the middle of the dining room. The older gentleman padded to the table and laid out that morning's papers, a few handwritten notes addressed to Lord Cabot, and, lastly, a sealed envelope. He looked at me with kind gray eyes.

"This one is for the Lady, m'Lord."

My eyebrows shot up, I hadn't received any letters since the one that announced my Father's passing. My fingers trembled at my side as I stepped towards the table in confusion. Lord Cabot swiped the letter up before I could fully take in the envelope.

He tore it open roughly, pulled the letter out, and let the envelope fall to the table. I stood at his side and collected it, turning it over curiously in my hands. It was addressed to me but, strangely, there was no return address; it must have been hand-delivered. Curiosity tickled the back of my neck. Odd.

"How do you know Agatha Warren?" Lord Cabot sharply asked me.

I gaped at him blankly, turning the name over in my mind. Possibly one of the ladies I had met at tea last week? I grew so tired of the society events he insisted I attend that I often daydreamed through them, never really hearing any inane gossip or prattling the other ladies went on about.

Mostly they were willing to let me stare off into the distance and pass my time. The name sounded vaguely familiar, though, and I remembered one of the ladies mentioning the *'local shut-in'* Agatha Warren. Deemed a bitter hermit, *Widow Warren* was how she was most often referred to.

"Agatha Warren? I have heard of her but never had the pleasure of her acquaintance. Miss Walsh mentioned her at tea on Thursday. She lives just outside of the city in one of the Manors. Why?" Curiosity raged beneath the calm appearance on my face. If I showed him that I had any interest in the letter, he would withhold it before I could figure out the meaning behind it.

"Apparently, she would like for you to visit her. It's written here that she heard you were an excellent conversationalist and wants your company for tea." He sneered. "I don't know who she would have spoken to. That woman has been away with the faeries since her husband passed years before I was even born." He looked to Kingsley for agreement, to which the old doorman gave a slight nod, though I could tell it was not meant with the same malice. "Somehow, despite being alone there, she's held on to that Manor for ages. She has no children that I am aware of..." I could see a thought forming in his mind.

"Thank you, Kingsley," he said, nodding to the doorman who bowed and excused himself. "Gentlemen, you are excused. We are finished with the meal." The two remaining waitstaff collected our place settings and quickly removed themselves.

If there was one thing I was absolutely certain of, it was my ability to read my husband's thoughts. Matthew was easy to read. His desires showed so plainly in both his features and his actions. He was a violent man— not a clever one. His utmost want in this world was status and power. Always wanted what others had and, if he could not earn it himself, he was happy to take it, maybe more so. If the widowed Ms. Warren had no children and no family to pass her Manor down to, perhaps there would be an opportunity to take it?

"May I please read the letter?" I asked, trying not to let the frustration of asking for something intended for me seep into my voice.

I thought he might deny me for a moment, but he handed it over. I could see the cogs in his mind working now, practically smoking, and if there was something equally frightening to Lord Cabot in a rage, it was when he started to plan. I looked down at the letter and could see the telltale signs of quill and ink, which softened my heart. My Father had never mastered the pen and preferred using the quill. I spared a moment of thought for him and continued reading until I confirmed the letter was as he had said. It was an invitation to the Manor on Orchid Lane for this afternoon's tea. Questions about her intentions flooded me.

"I will arrange for the coach to take you this afternoon," he said.

"What?" I sputtered, surprised at his willingness to send me away after his explosion over breakfast. I had expected the typical treatment of being locked in my room until he decided how best to punish my outburst.

"You are going to visit with the Widow Warren, and you are to charm her as best as you are able," he said, sounding doubtful while he took in the length of me. "And I will arrive in the evening to escort you home, where you can make introductions."

"Matthew, don't be ridiculous. I don't even know this woman. I—" I was interrupted by an explosive pain across the right side of my face that almost knocked me off my feet.

I looked back at him in surprise as he massaged the back of the hand that struck me. He never usually beat me in places where bruises could show so obviously. I swallowed down a surge of surprised tears for the second time this morning, feeling the blood trickle from my brow that was now split open.

"No. Don't *you* be ridiculous, Florence. You seem to forget yourself today, *wife*. Serve your purpose and do your duty to your husband. You will go to the Manor, you will make pleasantries with the old woman, and you will do it with enthusiasm and, so help me, God, if you use your fecking tongue one more time to speak against me today, I will cut it out of you. Do you understand?" He seethes.

"Understood, my Lord." The pit of despair and anger in my stomach grew.

"Good. Now go get your maid. She'll be accompanying you since you obviously cannot be trusted to follow instructions today," he spat disgustedly and waved me away. And tell her to clean you up; you look a fright."

That time, I managed to keep my mouth closed, sick to my stomach and tired of him placing the blame. A disheveled mess was correct. I pressed my hands to my skirts and forced myself into compliance as I turned from the dining room. *You look a fright.*

And whose fault was that I wonder?

FLORENCE

"I'm so sorry, m'Lady, I should have just told you what he said and let come what may, but I wanted to protect your feelings. You've been through so much recently..." Aisling's eyes dropped to my stomach as she tripped over her tongue, and whether it was from her endless apologizing or Matthews's blow to my skull, I was starting to have a persistent pounding in my temple. The carriage jostled from side to side as we left the more well-trodden roads of the city to traverse the countryside.

"Aisling, please—you didn't do anything wrong. He is the master of the house, and he makes that clear enough for us all. I don't blame you." I took her hand in mine. She sat across from me, her pale blue eyes wide with concern as she again reached to push aside the hair I had let fall over my face, hoping to disguise the tender flesh and sizable cut on my brow. Her lips trembled.

"He shouldn't be able to hit you. You're a Lady." She frowned, knowing intimately what he was capable of and that he had done much worse—to both of us. I gave her a look, painfully raising my brow, that said just as much.

"He shouldn't be able to do any of it. To anyone. But that is not the world we live in." I sighed, allowing myself a moment in the company of my only friend to feel slightly defeated.

Aisling had been my Ladies Maid for three years now and, for almost two of those years, she unfortunately shared the attention of Lord Cabot. I remembered the morning after the first time it happened. She had come in to dress me and could not look me in the eyes which, up until then, was extremely unlike her. When I had finally forced her to look at me I recognized the pained and haunted look on her. It was the same one I saw so frequently in my own reflection. Her lips, neck, and collarbone were all bruised, and her eyes were red and swollen from crying. I had gathered her into my arms immediately and sobbed along with her. I could never forgive him for the things he did, but now I could never forgive myself for the slight tinge of relief I had felt for no longer holding the burden of him alone.

God knows I have enough bastards in Ireland...

His words repeated in my mind, and I returned Aisling's gaze.

"Have you been drinking the tea?" I demanded.

Her eyes widened at me, asking so brazenly out in the open—but there was no danger of the Coachman being able to hear us as we traveled these roads; it was too loud. She nodded furiously and a few pieces of her dark hair escaped their pins. They were a drastic contrast to the linen headscarf they were tucked beneath.

"Every day?" I insisted, "And twice on the days that he... visits?"

Growing up as I had, reading whatever book found its way to me, with a very intimate knowledge of botany and many different animal life cycles, it had not been overwhelmingly challenging to come across a mixture of plants that created a perfect combination to effectively stave off unwanted pregnancies. And any pregnancy conceived by rape was unwanted as far as I was concerned. I had been drinking it since the first moment I knew without doubt that Matthew was an unredeemable monster.

We had just moved into the estate in the city. I had been grieving the loss of my father, staring out at the street in the front parlor when a starling crashed into the window. I ran outside and cradled it carefully in my hands, bringing it inside and upstairs to my bedroom, blessedly not shared with the master of the house. The poor thing was dazed and seemed to have broken its wing upon impact with the window. I kept it secret for weeks as it healed, I had grown so fond of it, and it of me. I always left the window open and, when it could fly again, it would depart, always returning to spend the small hours of the afternoon with me, singing sweetly in a way that reminded me of home.

One day it flew in through the window while Matthew had his focus on me. His anger lashed out in every way imaginable. He had paused in his fury and noticed the bird, managing to grasp it before it could escape, and I watched in horror as he crushed it in his fist and threw the limp little body against the wall.

I knew then it was not just me. No one could ever be safe around him, and I would do whatever it took to protect others from him. Especially a child, whether it was mine or Aisling's.

"Yes, every day and twice—sometimes three times—on the days he..." she trailed off, unable to finish the thought aloud.

"Good. It only works if you drink it consistently. The alternative is ghastly and painful." I reminded her as one of my hands floated absently to my stomach and rested there.

Unfortunately, the tea was not always completely effective, especially if it had been forgotten, or as in my case, he forced himself upon you during your courses. I alone had the lamentable experience of having to forcibly miscarry and, though it was only once, I would never forget the feeling of the tincture wracking my body. Aisling had held me through the entire ordeal.

The road noise lessened and I changed the subject in an abundance of caution, knowing the repercussions would be unimaginable if we were overheard. I wasn't sure whose reaction would be worse—Lord Cabot's or the Catholic Church's. I shuddered at the thought. I sat back and leaned against the wall of the coach, urging my heart to slow its unsustainable pace.

"Why do you think Mistress Warren sent the invitation?" I posed to Aisling while drawing the carriage door curtain enough that I could just begin to see the Manor in the distance. I chewed the inside of my cheek while I mused, "'*Excellent conversationalist*' seems an extremely unlikely moniker to have obtained when I barely speak to the women at tea..." I looked over to Aisling, who shifted in her seat uncomfortably and avoided my eyes. My suspicions grew, and I pressed her insistently. "Aisling... why am I being solicited by Agatha Warren?"

Her blue eyes darted from mine to her lap, and she cleared her throat. She removed a small vial from her apron pocket. The green-tinted tincture swirled inside. I had made four vials of it at the end of last year when I realized my courses had been weeks overdue. Having never taken it myself before then I did not want to leave it to chance that the babe would still be viable if one dose was not enough. Thankfully, it had been. This was the last of them.

While the Ladies would chatter during tea, so too would the Ladies Maids. Aisling had a particular aptitude for gossip and would share the goings on during the evenings as she would dress both myself and my room for the night. It was not long before I suggested that she clandestinely slip the tincture to one or two maids who needed it. She assured me she was meticulous in her admissions to the women she spoke to. She kept my name out of it as best as she could. But it only took someone with half of their wits about them to know access to these medicinal plants had to come from someone who had experience growing them, and that was not any of the Ladies in this city, except for one.

"Agatha Warren is, by my approximation, *one hundred* years old! And a widow, what's more!" I hissed exasperatedly as she popped the vial back into her pocket. "What could she possibly need with *that*?" The carriage jostled again as it descended the long gravel path to the Manor on Orchid Lane.

"A servant of hers approached me. *I don't know how*, maybe one of the girls told her," she swore. "But she said Mistress Warren knew what we had been doing, and she wanted to *help!*" Her eyes were bright with nerves, but excitement was also there. Aisling, bless her, had a heart too large for her chest, and sometimes I wondered if it had affected the growth of her brain. "Her maid said that she wanted to let you use the grounds of the Manor to grow the herbs. Think of that!"

Unlike Aisling, I was alarmed by this. Passing the tincture out to those who desperately needed it was already dangerous–but a risk I had been sure was worth taking. But to be seen by someone with it in hand—and to admit to its effect and having produced it? If the widow was not being truthful in her intentions...

"Aisling, we have spoken at *length* as to how dangerous it would be for anyone to know what we were doing or if we were the ones behind it!" I whispered ferociously. "If the Church finds out–" I was cut off by the whinnies of the horses as the carriage came to an abrupt halt.

Aisling shushed me and smoothed my hair to cover my brow before whispering confidently, "all will be well," before the Coachman opened the door and assisted us out onto the drive.

It took a moment for my eyes to adjust back to the daylight, but I squinted and realized we hadn't entirely made it all the way to our destination. We were outside the Manor's gates, by twenty yards at least. I looked at the Coachman, confused. He must have been anticipating my question as he immediately began to explain.

"Sorry, m'Lady, but the horses refuse to go any farther up the way. I've been tryin' to coax them along, I have, but the stubborn beasts won't move." He leaned in conspiratorially and nodded his head back in the direction of the Manor. "Animals can sense when a thing is off, aye? I never saw a more off thing than the Manor on Orchid Lane, I reckon." He chuckled with a wink.

"Oh, I don't know about that. I can think of a few," I said absently, looking up the path to the stately mansion on the hill.

It wasn't a far walk, and the fresh air would do me good. I wasn't often afforded the opportunity of leisurely strolls—even less so outside of the city where the air was so fresh. This would also allow me to interrogate Aisling further. However, she seemed to have predicted this and had already excused herself in the guise of announcing our arrival. I scowled off in her direction.

"I am that sure y'could *àilleach*. I'm that sure y' could." If his sad tone did not convey his thoughts, his quick glance at my bruising cheekbone did. I gave him a small smile and a nod and turned to begin making my way up to the estate. I could still hear him crooning to the horses in Gaelic when the noises of the coach turning away eventually drowned him out.

Orchid Manor was one of the largest estates I had ever seen. Three levels of dark stone were engulfed with thick, twisting vines that grew up and around the giant, beautiful windows framed in iron. Untold age gnawed at the bars around the junctions and turned the corners of the windows a slight turquoise with patina. The steep peaks of the roof seemed to pierce the sky, calling back images I had only ever imagined from reading novels. It was nothing short of a castle.

Many inhabitants of the city quipped that *Widow Warren* had been 'away with the faeries' since the passing of her husband decades before, and I could believe there may be some truth to that, now that I was standing just outside the gates. Even from here, I could see that the gardens were immense. There was plant life everywhere, from fields of clover to wild bluebells, and bushes of flowers so purple they were nearly black. They perfumed the courtyard beautifully and it truly felt as though this place could be home to multitudes of magical creatures, not just the fae.

I examined the courtyard more closely as I passed through the gates. To the left of me was a large round fountain ringed in fuchsia foxgloves. Perched in the center was a beautiful woman etched out of stone, carrying a basin. The water surrounding her was dark and sparkled in the gray afternoon light; atop it grew numerous lily pads, their white flowers just beginning to open. A hundred yards away from the fountain leading off to the side of the Manor, I could see the signs of a twisting hedge labyrinth. Two giant lion statues sat at either side of the entrance as sentinels.

"Aisling, look at this garden!" I exclaimed excitedly, despite myself. I could spend hours out here wandering these grounds. I looked over my shoulder to find her and point out the statues. There was no sign of her. I had been right behind her moments ago and I had seen her go through the gate. *Where could she have gone?*

I rounded back past the fountain and up the front steps to the Manor's entrance. It had an ornamented wooden door with a slick brass knocker in the center. It was cold as I took it in my hands and rapped it against the door. I heard no noise from inside the Manor and I turned to look out at the courtyard again. *Perhaps she went around the side yard but I hadn't seen her?*

About to call for her again, I heard the door latch click open behind me. I turned to greet whoever had opened it–but they were no longer there. The door was ajar into the foyer, but no one was at the entrance to receive me. Unease washed over me. This was the strangest reception I had ever had. *Where* had Aisling gone? It was not at all like her to disappear.

"Hello?" I called out into the foyer through the opening, unsure how to proceed. "Mistress Warren? Aisling? Hello?" I stepped toward the entrance, the toe of my boot grazing the threshold of the Manor. It took more strength than I expected to push open the heavy door, "I received a letter that Mistress Warren requested my company this afternoon…" I trailed off as I stepped fully inside and took in the scale of the room. This was not a foyer so much as it could be a grand ballroom.

Above me hung an imposing chandelier made of crystal and candles which painted the high ceiling in a glittering haze, making my breath catch in my throat. I had never seen something quite this intricate and delicate and here it was, suspended above me in the air, held aloft as if by invisible chains. It was something of a magic trick that left me in awe and nearly forgetting my uneasiness entirely.

The two front windows behind me were curtained with thick dark drapes that hung an impossible length from ceiling to floor. The chandelier was the only light source in the room. It cast shadows everywhere, leaving an eerie darkness to spread across the wooden flooring where its fluorescence could not reach. Two sets of wide, carpeted stairs climbed to the second floor in mirrored curves and met at an open mezzanine that overlooked the entrance. I moved to open one of the heavy drapes, as much as I was able, in an effort to illuminate the room more. I was rewarded with only the slightest bit of light that barely made a dent in the shadows.

"Hello?" I called out louder this time, and a shrill scream sliced through the dense silence like a sharp blade.

FLORENCE

A deafening crash shook the second floor causing the chandelier to groan and shudder as if it were a beast being awakened by the noise.

"Aisling?!" I cried out her name, not knowing whether it had been her I heard or someone else, but urgency licked at my heels and propelled me up the stairs towards what was now a cacophony of screaming and thundering. The walls seemed to shake around me with each new and terrible sound. As I propelled my way up the stairs, it got louder and louder until I reached the top step and, suddenly, it stopped. The silence was almost unbearable after such a malevolent commotion.

"Where are you?!" I cried out to the voice that had been screaming, unsure what I was actually going to be able to do once I found them—but knowing I had to help. The hallway was dark aside from the orange flickering glow emanating from the sconces on the wall. All the drapes were shut and the darkness in the hall made it seem as though it was the dead of night, rather than the middle of the afternoon. Though the temperature was cool, the air felt thick and musty, and a shiver raced down my spine leaving a trail of gooseflesh raised along my arms, despite my sleeves. My heart continued to rattle against my ribcage so hard I swore I could hear it.

Multiple doors lined the hallway but only one at the end was wide open. Despite my own fear I moved quickly toward it. It was a bedroom and, thankfully, more sconces and lanterns were lit brightly inside so I could see much better than in the hall. There was a smell in this room that I recognized immediately. I began to breathe through my mouth instinctively as my eyes watered. It was putrid and sulfurous and slightly sweet. *Decay.* It blanketed the air of the room like a fog. I had seen no signs of what could have made the enormous crashing noises while I had made my way to this space, but the evidence was all around me here. Not one single piece of furniture was left untouched in this room.

There was debris everywhere. A writing desk against the far wall was upturned and scattered papers littered the floor, dark splotches of splattered ink drying on the wall behind it. The drawers of a substantial wooden wardrobe seemed to have been yanked out with extreme force and whipped across the room. Its doors appeared to have been thrown open so hard one was nearly entirely off its hinges. A trunk that I was sure had been resting elsewhere was open and upside down in the middle of the room, its belongings pitched around it. The large four-post bed was the only piece of furniture that remained unmolested, and it was occupied.

I tried to swallow the knot in my throat and take a step towards the bed, glass crunching beneath my boots as I attempted to pick my way through the wreckage.

"Hello? Is anyone..." I trailed off, not knowing how best to finish my sentence. *There?* Yes, evidently. *Alive?* I wasn't so sure. I narrowed my eyes, rapidly blinking away the tears that continued to fill my eyes due to the acrid stench in the room. It grew stronger the further I went. The small shape in the center of the bed rustled, and I choked on a startled shriek.

An almost imperceptible voice croaked from the body of Agatha Warren. I could see her frail figure more clearly now. She was turned away from me, curled pitifully around herself like a small, frightened child. Her gray, almost white hair was long and matted around what may have once been a braid. *What* had happened to this poor woman? I lifted my skirts and half-clambered onto the bed far enough to be able to reach her. As gently as possible, I rolled her so that her back lay against the mattress and I could see her better. Bile rose from my stomach as I looked upon her face, and I swallowed thickly to force it back down.

Her body was covered in innumerable painful, bloody boils that appeared to have blistered and festered continually on top of themselves. Her face was gaunt, the already decomposing flesh was a gruesome yellow hue, and her eyes searched blindly for me with milky pupils. I forced myself not to gag as the stench that permeated her and threatened my composure. I had seen animals in various states of decomposition before, but never while they were *alive.*

"How long have you been here? How long have you been *like this?*" I choked out quietly, my hands shaking as I reached out to brush the hair off her face—and then abruptly stopped when I realized it had all but fused to the abscesses beneath. Her arm shot out from under the blankets with impossible speed and the movement shocked me. Her fingers found my wrist, and she squeezed tightly, digging her long, overgrown fingernails painfully into my skin. A shrill breath left her cracked and bloodied lips as she moaned.

"You came, you sweet, stupid girl."

The words left her throat in a tangled mess of strained groaning and painful coughing. Blood began to trickle from the corners of her mouth.

"Mistress Warren!" I cried out, and tried to pry her grip from my skin. She was incomprehensibly strong. Much more potent than any old woman had the right to be, even in a healthy state. "Please let go! I-I-I only want to help!" I stammered out, my voice high and frightened.

"There is no…" She was cut off by a fit of coughing, her whole body convulsing from the violence of it. Blood sprayed from her mouth and splattered across the lap of my dress. "You can't," she spat venomously. "You can't! *You should not have come!*" Her fingers squeezed hard enough into my flesh to draw blood from the sharp crescent peaks of her nails through my sleeve. I exhaled in surprised pain and scrambled backward away from her and off the bed.

I clutched my wrist to my chest. "*You* sent for me!" I bit back in alarm.

Her body shook as if being wracked with bone-shattering coughs again, a terrible wheezing sound filling the room. It was sharp and discordant, and the hair rose on the back of my neck. I finally recognized it as *laughter.* It tumbled from her ominously into the stale air, and her white eyes looked through me and almost seemed to focus behind me.

"It tires of me," she croaked painfully. "You are so young and beautiful. What a shame." Her split and bloodied lips twisted into a smile that almost looked… relieved?

"There is nothing to be done now. I have served my purpose. It takes what it wants." Her body tensed, and it looked as though every muscle in her had been pulled taut all at once. She howled in agony and repeated:

"*It takes what it wants! IttakeswhatitwantsITTAKESWHATIT-WANTS!*"

Over and over, the words tumbled out of her, booming impossibly loud from her tiny frame. Her body vibrated, teeth gnashing while her head shook violently from side to side until it stopped entirely, and I feared she was gone. The silence seemed to echo and a new eerie sickness washed over me. The room and the woman were unsettling enough but now it felt like there were unseen eyes on me. At a glance I knew it was only the two of us in the space, but I could not help but feel the overwhelming sensation that someone or some*thing* was watching me.

Agatha's head snapped towards me unnaturally and her blank eyes bored into mine as if truly seeing me. "I belong to the house," she said. Her voice sounded abnormally clear and almost untouched by age—nothing like it had just moments before. "I belong to the house," she stated again matter-of-factly.

"*And so do you.*"

Her deafening wail split the room, and her back arched as if she were being gripped and yanked in half by the spine through her stomach. Her body created a perverse imitation of a triangle before it was released and thrown back against the mattress. A finallabored breath left her lips.

Agatha Warren was dead.

Tears pricked at the corners of my eyes and felt like ice as they streamed down my hot cheeks. Though my body was ablaze with fear, my feet seemed nailed to the floor, and I began to shiver in a cold sweat. Adrenaline coursed through me, and I could not catch my breath.

"*And so do you.*"

The Manor seemed to tremble around me, vibrations coursing through the floor and into me through the soles of my shoes. I wanted nothing more than to run from this place but my feet wouldn't listen.

My body was rigid, paralyzed with fear. I opened my mouth to scream when Agatha's body was lifted from the mattress in a sharp, unexpected movement. In death, her neck no longer supported the weight of her head, and it swung limply as her body was suspended in the air like a marionette being wielded by an invisible puppeteer.

Unable to run, I squeezed my eyes shut, trying to block out her bloody and contorted figure, willing this to be a nightmare. But something that wasn't quite a voice, whispered in the back of my mind. An eldritch darkness dug its claws into me and forced my eyes back open. What had once been Agatha was now standing before me, lifeless eyes mere inches from my own. I was unable to hear if the scream that was building in my throat managed to escape over the thunderous beating of my heart in my ears.

What was left of Agatha cracked, her spine curling backward, bones audibly creaking until they finally snapped as her limp head grazed the floor behind her. The stretched and decomposing flesh of her stomach split open, blood and viscera seeped from her and pooled beneath the floating body. It was as if she was being turned inside out. Her mouth remained twisted open and unmoving in a permanent scream, and I swore I could hear her voice reverberating from every corner of the room. *Goodbye, goodbye, goodbye.*

It repeated again and again as she writhed in front of me until the streams of blood were thin, and all that was left of her was a deflated cadaver of skin and dust. I watched in horror as what was left of the body was released from the force that held it, and it slammed into the pool of gore below, violently enough to coat both me and the wall behind me.

I blinked the blood from my eyes, clearing them as best as I could while still being unable to move. When I was able to refocus, Agatha's body was gone, the blood seeping down between the floorboards as if it was being absorbed by the Manor until nothing remained but the stain. Terror gripped me, forcing me still as my heart thumped painfully in my chest. The disturbing thought that was not my own echoed within me loudly, tattooing itself onto my psyche.

You belong to me.

S uddenly, she jolted. As if struck by a bolt of lightning. Her feet started beneath her and carried her clumsily out of the room, stumbling on the edge of the ornate rug and barely catching herself against the door frame. Her breasts heaved as her lungs strained, unsure whether to scream or struggle for more air. Eyes wide with horror, she spared a backward glance into the room and nearly collided with the wall upon entering the hallway, upsetting the side table and causing the glass shade of an oil lamp to shatter at her feet. Flames licked down the table following the line of oil that now dripped from the base and pooled to the floor.

Her fear was already at its limit and she spared no thought to the growing flame she left behind her as she pulled wildly at her skirts to descend the winding staircase. Stairs that felt steeper and wider with every step. They seemed to wind impossibly long until suddenly her foot hit the main floor, which she swore hadn't been there before she stepped off the last stair. As though the staircase had been rearranging itself as she ran. Her ankle bent to an uncomfortable degree, and her knee slammed against the floor, causing her to hiss between gritted teeth.

The sizable baroque door, still open from her arrival, began to close as if pushed by an invisible hand and she forced herself upward, panic surging her forward. One bruised arm outstretched with her fingers grasping as if to hold it open by sheer will alone -but something else outwilled her. The door slammed shut just as she reached it and both her hands braced against the heavy brass handle, jostling it with no success. It remained immovable. She screamed, terrified confusion mingling with frustration as she began to pound her fists against the door, again and again, the sides of her hands reddening with each strike. The door hardly creaked at the impact.

She spun frantically, the auburn hair once held tidily in a loose braided bun at the back of her head was now wildly undone and unkempt about her shoulders and back. Her green eyes scanned the foyer for an exit, catching the orange glow of the flames she left behind on the floor above her. It began to descend the staircase. Smoke billowed down, step by step. She lurched towards a window, open almost imperceptibly but enough that she could slide her fingers underneath and feel the cool air outside. She heaved the pane upward but, again, it didn't move. She tried a second and a third time but, despite the effort, it didn't budge.

The smoke crept along the base of the stairs and red-hot flames engulfed the banister and jumped from the open mezzanine to the thick velvet curtains that framed the windows. Her screams choked off into fits of coughing and her hand grabbed the nearest thing to her- an unlit candelabra that she hurtled at the window. It bounced off as if the window weren't made of glass at all. Another item was flung from her hand before she even registered what it was. Again, the glass remained unbroken. The mezzanine above her began to creak and debris fell, crashing to the main floor as the blaze now fully consumed it behind her.

She covered her mouth with part of her skirts in an attempt to breathe through the smoke. Eyes red and watering she ran, stumbling from the foyer and into the adjacent hallway, the wallpaper already curling from the heat in the other room. She stopped at every window but nothing budged or broke. Her exits were few and her panic was suffocating.

She shrieked and coughed and wailed but, even if there was anyone around, they wouldn't hear. She crashed into the kitchen and threw herself at the back door. Rattling it so hard that it should've come off the hinges. Futile. She grabbed a cast iron pan resting on the large range and tried to smash it against the window on the door- but it held firm, barricading her from escape.

Smoke, thick and heavy, almost brown in color, completely consumed the hallway behind her now. Like an animal surrounded, such as she was, she began to throw herself at the door, the walls, directly into the windows, with force enough to break bones. Battered and bruising, blood trickling from her nose and fingernails as she used her body as a tool for escape, her eyes began to glaze as she lost her will, realization coming to a head.

Trapped.

Her back up against the door, her breathing was quick and sharp, but each breath drew in less and less air as the fire burned up the oxygen in the Manor.

Tired.

Shaking, she collapsed onto the floor, choking on smoke.

Sleep.

Her eyes closed.

FLORENCE

I felt a cool breeze on my face. Somewhere, a window was open. I took a long inhale, and the smell of clover mixed with fresh air filled my nose.

I could hear the tinkling of distant birdsong, light and bright like so many small bells—a simple melody that gently tugged me from sleep. I opened my eyes, disoriented. I was staring at a tall ceiling framed in wide, exquisite molding, and *I was lying on... a bed?* Confusion rippled down through my stiff muscles. I flexed my fingers beside me and felt the cotton fibers of the bedclothes beneath me.

My hair was loose. The soft curls tendriled around my face and fanned out into long waves, consuming the pillow in the way that Matthew hated. He always insisted I wear it in tight braids before going to sleep—even though we hadn't shared a bed in three years. *Surely I wouldn't have forgotten to plait it before falling asleep?*

I looked down at myself and saw that I was still fully dressed. Aside from my jacket, which hung on one of the bed posts, the skirts of my dress spread out beautifully over the bed linens. They were not crushed or wrinkled at all, as they would have been if I had slept on them.

I would never have slept fully clothed. My thoughts shifted to Aisling and dread filled me. Tangled with the memories of our evening rituals, she would prepare my room for sleep, hang my dress for the morning, and stoke the fire carefully. Her sweet voice so soft against the crackling wood as she repeated back what she had learned from any spare knowledge I shared with her that day. My sweet, inquisitive Aisling...*Aisling*. My memory was drenched in fog so thick it suffocated my rational thoughts. Where had she gone...

"Where am I?" My voice was raspy from sleep and my throat constricted sorely as if I had been screaming—*screaming*? My eyes scanned around the room as a vague memory gripped me, raising the hairs on the back of my neck and arms.

"You belong to the house now." I remembered Agatha's voice in the back of my mind.

I shot off the bed and my legs wobbled uneasily beneath me.

How long had I been sleeping? How did I get to this room? This bed?

I shook my legs as they were flooded with the sensation of being pricked by needles and, again, I wondered how long had I been unconscious? Unsteadily, I made my way to the large bay window. One of the side panes was open and I stuck my head out and saw no signs of the birds I heard moments before. Instead I saw the labyrinth and the gardens, and fully remembered where I was and, more importantly, how I came to be here.

"Agatha," I whispered.

Despite the comfortable temperature in the room the blood in my veins turned ice cold; upon quick inspection it was clear I was no longer in the room where I had found Agatha Warren before—I shuddered. My brain turned over the events slowly as I explored my surroundings in greater detail.

I'd come to the Manor on the hill in the early afternoon.

I glanced out the window again and saw that the sun was high in the sky and, despite the cover of some clouds, it appeared to be morning.

Had I spent the night in the Manor? Matthew would be outraged.

Though the thought was tinged with a familiar fear of having to deal with his ire eventually, a small part of me—no matter how beaten down—was pleased to anger him.

I came to the Manor to meet with Agatha, but then that gruesome *thing* happened to her and...*I ran...and... there was a fire?*

The memory of thick smoke and the sensation of choking made me cough. The movement caused my attention to be pulled by my reflection in an oval mirror framed in a beautiful freestanding walnut frame on the other side of the window. I took a moment to look myself over.

My head tilted to the side as I took in my complexion. *Curious.* My jacket was still hanging on the end of the bed so my arms were completely bare—something they seldom were due to the need to cover the constant array of dark purple and yellow fingerprint—sized bruises that peppered my pale flesh. Only, they weren't there. I stepped closer to the mirror to inspect my porcelain skin. Unmarred by any scar or scratch—no sign at all of the violence I had so often seen.

"How is that possible?" I whispered to my reflection.

I had spent years with bruises and knew intimately how long they stained my skin. The darkest of them would not have entirely faded for at least a week or longer. I stepped closer and pushed back the auburn curls that fell over my right eye to inspect the split brow Matthew had given me. The once painful laceration was gone entirely as if it were never there to begin with.

"What kind of magic..." I trailed off as I heard a creak, and the door to the room opened slowly in my direction.

"H—hello?" I stammered.

I waited as the door fully opened into the hall but, much like when I first arrived in this place, no one answered.

I had arrived. The door opened and I came inside. *Agatha...died? Was... destroyed?*

I shivered again at being unable, and frankly unwilling to fully describe the thought.

The shadowy claws of an invisible threat loomed, peeling back my logic and replacing it with illusions.

I ran. There was... Fire.

The heat and the smoke. The feeling of being pursued by the flames. It all came rushing back to me. I hit the sideboard and broke a lamp. The carpet caught ablaze and burnt the Manor around me as I tried to escape. The doors all locked tight against my efforts, the windows impenetrably strong.

My hand went to the base of my throat, I could almost feel the suffocating smoke in my chest. I could remember all those things, yet it felt as though it had happened to someone else entirely.

I walked cautiously towards the door and looked out into the hallway. It was long, with high ceilings that had the same intricately detailed molding as the room I awoke in. To the left of me, at one end of the hall, was an impossibly tall window, inset with iron in starburst and diamond shapes along the top that refracted the light into beautiful prisms onto the dark carpet. The window was framed with long, heavy drapes, held open with a corded gold rope that looped around itself and ended in an elegant tassel.

Venturing further into the hallway I noticed no sign that anything was out of place or amiss, let alone had been set ablaze the night before.

Surely I hadn't dreamed it all? Had I fallen and cracked my head open before arriving? Was I dead?

The thought forced me to still.

Could I be? I felt alive.

I always thought if I were to die young, it would be due to one of Matthew's raging episodes. Dark thoughts, produced from dark realities.

I mused over the speculation as I inspected the sideboard. It was made from wood similar to most of the furniture I had seen so far. The fine piece held two oil lanterns that were lit and emitted a low glow, and neither one of them was broken. There was a large ornate frame that hung above it. Inside it was an oil painting of pink and red roses in a white and blue vase, delicate against the rich wallpaper and dark wood.

I love flowers.

The thought surprised me at its absurd timing and made me snort quietly. I briefly wondered if anyone was around to witness such silly, un-lady-like behavior. But I heard nothing but the sounds of my own footsteps on the carpet.

I turned to the right of the hallway, which led me to the mezzanine, the balcony that opened out to the curved twin stairs that led down into the foyer. Again, nothing was amiss.

I bolstered my courage to raise my voice louder.

"Hello?" I waited for a moment and received no response. "Hello! Is anyone here?" I shouted.

I descended the stairs, one hand holding my skirts and the other loosely sliding down the smooth curve of the banister. The staircases mirror each other and made a beautiful frame for the lavish chandelier that hung high in the space's middle. Hazy flickering lights danced across the rich floral baroque wallpaper like stars. The imagery filled my chest with a lonely, longing feeling. Were this a different circumstance, I could easily get lost in daydreams of long grass tickling my skin as I stared at the stars back home.

I rolled my eyes at myself. Another absurd thought when one was trying to figure out why they had woken up in a strange place with strange memories. When I reached the end of the stairs, I walked straight to the door. My hand clasped the handle and it was cool to the touch. I took a deep breath and straightened my back. I turned the handle, and the door opened. I scoffed.

What did you think would happen, Florence? I scolded myself.

But still, I recalled pounding against this door as though my life had depended on it— because *it had*. Hadn't it?

I stepped out of the Manor to the entrance under the terrace. The air was fresh and slightly damp and I could hear the rustling of the wind and the smell of the clover... but something was different. I couldn't quite put my finger on what. I walked further out and away from the house, and the gravel crunched under my boots.

Was the garden quite this unruly yesterday?

The collection of foxgloves by the fountain I had noted when I arrived seemed to have grown three times in volume overnight, and a creeping vine completely covered the stone woman bathing in the pool of water in the center. In all my years of living in the countryside, I'd never known a single plant to be able to grow that quickly... the hairs at the back of my neck began to stand on end again.

I surveyed the expanse of the property in front of me and quickly began to notice more and more differences. The grass was waist-high now, where it had barely reached my ankles before. The shrubs surrounding the iron gate had been uniform and clean but now they stood out in all directions and disguised the fence entirely. I turned around and gasped.

Orchid Manor—once bright and polished, a building of untold extravagance, was hidden beneath a legion of ivy. The once-white shutters that framed the windows hung askew, some gone entirely, and the remaining ones were peeling and covered in grime. The windows were covered in a film of dust so deep they were no longer translucent. It looked as though the Manor had aged a hundred years.

"How is this possible?" I whispered as I wrapped my trembling hands around myself.

Everything was the same, yet so completely different. The Manor appeared abandoned, and yet how could it be? I arrived at the grand building only yesterday... I scanned my surroundings and looked for someone, *anyone*, who could explain to me what was happening. The sound of my heartbeat picked up to a thunderous drumming in my ears.

"*Hello?*" I cried out. There were no sounds besides the scattering of dried leaves in the breeze.

No birdsong as I had heard before. There were no human or animal noises, nothing but my voice echoing back solemnly from the Manor. I turned to face the large iron gate and rushed to it, my shoes skidded against the gravel as my body connected. It groaned but opened enough that I could fit myself through. I tried to squeeze through it when I was lifted violently, gripped by an invisible hand and thrown back several feet from the gate.

The air was shot from my lungs as I hit the ground. I took a moment to painfully regain my breath and reach an uneasy stand. I looked around desperately for the unseen force that had propelled me back—and saw nothing but the Manor and the surrounding grounds. My head swimming with panic, confusion, and pain... My only clear thought was to try to escape. I lifted my skirts and ran with what effort I could manage.

I grabbed the decorative curling bars of the iron gate, clinging desperately. This time, I noticed the feeling of being wrenched before my feet left the ground. My grasp slipped from the gate, pulling the vines that wrapped around it with me. They snapped and remained in my fists as I was yanked through the air and hit the ground at the base of the Manor's entrance.

I tried to orient myself enough to stand, but the invisible pulling did not stop. I fisted the loose gravel beneath me, looking for any kind of purchase, to no avail. My nails bent back painfully as I was snatched from the grounds and thrown inside the Manor. The heavy door slammed hard enough that it felt as though the stone walls shuddered around me. They seemed to almost *breathe*.

Mine.

FLORENCE

It had been months alone in this Manor, moving about as if I were a phantom within its walls. I never was able to breach the property line, confined to the barriers set by some unknown power and its inconsistent regulations. There were days when I was able to spend hours exploring the farthest corners of the landscape that the Manor stood on and days when I would not even be able to press a toe past the threshold of the building to the outdoors.

I had begun to explore my surroundings with caution. I found hidden doors and hallways that had surely been built for a significant team of staff who no longer inhabited the Manor. I was alone here, yet I always felt like someone was watching me. Despite the awareness of being constantly surveyed, it did not feel as though the unseen voyeur had malicious intent. More curious than anything else. At every corner I turned, it felt as though I might finally end up face-to-face with the eyes that followed me.

The first thing I noticed about the Manor was that it seemed to be completely self-sufficient. There were no staff to light the sconces, candles or chandeliers, or to monitor the abundant fireplaces that were somehow always lit and perfectly stoked. There was no one to stalk about the place, shine silverware or polish furniture, or maintain the expansive grounds. Yet there was never any dust, dirt, or disrepair in need of seeing to. I was at a complete loss as to how to explain it.

I had claimed one room for myself on the third floor. It was sizeable, bigger than any room I had in the past, including the ostentatious estate in the city, but it had a softness about it. A large bay window was trimmed with white gossamer fabric that bathed the room in the most elegant filtered light in the mornings. The bed was generous, a four-poster placed against the far wall with the fireplace across from it. It had the most luxurious feather mattress I had ever slept on. Though the temperature seemed to remain perfect in the Manor, comfortable blankets were always neatly laid out at the end of the bed, ready to cozy into. A beautiful walnut wardrobe stood grandly against the wall beside the window. It housed every combination of clothing I could possibly need, in all assortments of colors and fabrics. The ones that I gravitated to most often were the dresses made from soft green linens.

Beside the wardrobe was a door leading to a smaller room. This room also had a fireplace, though it was much smaller than the one in the bedroom, and held an oversized clawfoot tub. Like everything else in this place, the tub was always inexplicably filled and ready for me, the water never seeming to dip past my preferred temperature. Steam misted up in languid tendrils, dancing above the hot water until it eventually dissipated. The water was always clean and clear despite hours of soaking. It seemed to renew itself when I turned my attention away from it. It felt like the Manor itself offered me every luxury it could fathom.

The kitchen cupboards were always stocked but, the longer I was in this place, the less I hungered or tired. I could still eat, and at times did, if for no other reason than for the comfort of routine. But the food was never as good as it had once been, flavors seeming somewhat dull and unsatisfying. So I filled my time opening doors, peering inside to discover every possibility the Manor had to offer. There were many parlors and drawing rooms, and their furniture was ornate and positioned facing inward in order to entertain. Early on I got the distinct impression that I would have no such use for these spaces, but I took my time going through them anyway, collecting books on side tables or shelves to bring to my room for company.

As the weeks passed, I began to grow more confident. Even so, the Manor remained a labyrinth to me. I swore rooms had changed places, one corridor never leading to where it had the day before. It was impossible, like everything else in this place, but with my only choices being to let it drive me mad or just accept it, I chose the latter. There were a plethora of bedrooms and sitting rooms. I looked closely to see any signs of inhabitants but there were never any telltale signs of depressions in the chairs or beds, nor any books or journals for me to pour over.

My favorite days were when I was able to go outside. These days were typically when I awoke in a sunnier disposition, less horrified and frustrated at the knowledge of being trapped. I noticed that the outward appearance of the Manor had begun to change. Unlike the abandoned facade it had presented when I first awoke, it had begun reverting to the splendor of when I had first arrived. Windows, cleared of grime, glittered in the sunlight. The roof shingles were all realigned and straightened. Even the missing white shutters that framed the windows were all back where they had been.

Though I had never considered myself a woman of faith, I prayed often that Aisling had escaped this place. I implored whatever magic, or evil, that kept me here that Aisling had been spared from a similar fate to Agatha's or mine. The first few months I had spent in the Manor I had initially hoped I might find a door that would open and reveal that she had been here with me, trying to find a way to me as I had been to her. That hope had died quickly and I regretted even for a moment wishing she would have been trapped here with me. I wanted her to be free, to experience life in a way I knew I never would, free from this Manor and free from Matthew.

Matthew.

I had given up wondering why my husband hadn't come storming up to this place after me. Mostly I was just grateful that he hadn't. Though the loneliness that followed me through the empty corridors was always looming, the Manor was a haven away from that man. The rage that I had felt so palpably at the mere memory of him simmered, and began to dissipate as time went on, and I began to feel haunted by him less and less.

I was delighted to spend time in the gardens. I would care for the flowers, pruning back the overgrown shrubs that dwarfed and blocked the light of the young growth beneath it, and identifying particularly with the many rose bushes that I spent hours deliberately untangling from overgrown weeds that threatened to choke the life from them. Spending untold hours outdoors without having to worry about the shadow of Lord Cabot looming down my neck was cathartic. I did miss the companionship of Aisling greatly, but I also missed the even smaller companions I would so often have with me in the gardens. There were no birds here, hares, or hedgehogs; I had not even seen a fox nor a badger along the treeline of the forest to the far left of the property. Animals seemed to stay far away from here and, knowing what I did now, I cannot say I wholly blamed them.

Here, in the heart of the Manor, I was utterly and completely *alone*.

She wandered the halls cautiously, never the same path. She paused for a moment as she came to a new door to inhale deeply—perhaps steeling herself for what new wonders awaited her beyond it? Her small, unmarred hand reached out and her delicate fingers wrapped lovingly around the ornate brass handle; the mechanism clicked open at her touch, allowing her to push through.

The light filtered through the colored glass windows, illuminating the motes of dust that began to dance through the air as the space that had gone so long unexplored welcomed her into it. She laughed, an exhilarating sound that pierced the silence of the space, and rushed forward.

The books that lined the walls ranged from masterpieces untold to handwritten diaries of those who had come before her, stories of great adventures, poetry, Bibles, historical texts, and discoveries unknown— all awaiting her. The shelves reached the full height of the impossibly tall ceiling of the space, made of a dark, smoky wood that still inexplicably smelled of the forest it had been cut from. A commanding desk in the center of the room held space for many such stories to be poured over in earnest, oil lanterns always set aglow to read, even in the daylight.

Her fingertips tickled the spines as she read the titles, eyes wide and excited. Her tongue darted out to wet her lips as she mouthed the names aloud breathily to herself. The life she breathed into each new crevice was vibrant and enticing. She removed a leather-bound book with gilded pages and settled in the dark green settee in the corner of the room by the windows facing the garden. Stepping out of her shoes, her skirts draped haphazardly about her as she lifted her knees to rest the book against them.

This room became one of her favorites.

FLORENCE

I realized that the Manor was in some way speaking to me the first time I thought about ending my life. Mentally exhausted from the monotony of my confined existence, I began to be less interested with the things I had been doing for the last few years to pass the time. There were fewer surprises behind every door and hallway and I was finding my own company to be increasingly unsavory by the day.

I missed human contact. While it was almost inconceivable to think I would ever see a day where I would feel the loss of society functions, or the ostentatious estate with Matthew that had *never* been home, I did long for the company of others, and the friendship I had had with Aisling.

I missed her sky blue eyes that would sparkle inquisitively whenever we had the chance to explore each other's interests. I missed her light laugh and soft touch when she would brush my hair and help me dress. Despite the adversity of our situation, she never let it consume her like it had me. There was hurt, fear, and a fair bit of anger, as of course there would be, but Aisling always had a way of making things around her brighter. Without her company I was completely in darkness. The rage that had long been pent up inside me from the injustices I experienced at the hand of my husband, only seemed to grow and thrive in my solitude.

"Why am I here?" I had screamed once, not having anyone to direct my anger at, but feeling those ever present eyes on me all the same.

I grabbed the nearest item to me, a decorative vase, and hurled it at the wall. It shattered loudly and hit the floor in a million tinkling porcelain pieces. I stood there, breathing heavily as the cloud of rage began to clear. Feeling frustrated and foolish I crouched next to the mess and began cleaning. I palmed a large shard and stared at it. The glaze of the porcelain was ivory and decorated intricately with blue hand-painted florals. I turned it over in my hand and took in a thin breath when the sharp edge sliced cleanly through my skin. The cut was a fine deep slash that stayed pink and cavernous before it began welling with blood.

I shifted from my crouch to the floor, my legs crossing beneath me as I examined my hand. I extended my fingers and it pulled the cut open wider, blood seeping in the cup of my palm and dripping down my wrist to collect in my cuff. It stung something fierce and it was exhilarating. Like a cork being released on a bottle of champagne, it was as though the built up pressure of my mental anguish finally had a release through the physical pain. I flexed my hand again and relished in the stinging sensation it produced. I sat in contemplation until the sunlight from the window passed from one end of the room to the other, and then disappeared altogether. My head was not only dizzy with the loss of blood, but the thoughts that were seeping from the dark corners of my mind.

I never really tired anymore, not like before I had come to the Manor. I could still sleep, but I very seldom dreamed and though I never hungered, I could eat... with my basic needs always met it left a lot of time for getting lost, whether it be wandering through the Manor or the grounds, or most dangerously— in my mind.

Now, my mind had wandered to a place I had not yet explored; would death be the ultimate escape? I had not truly considered it before as I honestly was not sure I wasn't already dead. I thought back to the gruesome scene with Agatha, and the fire that had consumed the Manor after. More than a small part of me believed that I had died that night and that this façade of a life I had been living these last few years had been perhaps... purgatory? But though I did not hunger, or require sleep, I did feel pain, and I *could* bleed. That much I had just proven.

I came back to myself slowly and registered that the cut on my hand, though still painful, had stopped its steady flow of blood, and spectacularly seemed to be starting to heal. But the shard that I had cut myself with was missing. I glanced towards where the vase had shattered and gasped at the sight of the decorative vessel sitting in front of me, inexplicably whole. I stood and collected it, inspecting it closely. I could see no evidence that it had ever been broken at all, let alone shattered into a million pieces. It was not the first time something like this had happened. Often I would put something down, only to come back to it in a completely different place from where I left it. I equated it to the madness of the situation, the delusions of a confused mind, but this... I had evidence that this had happened, it was torn into my palm.

I had spent years wandering the seemingly never-ending twists and turns of corridors and hallways. Probing room after room content at first with just satiating my urge to explore, rather than searching for answers to questions I honestly was not fully prepared to ask. Now though, I wanted to know. I *needed* to know.

"Why am I here?" I called out again, my voice hoarse from disuse. I had long since given up hoping for an answer, but was feeling somehow renewed in purpose.

"Who are you? Why am I trapped here? What am I?" I said to no one, if only to hear the sound of my own voice echoed back to me.

For years of exploration of the Manor, there was only one place I specifically avoided altogether. The hall that lead to Agatha's room. I shivered involuntarily at the memory. A cold fear nipped at the base of my neck and caused the hair on my arms to raise uncomfortably. There were answers in Agatha's room, I did not know how I knew, but I was *sure*. I made my way up the stairs, and then down the hall, time passing in a blink before I stood at the door of the room, as if I had been placed there lovingly like a doll in the hand of a child.

I took a deep breath in an effort to prepare myself to open the door when it opened before me. Though I had been extremely uneasy, out of nowhere there was an overwhelming sense of serenity that consumed me whole. As if it had been whispered into my subconscious, I was being urged into the room with the promise of answers. The room I entered now was worlds apart from the one I had been in all those years before. Where before everything had been ravaged and thrown asunder now the room glowed warmly, with everything in its proper place, untouched by whatever malice had once devastated it.

I glanced at the bed, remembering the shape of the woman who had once inhabited it. There was no indentation, or sign that she had ever been there. The bedclothes appeared fresh and neatly laid out, an alabaster cotton blanket trimmed with fine lace lay over the mattress of the four-poster bed. It would have been beautiful if the memory of who had lain there before was not painted behind my eyes. I scanned the rest of the room with increased curiosity, and my sight set on the writing desk. I took a step towards the desk and, to my astonishment, the chair gently pulled out and away from under the desk where it had been, as if inviting me to sit.

I was aware that this was objectively terrifying and, though my years in this place had made me apathetic to some things, inanimate objects moving of their own accord was not one of them. Despite this, I was oddly unafraid. That unknown feeling of calm washed over me again, ensuring me I was safe to continue. I closed the distance between the desk and myself and noticed the many pieces of parchment neatly stacked, under the folded envelope with my name written on it. I let out a shaky breath.

I reached out behind me for the chair and felt it move to my hand and slide underneath me gently, tucking me comfortably under the desk. I again recognized that I would normally be frightened by this—but was not. Instead I was entirely focused on the letter that was addressed to me. Almost, as if involuntarily, my hand reached out and began to unfold it. I immediately recognized the penmanship as the same that had written the letter that had originally brought me here.

FLORENCE

*F**lorence,*

We have never met and it is my hope, for your sake, that we never will.

I could not remain any longer, I did not have the constitution for it. One day you will understand why, and I hope that when you have to make the same choice I did, you will forgive me just as I have now forgiven........

The handwriting that had begun clear and concise started to turn sloppy. Almost as though the hand that wrote it did not have the strength to hold the quill for long periods of time, I speculated as the sentence trailed off in a section of words that were too shakily written to understand.

I came to know of you, the circumstances of your marriage, and your strength of character in regards to helping those who needed your aid. I know it is an extreme unkindness I do to you now but, if it is of any consolation, I am in desperate need of help—and I hope that perhaps you may find this alternative favorable to life in the shadow of a man like Lord Cabot.

The writing continued to become more unsteady, difficult to decipher in some words and entirely impossible in others, but I was desperate to continue, desperate to understand.

The Manor..... I do not know how or why. All that I do know is that............ and it requires............For years I have been.............but I was never enough...........it tires of me. I can feel it tearing................at my bei ng..........punishing me, always punishing...

The following words bled together in a smudge of ink and wobbly writing, and though I strained my eyes to read it—it was completely illegible. I scanned past the mess of words to the end where it was still smudged and messy, but at least every few words were legible.

You cannot leave..........you mustn't try, only pain........

I turned the key of the oil lamp beside me on the desk and the flame flickered higher and brighter. I held the letter up to it in hopes that the words would be easier to decode with the light.

The Manor will provide. If you provide.

I belong to the house, and now so will you.

Forgive me,

Agatha Warren

I sat back in the chair and re-read the letter, twice, four times over. Every time I got to the end I would find myself back at the beginning, straining for the illegible parts to become clearer, praying to glean a little more understanding. This note, so clearly written in a state of distress, did little to satiate the questions that swirled in my mind. In fact if anything it created more.

What had she meant she did not have the constitution to remain in the house?

Who had she forgiven? Had someone lured her here as she had me?

You cannot leave, you mustn't try, punishing me... always punishing... I belong to the house and now so do you.

Those few lines of the letter made my heart thrum faster, *what does that mean?* She wrote as though the house were alive.

Almost immediately after the thought the flame from the desk lamp burned noticeably higher and brighter. I turned the key down but it did not affect the height of the flame as it should. If it had been years before I may have been more skeptical at the idea of the Manor itself being alive... but I hadn't felt the normal passing of time in years. I hadn't been able to leave the property, and the house seemed to be ever changing, evolving around me by the day, hallways constantly reconfiguring themselves so that no door ever opened to the room I expected. The feeling of always being watched and yet never seeing any evidence that there was anyone else here with me? It made just as much sense as anything else I had theorized.

"Do you...understand me?" I felt foolish as I mumbled the words, but I looked out into the room and awaited a response. I felt the chair underneath me move gently backward and I startled upward.

I swallowed a nervous laugh. "I'll take that as a yes."

There were no open windows in the room and yet I felt a breeze flow around me, gently pushing me in the direction of the hallway. I followed. As I reentered the hallway the sconces on the wall burned more brightly as I passed, almost as if directing me back to the stairs. I looked down at the grand entryway and waited for some kind of sign, my brain at odds with my gut. I felt embarrassed as I thought about waiting for a sign from...what? A haunted house? A living Manor?

The light at the base of the stairs flickered and I continued onward, down the stairs and to the right, away from where I knew the kitchen typically was. This hall was papered dark green, with gorgeous leaves twisting and climbing up the wall in shiny gold detailing. The sconces continued to shimmer as I passed and walked to the one door at the end of the hall. It was glass and ornate, the panes of the windows edged in iron that tapered up to high peaks ending in twists connected to the doorframe.

The door opened softly out into the unknown space just as I reached it. A warm breeze caressed my skin as I stepped out and down into the most extravagant conservatory I had ever seen. The steep glass roof was pitched high, each panel interlined with the same iron detailing as the door I had just passed through, with intricate curves that created dazzling refractions even in the low evening light.

The parts of the conservatory that were not glass and iron were ornate carved wood columns and beams that arched and stretched dramatically to the ceiling, connecting in the slightest whisper of a touch. The entire place was lit with varying sizes of pillar candles. They were in groups on shelves and on the stone floor in the corners, wax dripping slowly from the sides and pooling around them. Every column had a candle sconce with a lit tapered candle that emitted a soft warm glow. The windows caught the flickering of the flames and it reflected back like shooting stars across the glass surfaces.

My heart fluttered in my chest as the heady scent of earth burst from every part of the room. There were large garden beds that skirted the walls on either side of me that erupted with lush greenery. Many plants I recognized, but many I did not. There were shrubs with leaves that swirled with deep magenta and pale green, veined through the center with velvety maroon that came to points at the end like bat wings. A lavish lavender that was thick with blossoms, the center petals a dark vibrant purple that were framed in pastel. Peonies breached tall grasses that grew beneath them, the flowers a deep crimson against the almost silver of the grass. Ferns, larger than I had thought were possible, glittered with beads of dew. I walked the perimeter of the garden, my hand extended to investigate every new discovery.

In the middle of the room was a considerable-sized tree, unlike any I had seen before. It sat on almost an island in the center of a rectangular stone pool that spanned the length of the space. The water appeared deep but was densely covered by black and fuschia lotus flowers. The tree's limbs arced and flourished randomly, contorting itself into both interesting and unnerving shapes. Instead of leaves, magnificent yellow catkins hung, scaly and almost spike-like. I had seen something similar on the willow trees that grew by our barn back home.

The base of the stone pool seemed to be alive with flowering ivy, and copper lichen. A bright green moss grew along the top edge and I reached out to press my fingers to it. It was soft, and pillowy and briefly I imagined what it might feel like to lay on a bed of it, with just my skin against it. I stared into the dark fathoms of the water, and then studied a small bud of a lotus flower that had not yet opened.

"How have I never found this place before?" I asked, all pretension wiped away by the wonder of this new Eden. "Did you make this for me?"

As if in accordance the small pink flower began to blossom, its outer petals shuddering and reaching out to explore the space around it. This was a gift, and without a doubt, the most considerate one I had ever been given. A warm glow settled within me.

"The Manor will provide, if you provide." I quoted the words from Agatha's letter.

Another layer of the flower stretched outward, the first layer's petals dipping softly into the water below it.

But what was I providing? What did this place want from me? What could I even have to offer?

"But I don't have anything I can offer you—I." I wracked my mind for anything but the pathetic admission that left my lips next was: "I only have myself."

The lotus burst open, an incredible canary yellow center to complement the warm bright pinks of the petals. A stunning response, as if it were telling me that the offer of my company, that being here within the walls, was enough. I was enough. The beautiful imagery did soothe the message the Manor was trying to convey, but not entirely. The warmth of the room was not able to keep the small chill from trickling down my spine.

"I belong to the house," I conceded.

T he walls thrummed about her as she flitted delicately through the halls. Carpets cushioned her steps and a warm, ever-present breeze rustled delicately against her skirts and skin. An understanding had been come to. A union of sorts. Years spent learning every inch of her, from the countless flecks in her irises to copper curls of her hair, were reciprocated in kind by her inhabiting the Manor. Unknowingly she breathed life back into spaces that had long been forgotten and left untouched.

Countless hours spent reading in the library, using her boundless imagination to explore and live vicariously through the pages, seemed to inject energy into the house. Back into the walls that held her, cocooned around her with care. The plants that blossomed under her hand brought life and wonder to a place once dark and dying. Both inside the conservatory and the outside gardens bloomed and thrived to please her. She was loved here, and often loved in return.

As the trust continued to grow, a field of wildflowers did too, flourishing among the rolling hills of grasses in the expansive acreage behind the Manor. A gift, a loving gesture and an extension of freedom, however limited. It was always met with gratitude and excitement, and also a hidden unshakable sense of sadness. Despite it, to the Manor she shone.

Something so light, only able to shine so brightly due to the dark that constantly threatened to devour it.

FLORENCE

No part of this Manor had been left untouched by me. It offered solace and comfort within its walls and I did as much as I could to care for it the way it did me. Even still, routine was the best way I had found to stave off the stark raving madness that could easily consume me due to having unlimited time. My first few years in the Manor should have ended violently and abruptly at the end of a rope because I hadn't understood that. Unfortunately, there was no escaping that easily.

Though I had tried to end my own life, the Manor would not allow me to follow through. The post I had tied the rope to on the mezzanine had snapped and sent me plummeting to the floor before the noose had a chance to do its job. It was my first of a handful of failed attempts and it was also the first time the Manor had put me to sleep for an extended period of time. When I had awoken, I could tell a significant amount of time had passed due to the change in the seasons. It had been the dead of winter, and I woke to spring blossoms.

That was the first time, though it certainly hadn't been the last.

I did my utmost to follow a routine to keep myself distracted, to keep myself feeling *sane.* As time had gone on I was granted more freedom in the form of the boundaries I was able to push out on the property. I was never able to pass the gates, always being flung back and locked up tight until deemed trustworthy again to go outside. But a field of wildflowers that seemed to go for acres had sprung up, another reminder from the Manor that I was loved and cared for. I was able to wander. I could walk out and explore, and press my favorite flowers. Often I would just settle down to read amongst them for hours.

I would cultivate the gardens, growing vegetables I didn't hunger for, and saplings and flowers that no one but me would appreciate. I would explore the halls, looking for new rooms I'd yet to discover—though as time went on they became fewer and farther between. Some days, when I could feel the darkness in my mind clawing at my peace, I would float unclothed in the bathing room. I would expel my lungs of all the air I could manage and sink to the bottom, waiting until the burning in my chest was so great that I had to break the surface for oxygen, to remind myself what it felt like to be alive. To be grateful of the sanctuary I had been given. I kept a daily record of my goings on, as mundane and repetitive as they were, as a way to both fill and mark my time. Most nights I would sleep, though it wasn't necessary. It passed the time in a way that helped to keep away the darkest thoughts that would creep in when the nights were unbearably lonesome.

Since the discovery of the library I had made it a habit to write in the mornings. I spent hours pouring over pages with a fountain pen that never seemed to run out of ink. I had filled multiple journals, with the memories of my life before I came here, the ones I could not bear to forget. The color of my mother's eyes, the layout of our countryside home, the feeling of my father's arms around me, the sound of Aisling's laughter.

Time had a different way of moving in this place, and I seemed to have a different place in time altogether. I had marked what I thought could have been well over two decades in my journal, and still I remained unchanged. Any injuries I sustained, whether purposeful or accidental healed quickly, and left no scars. There were no signs of the extreme aging or sickness as I had seen in Agatha visible on my flesh. While I was relieved to not be deteriorating in a similar fashion, I did long to see the signs of time mark me in some way. Whether it be wrinkles at the creases of my eyes, or white hair growing amongst the auburn. But there were none when I studied myself in the mirror. My hair retained its natural vibrancy, my skin stayed taut, and the only thing that changed was the weariness behind my eyes.

Despite my efforts in routine and normalcy, I could feel the familiar shadows reaching for me again. Always there in the back corners of my mind, coating every day, every moment, every *thought* in a dark ichor that threatened to pull me under. Days where the loneliness was just too much for me to bear and everything I touched seemed to curdle and molt.

No book could hold my attention, no breeze could be sweet enough, no room in this blasphemous Manor worth looking through. The nights would stretch on forever and try as I may to sleep my eyes would remain open. Madness setting in. The blackness would take hold and over and over again I would picture the people I had lost, the years I had suffered and the inescapable endlessness of it all.

"WHY HAVE YOU BROUGHT ME HERE?" I screamed out, grabbing the closest candle and throwing it directly at the glass wall of the conservatory.

It thumped unsatisfactorily against the panel. I shrieked and fell to my knees, my hands fisting the earth in an effort to keep from trembling with rage. As of late the downward spirals into unfathomable dark moods had become almost daily occurrences. The heated hatred rolled through me, my throat thick as I seethed.

"Why me? Why?" It was a question I repeated many times through the years, but never more than when I was in such a desolate state. I could not see beauty, it did not matter. There was no joy, no interests, no peace. Just loathing and suffering and a mind that never stopped turning.

The Manor never responded when I was like this, or at least I had never been in a state to notice if it did. I couldn't feel the usual gratitude and love I normally felt for it in these moments. I hated it. I hated myself. There was no room for anything else. I was about to stand and storm off when, from the corner of my vision, I noticed a familiar plant growing beneath the Azaleas.

The small umbrella shaped white flowers of a hemlock plant were clustered together, almost completely out of sight. I leaned down further to inspect closer. Yes, it *was* a hemlock plant, one of the most poisonous plants that I knew of. My mind began to spin, the melancholy that moved me made a plan before I had fully thought it out, and perhaps that is why the Manor did not notice.

I fisted the flowers and pulled them out of the ground. I stood and hastily moved to my planting table, my mortar and pestle exactly where I knew it would be. Quickly I pounded the flowers, crushing them into a fine syrup. I then retrieved a propagation glass from the shelf above the table, and filled it with water from the pool.

I could see the branches of the tree begin to extend out in intrigue, the Manor unsure of what had derailed my tantrum and pulled my focus. If I wanted any chance in succeeding it would have to be now.

I poured the lethal liquid into the tube, covered it with my thumb and mixed it with the water. The color reminded me briefly of the tincture I used to make.

Maybe this time I would finally be set free.

It was that thought that did it. The Manor's walls shuddered and the glass of the atrium creaked and moaned.

NO.

I drank.

PART TWO

WESLEY

The box of beer dangled from my three fingers as I grabbed the two bags of food and kicked the door of the Bronco shut with my boot. I adjusted my grip on the box and stuck the bags between my teeth as I wandered toward the motel door.

A long stretch of doors spread across the two story, mint green motel on the side of the motorway. The bright vacancy sign flickered in red neon bursts that illuminated the wet parking lot and reflected off the rows of dirty windows.

I used my free hand and opened the door, pressing my back against the damp wood to spin into the cramped, musty room slamming it behind me.

"What the hell took you so long!" Koen was on his feet in seconds, all six feet of him moving toward me. His blond hair matted against his forehead, wet from a shower, and the cut on his cheek from the hunt hours before finally clean and looking less irritated. He snagged the food from my mouth so quickly I barely had the chance to unclench my teeth before I registered the sound of the bags ripping.

"Wow, yeh, thank you for the help," I grumbled and set the beer down on the dresser before I grabbed his chin. He tried to tug away from me, mad that he couldn't start digging in the bags, but I tightened my grip.

"Was it deep?" I asked him and he shook free of my grasp. The cut made his usually soft features look tired and sore.

"No," he huffed and went back to digging in the bags for something to eat. "Are there onions on this?" He held up one of the burgers.

"What's wrong with onions?" I scoffed and grabbed one, tossing it to Clay who sat at the table across the room.

He caught it without taking his focus off the newspaper he was reading and started to unwrap it with his teeth. His sweater was pushed up around his forearms, exposing the tattooed skin beneath that made him look less like a posh dork. His wavy dark hair was pushed back off his slender, sharp features and inquisitive, almond-shaped eyes were framed by a pair of glasses that sat on the bridge of his angled nose.

"He hates onions," Clay piped up and sniffed the burger, his blue eyes lifting from the page to look at me. "Bring it here," he instructed Koen, who stuck his tongue out at me and threw his burger to Clay.

"Sorry, I was a little busy cleaning up the decapitated body in my boot," I groaned and dug into my burger as Clay picked the onions off Koen's without fuss.

"Have you ever noticed that when there's a body stinking up the vehicle and it's his turn to deal with it it's '*my* boot' and whenever she needs gas or a wash or new tires all of a sudden it's *our* boot?" Koen joked through a mouthful of chips.

"What did you do with it?" Clay asked, ignoring the comment and sliding the tin foil toward Koen who started eating without a moment of nausea affecting him.

"Took it down the motorway and burned it in a field," I said with my cheeks full of greasy burger. "That was the easy part. Someone didn't wrap the tarp properly and it took me an hour to scrub skinwalker guts out of the upholstery."

"Did you just refer to the twenty year old brown carpeted boot in the Bronco as upholstery?" Clay's tongue darted out over his bottom lip as he tried to stifle his laughter.

"That's what it is, and I like *my* truck more than I like both of you," I grumbled, digging my boots into the ugly shag rug beneath me and setting my half eaten burger on the bed. I pushed up, shucked from my jacket and grabbed a beer for each of us from the box. The caps popped with a long hiss and I extended them out to Clay and Koen.

"I can feel you blaming me for the tarp but the problem is, I don't give a fuck," Koen leaned back in his chair with a smile and brought the bottle to his lips. "I did all the hard work last night anyways, it took me two showers to get the bodily fluids out of my hair and the stench off my skin. I had to throw out my favorite Queen shirt!"

"Boo hoo," I laughed, crossing the room and settling down against the foot of the bed to finish my burger. "And you didn't do anything. The reason you were covered in bodily fluids is because you were beneath the walker when Clay finally got his hands on it."

"That's not true, it was already bleeding by then!" Koen argued, his hands flying out in defense. "You know that's not true!" He looked to Clay for backup.

Clay laughed and noncommittally shrugged his shoulders. "You did look pretty helpless." He took his glasses off and rubbed his face with his hands before starting to work on his own burger. "This is disgusting." He scowled after the first bite.

"It's all the services had." I shoved the last bite of burger into my mouth without concern.

"You got these from the services?" Koen gagged and set the burger down to look at me with disgust on his round face. "If the monsters don't kill us, Wesley's choice in dinner will always finish the job."

"It's not even the dodgiest place we've eaten from." I stared at him with a blank expression, unsure why he was so outraged.

A pillow hurtled through the air and narrowly missed my head.

"Yeah? Well you get to shit in the street if the bathroom is occupied tonight because the burgers have torn through us. I call the toilet–Clay you can have the shower," said Koen exasperatedly.

I picked the pillow up and threw it back at him, getting him square in the nose before he could duck.

"And *that's* why you lost your Queen shirt. You need to practice your aim, little brother."

Koen bristled at my jab. "You aren't considering all the facts. The odds were stacked against me. In any other scenario I would have won that fight!"

"Against the monster or the pillow, Koen?"

Laughter echoed from Clay behind his screen.

"It's fine, luckily for me there's always another monster to prove my-self against." Koen leaned back in the motel chair and the wood creaked and collapsed out beneath him. He tumbled to the floor in a clumsy mess of limbs, blond hair and chips, sending both Clay and I into a fit of laughter.

"Did the chair bite you?" I barked out, still chuckling as Koen grum-bled and picked himself up from the floor.

Koen straightened himself out and lunged for me, his face pushed up against my stomach, arms wrapped around my waist, toppling the two of us over onto the dingy carpet. He wrestled with everything he had, tossing light-hearted punches to my stomach, but I flipped him over and pinned him to the ground.

Laughter filled the room as he fought against me, wiggling just enough to knock me off balance and against the foot of the bed. As I primed for another attack, Clay cleared his throat and the bugger lunged again, capitalizing on the interruption. His fist landed and a surprised cough was knocked out of me as I doubled over and he climbed on my back. His arm wrapped around my neck and pulled upward, locking my head between his bicep and forearm.

"Tap out!" He laughed, choking the air from my lungs.

I drove my elbow back and caught him in the side, loosening his hold on my throat just long enough to push him off when Clay played the sound of an airhorn from his laptop at full volume.

"Excuse me," he scolded. "When you two are finished I have a case."

We both rolled back in unison, I rested on my elbows out of breath as Koen fell to his back on the carpet and stared up at the water-stained ceiling.

"Another one?" Koen whined. "Dude, the body from the last one isn't even cold yet! *Literally.*"

He stared up in silence for a moment, sulking, before he pulled himself up exaggeratedly into a sitting position with his legs kicked out in front of him, and leaned his back heavily against the dresser.

He was the youngest and it never showed more than when he sulked. His brow knitted together as he shot puppy dog eyes at Clay—the better target for that particular weapon between the two of us.

"We haven't had a break in..." He paused for effect while he mimed out a long mathematical equation "...like a year!" He finished exasperatedly. "I haven't had a smooch in months! Can't we take a break? Meet some people who we aren't trying to kill, or them us?"

"I distinctly remember a girl a few weeks ago... What was her name? Carmen?" Clay responded with a raised brow, poking holes in his argument. "And wasn't there a Liam before that?"

"No before Carmen was Quinn, Liam was before Declan," I corrected, laughing at the look of incredulousness that was forming on Koen's face as we continued to name off his long list of conquests.

"God, Declan was an ass," Clay said behind his laptop.

"And your opinion is moot because you just got with that pretty thing before the vampire case, Annabeth?" Koen pointed at me. "Clay's really the only one here that is celibate."

"Not by choice," he scrunched his brows together. "It's not my fault I put standards over needs," he grumbled.

"All you have to do is ask." Koen pouted at him and, even though Clay didn't engage, his cheeks flushed pink. "Tell me what you need," Koen purred.

The blurred lines between the two of them showed in a hazy vibration as Koen's green eyes grew wide and flirtatious. Luckily Clay wouldn't give in to whatever Koen was trying to cook up; flirting kept them satiated on the road and it kept everything else clean when we were held up for days with each other. I couldn't be bothered by either. I enjoyed the company of a woman when she'd be so inclined to fall for my terrible flirting tactics and what I'd like to think was a charming smile. And Koen was my brother, blood or not.

I understood Koen's gripe, it would be nice to slow down, to find more than just brief moments of human interaction outside of our circle. But for now, just the three of us would manage. I smiled at the two of them, grateful we were all still together.

It had been a long road, never as easy as I wished it could be.

When I was ten, my parents saved a group of people from a vampire den in Northern Ireland, outside of Donegal. A day burned into my memory as the worst day of my life. Koen was the only survivor and had no family left. At four, we had taken in the petrified, green-eyed spitfire and raised him like our own. I had no blood siblings, only Koen and Clay. But family didn't end with blood. Not for Hunters.

Clayton had come later. The day I turned eighteen, my parents were investigating a string of fires in Chelsea. Turned out to be a wraith who was burning down the victims' homes after consuming their brain fluids. Cruel, horrible monsters. Among the handfuls of monsters we have taken down, I held a special hatred for wraiths. They had no moral code, they were selfish, greedy monsters. It was that day I pulled an unconscious Clay from his bed and ever since we'd been inseparable.

Koen's muffled complaints pulled me from my thoughts and I turned to find him ranting about how people need human connection to survive.

"One more hunt then we can take a break," I laughed.

"It's always one more hunt!" Koen's groaned, his hopeful eyes trained on Clay, pleading for assistance but Clay's gray eyes were focused on his laptop screen.

"I promise this time," I nod, lying through my teeth. I couldn't exactly explain it, but whenever we took too long of a break I'd get restless. If we relaxed for too long we'd get too comfortable, too soft. There were so many evils in the world and too few Hunters around anymore to deal with them.

There were more Clay's and Koen's out there needing people like us to help them. If we didn't go, who else would? Stopping felt like accepting that the nightmares outnumbered us. Our home was with each other, on the road, if we stopped... *What were we anymore?*

"Shut up." He looked back at me. "We're exhausted."

"You're exhausted." Clay corrected him.

"You are both *exhausting,*" I huffed.

"So it's decided then, we're taking a break?" Koen lifted his eyebrows at me but his mood quickly deflated when I told Clay to keep talking.

"No breaks," I hushed him when he whined something under his breath. "People are dying Koen, and–"

"Yeah, yeah." Koen shook his head but added as he turned his attention back to Clay, "they need our help."

"Atta boy," I said, handing him another beer in reward.

"Unfortunately so." Clay turned the laptop in our direction and I pushed off the floor to get a closer look at the news article he had brought up. It was a nation wide alert. "Six kids dead, three more missing. Cops say they're doing everything they can but it's out of their hands. The only body that turned up was mangled. Coroner said it was as if something had feasted on the kid. There's no leads, no warnings, parents all say they were taken in the middle of the night. It's out of control and it just feels..."

Supernatural.

"My best guess? A ghoul."

"Shit," Koen was the first to express, with a sad huff of air as he listened to Clay spew the facts. The mood in the room instantly killed by the thought of dead children. Gone was the urge to goof around with my brother and Clay.

"I call first sleep." Koen moved from the floor and started to shove his clothes back into his duffle bag.

"Let me shower first." I rubbed my hand over my face. A cold shower would wake me enough to do the first driving shift. "Go get us some coffee." I tossed the keys to Koen with a tight nod to Clay confirming that we were all on the same page over the urgency that surrounded the situation. "Map out where we're going and find out if we can get in to see that body. We need to know without a doubt that ghouls are what we are dealing with. No room for error."

WESLEY

A WEEK LATER

"It's behind us," Koen whispered in the darkness. The only light between us reflected off his hunting knife as we huddled back to back in the cellar.

"No," Clay argued, "above us."

I turned my head upward, chin to the ceiling, and listened. An eerie hush fell over the three of us, only the sound of our shallow breaths echoing off the walls of the decrepit house we found ourselves trapped beneath like prey for the taking.

I swallowed tightly, rolling my thumb over the barrel of my pistol, and sunk my large frame closer to the floor. We had been hunting a ghoul. Or actually, what seemed like a pack of them, leading to a house in rural Ireland that stood crooked in the soil. I wasn't even sure how the old thing was still standing, and I hated that we had gotten ourselves cornered in the cellar.

"There's more than one," I finally said, and both men huffed in annoyance.

Ghouls are known for feasting on the flesh of dead bodies, but these ghouls apparently had a taste for something fresher, and started to steal the children from town. Ghouls were predominantly large, lanky, ugly creatures with milky gray skin and claws that mimicked those of bird talons. They were solitary monsters, keeping to themselves and moving through the darker areas in life. But they were known for their ability to shift into something more human, passable to the average eye and not quite so horrifying in the daylight.

If I had known following this lead meant we'd be cornered in the cellar of a condemned house, I would have never let any of us step foot in this shithole. Now we were in this mess because I had insisted we look into the disappearances—and it pissed me off that we were in this situation and I had no one else to blame but myself.

Turning to Koen, I handed him the machete I rolled in my left hand. "Don't swing that unless you have to."

The moonlight glimmered, trapped in the deep moss green of Koen's frustrated glance as he flipped the handle over in his hand. "I've used a machete before, asshole."

"Not in this tight of a space." I took two steps left and my boot found the shelf's base, "Clay, keep your head on a swivel."

"For the machete?" Koen jokingly huffed.

"For the ghouls." The sound of Clay slapping him on the back of the head rang out and I almost laughed through the blanket of stress that smothered me... I hated being trapped.

"Cut it out," I warned as another shuffle of footsteps echoed from above.

The ghouls descended quickly down the stairs without worrying about the ambush they ran headfirst into. Four sets of feet. Four sets of claws.

I tapped the metal shelf with my knife four times and felt the space on my right become vacant as Clay moved to the opposite side of the basement, setting us up in a triangular formation. Koen shifted to my left, creating a dead space between us that the monster moved through not seconds later.

A reflection of light flickered off the machete, and the ghoul whipped its ugly head toward Koen, but Clay was faster on the draw. Two shots rang out through the air and echoed against the basement walls.

"That was too close!" Koen panted out in disbelief.

"It was perfectly timed," Clay's posh, husky, Chelsea accent whispered. "Not a scratch on you."

The second ghoul gave us no time to recover, it moved quickly. Its feet shuffled faster than I could calculate and it was on top of me in seconds. Teeth snapped mere inches from my face as I fought to angle the blade I carried into the monster's abdomen. A set of heavy claws sliced through the concrete beside my head, nicking my cheek and drawing a trickle of blood in a thin line through my skin. I grunted in struggle, feeling the blade sinking into the ghoul's stomach but it wasn't enough.

Fuck.

Blood sprayed across my face, coating my mouth and eyes in warm liquid as the ghoul went limp. I shoved the dead body from me and pushed to my feet behind Koen, who whipped the machete around in his hand and scanned the room.

"I could have done without the shower Ko," I quipped while trying to clear my eyes of the ichor.

"You're welcome," Koen responded sarcastically.

Clay was breathing heavily to my right but it was almost impossible to see precisely where he was in the darkness.

Watching its friends meet their end, the next ghoul's movements were more intelligent and calculated. I knelt in the pool of blood beside me and used the flash on my phone to examine the body.

"Shit." I swallowed tightly and ripped the badge from the jacket.

"What?" Koen asked quietly, a new sense of urgency in his voice.

"They're *cops*," I slapped the shiny, blood-covered law enforcement badge into his hand.

"Fuck," Koen swore.

The worst case scenario had quickly become a reality. The ghouls had blended into society to make it easier to eat. Most chose something less obvious: morticians or lab assistants. These ones were gluttons and law enforcement.

The last ghoul laughed into the shadows. "You're deadmen."

"We've heard that before," I groaned and used the hem of my shirt to clean the blood that dried across my face, hissing quietly as the fabric of my shirt tugged at the cut on my cheek.

"We weren't bugging anything. We were just surviving." It hissed from the right of us. It was circling.

Koen moved his body, machete first, and watched. He turned to me, lowering his voice. "Do you see the fourth bastard?"

I shook my head in response, holding up my hand to Clay with four fingers. In the darkness I watched his head bob as he shifted back into the shadows below one of the dirty cellar windows.

"Killing children isn't really a fair fight," Koen said indignantly, unable to hide his outrage as he became a distraction. He had always been good at getting the monsters to monologue, it usually kept their attention long enough for Clay and I to ambush them.

"Food is food. They fought back all the same." The ghoul laughed. "Until we broke their bones and scooped them clean."

"That was unnecessarily detailed," Koen made a loud gagging sound to pull the ghoul closer as his hand shot out to alert Clay of movement to our left. The fourth ghoul circled, surveying from a distance.

I shifted down behind my brother, trying to create space as the ghoul circled the shelf between it and us. I held up my hand to Koen, who contemplated following but stopped when he saw my stern look of authority.

"Stupid," he clicked under his breath at me but backed against the wall, his weapon still at the ready.

With all my strength, I pushed up and shoved my body against the rickety shelf and sent it toppling to the ground. The glass jars that lined the shelves smashed to the ground, and the ghoul took off to the left.

"They're going for the stairs!" Koen yelled, pushing off his feet.

He was the fastest of the three of us, and I'd never admit it to him out loud, but some days, I was thankful for how quickly he caught on and caught up.

Clay hollered out as one ghoul collided with him and the other bounded up the stairs and out of sight. *Fuck.* There was no time to pick which ghoul to deal with. The impact of Clay's body slamming into the wall sounded painful and they tumbled to the ground. The ghoul was fighting for dominance. A guttural cry left its throat, ringing out into the darkness before a shot rang out.

The ghoul stumbled off Clay into the streak of moonlight from the window, giving Koen the upper hand. The machete sliced through the flesh and spinal cord with ease, separating the ghoul's body from his head.

"It's almost like I know how to use a machete," Koen quipped through the gag that bubbled from him. He recovered well, kicking the head away from him the second it hit the ground. "*Weird*." He rolled his eyes at me and turned to Clay. "Shit," he stopped fooling around and slid to his knees next to him on the ground.

"Surface wound," Clay grunted through tight lips.

I squatted next to them, flipping the flashlight out of my jeans pocket to shine it on him. His stormy blue eyes squinted and blinked a few times as they adjusted to the light, and then he turned his head to look at the gash that severed the skin on his bicep.

"Shit, that hurts," he hissed and gripped his arm, blood seeping through his pale fingers.

"You need stitches," I started, but blue and red lights flickered from outside. "But not here," I ordered both of them. We were no good to anyone locked in jail. "One of those bastards got away, we aren't safe here."

"The call came in an hour ago." We startled at the voice that pushed through the radiostatic that came from inside the ghoul's jacket beside Clay's foot. "Three male suspects."

"We need to go." Koen slotted his six-foot frame beneath Clay's good arm and hauled him to his feet.

I found the cellar door on the South wall, away from the main stairs where the fourth ghoul had escaped, and pushed it open quickly and quietly.

"Come on." I ushered them up the stairs. Clay left a trail of blood as it seeped from the twisted cut on his arm and,although he was moving decently, he would leave a scent.

"Wes—" He swallowed tightly as I closed the doors behind us.

"Leave it. You're not gonna be winning any battles with that arm as it is…" I didn't like leaving loose ends any more than Clay did, but I did not like the look of how quickly his sleeve was turning red. "It'll likely lay low and lick its wounds. The chances of it being able to gather up any others to cause real problems is low."

But not zero. I could hear the words from one look at Clay, but we didn't have the time to deal with it. "Move your ass before you get us caught, then." I shooed him.

Koen grunted under Clay's weight, who eclipsed him in size by nearly four inches. Clayton was Koen's opposite, with dark wavy hair that I wanted to take scissors to, and stormy blue eyes, so cloudy they were practically gray, framed by a pair of dark-coloured glasses. His looks contrasted Koen's short, shaggy, dirty blonde hair and curious, moss-green eyes. While shorter, Koen was sturdy and fast because of his size. Clay, born with his nose in a book, was a little less graceful in the art of fighting but he managed.

"I keep telling you to carry a smaller knife," Koen scolded. We broke the tree line and stumbled toward the old white Bronco left on the side of the motorway, tucked into the trees and out of sight.

"Be quiet." I turned as they opened the passenger door to the Bronco. I listened for a long moment, only satisfied when I couldn't hear the sound of following footsteps or a police radio on our tails. "In, now." I hurried them.

We were on the road as soon as Koen closed his door.

"We need to find somewhere to rest. I need to stitch him up." Green eyes found mine in the rearview mirror, illuminated by the dim light of the moon. I could hear the sound of ripping fabric as Koen fashioned a makeshift tourniquet and tied it tightly at the top of Clay's arm. "I'm not asking, Wes. I'm *demanding*."

Clay groaned. His lanky body didn't fit in the Bronco well in the first place, but he was fighting to find a comfortable position as Koen was practically on top of him trying to staunch the blood that seeped from the open wound.

"Fine," I snapped. "But only because I'll never get that blood out of the leather."

"Oh, boo hoo," Clay coughed with a lopsided smile on his slim face. "Not the leather!"

"This is a classic." I rolled my eyes and pushed the truck further down the motorway.

"It belongs in a rubbish heap," Clay joined in weakly, his head leaning heavily against the back of the passenger seat.

"You're both one more comment away from living in a ditch, permanently."

"Does that mean we both get to slag off the Bronco once more each or do we share the one between the two of us?" Koen joked. The distant sound of sirens flooded the night air, and all three of us went silent. Ten or so minutes pass with our ears strained for any signs of being pursued.

"There." Koen pointed to a service road hidden between tangled trees and brush.

"Orchid Lane," Clay huffed as the headlights illuminated the rusty road sign. "Did you know that one orchid plant can survive nearly a hundred years?" He spewed the fact through a clenched jaw.

"Be quiet before you bleed to death," I groaned and continued driving until a Manor came into view. "Somewhere to rest," I clipped at Koen who merely grumbled something from the backseat.

It grew more prominent as we drove down the unmanaged road. I stopped at the gothic iron gate that was covered in masses of tangled vines. I stopped the Bronco and hopped out of the driver's seat, quickly using my knife to hack at the dead growth that kept the gate woven closed. Once it was clear enough to push open, I jumped back in and we passed through the gate and up the driveway. More vines tangled across the dark gray bricks and covered the Manor in lush green, matching the trees and bushes surrounding the building. Dark arched windows stared down on the three of us, and it was clear that no one had lived here for a very long time as the chill settled over the truck like a blanket.

I looked back at Koen, meeting his gaze. His eyes had grown wide. "Great, *another* haunted house."

CLAYTON

"**D**o you think anyone is home?" Koen leaned forward with bloodied fingers curling around the headrest of the seat. He pulled forward as far as he could, his chest brushing against my face as he peered up at the derelict building.

"Do *you?*" Wes asked, the sarcasm rolling off him in waves.

The Manor was clearly empty. All of the windows were buried behind thick, dark vines that curled around the house and hugged it tight. The stone was decaying around what was still an expansive, intricate overhanging that protected a large, decorated wooden entrance.

The garden beds that would have once been filled with flowers now overflowed with weeds and dead branches that sprawled across the messy gravel drive. The moonlight slithered across the sloping moss and vine covered roof. I swallowed tightly, not exactly sure what to expect from the inside. A thin film of weathered grime covered the window panes, clinging to the metal frames and turning everything a murky shade of brown. I collected a full breath, swallowing down the nausea and pushing away the dizzy feeling overwhelming my rational thoughts.

There was something...wrong about this place.

"You up for a sweep?" Wes's bright hazel eyes turned on me and I nodded, shaking off the sharp pain that radiated through my muscles and burned the ends of my nerves.

I sat up and shifted, extending my uninjured arm to the dash and gripped the butt of my gun. "I'm shooting anything that moves," I hissed as I climbed from the truck.

Koen jumped out behind me, his feet crunching on the gravel as he landed. He extended his hand in my direction but I pushed it away. "I'm alright," I grumbled.

I was far from it but I was standing, despite the dizzying blackness that crept into the sides of my vision. All things considered I thought I was doing a pretty good job pretending. My sleeve was soaked and, even though the tourniquet Koen had applied was holding, I could feel how deep the cut ran with every small movement I made. It needed stitches.

"Let's get this over with." Wesley nodded, leading our way with his gun first. He leaned forward, checking the doorknob and found it unlocked. The door swung open lazily, hinges squealing as they rotated.

Koen stayed close to my back, keeping an eye behind us as we carefully crossed the threshold into the colossal Manor. The inside was much the same. Worn down from years of neglect, vines had forced their way through the wood flooring, filling the cracks with greenery that climbed the walls and overran the foyer. Hanging in the center of the ceiling, framed by two rotting staircases, was a cobweb-covered chandelier. It was coated with so many years of dust that I wasn't positive if it was made of gold or brass. Regardless, it was extravagant and once would have been an impressive display of wealth. It was precariously suspended in the air with most of the glass shattered beneath it, scattered amongst errant pieces of fallen plaster and dried leaves.

"It smells like death in here," Koen coughed as his shoes dragged lines through the dust that covered the warped wooden floors.

I stumbled, my knees shaky from the blood loss. Koen's fingers found my good bicep and dug in to hold me steady. Usually I'd fight it but there was no way I would make it much further without his help. Wes went ahead, sweeping through the closest rooms, calling out to us with each one he found empty.

"Judging by the amount of vines I had to hack off the gate, and the leagues of undisturbed dust, I don't think there's been anyone in this place for a while. We should be alright," he said on his way back through, stopping in front of us as he shoved his gun in the back of his pants.

"That's not a guarantee..." I grumbled.

"Keep your percentages to yourself, Clay. You wanted a place to hide, I found you a place to hide." Wes shrugged in his jacket.

"I would have preferred a place that didn't look like it was full of black mold." I shifted my stance against Koen and groaned under the dull, throbbing pain.

"Beggars can't be choosers, and that arm will kill you faster than the mold will," Wes sniped as he helped Koen, slipping under my arm and guiding us toward the empty sitting room.

There was an enormous stone fireplace that looked like it hadn't seen a fire in a century and two large chairs, which appeared to have been devoured by animals and insects. The fluff torn and pulled from within the ugly graying fabric. Once upon a time they might have been beautiful, but now they were void of any comfort as they sat across from a long settee with a high back and exquisite wooden details.

They lowered me onto the ruined cushion, making sure I was balanced before pulling away and surveying the room more closely. The wallpaper peeled away from the decaying and cracked molding in the corners of the room. Vines pushed their way through the separated walls and made home within, thriving in the darkness.

"This place gives me the creeps." Koen stayed close, his green eyes flickering over the space with caution.

"I'm going to bring our stuff to the door and hide the Bronco," Wes said as he started to walk away. "Koen, come get the kit and sew him up. The sooner he stops bleeding all over the place and feels better, the sooner we can leave."

Koen followed Wes to the front, his sneakers tapping impatiently on the floor as Wes hauled everything inside unassisted. Wes mumbled something to him and Koen responded in a grumbling tone that could only mean they were arguing again.

Blood was still continuing to seep down my arm despite the makeshift tourniquet, and was staining my fingers crimson.

"Don't worry, I'm sure I won't bleed out before you've finished fighting..." I yelled from my slouched position on the couch. That got Koen moving, the heavy door slamming with a vibration that shook the walls of the sitting room.

"Sorry." He knelt beside me on the couch, working at the knotted fabric on my arm. It only took him a moment of fussing with the knot before he discarded the soaked scrap at our feet and scowled at the damage.

"Remember the steps." I closed my eyes, just trying to remain conscious long enough to walk him through the important stuff. I opened them when he didn't respond. "Hey." I clapped a hand to his face, leaving a tiny smear of blood across his flushed cheeks. "Take it slow, clean it, sew it up. Easy." Typically I was the one who did the sewing in this group, so this was a step out of his comfort zone.

Koen nodded, worry rippling over his face as he started on the buttons of my shirt. He rolled the fabric down gently. I leaned forward for him, so he could work the shirt down over my arm to give him better access to the wound.

"It's deep, Clay," he mumbled, grabbing his flashlight from the pocket of his jeans. He flicked it on and popped it into his mouth. The light shone over the wound, and he was right in his examination. The long jagged claw marks had sunk deep enough to pull apart the tattoos on my bicep, leaving them in shredded pieces between the three gaping slashes.

"Damnit, that was my favorite one." I offered a small joke to break the tension as I stared down at the once elegant tattoo. A portrait of a woman; her delicate black and gray features were strewn into fragments, eradicating what she had been.

Koen's hands trembled, noticeably silent compared to his usual playfulness.

"It was a joke, Koen, It'll be alright," I said, and leaned my head back against the couch, closing my eyes as he flicked off the cap of the antiseptic we kept on hand and dumped it out onto a cloth.

"This is going t' fuckin' hurt," he hissed as he pressed the cloth to my open wound.

"Bugger me," I growled as he quickly cleaned the deeper spots around the wound. I could tell he wanted to apologize for hurting me but the last time we had been in a similar situation Wesley had not so politely reminded him that it wasn't his fault and that I would likely die from infection or blood loss if he didn't just 'get on with it'.

"Almost done," he huffed. Sadly we were far from the finish line.

The next few moments were tense as the silence between us filled with small groans of discomfort and Koen's mumbled thoughts. He cleaned the needle and cut the thread. Pausing for a moment to steady himself before he attempted to thread it, once, twice...

"Koen." I pressed the back of my hand against his thigh. "Breathe."

His wide, panicked green eyes looked up from his shaky hands to meet mine as my head rolled to the side. It took him a moment, —a long, painful moment—and one rough inhale before he started again. The needle pushed roughly into my skin and I did my best to stifle the sound to protect him from the pain he was causing, but I couldn't. The groan left my lips and Koen paused, hand on my arm, needle in the air.

"Listen," I said to him, pausing to take a short breath. "I'm going to pass out," I said tightly, trying to keep my eyes open through the excruciating throbbing that wracked through my body. "Monitor my breathing, keep sewing, clean it when you're finished," I instructed him slowly, my breath getting harder to manage through the ache.

"Wait—wait, wait!" Koen's words were strung together roughly in his panic. "Isn't falling asleep bad?" He asked.

"No, there's a laundry list of—" I moaned through a wave of pain. "I'll be okay. Just finish your job." I promised him. I needed sleep, days of it, but a few hours would suffice.

My eyes grew heavy as Koen talked himself through each tedious stitch, the skin pulling and stretching in a new agonizing way each time. Shadows claimed the corners of my vision as my blinks became longer and eventually I drifted into unconsciousness, passing out from the pain.

She lay in the conservatory. Still and untouched since the moment she had fallen. Hair splayed out about her shoulders and entangled with errant petals and leaves that had reached for her and grown about her during her compelled rest. A contented thrum wavered in the air as she laid peacefully among them, on the bed of moss.

She had been happy here once, with the blossoms and the dirt for company, and she would be again. Time to reset was all it took to pull the light back from the shadow that had consumed her. She had a gift for nurturing, one that came so easily to her that the plants yearned for her touch. Even now in her sleep they leaned toward her, in bundles and tangles, longing for her attention.

The front door opened. The disturbance shuddered through the walls in the foyer and stirred up hostility and covetousness where previously there had been calm. Darkness descended from the top of the Manor through each floorboard and beam. It crept over every brick, encasing the building in an imposing unease.

Three men stumbled over the threshold, dripping with blood not entirely their own. They stunk of violence and danger and, one especially, of death.

The lock clicked responsively on the atrium. A possessive barrier between *her* and them... and then unlocked all within the same moment. A twisted curiosity settling within the walls.

The shadows that wrapped around her seemed to stem from a consuming lonesomeness. Despite the companionship that had formed between her and the Manor she had a tendency to fall into despair, never lasting long before trying to escape it with finality. The walls rippled malevolently, the most recent attempt had caused the longest stretch of unconsciousness yet. Punishment for using the gifts it created especially for her against it.

Perhaps a change would stave off the madness for longer? Perhaps a reminder of what *could* await would steady her against repeating her actions again. The air swirled with sick fascination and contemplation. A short time then. It had been a while since things were interesting.

Open your eyes.

KOEN

There was a note stuck to my forehead when I finally managed to open my eyes the next morning.

Gone to get supplies.

It was scribbled in Wes's horrible handwriting. I crumpled it and chucked the paper to the side. We wouldn't see him for at least a few days. After challenging hunts, he would disappear under the guise of making sure we were safe. He'd walk his six-four frame with his perfectly coiffed, honey blond hair and hard, hazel eyes out the door of wherever we were sleeping and wouldn't come back until he shook free of the nightmares. And only after he knew we would survive whatever had happened. He must have determined Clay to be in a decent enough state to slip away in the middle of the night.

Clay was still sleeping on the couch where we had dropped him.

I managed to stop the bleeding with a handful of sloppy, sleep-deprived stitches as he passed out cold. He was going to be pissed when he woke up to find out I maimed one of the delicate fine line tattoos that ran the expanse of his bicep. It would heal okay but the tattoo would suffer from scarring once it did.

I stumbled to my feet and wiggled them into my Converse before pressing my fingers to his throat to check his pulse. He stirred at my touch and that was good enough for me. I messed my fingers through his dark curls, saying a silent thank you to whoever was listening for protecting him. I looked around at the room we had thrown ourselves down in for the night. The light from the sun peeked through the cracks of thick curtains that covered a set of east-facing floor-to-ceiling arched windows.

I turned in a circle, admiring the once rich blue wallpaper, now dull, peeling, and cracked. Dust and dirt settled over the furniture and the floors.

"I'll be back." I patted a sleeping Clay on the shoulder and flipped my knife through the air into the palm of my hand, just *in case.*

In the dark, I would have bet my life that no one had lived in the Manor for nearly a hundred years; in the light I'd have doubled that bet. I tapped the blade of my knife against the solid oak bannister and stared up at the high ceilings in amazement. Even in disrepair, the house's architecture alone was incredible; gothic and extravagant. It was a mystery as to why it was empty.

My thoughts were interrupted by a loud crash echoing down a hallway to my left.

An intelligent man would have woken Clay but curiosity ate at my good sense and I was already walking towards the sound before I had fully decided not to wake him. I rolled the sleeves of my navy shirt over my forearms and shook out what was left of the sleep from my sore muscles.

Every hall of the Manor was the same; crumbling wood and dusty floors. Each step toward the source of the noise only fueled regret at leaving Clay to sleep. *It was probably a large rat.* I looked closer at the holes in the baseboards. *A colony of large rats, more like. I hated the things. Disease carrying, no good rodents...*

"Hello?" I called out, but it was stuttering and weak. *Get your shite together, Koen. Wes would take the piss out of you if he knew you were this out of sorts.*

I had been hunting monsters with Wes for as long as I could remember. One of the first memories I had was being in the backseat of the car with Wes, sharpening his father's hunting knives with the utmost focus.

He had always been like that, dedicated to the hunt. I wasn't sure if he even had personal hobbies outside of killing monsters. It was just Wes. Dedicated, driven and focused. He tried to raise me with those same values and the jury was still out if I managed to uphold those ideals to a satisfying level yet. He had been stuck with me more often then he would have liked when we were young. I knew he had had an older brother, Wyatt, who he never spoke about by choice, and his parents weren't around often. And when they were, they weren't very nice. They missed birthdays and holidays. By all accounts and from what I could remember, his father brought me home, but it had only been Wes and me from the beginning.

The sound thumped through the wall again. *Totally a fucking rat.* It was coming from just beyond the dark corner ahead of me. The hallway led in both directions, covered with moldy framed artwork and fading intricate floral wallpaper. There were heavy brass sconces every few feet that I wasn't even sure had working bulbs inside, but when I stepped to the edge of the hall, they all flickered on simultaneously. But they weren't bulbs...they were candles.

"That's super chill," I whispered, running my hand through the messy ends of my blond hair. "I'll take 'haunted house' for three hundred, Alex."

Clay would have snorted at the joke. Hours had been spent arguing over reruns of Jeopardy until the three of us melted into shitty motel carpets with our eyes half open.

Again, two loud crashing sounds. *Thunk, thunk.*

"Is anyone there?" I said louder that time, and the sound abruptly stopped. "That answers that question," I huffed, wishing I had brought something other than the small, steel hunting knife.

At the end of the hallway was a large ornate glass door that stood out against the crumbling architecture. I looked around at my surroundings once more with confusion and then back to the glass. It was pristine. The glass was polished and the iron frame that twisted around it came to a peak.

"That can't be good," I whispered, and the candles flared against the wall.

I started slowly toward the door, each step revealing more and more of what I might be in for. The glass reflected soft morning sunlight in rays and illuminated what looked like a greenhouse. It didn't explain the sound, which rang out again in three quick thumps, nearly scaring me off my feet.

"Don't be a rat," I whispered as my hand wrapped around the doorknob.

I wandered into the bright space and took in all its beauty. I looked back at the hallway, still dark with nothing but a quick flicker from the candles to remind me that it was derelict and abandoned.

"But not you," I murmured as I studied the high glass ceiling, the curved panes soaking up the sunlight and reflecting them back onto the lush garden that grew within its walls. Flowers in every color, shape, and size bloomed around the floor in planters, and climbed up the iron that framed the entire conservatory. In the center a massive old tree grew tall, nestled into a concrete pool of still water. It was magnificent and unnerving all at the same time.

The sound banged again, loudly and from my left. I turned with my knife forward, waiting for the attack, to find a hanging planter swinging against the wall. It spun in lazy circles, only hitting the wall every so often; *thunk, thunk.* I stepped toward it, reaching my hand out to slow its motion and leaving it still. The sound quieted but my mind was still running rampant with questions.

A stream of light caught my eye and pulled my attention to a dainty hanging decoration, a suncatcher, that shone in the sunlight and created a pattern of refracted colors that danced across the floor. My eyes followed the skittering colors along the stones and over a mass that took my brain longer than it should have to register what I was seeing.

"Mother of–"

Dark copper hair was tangled in the vines on the floor. A soft round face, deep in sleep as the plants seemed to overtake her, blanketing her in blossoms and vines. She didn't look dead...

Her skin was pale but still held a considerable amount of color in her cheeks. She certainly didn't look dead.

"Not a ghost?" I said, confused, still holding the knife. I knelt down beside her, hovering my hand over her lips, a perfect cupid's bow that matched the color of the blossoms around her still body. "*Maybe* a ghost?"

As I took a better look at her, I noticed she was wearing a pile of skirts and— "Is that a corset?" I said out loud.

Vibrant green eyes whipped open.

My grip on the knife faltered suddenly, shocked that she was alive.

She stared at me with fear in her eyes and I could confidently say I returned the sentiment. She flexed her fingers and started to wiggle free of the plants' confines. I kept my knife pointed at her, unsure what her next move might be, but she remained silent, observing me with every tiny movement she made.

With a tiny whimper she shifted off the floor to a sitting position, scooting backwards to create space between us. Her loose curls fell as she tilted her head to the left and raked those doe eyes down my body. Delicate features and blushed cheeks complimented her scowl and furrowed brow line. Her curves in the corset left nothing to the imagination and, suddenly, I was made aware again as to how long it had been since we had taken a break long enough to *touch someone.*

Heat licked at my neck.

Okay, don't get turned on by a ghost. You'll never hear the end of it.

The feeling washed from me as quickly as it had built, as the plant pot nearest to her flew from her hand and hurtled just past my head.

"Okay, okay!" I yelled, dropping my shoulder to the left, barely missing the terracotta pot that smashed against the floor.

She responded simply by throwing another pot. It clipped my shoulder but didn't hurt; it startled me enough to push to my feet and walk backward toward the door away from her, hands raised in submission.

She clambered to her feet, shaky and off balance, but picked up another plant-filled clay pot. It smashed against the wall behind me, just inches from making a direct hit to my face.

"Will you stop throwing shit at me!" I dodged another and managed to wrap my hand around the doorknob.

The pot shattered against the wall behind my head, a splinter that mimicked the spidered, cracked glass of the atrium biting at the skin on my cheek as I popped the door open and slid out of the room.

I slammed it shut behind me and held it there momentarily as quiet fell over the house. I counted the seconds before she appeared on the other side of the glass and started to rattle at the door knob. I gripped it tighter when she began kicking the door and looked around for anything that might help keep her trapped while I ran for Clay. He'd know what to do.

"Curiosity killed the cat," I mocked Wes's voice as I spotted an old high-backed chair at the end of the long hallway. "Gotcha."

I waited for a pause in her panic and took off, sliding on the thin soles of my shoes against the old carpet, my hand gripping the back of the chair clumsily. I shoved the entire thing up against the knob and watched as she tried it again without luck.

Emerald eyes widened with crippling fear.

"I'm sorry," I blurted as an odd guilt weighed on my chest. I backed away, never taking my eyes off the glass door until I reached the corner and ran at a pace that matched my racing heart all the way back to Clay.

CLAYTON

The book that had been within reach was boring.

Or maybe the dull throbbing that cut through my bicep was more distracting than expected. I had been trying to wake up from my injured haze and figured a book was my best way out of the fog. But half its pages were missing and it smelled of mold, which didn't help the distraction, it just made me disgusted.

"Clay!" Koen slid into the room on his heels, fresh blood on his cheek, and I sat up gingerly on the couch.

"You're bleeding," I said, and his response was simply to nod as he caught his breath. "What happened?" I asked.

"There's a woman in some crazy glass greenhouse at the other end of the house," he said between shallow breaths. "I don't know where she came from, but I heard a strange noise, I thought it might be an animal."

"It's never an animal," I said, and he nodded, exaggeratingly mocking me under his breath.

"I know, I know!" His chest thudded beneath his dark t-shirt as he worked to collect himself. "It obviously wasn't," he huffed, frustrated and frazzled. "It's a fully-grown woman in skirts and a corset. Clay, she..." he stopped, finally looking up from his feet. "She looks like she walked out of a Jane Austin novel."

"How do you even know—" I let the rest of my sentence trail off. "Koen, we're exhausted. Are you sure you weren't seeing things?"

"I'm bleeding, remember?" He pointed to the trail of blood that dripped down his face, curling around his jaw and down his neck. "She threw a bloody pot at me!"

"Is it a ghost?" I asked, sitting up and reaching for my pack. "Come here," I said, grabbing a dirty shirt from inside.

He sank to his knees beside the couch and offered his chin to my outstretched hand. "It's not a ghost," he said, his eyes flickering closed at the contact.

"Are you sure?"

"No—" Koen shrugged his slim, muscular shoulders at me and winced when I rubbed away the blood. The cut wasn't deep, but it was real. "–Yes!" He corrected, as if Wes were picking at the back of his head, teasing his confidence. "Whatever she is, she's not a spirit."

"Alright... I don't believe you," I said, fingers still lingering on his skin.

Koen rolled his exasperated green eyes at me. "Of course you don't."

"But I am curious." I balled the shirt up and set it to the side, climbing from the chaise.

A cloud of dust kicked up in my nose as I moved. My entire body was sore, and the stitches that Koen had threaded into my arm hurt in unexplainable ways. The muscles itched and stung as I pulled my shirt on and buttoned it to the collar.

"The stitches are too tight." I slapped his face playfully, trying to ease the tension from his shoulders, and pushed past him, still sitting on the floor. I shoved the barrel of my gun into the waist of my pants, resting it at my back and covering it with the shirt. "But they did stop the bleeding. We can pull them out and try again later."

He was learning. I even had him read books on medical procedures, but his nerves were constantly getting the better of him. He stared at me for a long moment before compiling his out-of-order thoughts and nodding.

"Good." I nodded toward the archway from the sitting room. "Lead the way."

His stocky frame straightened out as he ran ahead of me. It's not that Koen is short, but his six-foot frame seems lower to the ground than my six-two. His shoulders are broader than mine and built with rugged, sculpted muscle that he works tirelessly to acquire. All so he can measure up to Wesley, who towers at six-four and basically looks like he's related to the Ents in *Lord of the Rings*. It was the simplest way to tell the two weren't blood-related.

Koen scrunched up his nose as we reached the opening to a dark hallway. The entire house seemed silent. There were no creaking floorboards or drafty breezes. It was merely the sound of our breathing and nothing more.

"This way." He led me down the hall.

The chair propped under the door was still held tight and, as we approached, I started to think that Koen might require more sleep; but as we got closer I could hear a faint tapping against the glass.

Resting against the frosted glass of the door was the silhouette of a woman, her finger lightly tapping the glass in a soft pattern. His eyebrow was raised when I looked back at him. "Not a ghost."

"Tapping doesn't rule out a ghost," I said. "Remember the spirit in Kingston?"

"It's not a poltergeist, Clay," Koen said. "I know the difference."

I wanted to tell him it was okay to make mistakes. We all get tired. Wes drove the notion that mistakes get you killed into him so early that it's been torture trying to yank it out of him.

"Let me out," a voice whispered, so quietly I nearly missed it.

I turned back to face it, pulled out my gun, and wandered closer to the door. Knocking gently on it with my knuckle, I waited. Feet shuffled backward. Removing the chair from beneath the knob, I set it aside and turned it until the latch clicked and the door swung open gently.

"Stay." I pointed to him and when he didn't move I followed it up with a quick, praising *'good boy.'*

The room was in shambles, which was nothing less than expected from the state of Koen's face. I stepped inside, eyes scanning the room, and was met with a fiery gaze. She stood in the corner on high alert, her hands balled around objects at her side.

The first thing I noticed was that Koen hadn't been wrong; she wasn't from this era. The fabrics of her full skirts and tight bodice gave that much away, but the confusion on her face was unreal as her gaze lowered to the gun in my hand.

Her jaw tightened and she threw hard the object she had been holding in her hand. It smashed against the ground at my feet, splintered into tiny porcelain shards.

"Get out of here!" She said, her voice commanding, but her panicked eyes flickered around the room as if someone were listening.

"Out of the room?" I asked, feeling Koen sneak in against my back.

"Out of the Manor!" A chill ran through me. "You must leave."

"We were just—" I started, but she threw another item she'd been keeping behind her back. It hurled through the air harder than the first, but I was faster and more prepared and caught it in my hand. Her eyes narrowed as I carefully set it on the shelf beside me.

"Please stop throwing things at me."

I walked toward her, hands in the air to show her I meant no harm but she scrambled away, scared nonetheless, and pinned herself in the opposite corner of the room away from us. Her auburn hair slipped from the bun it had been wound into and fell in thick, soft bundles around her throat.

She was terrified, but gods, she was *beautiful*.

Koen scoffed from the right of me, reading the expression on my face better than he had any book.

"We were just squatting. We thought the house was empty. We're sorry for intruding," I said to her.

"You need to leave!" She repeated, her jaw tightened with anger as her eyes flickered around the room for anything she could defend herself with.

There wasn't much left that she hadn't destroyed short of the furniture, but I also didn't want to tempt her strength. I still wasn't sure if she was a spirit or a monster, but there was something very clearly wrong with the woman. She observed me. I wasn't in the condition to get in a fight with her regardless, but I needed to keep her and us safe until I could figure out precisely what she was.

"I'm sorry we can't do that," I said, snapping my fingers.

Koen took the hint and moved from the room.

"No!" She screamed when she realized what was happening. I slid back toward the door as she ran toward me. "You don't understand!" She screamed again as I shut it in her face. Her fists pounded against the glass, making it groan under her strength. "You have to leave!" She pleaded with a strained voice over and over as we barricaded the door.

"Not a ghost," Koen sighed.

"She might still be, Koen. We can't rule it out," I warned him as I stepped back from the door.

"She's *really* pretty for a ghost," he said quietly, and I looked back at him. He was staring with his head cocked at the door as it strained.

"We need to figure out what the hell she is before you start flirting with death," I groaned and walked back toward the stairs.

"Please don't make me read," he whined and followed.

"First things first," I said. "We need to redo these stitches."

I pointed to the blood seeping from my shirt. The stitches had popped when I caught the glass she had thrown at my head, and I was already starting to feel dizzy from the pain that throbbed up through my shoulder and into the base of my neck. Koen's eyes widened at the stain and he followed back down the hallway after me.

The air crackled with electricity from the energy exerted by all parties, but especially *her*. She heaved once more at the handle on the door before giving up and slamming her palms against the splintered glass. A stray shard slid into her hand and she hissed, shaking it out, and spun into the center of the room to address the walls.

"Who are they?" She croaked, her voice hoarse from years of silence.

She marched towards the stone pool with purpose and sat on the edge of it with a 'hmph'. The sullen sadness that had once permeated from her was replaced with frustration and calculation, and a haughtiness that seldom appeared. The Manor buzzed with pleasure around her.

She focused for a moment on removing the sliver of glass from her hand before submerging it into the cool, glittering water. She surveyed the growth of the space around her and said to herself in wonderment, *"How long was I gone this time?"*

She removed her hand and inspected the palm and, while there was still the faintest silver line to show that the skin had been opened, it was almost completely healed over. She growled in the back of her throat and looked up at the closest cluster of pillar candles.

"I assume I've been forgiven then?"

The group of candles flickered alive briefly in confirmation. She nodded absently and chewed the side of her cheek in thought. She moved breezily about the space, collecting the debris of shattered terracotta and clay, and coaxed the remaining plants gently from the surviving pots. She took a moment to dig her fingers into the damp earth of the garden bed and placed each one into the dirt, an apology present in the tender way she buried each set of roots.

She stood, brushing her hands against her skirts and cleared her throat.

"You let them in. Am I to assume you want them here?" She addressed the newly cultivated plants. Fresh leaves burst forward in response, vibrant and green from one of the flowers she had sent flying through the air toward the smaller man's head.

"Am I to play nice?" She asked, curiously. A flower that had been wilting rustled gently and perked its freshly invigorated face to the sun. Her eyebrow cocked inquisitively.

"Will you *play nice?"* She waited, her keen gaze watchful for any sign. None appear.

"I thought not," she sighed in response.

Her toes tapped on the stone floor for a moment as she puzzled out how to proceed, and then determinedly walked to the furthest back corner of the room. The opposite direction of the ornate glass door that led into the hallway where the men had retreated. It took a moment for her to uncover it but there, nestled between two large ferns, was the door to the back garden.

FLORENCE

They had caught me off guard.

Of *course* they had. I could not remember the last time I had seen another soul. I shuddered; that was not true. I remembered all too vividly the last person I had seen in the Manor with me, and I had watched her be gruesomely devoured in front of my eyes.

Though I hadn't seen or experienced such evil or cruelty from the Manor, or anything within its walls myself, every fiber of my being buzzed with the need to protect. Protect the Manor, protect myself, but also protect the men who had no idea what they had stumbled into.

I brushed aside the overgrown greenery and pried open the nondescript door that led out to the back garden. They had been clever. I could award them points for thinking they had locked me in but I knew the Manor better than anyone.

The latch popped free of the wall and the door swung open. I could guess that they would be somewhere by the hallway, keeping an eye on the glass door to be sure I didn't escape. If I skirted along the north side of the Manor I should be able to re-enter through the kitchen.

The men that had crashed into the room looked funny, dressed in clothing I had never seen before, but it had been a long time since anyone had dared wander close to the Manor; and in all my years here– however many there were, I had never seen another being be *let* in. I had no idea when in time I was.

The problem was that Orchid Manor had the tendency to put me to sleep, typically as punishment for acting out against it in some fashion. Sometimes only for a few days or weeks at a time, if I was behaving in ways that endangered me, like pushing against the barrier at the property line until I was thrown back so hard my ribs cracked.

Sometimes I was gone for what felt like years, especially if I tried to end my life. I shuddered at the memory of that most recent failed attempt. It made it impossible to really know when it was, all I knew is that time had passed. Regardless, the time did nothing to ease the burning need to be free. It never subsided, no matter how long I spent in the house.

I yearned for release; for freedom.

You belong to me.

The stone wall of the Manor seemed to vibrate against me as I quietly closed the door and leaned back against it. I was struck with the sudden urge to apologize.

"You've been so good to me," I hummed quietly, a little piece of my resolve chipping away. I took in a deep breath of fresh air and, for the first time since waking, surveyed the expanse of the property around me. I was immediately struck by the height of the grass and the state of the overgrown and abandoned garden bed. *I may have been asleep for longer than I imagined.*

Quickly I picked my way through the overrun garden, careful to keep my body low and out of sight of the windows that covered the Manor. Hugging the wall, I made my way up easily to the kitchen door and slid in without issue. I let out a sigh as I managed to shut the door silently.

The kitchen had access to the servants' stairs that led up to the third floor where I most commonly found my favorite rooms. If I was able to make it all the way up unseen I might be able to have some time to myself to determine how best to persuade them to leave without upsetting the Manor.

It struck me as almost ridiculous, getting worked up over strangers, when I had spent years driving myself to madness in this solitary confinement. But the Manor had never allowed guests in before to my knowledge, not since I had arrived. Being the last to have entered, I was intimately aware of how Orchid Manor treated its guests, and if these men had families or lives out there they would want to return to... I needed to get them to leave as soon as possible. If the Manor would allow it.

I could hear them in the front parlor off the entryway. Their voices were deep and melodic murmurs through the walls that separated us. I paused in my path towards the servants' door and instead re-routed and nestled myself between the wall of the parlor and the china cabinet in the staff dining room off the kitchen.

"It looks angry." I recognized the voice of the one who was in the conservatory with me when I awoke.

*"It **is** angry—we've been at this for ten minutes! This is the last stitch, you can do I— no, no, no, tie it off before you cut the thread you gobshite."* It must be the dark haired one that hissed but, despite the words, the delivery was light and jovial.

*"**I'm** the gobshite? You're the one who got slashed open and then passed out while I stitched you up out of the very goodness of my soul. If anyone here is a gobshite it's **you**..."* The first voice responded, clearly enjoying

the conversation. There was a softness between them that was easy to decipher even from behind the wall. *"...Now apologize or I won't kiss it better!"*

"Oh shove off you!" This was followed by some unplaceable noises—furniture being knocked over? And loud grunting until finally I heard *"I tap! I TAP!"* Followed by laughter.

Despite having looked around the same age, the blond man with curls and big green eyes was slightly shorter and had been wearing a black shirt with a strange image on it and denim that looked painted to his muscular legs. The taller one that arrived second had been dressed in a well-fitted, button-down and trousers. His dark hair had curled back off his forehead, and his blue eyes had been pensive, careful, and curious.

I pictured them now as I overheard the camaraderie going on in the other room. They seemed almost harmless in a way that I could not explain, like puppies, wrestling for dominance. But, in spite of my years of solitude, I was not about to go blindly trusting anyone—let alone any *man* who wandered into my home. I slid myself out of my hiding place and back into the kitchen. The Manor wanted me to play nice, and I would, but I would be a fool to not protect myself *just in case.*

At the opposite end of the range there was an assortment of knives, and my fingers kissed the handle of a small paring knife.

I stopped short of grabbing the handle completely, thinking about the reaction it would cause. They had guns and, well, I had tested the limits of injuries more than a few times over the years, but I had never tested guns.

I look toward the living room, their voices echoing softly among the books and furniture.

Would a gunshot end this nightmare?

"Turn around. *Slowly.*" A deep, thick voice with a muddled European accent spoke behind me and turned my blood to ice. My eyes flickered to the knives again, the shining metal staring up at me, tempting me to grab one. "Don't," the voice demanded.

There was a shotgun directed at my head, double barreled, similar to the ones that Matthew had used for hunting, except this one looked to have been sawn off to shorten it. I shuddered. Perhaps that would do the trick. In my time in the Manor, I had quickly learned that skin healed, blood cells reformed, and I couldn't die. No matter how much I wanted to. A demented wonder filled my mind... *could my head grow back?*

He was tall—taller than the other two—and meaner-looking as well. Golden hair curled around his ears and licked at the nape of his neck, tucked messily into the collar of his leather jacket and tartan shirt. His hands flexed around the gun, his finger off the trigger, and his hard hazel eyes were trained on me. A feeling of familiarity thrummed through me, tangling with the caution that gripped my logical thoughts.

"Who are you?" He asked, tongue darting out over his bottom lip.

"I *live* here. Who are *you*?" I steadied my voice in an effort to appear more confident than I felt, but I couldn't seem to brush off the tone in his voice. Rough and demanding. A tone that was almost always followed by undeserved violence.

"No one lives in this place." His broad shoulders angled around the long table in the middle of the kitchen, paper bags overflowing with food carefully set out on top. "Have you seen the state of it?" He scoffed.

How had I missed his arrival?

His eyes roamed down my body, no doubt taking in my odd attire, compared to his. I'd never evolved past wearing the clothing of my time. I didn't know what was happening outside of this place, and it didn't matter as I'd never needed to dress in order to impress anyone.

I narrowed my eyes at him.

"You're very quiet for such a large man."

"You're dressed pretty silly to be judging other people." His brows furrowed.

"You're being awfully aggressive for an intruder," I noted, my agitation growing.

"I have a gun," he responded.

His jaw ticked. I could see fire dancing in the golden flecks of his eyes and I angled my hand cautiously behind my back for the knife. He didn't blink as the shotgun fired off to the left of me. My ears rang from the explosion of the gun at such a close range. Tiny shards of metal ripped through my shoulder and arm, blood pooling as my skin pinched and tore open.

"You shot me!" My mouth popped open in shock.

"I told you, I have a gun." His voice was cool and calm, even as the blood rolled down over my skin and soaked through the sleeve of the blouse.

"Hey!" The blond, green-eyed man flew into the kitchen, the brunette on his tail without a shirt.

He slipped on his glasses and tugged the shirt over his painted arms, swirling black designs that covered every inch of his skin from wrist to neck. The markings disappeared as he buttoned it up.

"You shot her?" He exclaimed, walking toward us.

"It's not a *her*." The shotgun held steady, pointed at my face as he turned to give them a look. "It's a ghost."

"She's not a ghost, Wes," the blond said, putting out his hand.

"Look." The dark haired one with the glasses moved closer, pointing to the blood seeping down my arm, and dragged Wes's eyes to the scene. "She's bleeding."

"So it's a ghoul." He shook his head. "It's not out of the realm of possibilities with the cops all being in a nest."

"Wes," the brunet barked. "You're just pulling answers out of your arse."

"Clay," he sneered in response.

Learning their names was a small consolation for the holes in my flesh. The Manor seemed to throb in response, picking up on the racing of my heart. The cups in the cupboards rattled together as if the entire Manor was shaking, and a soft noise vibrated off them. The gunman, Wes, could hear it too, his eyes flickering to the space behind my head.

"Take a moment, think about it." Clay turned his body, his back muscles straining under his shirt as the blond continued to inch closer to me out of their view, "Look at her hands," he whispered, but the sound echoed in this old house, and nothing was sacred.

They were shaking, and I couldn't get them to stop, no matter how much I tried to control them. Wes and Clay seemed locked in a hushed conversation as the other skirted closer. He put his hand out, wiggling his fingers in my direction, and smiled.

Green eyes twinkled. "I'm Koen," he said.

He was talking to me directly, ignoring the look his counterparts tossed him for doing so. Wes tightened his grip on the gun and Clay turned to watch.

"I'm..." My eyes dropped heavily even though I could feel the Manor beginning to heal me.

The counter I was leaning on seemed to hum against me possessively.

Mine.

"Is she okay?" Clay stepped forward, lowering his face to look into my eyes. "Are you okay?"

"I'm..." Everything seemed to spin around me, and I let it sink me to the floor.

KOEN

"Is she alive?" I asked Clay, who hovered over her on the couch, fingering the material of her skirts.

"This cotton has to predate anything in the last century; it's pure, and there doesn't appear to be any trace of synthetic materials in it," he mumbled to himself, brain stirring with endless dramatic, and brilliant thoughts.

"How would you even..." I shook my head. "Never mind."

I knelt in front of her, tracing the delicate round features of her face with my eyes. Full cheeks speckled with freckles over the bridge of her swooping nose. Her cupid's bow lips and long, soft-looking neck. I'd collected her into my arms before she hit the ground, scooping her against my chest despite both Wes and Clay growling in protest. I laid her in the sitting room as Wes followed closely behind, whispering to Clay about something they didn't want my input on.

She was a magnet.

"Where did you find it anyway?" Wes snapped.

"There's an atrium." Clay pointed lazily behind him as he moved to stand with Wes on the far wall by the door. "And yes, Koen, she's alive."

"Alive?" A ragged scoff left Wes' lips as he rolled his eyes. "We know nothing about this thing."

I looked over at him, disapproval on my face.

"Don't do that." He looked away from me, his hands still gripping the shotgun, his jaw still tight enough to break teeth. "It's a case, just like any other."

Wes doesn't budge on his code. I could see the gears turning behind his eyes. Going through the catalog of all the horrible threats she could turn out to be. All the ways he would end her life if she was. He licked his bottom lip and turned his gaze on Clay, but not the gun. That stayed trained in her direction.

"Clay, do you have any idea what it might be?"

"*She*, as far as I can tell," Clay noted, much to my content, "seems to heal, not instantly, but fast—there are no traces of the shotgun wounds on her skin."

Her shirt was still soaked with blood but the peppered gashes on her throat had closed before I even laid her on the couch. There was no telling what was under the tattered fabric but the bleeding had stopped. By all accounts it looked as though it had taken the time to walk from the kitchen to the sitting room for them to heal. Even Clay sounded confused. Which, frankly, was some pretty foreign territory.

"She's not cold," I added, and Wes growled. "What was I supposed to do?"

"Let her hit the ground! You had no idea what you were doing. What if it had been a ploy to get you close enough to turn on you?" He barked at me, rage flickering like a wildfire behind his hazel eyes. He stripped from his leather jacket, juggling the gun before throwing the coat against a nearby chair.

"She wasn't going to," I argued.

Not knowing for sure, I enjoyed how the argument seemed to rile Wes up to no end.

He mocked me. "You're reckless."

"Learned from th'best." My words were clipped as I rolled my eyes.

"No, I taught you to be cautious, always. Whatever the hell you're pulling now is bullshit." He raised his voice.

"You taught me to assess the situation and act! She's not a threat!"

Wes tensed. "We're leaving, pack your bags."

"And leave her? Don't you wanna know why?" I argued, considering standing up from where I was crouched beside her, but my body felt like lead, my fascination manifesting as a rope tied tight between her and me.

"No." He shrugged. "I want to get out of here before someone comes looking for us. We killed three cops with a fourth still out there." Wes shook his head, golden curls falling out of place around his square jaw.

"Three ghouls."

"Three men that don't look like monsters on the outside. Not to the public," he argued. He had a point.

He looked over at the woman, who seemed perfectly normal from the outside. She looked so peaceful as she slept. Her auburn hair fell out of the bun laying against her jaw and throat in long waves that I wanted to touch.

"But we have extensive research on ghouls," Clay finally piped up.

I pointed at him, snapping my fingers in agreement. Hope ignited as Clay joined the conversation productively. Wes watched him with restraint, knowing that if he was going to get control of the situation he needed Clay on his side.

But Clay, the most intelligent of all of us, would always throw caution to the wind in the name of lore. Especially lore he had yet to study.

"So you're siding with him?" Wes snarled at Clay.

"He's siding with his incessant need to be a *know-it-all*," I scoffed.

"All I'm saying is maybe a few days to learn more?" He sighed, his chest heaving beneath the dark dress shirt, buttons straining to expose pieces of the large, wispy black artwork of an angel across his chest.

"He still needs to heal," I added.

Wes just rolled his eyes. "That excuse is shite."

"He's right," Clay said, tilting his head to the side. "I'm in no condition to fight anything."

"So we drive, get out of here before we find more trouble."

"It's too late for that." Clay nodded to the woman on the couch.

Trouble had found us, I thought and looked back at her to find a set of emerald eyes observing my every move.

Wes instinctively raised his gun back from the slack position it had fallen into during the argument. Clay tensed from his spot on the far wall as she shifted to sit up on the couch. A stiff grumble fell from her plump bottom lip as she managed to do it herself. I kept my hands off her but close enough that if she needed it, I could assist.

Her eyes widened as she took in everything around her: Wes on guard, Clay watching and scribbling in his leather-bound notebook, and then back to me. Confusion, frustration, and fear ticked across her face as she opened her mouth to speak but closed it again.

"Koen," I pressed my palm flat to my chest, unsure how much she remembered from before, in the kitchen. "Clayton." I point to Clay, who nodded at her gently, only looking up from his notes for a split second.

"Just Clay," he added.

"Do not–" Wes huffed in a pitiful attempt to silence me.

"Wesley." I ignored his order.

I turned back to her, hoping that she understood that by giving her our names, she was safe to do so in return. A name could mean figuring out who she was. At least it would help Clay. I just wanted to know out of selfish curiosity. Was the name as beautiful as the woman?

"Florence."

Florence.

The name seemed oddly appropriate to her, as if it had been made for her in some way. It didn't make sense, but it sent a tickle of euphoria through my veins. Her brows furrowed as Clay stepped toward his bag, her body tensing back against the ratty couch. I could see her searching her vicinity for a weapon to defend herself.

"They aren't as scary as they look." I tried to calm her. "As long as you aren't hurling plants at them."

Clay snorted from behind me. The human noise seemingly made Florence relax a touch.

"Wes." I turned to him when her eyes didn't move from the shotgun. "Put it down."

"No," he instantly responded, practically cutting off my request.

"It won't work," she spoke.

All three of us listened. Her voice was soft, with an Irish lilt that was even thicker than my own and it made me wonder where, and weird-ly–*when,* she was from.

"Guns." She pulled at the collar of her blouse, exposing the skin stained with blood but perfect otherwise. There wasn't a trace of injury. Not even a scar. "Neither will knives," she added her sharp gaze clocking the hunting knife tucked in Wes's belt, "or toxins, falling from great heights, or rope."

The last one made us go still.

Clay was the first to move, inching closer to her with his notebook, studying her like an animal. He did the same to everyone, person, ghost, or monster. He craved knowledge, the unknown.

"Are you saying you've tried to hang yourself?" He asked her, and she nodded. "With no long-term effects?"

Her eyes twitched briefly in the direction of the open landing at the top of the double staircase out in the foyer. I swallowed the lump in my throat that formed immediately at the thought of her swaying lifelessly beneath the decrepit chandelier.

"Why would you do that?" I asked in a short breath.

"Not that I'm aware of..." She answered Clay. "Desperation," she whispered when she looked back at me before she went quiet again, retreating into her shell.

"Fascinating," Clay whispered, his glasses sliding down his nose as his eyes roamed over her stiff posture. He opened his mouth to ask more, but Wes was quicker.

Heartbreaking.

"What are you?" Wes asked. "And don't lie to us."

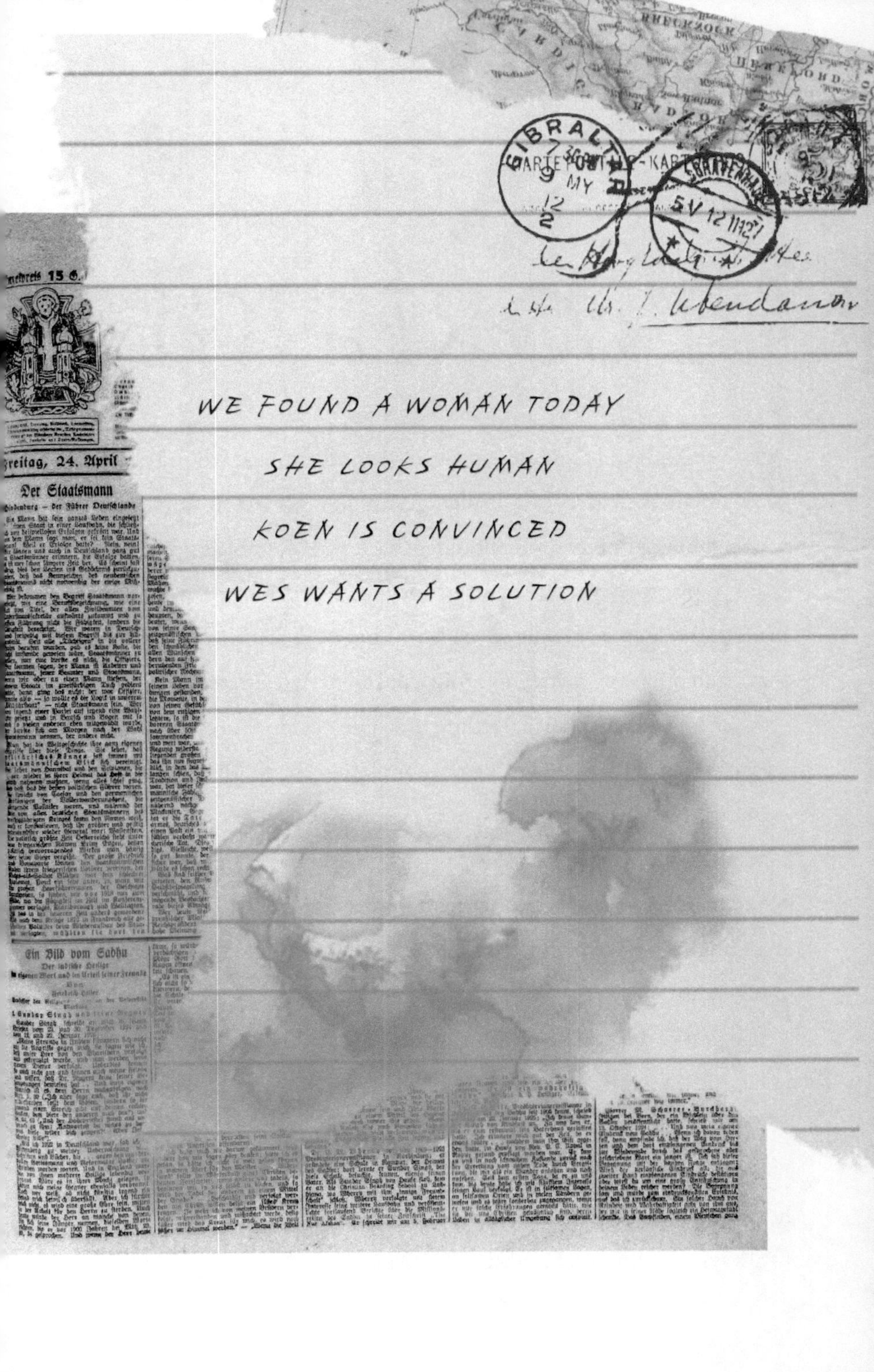

WE FOUND A WOMAN TODAY

SHE LOOKS HUMAN

KOEN IS CONVINCED

WES WANTS A SOLUTION

FLORENCE

Even knowing the outcome of surviving a gunshot wound, staring down the barrel of a loaded gun, made it hard to think. They watched me as I pinned my shoulders back and scrambled through my brain to put together the events of my life so far; at least the ones that made enough sense for me to explain. I began telling pieces of a story that I had only ever written in a journal, and never expected to tell.

Koen seemed enthralled, settling down on the floor and crossing his legs to watch me in awe. The demeanor was almost childlike, and it was extremely endearing. He was handsome in a nearly indescribable way. His heart-shaped face, full cheeks, and boyish smile drew me in. His blond hair was messy and longer than the other men's and his green eyes were bright. Unlike my own dark emerald, his reminded me of vibrant spring grasses, and sparkled with humor.

"So you're trapped here?" The words fell off Clay's tongue smoothly as he studied me.

"Yes." I nodded.

"How long?" Koen's voice was lighter with a familiar Irish lilt. Clay however, had an accent that was posh and husky. Curiously, he seemed to always talk through his teeth. Wesley barely spoke.

I tensed. "You believe me?" I asked incredulously. "How are you not..." I couldn't find the words. *Panicked, angry, confused?*

There were a thousand different reactions they could have experienced during my recounting but instead each seemed to be a different kind of calm. Koen leaned forward, hopeful and helpful. Clay exuded a sophisticated curiosity that had him scribbling down my every word. Wesley was on the verge of snapping the metal barrel of his shotgun in half and, while with any other person I wouldn't normally consider that a possibility, he may just accomplish his goals.

"We're Hunters."

Wesley's accent was stern, and thick with English notes.

"Hunters?" I asked, my mind giving me images of men on horseback, chasing poor foxes with loud howling dogs close at their heels. I tried to picture Koen on horseback and could not fathom it.

His hazel eyes narrowed on me. "We kill monsters."

His words shot the image of Agatha's spine cracking in half and turning inside out in front of me in my memory. But she hadn't been a monster, she'd been a victim. I was sure of that.

"Monsters? Like *bears, or wolves?*" I tried to understand.

He scoffed at me and shot a look over to Clay, and something unsaid seemed to pass between them in just a gaze.

"Like *demons and wraiths and lycanthropes.*" His voice was mocking, and then hardened. "And *phantoms* and *poltergeists.*" He finished pointedly. "I'm sure you're familiar."

I nodded. "Of course, I have read novels, *fictions,* with the creatures. Are you saying you know them to be real?"

And you think I am one of them? I couldn't help but think, it was written all over how he gripped his gun and watched his friends' every move. He believed I aimed to hurt them. His eyes narrowed as he watched me think. He nodded.

"Like a fairy tale?" I asked.

"Like a nightmare," Wesley barked.

"I'm not a monster." I inhaled. "I've never caused harm to anyone."

"Just because you say it doesn't mean I believe you," he responded.

Koen shook his head in disapproval from where he sat at my feet. The shoes he wore were funny. White in color but dirty with mud and flecks of blood. They were long and made of canvas that laced up the front around his ankles.

He followed my gaze and wiggled them at me. "They're Converse," he said like I should know what that is. "It's a type of... never mind." Koen looked at the other men, a twinkle in his eyes, and laughed. "C'mon, Wes, *look* at her. Do you really think she's a monster?"

Wesley wasn't amused.

"She's not human!" He argued.

"Alright then." I shifted and stared at my feet.

I detested being spoken about as if I were not present in the room. It had been years since I felt myself try to slide into the small mold of "wife" or "woman", and it was alarming to me how quickly I tried to shrink myself to fit back into it.

I fidgeted with my hands in my lap as they argued, yelling back and forth about how dangerous I was without considering that I could hear them. I noticed out of the corner of my eye the crystal shards of the chandelier beginning to tremble, and I hid my smirk. The arguing was agitating the Manor. Perhaps I wouldn't have to convince them to leave for their own safety afterall, the Manor may just get fed up and expel them itself.

This is the companionship that you missed?

I could all but hear it ask.

Their voices rose higher and more heated. Hands waved comically in exaggerated motions that pointed and punctuated. The walls of the parlor shuddered around us in revulsion. They were so focused on shouting over each other that they did not even notice the corners of the paper peeling back from the walls. I began to worry slightly that it wouldn't just change its mind and expel them, but that it may become violent... like Agatha...

I could feel my panic rise.

"Excuse me." I cleared my throat but clearly my voice hadn't pierced the cacophony of the men. "*Excuse me!*" I shouted.

They spun to face me, Wesley's gun at the ready and trained on me.

The floorboards groaned beneath us and a book whipped off a shelf at lightning speed, dislodging the gun from his hand.

Mine.

I felt a touch of relief knowing the Manor was protecting me, but also not enacting any violence worse than flying books at the men.

For now.

"What the hell was that?" Wesley spun on me. "You keep doing shit!" He said to me as Clay inspected the dark, elegant wallpaper.

"It's like..." He stopped, looking over at me with his glasses low on his nose. "It could be that the house is just old..." But the lack of conviction in his words spoke volumes.

"Clay! This is classic poltergeist shit. Pure and simple." Wesley glared at me as I worked to control the nervous feeling that rippled through me like a wave. There was a weight to his gaze that settled against my chest. Danger in a way that was mesmerizing.

"You need to leave," I said, finally snapping from the trance. I looked to Clay, whose arm was tucked against his body. "It's not safe for you here."

"You see, *it* even agrees," Wesley growled and dropped to collect his weapon, turning away. "I'm going to search the house."

"Wesley," Koen snapped at him as he stomped from the room.

"What do you mean it's not safe?" Clay asked when the heavy footfalls disappeared down the hall. He pulled off his glasses and shoved them into his pants pocket before closing his notebook.

I didn't know how to answer him.

"Do you truly hunt *monsters*?" I asked instead.

Koen sank on the couch beside me, tucking one of his long legs beneath him, and rested his arm over the back of the ornate settee. Heat tickled my neck under his gaze as he contemplated an appropriate answer before nodding. I kept my distance from him but could feel the curiosity blossoming in my chest at his proximity. I wanted to know more about them.

"What kind of monsters?" I looked at Clay, pursuing further.

"Are you trying to figure out if you fit into one of the boxes?" He asked me. His face was slimmer than Koen's, angular in comparison to Koen's softness. Full lips and piercing, almond-shaped blue eyes that looked like the gray sky before a storm trapped inside. Clay was a fox, and Koen could be described as a lion cub or a stuffed bear.

"Perhaps." I chewed on my lip.

"If it's any consolation, I don't think you're a monster." Koen tapped his finger on the couch, his smile bright when I looked back at him.

"We hunt monsters with no regard for humanity," Clay said.

"Like the…" What was it that Wesley had called them? "…ghouls?"

It had been easy enough to pretend to go unconscious. Though it had surely been decades since I had even attempted to do such a thing. I had felt off, and could feel the Manor's rage at my being hurt, but pretending to pass out was merely a defense tactic to eavesdrop on these unexpected guests. A way to gauge just how much danger they might be to me, or to themselves.

"Ghouls," Koen helped, his brow raised, surely putting together the pieces; they had not been in the list of monsters Wesley had offered.

"They're foul creatures. They feed off of brain matter."

"And you found your way here because of that?" I asked, pinning back my shoulders to stave off the shudder that wracked through my body in disgust at the thought.

"They were…" Koen trailed off, searching for words.

"Feeding on children," Clay finished for him.

All of this was very strange and overwhelming.

"I apologize. I must seem so rude, telling you to leave, and then inter-rogating you with questions." I sighed. "I've been alone here for so long… I haven't had anyone to speak to other than myself in years." I faked a smile. "I am not always my favorite company."

Clay's jaw ticked and his lips pressed into a thin line as he nodded his head. "We understand," he offered, "and I can't speak for Wesley…" He paused.

I had a feeling no one honestly could.

"But we're sorry for barging in." He shifted uncomfortably in his chair and offered me his hand. "A proper introduction might help. I'm Clayton Dunn. The brains of the bunch."

I stared at his hand. It had been a custom to shake hands with close friends and well known acquaintances, but Lord Cabot had been very clear that he found it improper for *his Lady* to be so familiar with anyone of the opposite sex .

"You shake it." He smiled at me and his full lips transformed into a vast, cheek-splitting grin that only cemented my description of a fox.

"I know that much," I said, extending my arm and placing my small hand in his. His was warm, and soft. I hid the small jolt of electricity that ran up my skin at the contact. "Florence Cabot." I gave my own full name in return. His eyes were kind as he cupped our hands with his other with a reassuring pat.

"Lovely to make your acquaintance properly, Ms. Cabot." He released my hand and looked over at his companion.

"Koen…" I turned to him, and he nodded.

"Cameron," he finished. His hand reached out to mine immediately. The corner of his lips curling up on the left side with perhaps pride? "Wesley is my brother, *adopted*," he quickly cut in the information. "He seems rough, but he saved the both of us."

"I see," I said. "As overwhelming as this all is for me, it must also be for you."

"Less overwhelming, and more curious." Koen shrugged. His hand was still holding mine in a way that was much too familiar considering we had only just met, but was surprisingly comfortable regardless.

"We've dealt with many monsters, things that are hundreds of years old, but nothing so unaware of what they are?" Clay said, his eyes flickered down to Koen's hand, still holding mine and I pulled it back to my lap, feeling a little sheepish.

"Well, I'm *not* a monster. I'm just me," I said.

"Seemingly undecided by the crowd," Clay laughed. "But I want to learn more about you. We promise that we'll vacate your space the moment we can, given that you aren't a threat to anyone."

My heart raced in my chest, "And if it's decided I am?"

Neither spoke, but a grim flicker of realization passed between them.

"Then we do our job," Clay said, in a tone that made my blood run cold.

KOEN

After more than a little bitching from Wes, we had all managed to agree to lay low in the Manor for a few weeks. At the very least it would give us enough time to take a break and regroup. Clay could heal and research to his heart's content, while Wes followed up on the rogue ghoul. And *I* could let my curiosity run rampant in the form of exploring the spooky place with its extremely tantalizing built-in tour guide.

The first major hang up to the plan was that the mansion itself was ancient. No electricity, no outlets, *no indoor plumbing.* Electricity was an issue that was easy enough to remedy as we always had our generator and the gadgets that Clay insisted on keeping at the ready at all times. *'You never know when you'll need to look something up.'*

He was absolutely the biggest nerd of the three of us and I was almost certain it was a point of pride. On long road trips, Wes and I would take turns asking inane questions to see which of us could get him monologuing the longest. It was an unspoken agreement that whoever won got to choose dinner. It wasn't the most exciting road game but, begrudgingly, I had to admit it was informative.

The plumbing issue was where we almost lost Wes again.

"The fuck do you mean you want to stay in this shithole? It's bad enough that it's basically one gust of wind from falling down on top of us. Clay,

*you can barely stomach roughing it without bathrooms on the rare occasions we camp. **You**, of all people. want to stay in a place that only has chamber pots?"* In Wes's defense he had a point, but Clay had cracked back saying that a chamber pot was much more sanitary and easy to manage one arm down than digging a hole to shit in in the woods. So we stayed.

I grinned at the memory of Florence's face during the plumbing discussion. Her pale skin could do nothing to hide the rosy blush on her cheeks, and her eyes had twinkled ruefully with laughter. She was taking the intrusion of three loud idiots with an admirable amount of humor and grace. I was impressed, and completely captivated by her.

"It's sad that someone so pretty is trapped in such a trashed place," I said to her, while we watched Clay and Wes lobby arguments back and forth at each other in the parlor room, like a pathetic game of ping-pong. She had looked at me quizzically, her head cocked to the side and eyebrow raised delicately.

"What do you mean? *Trashed*?" She seemed genuinely confused.

"Like—destroyed? In bad repair? Falling apart?" I explained, gesturing around us to the room pointing out molding baseboards and cracked furniture and crumbling stone.

"Oh, I *see*," She breathed out in a whisper. "The Manor has always provided for me, as long as I..." She paused briefly, seeming to search for the correct words. " ...as long as I have been here... Perhaps you only see what it wants you to see, while I see it for what it truly *is*," she responded. "This place is as grand and beautiful as the day I first stepped foot in it." There was an unexplainable look of pain behind her eyes, yet at the same time, an undeniable fondness. Her hand patted the fabric of the couch's arm absently, as if stroking a beloved pet.

I contemplated for a moment. "Hmm. So what you're saying is... it likes you better?"

She laughed, a mirthful giggle bubbling out of her plump lips. I fought with every part of what little willpower I had not to imagine what that pink pout would taste like... It was a slippery slope from there. Her eyes glittered mischievously.

"*Yes.* That is exactly what I am saying." She snorted softly and, honestly, it was the most adorable thing I'd ever heard.

It caught Clay's attention and he looked over at us. "What's funny?"

"Apparently this place isn't as gross and abandoned as it appears," I said, relaxing back into the uncomfortable couch with a little more force than I had before; when I had thought it was about to break apart from underneath me. It held strong and I started to think Florence may be on to something.

"What do you mean?" He asked, pushing his glasses up to rest in their proper place at the bridge of his nose.

"Well, Florence here." I nodded my head in her direction, mostly for Wes's benefit. I knew it would piss him off if I used her name, just as much as it pissed me off when he didn't. "Says that the Manor is in fine repair, *grand* even." I winked at her as I used the word, exaggerating it in her accent. She smirked and her eyes rolled skyward. "And that maybe it's just putting on a show of looking all crusty and dilapidated so we don't stick around too long." That last part I put together myself, but based on Florence's response to it, I didn't think I was far off.

"*A magic mansion.*" I heard Wes scoff under his breath grouchily. "*Next it will be a magic school bus.*" He kicked his foot at the leg of a rickety-looking table and we were all surprised by the fact it remained standing steadily. There was a hissed intake of breath from Wes and I tried not to snicker at the sight of him shaking out his toes.

Clay's attention was fully on Florence now. "When did you first come here?" He asked the question that had been at the forefront of my mind since finding her like Sleeping Beauty in the greenhouse.

"Eighteen Fifty-Two."

Oh holy shite.

Her hands tidied her skirt busily, brushing away imaginary lint, and she seemed almost embarrassed as she returned his gaze and asked.

"What year is it now?"

Clay glanced towards me, eyes wide, and I knew he was thinking the same thing I did. Though he had probably come to the math faster than I had. *1852 means...*

"It's the year Two thousand and Twenty-Four," he said gently. "You've been here almost *one hundred and seventy two years.*"

"Oh." The smallest sound escaped as all the air seemed to leave her body.

I could see that her hands were trembling, and she extended her fingers briefly before clutching them into tight fists that she then balled into her lap. A shaky breath inhaled through her teeth and I had to hold myself back from moving to her– to take her hands in mine, or rub her back, to hold her in any way she might allow. The urge to comfort her was overwhelming.

Her eyes were wet with unshed tears when she finally looked back up at us. "I hadn't realized it had been quite *that* long," she admitted.

She stood abruptly and straightened her skirts. "Please–please excuse me," she whispered, before darting from the room and down a hallway that I was not sure had noticed before. Disappearing from sight quickly, like the phantom Wes was so sure she was.

I stood to go after her but Clay's hand gripped my shoulder gently. "Let her go, Ko. I think she needs a minute."

I nodded, but it took a moment for me to be able to sit back down again. I felt an insane pull to go after her–and while yes I *did* have a habit of getting attached easily to beautiful people– earning me the nickname *lover boy* on more than one occasion, I had never felt anything this strong so fast. It wasn't just sexual attraction or general curiosity either, though admittedly there was plenty of both. There was something *more*.

"Oh no. *Hell no.*" Wes's voice pulled me from my thoughts before his hulking frame blocked the hallway my eyes had found following Florence's retreat. "I know that look, Koen!" He scolded me like a child.

"*What* look?" I said defensively, pushing him away from me gently and flopping back on the couch. I kicked my feet up over one arm and rested my back against the other. I threw my hands up in an exaggerated show of misunderstanding.

His scowl deepened and he pointed his finger in my face and I swiped it away.

"Like a lost puppy who will follow any pretty little thing without a thought, no matter what danger might be waiting!" He said in exasperation. "We have no idea what this place is or what that thing is. We *do* know it's been here for over a century and it looks like it hasn't aged a day over Twenty Five–"

"We also know she heals quickly from gunshot wounds," Clay offered nonchalantly as he settled into the chair across from me, pulling his laptop from his bag. "*And* that the Manor is a significant part of this whole mystery." He rolled his shoulders before opening the computer and beginning to type.

"I'm surrounded by morons," Wes groaned to the ceiling.

"I *think* you mean outnumbered by morons." I grinned up at him as he turned on his heel and left out of the front door, slamming it heavily behind him.

"Was that necessary?" Clay asked me, a grin in his eyes that he tried to keep from his mouth. He tried not to play favorites between us but, despite Wes being his best friend, he tended to enjoy it when I pestered him for being bitchy.

"Absolutely."

CLAYTON

I t had been three days and, usually, research was the only way to keep myself calm. Books rarely lied to me but I was starting to grow frustrated with the history of the town and the lack of information on just about everything surrounding the Manor.

The ache in my arm was fading, but the agonizing, tight, itchy feeling of the stitches healing was setting in. I was just praying it didn't get infected due to our condemned lodgings. I could feel the dust crawling across my skin as I spread out what little research I had on the sitting room floor and flipped through old notes that I had taken. Wes sat across from me in one of the chairs, his fingers methodically cleaning a set of knives in deep concentration.

"I can't find a single piece of information on Florence. It's like she was scrubbed from history," I mumbled, clicking back from the webpage into Google.

Wes's eyes flickered up to meet mine. "Probably because it never fucking existed outside of this shit hole. I've searched every room and haven't found a single T.V. This place is a black hole of boredom." Dust kicked up off the floor into his face, causing him to sneeze and drop the knife in his hands. "This place is taunting us."

"It's taunting *you*," I corrected him. The Manor, and whatever magic it held, had been somewhat pleasant to us since Koen had started paying more attention to Florence. Glimpses of her sweet smile flashed in my mind and, just like that, I was derailed again. I needed to focus. "If you took a moment to settle in and stop banging around…"

"You want me to play nice with a monster, and its monster mansion?" He mocked, leaning forward and scooping the knife off the floor by the handle.

"While we're living inside of it, it might be helpful?" I shook my head and started to type again, but Wes's groan interrupted me. "What?" I looked at him.

"Let me kill it," he said quietly, barely audible to anyone, but his lips moved slowly, and his intent was clear.

"You already tried," I reminded him.

"I missed on purpose. It was a warning shot," he snapped. '*Next time, I won't miss,*' was said in his determined stare. "I understand how badly you want to figure out what's going on here, Clay, but I just don't think it's worth it. No one is in danger, nothing has died except probably that thing." He rolled his eyes and I knew he was speaking about Florence but I didn't want to argue it.

"Listen." I pushed up onto my knees and straightened my shoulders. "Whatever is going on here, it's weird. I've never seen anything like it. The readings I've gotten from this place are like nothing in any of my books or notes. It's hardcore, Wes."

"So let it be hardcore from a distance. Keep researching it far away from here," he argued, setting the knife down on the table. "Preferably somewhere with beer and bad reruns."

"No." I shook my head. "If there is a shred of truth to her words, that this Manor has held her captive here, and living, which..." I shrugged and looked at him. "I'm estimating the likeness is around ninety percent by the evidence so far...."

He growled at the mention of percentages and it made me laugh.

"It could be very dangerous. I need to figure out if it's hurt anyone or anything in the past, before or after Florence," I explained. "And I need time to map out the layout. Did you notice it changes?" I asked him, ignoring his plea for retreat.

"A little, but for the most part I don't leave this room unless I have to go into the run-down, rat-infested kitchen for food that turns rotten in hours of being within the walls." He shrugged.

"We've had no actual confirmation of rodents of any kind since being here." I rolled my eyes at him, and let the important piece of what he said sink in. "The food spoils?" My brows raised in question, and he nodded.

"The fact that you haven't noticed is concerning. Have you stopped to eat at all in the last three days?" He asked me.

He wasn't going to like the answer. "Florence has been bringing me food."

Wes' hand gripped the cloth tighter, his jaw clenching tightly in frustration. "You're letting it feed you?"

"She's actually quite hospitable, you should get to know her." I shrugged. "And a very good cook. Yesterday she made–"

"Enough." Wes stopped me. "How do you know it's not slowly dosing the food? That poison isn't coursing through you right now? Have you lost your fucking mind?" He laughed incredulously, it sounded cold and frustrated.

A fire sparked in the fireplace beside us, raging hot and angry, gone in the same second, leaving nothing but ashes.

Wes glared at me.

"I'm fine," I said. "In fact, I've never felt better. You're blowing all of this out of proportion."

"Awesome, my brother is chasing ghost tail, and here you are being fed by it," he snarled. "You're both being infuriatingly reckless. Let me know if you find anything, I need a break from you."

Wes stomped from the room, leaving me in silence again.

I climbed to my feet, grabbing a pen and notebook, before starting to draw the sitting room into my notes. I moved on only when I felt satisfied that the drawing captured what I saw. I wanted to show Florence the difference in our perspectives. Maybe it would help her understand.

It took me half the day to get the foyer, main kitchen, and a few of the hallways jotted down on my map, but every time I thought I had it figured out, I turned around to find the hallway leading in a different direction.

I pulled out my cell phone, brought up the compass, and held it flat. I could find my way back to the main rooms; I just needed a little guidance. When I looked down at the compass, the needle was spinning out of control, a tiny blur of white and red that never stopped.

"Okay, well..." I sighed and shoved it back into my trouser pocket.

I stopped again, trying to orientate myself, but the same hallway now went straight, and the feeling of being incredibly lost started to sink in. It was heavy on my chest but not panic, just confusion, which for me was almost worse. I looked down at the notebook in my hand, studying the map I had created. The hallway in front of me had definitely turned left before. It had been the way I came, but...

"Your party tricks are less than to be desired, Orchid Manor," I whispered, chewing on my lip. "Are you leading me?" I asked, but nothing answered.

I walked down the changed hallway for what seemed like minutes but, after roughly forty-five seconds, I popped out by a set of doors. Dirty, like the rest of the glass, I could barely make out the back part of the property. I pulled my sleeve over my palm and cleared a circle in the dirt to admire the rolling farmscape. Wild grass grew for acres further than I could possibly measure. It was no wonder that Florence had gone so long unnoticed at the Manor. She was hidden deep behind farmland and miles of dense forest.

"Thank you for your help," I whispered to the Manor as I jotted down the appearance of the doors and everything that had happened to bring me to them. It was hard to imagine that the Manor was supposed to be elegant and pristine when all I could see for feet was decaying wood and dust that settled in thick rugs.

"Are you lost?" Her voice draped over my shoulders, and I turned to find her in a dark green dress, similar to the one she was wearing the first time we met. It was tucked in tightly at the waist over a structured corset that hugged her curves. Her hair was half up, and the auburn waves were tied back with a crème ribbon that matched the embroidery on her skirt.

"Ms. Cabot." I nodded as I acknowledged her. "It would seem that way," I confessed, tearing my gaze away from hers. "I was trying to map out the house, but the further I explored, the more lost I became."

She stepped forward and I couldn't help but close the distance between us as she angled to look at the map I had drawn. "You did very well," she praised. "Oh that is one of my favorite chambers, it faces the east side of the house. It has a thicker window sill than other rooms and in the winter, if you open the window, the snow falls against the sill. You can scoop it into a bowl and enjoy it with sugar." Florence practically hummed the story she was so excited to tell me.

I stared at her for a moment, taking in the innocence of her story and chuckled, slowly understanding why Koen was so enamored.

"I wanted to show you something." I flipped the page for her, matching her enthusiasm and showed her the drawing of the parlor and then the kitchen in all their rotting, old glory.

"Is this how you see—" She paused and reached out to the wall beside her, green eyes exploring the peeling wallpaper with wonder. "You've been living in filth for nearly a week just to help me?" She looked over at me, confusion filling her expression but also gratitude.

"We've squatted in worse places and none with such a gracious, beautiful host—" I said before I could stop the compliment from blurting out. *Who tells the most endearing stories from the prettiest of lips.* My tongue grazed over my bottom lip and my cheeks flushed with embarrassment as I took a step back from her.

"You're very kind, Mr. Dunn," she responded with that sweet smile I had been itching to see.

I shook the feelings of curious need loose and tried to focus once again. "Do you know what this door is?" I pointed to a spot on the map, turning to see if it was still where I had left it but it was gone.

If memory served, it looked just as old as the rest of the house, and I could have sworn it pulsed like an artery. But the feeling had subsided as quickly as I had felt it. I had seen it once or twice in passing, but it never seemed to be in the same place...Like it was moving on its own.

Florence's nose scrunched playfully, ignoring my question. Her hands still shook as she clasped them together and walked past me. "I think I have a room that will catch your interest."

Doubt ran hot through me. No room could possibly be more interesting than whichever one she was in. I wanted to know more, every little detail that made her so enticing. I wanted to read Florence like a book.

The sweet smell of rosemary and oranges wafted from her as she passed under my nose, wandering down the hall into the darker part of the Manor. I followed her, keeping my eyes trained on how her skirts floated across the floor with each step she took.

It was enchanting.

"This way." Her voice drifted toward me as I paused to shake free of the magnetism radiating from her. She stopped at the end of a long hallway, warm sconces on the wall that barely seemed lit but flickered as she passed each one.

"You aren't leading me to a kill room, are you?" I asked her, but I was only met with soft laughter as she pushed open large wooden doors. Their hinges, rusted and barely holding the panels, were tangled with cobwebs and dirt.

"Just look," she said, stepping out of my way.

CLAYTON

S idestepping through the door frame, avoiding any physical contact with her, I entered the room, unprepared for what I was about to see. The dingy, decrepit hallway opened into an enormous room with rich green wallpaper and floor-to-ceiling dark wood shelving. Each one was crammed tightly with more books than I had ever seen in my entire life. I looked back at her, still standing by the doorway, a soft, unusual smile on her face as she studied my reaction.

"How is..." I turned back to the library.

In the center was a grouping of tables, all with their golden lamps flickering with candlelight and a few comfier areas with long plush chaises and sitting chairs. Such a space couldn't exist in a place so worn down, and yet I found myself at a complete loss for words.

"Do you see its beauty?" She asked.

I stared at her for a long moment, breathing in her essence as she watched me with bright, curious emerald eyes. They flickered up to the high ceiling and down over the tall window panes that allowed light to spill inside like rushing water. I was amazed that mere moments before, we had been in a decrepit and drafty hallway in a building that appeared far past condemned.

I saw the beauty, but I wasn't looking at the library. "I do."

"After some time spent in the Manor, I found this room. I believe it was a gift..."

"A gift?" I asked her.

"I had explored the deepest corners of the Manor time and time again until I thought I had gone insane, and then one day–" When she finally broke eye contact a chill set in, as if she was the only warm thing in the room and, without her, there was nothing to stave off the cold. "–I was led to those doors and inside..." She looked around the library.

"This isn't a trick?" I asked her, shoving a hand in the pocket of my trousers to keep it from shaking as I inquired.

"Only a *monster* would play such a cruel prank," she hummed, raising a single brow at me. "It's real."

My stomach knotted at the sight of her amusement, something softer creeping up my spine as I studied her eyes. They were the darkest shade of green I'd ever seen in an eye color before; they were dark but caught the sunlight like a prism.

"Thank you," I said, setting down the book in my hand and wandering in to explore more.

"I thought you might be able to find something in these books, I'm sorry there's no..." She tilted her head to the side, looking for a word. "Computer?" She said, unsure of herself. Koen had walked her through all of my devices the day before as we sat in the parlor and I took notes on her life.

"That's correct," I praised. "This is much better than that. Computers are finicky and sometimes will only give you half the answer. Or sometimes they'll give you the wrong answer on purpose."

"Do they have conscious thoughts?" She stepped into the library, keeping her distance, but curiosity sparked in her eyes and I bit my lip to keep from smiling at her like an idiot.

"No," I said, "well, sort of. Their thoughts are nothing but code and information that real people have programmed into them."

"So people..." She wandered closer, intrigue lacing her voice as she worked through the foreign ideas. "Put information?" She asked, unsure about the word. I nodded to encourage her and inched closer to her. "From books and their lives onto the computers for others to find?"

"Atta girl." I smiled at her. "That's exactly it."

She looked up from her feet, and her expression relaxed. Under my gaze, her cheeks blushed a rosy pink color.

"Thank you for sharing your space with me," I said to her, clearing my throat as I ran a hand through my hair. A few wavy curls fell against my forehead, even in my attempts to keep them back.

With a curt nod, she blinked slowly and the curiosity died in her eyes, turning them a pale shade compared to seconds before. She wandered around me, keeping the space, and then walked to a shelf near the back of the library, the only shelf not crammed with books.

"I see the way you look at me, Mr. Dunn," she said. "Like I'm fragile or innocent, but I can assure you, I am not."

I watched her as she circled the row of books, her hair but a flash of red in my vision as she moved. "Then what are you, Ms. Cabot?" I asked her.

"Long before I was accused of being a monster, and before I was trapped. I was just a woman," she said, appearing on the other side of the row with a tight smile on her face. Her breath shuddered as she thought about something, and her lips parted to continue her thoughts. "I enjoyed risking everything, extending my kindness to help people, women specifically. Those who were unable or not allowed to help themselves. Women in particular situations, burdened by something forced upon them."

I watched her, a little confused but still very curious. I followed as she disappeared around another stack, listening for the honey sound of her voice.

"I was brave," she said, "curious, intelligent."

You are all those things still, I wanted so desperately to say, but she wasn't finished.

"Your eyes remind me of a friend," she said quietly, stopping her movement and scanning the shelves for something.

Finding what she needed, she pulled the two leather-bound books from the shelf and set them on the table beside me. I inched closer, our shoulders brushing as I reached to open the top. Inside were pages upon pages of handwritten notes, dates, and names.

"Is this a ledger?" I asked her, inspecting with more detail.

"No," she whispered. "It's stories." She brushed her hand down the open center of the book.

"I did not want to forget my life in old age, unsure of what the Manor had in store for me." A shaky breath interrupted her thoughts and the darkness returned to her eyes as she thought of something. "So I recorded every story I could remember. Some of them are simply silly days that made me smile or brought me joy. Some are sad and full of grief or pain." She briefly tripped over her words in an attempt to control her tone.

"The color and kindness in your eyes reminds me of a young woman I used to call a friend."

"Will you tell me about her?" I asked her, unsure if that was crossing an invisible boundary.

"Aisling. She was my ladies maid in my household before I was... before I came to Orchid Manor," Florence explained. "But she was more than that. We would spend hours together in conversation. She was so bright and always wanted to learn. She would accompany me and assist me with every woman I helped. Aisling was loyal and kind, and I will never have a friend like her again."

I looked over at her, eyes still glued to the page but now filled with tears that weren't there before. I wanted to reach out and brush the tear that trickled down her flushed cheeks but curled my hand deeper into my pocket.

"I apologize, Mr. Dunn. It seems that I'm still grieving for her. Up until your arrival, I was unsure of the passing time; frequently, the house—puts me to sleep, and it seems more time has passed than I ever could have imagined. To me, Aisling was still alive until a few days ago, and now she's gone."

"I'm sorry, about Aisling," I say, extending my verbal sympathies instead of touching her.

"Time is a thief," she mumbled, "except when you are begging it to steal from your own life, and it plays ignorant to your pleas."

"She will live on forever in your stories," I offered.

"Correct and I'm sure, with time, the ache of missing her will ease."

One hundred and seventy-two years she had been in the Manor.

I ran my hand over my mouth, trying to hide the raw emotion that rolled through me. There was nothing I could say or do that would ease her heartache.

"How long have you been a—Hunter?" she asked me, seemingly trying to change the subject.

"Fourteen years, which to anyone else would seem like a long time but," I paused, running my tongue over my bottom lip.

"To a one-hundred-year-old monster." She fingered the old page and sighed.

"One hundred-year-old *anomaly*." I corrected her.

Florence looked up at me and stole the air from my lungs.

She was like a supernova in the night sky, begging to be picked apart and explored for every inch she was worth. Bright and burning, but so far away.

It would take a lot of convincing to prove she wasn't a monster but, quietly, the determination snuck up on me; I was willing to put in the work. The moment that stretched between us was long and quiet, her eyes searching mine with her lips pressed into a thin line. There was a tiny freckle beneath her right eye that begged for attention and a fleck of dark brown in her left iris that seemed so harsh against the stark green of them.

I cleared my throat to break the trance.

"Do you have any family?" She asked and shifted away from me.

"I did," I said, rolling my shoulders back despite the stinging pain in my bicep as the muscles flexed. "I do," I corrected myself. "My parents died when I was eighteen, killed by a wraith that would have taken me too if Wes hadn't saved my life."

"And then?" she inquired, brushing a piece of loose hair away from her face.

"Koen's parents were killed when he was small. I don't even know if he remembers them. Wes' parents lived for a long time until they were killed during a hunt. Now it's just the three of us." I tried to explain.

"You mentioned before that Koen and Wesley aren't blood related," she asked.

"Yeah, Koen was... adopted into the family later, not legally or any-thing. His real last name belongs to the past now. Wes slipped into the role of older brother without a second thought." I left out small details, things she didn't need to know about Wes, stuff he would kill me for speaking about.

"You are all very odd," she said to me. Only then did I realize I was staring again. It was nearly impossible not to. "Do you believe you can figure out why I'm stuck here?"

"If anyone can, it's me," I said. "I've always been more interested in the lore and science behind the hunt. The hunting part is a little violent for my taste."

"You don't enjoy killing?" She asked me and leaned against the desk, staring into the books.

"Not particularly, not in the moment, at least. Once it's done and we've saved a family or protected a town... it feels satisfying," I explained. "But learning all the ways we can accomplish that, chasing that fulfilling feeling through research. That's the real high."

She turned to look at me, the green flooding her eyes again as she smiled softly at me.

"I'll leave you to it then, Mr. Dunn." She excused herself, wandering toward the door.

"Clay," I stopped her with my voice, and she turned toward me with her slender hands on the frame. "Please, call me Clay."

"Then you'll have to call me Florence." She smiled sweetly, sending a shiver down my spine as I nodded in agreement.

FOOD HAS
BEEN GOING
ROTTEN
DECOMPOSITIO
N IS RAPID
LESS THAN
THREE HOURS
BUT STILL NO
MAGGOTS
ONLY MOULD

WESLEY

Staring down at the bag of rotten apples, I nearly loaded my gun and started shooting holes in the walls of this damned Manor. It was playing with us.

I strode into the parlor to find it empty, the soft sound of laughter floating from one of the upstairs rooms. Anger coursed through me, knowing that Koen was up there with that monster, enjoying his time, and putting himself and the rest of us in danger.

While I was suffocating on the thought of staying in one place.

Pushing out into the night air through the front door, I wandered around the Manor's grounds. Void of sound, it ran a chill down my spine that stuck to my skin. There were no animals... at least in the week of being at Orchid Manor I couldn't remember seeing or hearing a single one. Not even a rat.

I rounded the corner, my eyes catching sight of Clay, his nose buried in a book sitting at a table that was surrounded by dried and wilted flowers and leaves. His back to the large maze created with cracked branches of dead bushes.

"We've been here over two weeks, I think I've got cabin fever." I settled down into my leather jacket to block out the chill of the night air. "You aren't going to find out anything about it because whatever the hell it is, it's old and dangerous," I snapped at him.

He laughed, eyes peering up from the book as he leaned against the iron-framed garden chair. It looked older than the house, licked with rust from the elements on it.

"What the hell are you laughing at?"

"I've never seen you get so worked up so quickly." Clay shook his head and closed the book he was reading. How he wasn't freezing was beyond me. Wearing a thin black dress shirt, two buttons undone and sleeves rolled up to his elbows, he leaned forward on the table and cocked his head to the side. "She hasn't hurt anyone," he started.

"That we know of," I interrupted.

"I've cross-checked all the police records, and there've been a few reported incidents on the property. A lawyer in the fifties was admitted to the hospital with what the records stated to be *thousands of splinters.* There have been no other reports that I've been able to find so far."

"We don't know what it's capable of," I said, crossing my arms. "Just because it's not reported doesn't mean whatever the hell is in that house doesn't have an impressive body count."

"You gotta stop calling her that." His smile grew lopsided, and he leaned back to look at me.

"It got to you, too." I closed my eyes, frustrated enough to lash out. "Have you thought it might be a siren?"

"She's not a siren, Wes." Clay palmed one of his books and spun it for me. "She told me that she used to help women in need, she wouldn't get into it but...I think she was making a house call." He pointed to the house. "I just can't find any records on who owned the house. It's like they were scrubbed."

"So you've gotten nowhere!" I slammed my hands down.

"Until you sit your ass down and start helping, you don't get to yell at me about my efforts!" Clay snapped back.

"You're working slowly on purpose. You haven't left the house even though that–" I point to his laptop, "is useless up here. You haven't even tried to use it."

"First of all, I have my..." I looked around for the little black box that created my wifi hotspot and furrowed my brows. "Well usually I have wifi, Buttercup, but in any case where exactly do you expect me to use it otherwise? In town? Where we're wanted by a police force that may or may not be further infected by ghouls?" Clay cocked his head to the side. "Because it's the only town within two hours of us that might be large enough to have internet, and you want to stroll down there?"

"I've been keeping an eye on the scanner. The search has died down for us. But you wouldn't know that because you've been too busy with that *thing*," I said. The reality was that just because I hadn't heard anything over the scanner didn't mean they weren't still looking for us, but I was frustrated and the cabin fever was setting in harder than usual.

"I've been working my way through the library. It's got a lot more information than I was expecting."

"But none on the house." I pushed the book away and ran my hands through my hair. "You're making fucking excuses."

"We decided as a group to stay until I heal and figure her out." He stared me down, his eyes meeting mine unwavering with defiance. "I'm still doing the first part."

"Do it faster," I growled.

"You're insufferable. Instead of wasting my time, why don't you try to help?" Clay huffed.

"I would, but this is the first time I've found you outside of that library and away from *it*." I accentuated the word, pissed off to no end that we're having this argument. Again.

"This isn't about the time frame or a looming threat. The only boot to our throats is yours. Wes, what is going on with you?" He removed his glasses and set them aside, rubbing his hands over his face.

"It's not *my* boot. You two are just enamored."

"What do you want to do? Leave here, leave her? What if you're right? What if she's a bloodthirsty succubus, just waiting for us to fall asleep to have her way with us? What then? We leave her to the town. Hope she keeps to herself for a few more years until a Hunter comes along with more sense than you."

I stared him down, a growl rumbling from my chest. I was fighting to control the urge to knock him out, but he was right. If it was dangerous, leaving the house and the town to the monster's control was just as bad as staying. At least we could monitor the activity this way.

I just disliked every single second of it.

"Perfect, so we're sitting ducks in a giant ghost house while you and Koen make eyes at the poltergeist? This is my hell." I slumped into the chair across from him with a loud groan. "You need to figure this out faster before Koen gets attached."

"Whining is a bad look on you. No one is making eyes," Clay protested. "I'm doing my best."

"Koen is," I snapped, making eye contact with him. "This past week, he's barely left her side; he risked going into town to get her treats. *Treats*, Clay."

"He was buying himself treats, and besides, he's just keeping busy." The excuse was flimsy. "And you just said activity has died down."

"No, it's..." I swallowed the foul taste of anger and fear back down my throat and lowered my voice. "We both know what happens when Hunters get sloppy."

"You mean when Hunters have a conscience." Clay arched a brow at me. "There's a difference. You seem to think having a heart is the end of it all."

"It is when that heart starts bleeding for the thing we're supposed to be hunting," I snarled. Koen would have flinched, but Clay just smirked.

"Humanity is all we have, Wes," he said, tugging on the fabric of his pants as he sat forward to come face to face with me. "If we lose sight of what we're trying to do in the world, we're no better than the things we hunt."

"Don't use that philosophy shite on me, Clayton."

I pushed out my chair, knocking it into the gravel behind me, and stormed from the property, only breathing when the truck door slammed shut. The old visor rattled and dropped, the picture tucked inside falling into my lap like a cruel twist of karma. I would have preferred to instead be slapped across the face or stabbed in the back.

My older brother Wyatt and I stared up at me.

My blood brother.

With his golden hair and big hazel eyes, barely nineteen in the photo, we were off on our first hunt together. I could remember the day like it was yesterday. Everything had been fine; we were hunting a ghost when he changed course and brought me to an old abandoned barn on the edge of town. Introducing me to his new girlfriend, but everything about her and where we were felt wrong; it felt unsafe.

The words he spoke to quell my nervousness repeatedly played in the back of my mind: *"There's nothing wrong with falling in love, Wesley."* I never scrubbed the sound of his screams that followed as the vampire tore into his flesh from my memory. At such a young age, there was nothing I could do; I had to run. He had sealed his fate, and forced me to be an unwilling accomplice to it.

He let his heart bleed when he had fallen in love with a vampire in the nest. Completely aware of what she was, he fell right into her trap, thinking she wasn't like the others.

I started the engine, tucking the photo away to forget what I had lost, and peeled from the gravel driveway away from the massive, haunted Manor that mocked me. The knowledge of what I had left behind, alone and at the mercy of a new threat, willingly letting her drain them of spirit until they were easy prey.

I wouldn't let her take my family.

I couldn't afford to.

CLAYTON

There was nothing worse than an argument with Wes. They were always the kind that cut deep and hurt everyone. He would go off and lick his wounds, but I couldn't afford to stop digging into Florence.

I needed to know everything about this place, about this house.

About *her*.

I would be the first to admit that the lines were blurring quicker than anticipated, and there was very little I could do to stop it once it had started. Florence was all consuming and my restraint was wavering with each small laugh and sweet smile. It was in the way she familiarized herself with each of us. With Koen, there was laughter, jokes, and brazen curiosity. She had seemingly come out of whatever shell she was in the day we met her.

She was unknown and fresh. Seemingly a creature we had never run into before and questions swarmed me faster than I could ask them of her. The lines that blurred were that of logic and infatuation but, slowly, I was caring less and less which of the two my head and heart were consumed by.

She wore her hair down more each passing day, her laugh grew louder, and her questions about society and life outside of the Manor became more frequent. Better yet, she appeared more often around the house, only hiding when Wes was stomping around. But, even then, I could see the intrigue brewing behind those sparkling emerald eyes. Florence was just waiting for him to come to her, which... spoke volumes about the attention and care she provided us all effortlessly. Shifting the way she cared for us individually. My mind wandered, wondering if anyone had ever taken the time to care for her the way she so naturally did us.

With each day, it felt less like we were squatting and more like we were—

Home.

I pushed into the library, shaking free of those consuming thoughts, and set everything down on the table before rolling my sleeves up. My arm was starting to feel better, stinging less each time I moved to card my fingers through my hair or lean impatiently against the table. I stared down at my research, bewildered and overwhelmed.

"There's got to be something in this library that explains you." I ran a hand over my notes and turned to the rows of books. Against the far wall of the library was an odd collection of leather-bound journals that I could have sworn were not there before.

I wandered toward them, fingering the worn and collapsing spines in passing before grabbing the one at the end. Unlike the ledger that Florence had shown me before, these were old. The most pristine of them all was made of dark red leather, almost brown in color, it was so dark, and engraved in the front was a small capital F.

"*Florence,*" I whispered and made my way back to the table, sitting down in the chair and flipping open the pages. A light smile formed on my lips at the sight of her soft handwriting. True to her nature it was a little messy but curved around the bottoms of the letters, and she left little doodles of flowers and birds in the margins. Every entry was a story, her writing fluid and easy to read. It was—simply put—a novel of her life.

I swallowed tightly, reached for my glasses, and continued to flip. The first entries were dark. They were mostly confused and pleading...

Florence marked the passing of time with seasons. The winter was seemingly her worst time of the year. Sadness consumed her in those months, without the sunlight to soothe her gentle soul. My heart ached as I continued.

There had to be over a hundred entries in this journal alone. Each page was a pouring, heartbreaking confession. Raw and straight from Florence, it was her experience with the house, with time, and with loneliness. But at times the entries became a softer, more genuine curiosity for herself and her surroundings.

I collected all the little moments where her light shone off the page. Her intelligence was astounding. Her thoughts on childbirth and abortion were far past her time, each one more in-depth as she started to work through it, but she noted every little idea she had in that journal. I stopped on an entry near the end of the journal, Spring:

I sat perched at the edge of the chaise and undid the laces of my boots. They thumped gently against the floor where I dropped them unceremoniously, stretching out my legs and wiggling my toes in the silk stockings before standing to remove my bodice.

My eyes wandered to the chaise, it's where I could always find her. Even when she disappeared, fading into the shadows and mazes of the Manor, she always showed back up, and she was always there. I leaned back in the library chair, holding the journal up to my face, and continued to read.

As I took to task removing the many layers of my dress, it occurred to me that being cooped up alone in the Manor, there was no reason to be fully dressed every day. Despite that, I always had. At first it had been due to the fact I never felt truly alone here, and always had a feeling of uncertainty that I was being watched by someone. Though since my discovery of Agatha's letter, I now knew there was indeed something watching... but it was a something and not a someone, and that put a lot of nerves at ease.

Agatha's letter... begrudgingly, I leaned forward in my chair, jotting down a note to remember the question before diving back into the entry. My chest was warm with anticipation for her next words.

Perhaps now, it was just to maintain some semblance of routine and normalcy.

I let the final petticoat hit the floor and stepped out of the pile of skirts around me. I wandered over to the closest bookshelf to peruse the titles along the spines of the novels. There were hundreds, if not thousands, of works in this library, and I had a mind to read every one of them—after all, I had the time for it. As I scanned the titles, my fingers worked mindlessly at loosening the laces of my stays— just enough to ease the unfastening of the busk closure. It opened easily, and I draped it over the back of the dark green velvet settee nearest to me and continued my exploration of the shelves... It only took a moment more before I settled on a novel by Currer Bell.

I smiled, recognizing the pen name of Charlotte Bronte. Of course out of all the books in this library she would manage to choose a literary canon, and a female one at that.

I selected the book and reveled in the creamy feeling of the leather and the weight of it in my hand. I hugged it to my chest and the tome felt tangible and cool through the thin layer of my chemise. I settled into the chaise longue that was tucked into the back corner of the library, next to the wall of floor-to-ceiling windows. The drapes were drawn open now. The Manor and I had come to what I believed to be a bit of an understanding in that respect. Windows stayed open now, and light and fresh air allowed both the Manor and myself to breathe.

I inhaled the scent of grass mixed with old pages and sighed. The weather outside was gloomy, and it appeared as if the sky could open at any point to drench the world in rain but, in my experience, that was the best time to be curled up with a book. I had so missed getting lost in a story. I flipped open the cover, luxuriated in the cracking noise, and plunged deep into the world on the page.

I adored her love of books and stories. It didn't matter the topic, she just always wanted to know more, and it excited me. I wet my bottom lip and unbuttoned the top of my shirt. The library was so warm in the mornings. I palmed the journal and ran my hands through my hair before flipping the page.

I was barely aware of the day slipping away from me, it had rained at some point in the early evening, I think—but I had only vaguely noticed due to the click of the window shutting to keep out the dampness. I was fully engrossed in the tale that was unfolding—the struggles, the longing, the pining for a forbidden love. I read enraptured, long past the sunset and into the small hours of the morning. Until, at some point, I was no longer reading—I was dreaming.

I dreamt of a man with dark features; deep-set brown eyes that seemed to pour into me and fill me with warmth in a way I had never known. His hair was unruly and curled at the nape of his neck, creating the perfect hold for me to wind my fingers through. His broad brow furrowed slightly as he took my mouth with his, gently at first and then with intensity that built until I was sure I would not be able to continue to stand. Seeming to sense this, his hand reached behind me to pull me in tightly, entwining our bodies so closely that there was no part of him I could not feel against me.

I shifted in the chair, my cock twitching instinctively at her words.

"Fuck." I closed the journal over my fingers and held it in my lap as the flush of heat rose up my neck and coated my ears red.

All of the other entries had been tame, no mention of her sexual frustrations, but... She had left the journal out in the open... was I wrong for reading it? Could I even stop myself if it was? I looked down at the journal and then around the library before flipping it back, opening and reading more.

CLAYTON

*T*he hand at the small of my back lowered until it fully cupped my backside, fingers pressing deeply and pulling my hips against his thigh. His other hand moved over the swell of my breast, his palm grazing my nipple and causing it to rise under the thin fabric. My breath escaped in a shocked sigh and his lips moved down my jawline to my ear, leaving a trail of heat in their wake. His teeth grazed the hollow of my neck and every nerve ending I had stood on end. His practiced fingers slid into the low neckline and dropped it off my shoulder to reveal my breast.

"I shouldn't be reading this," I grumbled under my breath, unable to stop as the arousal built between my legs. It was just so... *Florence.* I shook out the tension in my shoulders and adjusted in the chair, looking over at the chaise. I could see her there, laid across it with her hair pouring over the back, her lips parted. Completely undone in her dream.

The cool air sent a shiver through me for a moment before his mouth was on me, hot and wet. His tongue danced circles around my hardened peak, and my head fell back without my control. His teeth pulled softly, and it elicited a noise from deep in my throat that sounded more animal than I've ever heard myself. His hand was snaking high up my thigh, and the heat of wanting him ached within me. I felt simultaneously sharp and hollow, an emptiness that was somehow both pain and pleasure and...

I woke up with a start. The book had fallen from where it was resting on my chest as I slept and tumbled loudly to the floor. I relaxed back against the chaise, my heart racing. I could feel my pulse in my throat. My fingers touched my neck and I could almost feel the ghost of the teeth that grazed beneath my ear. My breasts heaved and I was still struggling to catch my breath, the pebbled flesh pressed tenderly against my chemise. It hadn't been real, but my response to it had been more real than anything I had ever experienced. I could feel the evidence of it slippery and aching between my thighs.

The room was a dull glow from the lamplight; the night outside was black, and the windows now bare my reflection. My long hair was fanned loosely around my pale round face, eyes wide and excited. I could see the chemise had ridden up significantly in my sleep, and my stockinged legs were bare from the knee to my hips, and what of me that was covered by it was doing little to disguise the soft curves of my breasts and stomach. The ache in my core pulsed softly, and without truly thinking, I watched as my reflection reached down and touched the wet center.

My grip tightened on the book as my eyes flickered to where she would be. Her long legs and full thighs would feel better than the leather between my fingers, and it drove me to the edge. My breathing grew shallow with every word she penned. The idea of her taking control of her own pleasure was unexpected and torturous.

I leaned back in the chair further, letting my head fall back between my shoulders with a huff of frustration. Knowing how wrong it would be to use her words, her newly explored pleasure, to bring myself relief. But my cock pressed painfully against my pants at the thought of my fingers buried between her thighs and her lips on mine. To feel her breasts in my palm, to sink into the wetness of her... I closed my eyes and could almost hear the sounds that left her, breathless and begging for more.

"Jesus," I growled and continued reading, my restraint waning with every word.

Warm and slippery, my fingers explored a part of myself I never had before. The memory of gentle hands slipping up my thighs spurred my exploration deeper. I slid a finger through my folds until I struck a nerve that felt as though I'd been shocked. My back arched in response and my hand moved instinctively, searching for that feeling again. My mind wandered back to the man as my hands picked up where my dream had left off; pinching at the swollen flesh of my breasts and stroking the tender flesh between my thighs as my hips rocked, until eventually, I succumbed. Exhausted and ecstatic all at once, the walls inside me shuddered and released, and I was undone.

"What are you doin'?" Koen's voice startled me upward, smacking my erection on the heavy wood table and buckling over against it with the book beneath my palm.

"Reading," I groaned as the pain rippled through me down to my toes, sharp enough to make my eyes water. I tugged off my glasses and wiped the tears from the corners with a knuckle before tossing them on the table.

"*Reading...*" Koen wandered into the library, his blond hair tucked under a backward hat and his arms exposed in a sleeveless *David Bowie* band shirt. "I've seen you get pretty worked up reading, but I've never heard you moan like that before," he said with a smug look on his face as he crossed his arms.

I inhaled through the next aftershock of impaling myself.

Karma.

"Shut up, Koen," I groaned and loosened my hold on the journal.

"What is it?" He pointed to the book, reaching across the table to take it from me, but I slid it backward away from him.

"It's a journal," I said, finally able to stand up straight.

Until I knew that Florence had left it out on purpose, I didn't want anyone else tearing through her personal thoughts. I shouldn't have even succumbed to my impulses without her consent.

"Who's Agatha?" He pointed to the scribbled note next to my laptop.

"Florence mentioned a letter written to her from someone named Agatha," I said, staring at the note, my mind still waffling between the image of Florence touching herself and reality.

"Are you all right, big boy?" Koen's green eyes flickered over me. "You look...flushed."

"I'm fine." I shook my head. "Do you think we're being ridiculous?" I asked him.

He shrugged, a funny little scowl forming on his face as he leaned against the table to study my expression. "About Florence? You aren't going to go all *Wesley* on me, are you?" He asked.

"Should I?" I countered.

"He thinks I'm losing my mind. I'm not." Koen shook his head. "I know that he's all family traditions and violence. You're all research and logic, but..."

Koen was emotional and had gut feelings. I knew that. He knew it. Everything that had transpired since our arrival at Orchid Manor had put Wes in a mean state. He slipped in and out of them when he felt like he was losing control of a situation, but taking it out on Koen wasn't necessarily fair. And Koen would let Wes use him as a punching bag because it was what they always did.

I didn't agree with it but arguing the point had gotten old, fast with Wes so I turned to make sure that Koen felt protected during those periods of emotional upheaval. It didn't happen often; Wes was his number one protector, but when it did it was always a balancing act.

"I'm sorry you feel like we don't believe you," I said, and he looked up from the table where his eyes had settled.

"I just know whatever is going on in this house, it isn't her fault, Clay," he said with conviction. "I've never been so sure about something."

"Alright, well, one time you said that about a Hugh Grant movie and were horribly wrong, so..." I teased him, but he didn't laugh. I leaned over the table and patted his cheek with the palm of my hand. "I believe you," I said.

"Mmm." That was the only response from him.

"I wouldn't be in here, reading hundreds of books with a dead laptop if I didn't," I said, and he looked up at me with trust in his eyes and a small nod. His brows furrowed at the end of my sentence.

"What do you mean it's dead?" That sparked his interest, the tension floating away from us as the conversation eased back to normal.

"I had the hot spot box for the Wi-Fi... but I haven't seen it in a few days," I said, looking around at the messy table. It was shortly after I found the articles on the Manor about the incidents. It was there, and then it just wasn't.

"I didn't notice," he said. *I've been a little preoccupied,* hung unsaid in the air between us. "I'll keep my eye out for it?" He said, standing up straight. He paused with a quizzical look on his face. "Actually, now that you mention it, I haven't been able to find my charging bank for my phone either. Weird." He shrugged it off and pointed to the mess of notes on the table. "Do you need any help in here?"

"Not unless you want to read through a bunch of books on ancient civilizations that believed the moon was a real person who took the form of a river," I said quickly, wiggling the journal at him, and Koen stared at me in confusion. "Transfiguration," I said, like the word would make any sense to him.

"Right, have fun with that," Koen said, backing out of the library.

When the door closed, I looked back down at the journal, worrying my bottom lip between my teeth as I tried to figure out my next move.

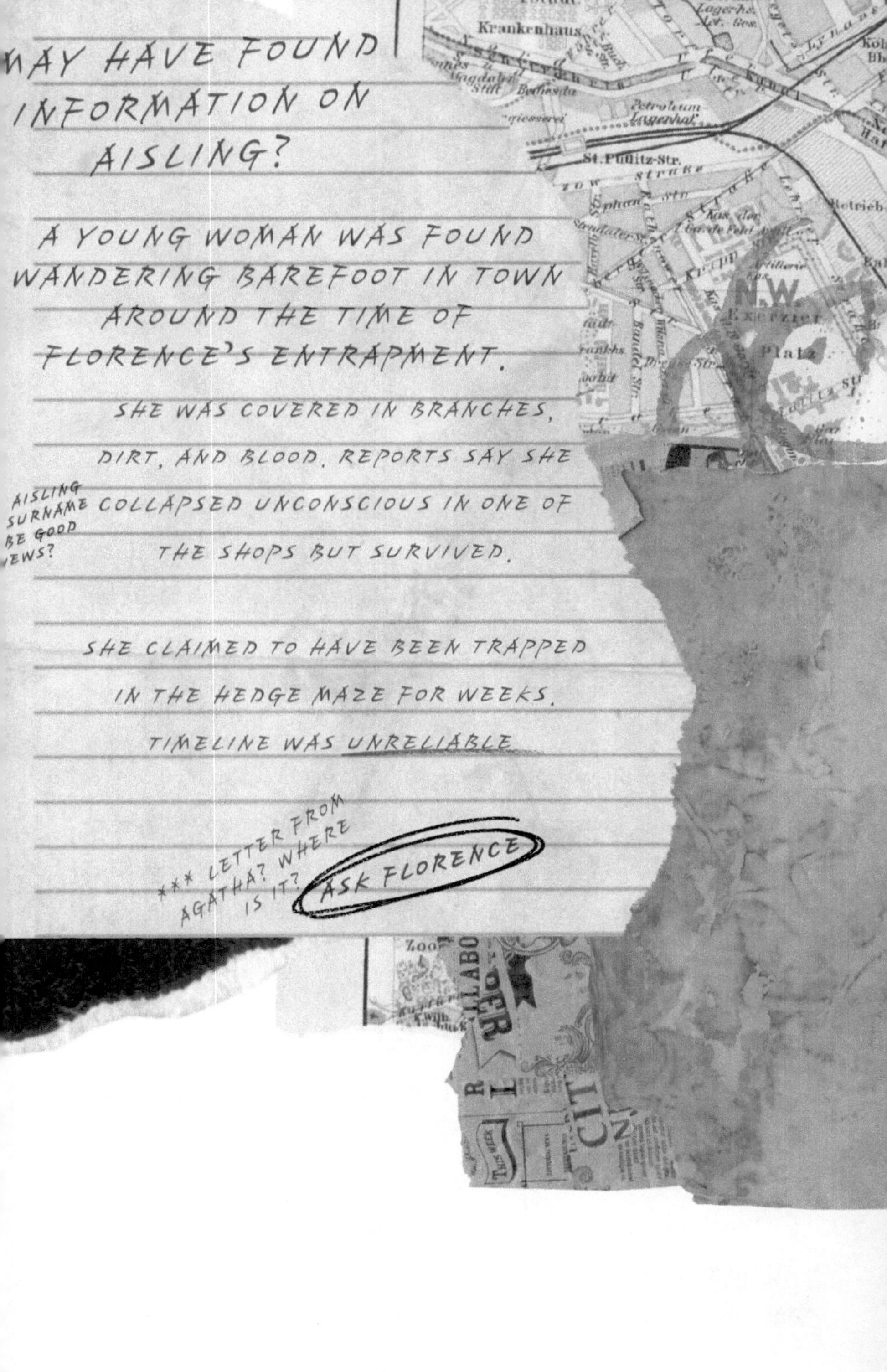
MAY HAVE FOUND
INFORMATION ON
AISLING?

A YOUNG WOMAN WAS FOUND
WANDERING BAREFOOT IN TOWN
AROUND THE TIME OF
FLORENCE'S ENTRAPMENT.
SHE WAS COVERED IN BRANCHES,
DIRT, AND BLOOD. REPORTS SAY SHE
COLLAPSED UNCONSCIOUS IN ONE OF
THE SHOPS BUT SURVIVED.

SHE CLAIMED TO HAVE BEEN TRAPPED
IN THE HEDGE MAZE FOR WEEKS.
TIMELINE WAS UNRELIABLE

AISLING
SURNAME
BE GOOD
NEWS?

*** LETTER FROM
AGATHA? WHERE
IS IT?   ASK FLORENCE

KOEN

I found Florence standing alone on the front stairs, staring at the moon. It bathed her in silver and highlighted all the darkest tones of her auburn hair. I wanted to touch it, run my fingers through it, and remind myself she was real. Her skirts hid most of her curvy figure but the corset she wore dug into her hips and tugged at her waist, forcing her chest to spill slightly from her pretty pale green blouse. She was breathtaking.

Wes had been on a warpath, trying to figure out how to convince us to leave the Manor. He was determined that she would destroy us in some way. I was convinced she might be an angel because no one, monster or otherwise, had ever made me feel the surge of butterflies in my chest that she did every time she smiled at me.

"What are you looking at?" I asked her, and she whipped her head around to look at me, arms folded over her chest.

"The sky," she sighed, and a tiny huff of warmth floated into the chilly air.

"Pretty," I said, not looking away from Florence.

"Your brother drives that metal coach like an insane person."

I laughed and came to stand next to her. Wes had left so fast that no one could ask him questions about where he was going or when he'd be back. But, knowing him the way we did, it would be a minute before we saw him again.

"It's called a truck. That one specifically is called a Bronco. And he just needs to clear his head," I said.

"I'm extremely envious of his ability to run away," she said, not looking away from the sky. Something devastating was in her voice as she said it, and then her eyes sparkled and she looked at me quizzically, "You got rid of the horses but then call it a Bronco?"

I snorted, enjoying the look of adorable confusion on her face and shaking my head. "Let's save the history lessons... future lessons?" I mulled it over briefly and then shrugged the thought away. "Whatever lessons they would be, for Clay." I watched her for a second longer and stepped off the stone steps in my jeans and a band t-shirt. "Show me around." I tilted my chin toward her, extended my hand to her, and smiled. *Just open yourself up to me*, I silently begged. "I haven't explored outside. Inside is enough of a maze."

"Alright," she said, voice thick with amusement as she offered me a lazy smile and took my hand. She gathered her skirts in her other hand and descended the stairs, starting the tour around the Manor with the front garden. It all looked the same to me, run down, falling apart but there had been small moments, when the floors didn't seem so cracked and the wallpaper looked brighter than before.

She pointed out every little detail she loved about the Manor, never complaining that she was bored with anything. She loved the vines that climbed the windows and the wildflowers that bloomed in the spring. Nothing seemed old or tired in her eyes. She appreciated every detail as if it were the first time she had seen it even if I couldn't.

I just enjoyed watching her talk. Her bottom lip jutted out when she was trying to find a word more progressive than her current language, and how her eyes twinkled like glitter when she told me that her favorite place in the entire house was the field outback because there was a tree to climb.

She tucked her hand into the crook of my elbow. The gesture was small, but it set off fireworks along my skin, and my eyes flickered down to how her fingers curled into my forearm. Florence pointed to the small running foundation surrounded by bushes of dark roses she described. As if she spoke them into existence, with a blink of my eyes the cracked, dying bushes bloomed. Doubling in size, each flower spreading its petals and soaking up the moonlight.

My lips parted in amazement and closed again, keeping my shock to myself. Trying my best to remain stoic in a righteous attempt not to startle her.

It was truly incredible how Florence's outlook on the Manor was so different from ours. To her there was no crumbling brick or rusted and dingy windows. Every piece of it was like it had been built yesterday. When Florence didn't respond, I tracked her gaze to the large iron gate at the end of the driveway.

"Have you ever tried to leave?" I asked her.

"In the beginning," she said, continuing our slow pace around the side of the house, "every day."

"And you never made it out the door?"

"Not at first. Over the years, slowly but surely, I could creep over the threshold, my boundaries increasing until I could walk around the front of the house. And then, eventually, I could get to the garden, and then the field."

"But never the gate?" I asked her. "Have you tried recently?"

Florence shook her head at me; her demeanor had curled in on itself, and she seemed terrified.

"What's going on in there?" I stepped forward, unlinking our arms, and blocked her path.

She was only a few inches shorter than me, but I lowered myself to look into her eyes.

"There are details about my past." She licked her lips nervously and looked away from me. I couldn't quite place why she was so upset but something was bothering her, and the fact that she wouldn't tell me upended my normally playful mood.

"Hey." I held my hands back in surrender. "There are a lot of scary monsters in the world with more teeth." I smiled at her, and her eyes flickered to the dimple on my cheek as they turned a shade lighter and her body started to relax. "I've been bitten, stabbed, and nearly beheaded by most of them."

"Koen," she stuttered.

"Nothing you say is going to scare me, and it stays between us," I added, knowing that if Wes could hear me right now, he'd have both hands around my neck. *Never trust them, no matter how much they plead and beg, Koen. Deep down, all they want is blood.*

"I'm never sure." She looked back at the Manor like something was watching us. "If I grew stronger or if I was given more freedom. But I'm grateful either way. Being outside makes me feel alive."

I straightened out, processing her words. She had done that before. She spoke about the Manor as if it were alive, but it seemed strange. She was fond of it but also feared it like a caged animal. I would have to break my promise if only to tell Clay what she had said. Any tiny detail from her was one step closer to figuring out how to free her.

"What if we try?" I asked her.

"That's not a good idea," she said, backing up a step. I reached out to her and wrapped my fingers around her wrist, which was always so warm.

"I'll be with you the entire time," I told her. "Can we try together?"

The word 'together' seemed to shudder through her like a chill. Her eyes flickered to and from the gate then back to me as she visibly forced herself to steady her breath. I tilted my head to catch her gaze and pressed my lips together in a thin line.

"I won't let you go," I whispered under the wind that brushed our cheeks, and her eyes snapped to mine.

I know how foolish I must have looked, tripping over my two feet just to garner her attention, but there was a magnetism to Florence that I had never felt before. And part of me, hidden under all the sense I had, was the hopeful kid I used to be. He held all the yearning for joy and tender care I hadn't felt in a long time. And it radiated from her like a sunbeam, calling to me like a moth drawn to a flame.

"Okay," she conceded, pressing her hand into mine a little tighter.

We walked down the path toward the gate. Each step Florence took felt a little more like walking through hardening cement. She got slower with every inch we gained closer to the gate. I kept my hand gripped around hers as I popped the latch on the iron bar and kicked it open with my foot.

Not letting go of her, I slipped in front, walking backward through the gate. Our arms extended between us as the space grew. "Are you okay?" I asked her.

She nodded.

"Are you lying?" I smiled.

"A little," she breathed out through shaky lips. "Don't let go."

"I won't."

But the promise meant very little as she stepped across the gate's threshold.

The toe of her shoe brushed against mine only for a moment, before she was lifted from the ground.

Florence was violently ripped from my grip, and I was sent flying backward as if a blast of energy had gone off between us and separated us by force. I rolled in the dirt, pushing to my knees and coughing up a sticky stream of blood that coated the inside of my mouth and then painted the gravel between my hands. Both impaled with tiny rocks, I couldn't take a full breath and realized that I must have hit the ground hard enough to knock the wind from me and possibly break a rib.

I blinked the tears and dust from my eyes, rolling to my back and curling into a ball, trying to get my body right before I looked around in panic for Florence. There was a deep track from what could have only been her feet sliding and grasping for purchase, but she was nowhere to be found.

"Florence!" I called out to her as the darkness settled deeper against my shoulders. I screamed her name until my voice was hoarse, but she never came back to me.

FLORENCE

My head was throbbing when I woke up, crushed up against the wall in my room. It's where the house put me when I tried to leave.

The main reason I had stopped pushing for them to leave was because there was a possibility that they could find the answers I had been searching for. Clay was determined to figure it out, no matter how much Wesley was against it. Koen- well he had an undeniable interest in me that was surely becoming more dangerous to us both by the day.

With one pitiful attempt, I pushed from the floor but could feel the pain that shot through my shoulder. It had been dislocated and hung limp at my side. I groaned and climbed to my feet, stumbling toward the bed, and crawled across the mattress. A shaky exhale left my lips as I settled against the pillow. I was silently grateful that I had chosen a front closure stay that morning and undid the busk with less effort than a regular corset would have been. As I became free, I could finally catch my breath, inhale as deeply as possible, and fully expand my chest, filling my lungs with air. My skirts and shoes were covered in dirt, and blood seeped through the fabric from a nasty cut on my knee that stung fiercely.

The mattress welcomed me as I sunk deeply into it with a groan. I would heal after some time, the cuts would close, and the shoulder would roll back into place. It always did. The Manor almost apologizing for trapping me here, it would always take care of me after the punishment came down on my head.

Another shaky exhale was followed by the prayer to fall asleep.

I closed my eyes and willed my body into darkness.

"Florence?" Koen's knock on the door woke me from my sleep. The cuts on my knee had stopped stinging and, by the grace of a high power, the throb in my shoulder had ceased.

"I've been searching everywhere for you." His voice was full of both concern and relief as he crossed the room and dropped to the side of the bed, reaching a hand out to me.

I gasped at the state of his skin, and he pulled back.

His hands were cleaned and healing but there were tiny cuts that maimed his palms and the skin of his arms. The house had hurt him, and my stomach flipped. His jaw had a small cut and his green eyes were so wide with concern that tears welled in my own.

"Are you okay?" I asked him.

"Me?" he laughed, pushing over the bed toward me. "I thought you were gone! It's been three days, I..."

He stopped, flustered and upset.

Three days. I had been asleep that long. I peered into the room's darkness and cursed myself internally. Of course the Manor would have hidden me away from them for so long, as far as it could tell, I had let

Koen convince me to try and leave. It was his fault I had been hurt by the barrier.

Safe.

The Manor seemed to whisper through the gentle rustling of the curtains, it was protecting me.

"The house changes," I said. "It's not your fault you couldn't find me."

Each man was defiant and unafraid of the goings on of the Manor. Koen stared at me unblinking and swallowed tightly before his eyes drifted down over my throat to my state of dress. The blouse I wore did nothing to conceal my body, and his brows furrowed as he took in the small pools of dried blood on my skirt.

"Are you bleeding?" He looked back up at me.

"Not anymore."

"But you were?" Koen licked his plump bottom lip as his fingers played with the hem of my skirt. "Can I check?" He asked quietly and I nodded, the skin on my calf warming as his fingertips brushed me. He tugged the skirt up and over my knees, careful not to risk my modesty, and ghosted his thumb over the pristine skin of my knees.

"See?" I forced a smile to my lips.

Koen's eyes flickered over my face with disbelief. "Your smile is cute even when it's fake," he sighed and sat at the end of the bed. After a long moment, opening his mouth a few times to speak but closing it again, he asked, "is it always like that?"

"Always."

"Why didn't you tell me?" He leaned forward, pulled my skirts back over my knees, and rested them neatly around my ankles.

"Would you have believed me if I did?" I asked.

"As someone who knows that skinwalkers and the Loch Ness monster exist," he scoffed, "yes."

He was right. I should have warned him but the fear of what he would see gripped me tightly. In the end, I still ended up with his sad, confused, evergreen eyes staring back at me like I had betrayed him.

"It's the property line," I explained. "I knew the chances of stepping through the gate were non-existent, but something about you gave me the courage to try."

Koen's brow raised, and his gaze danced across my face.

"No more secrets," he said. "Even if you're scared. I think I've proven that I don't care what you are, I just know that you aren't dangerous and I want to help."

So sweet and well meaning, and so naive. I might not have been dangerous, but the house swelled with hostility at his words. The bedclothes wrapped tightly against my legs, a flimsy yet visible barrier between us.

"Wes is making dinner." He smiled at me, that adorable dimple appearing on the left side that kicked up the butterflies in my chest. "Will you come downstairs?"

"Is he going to shoot me if I do?" I stared at Koen.

"What? Afraid of a little shrapnel, Blossom?" He teased, his accent thick as the nickname washed a warm blush over my cheeks. Consider me convinced.

"Let me change first?" I looked down at the discarded corset and crumpled, bloody skirts.

"Don't disappear," he said, backing off the bed. "I'll wait outside for you."

He slipped from the room, giving me the privacy to change from the dirty clothes into something nice. I reached around, only to be met by a sharp pain that radiated from my shoulder. I looked down at it. There was no bruising but it certainly wasn't fully healed. "Curious," I whispered to myself. I tried briefly to lace the corset with my sore arm before realizing it wouldn't be possible. I debated looking for a different set of stays, but did not want to make them wait. So I called out to him. "Koen, will you help?"

Without hesitation, the door popped back open.

"What can I do?" He asked from the door, his eyes on the thin fabric of my chemise that barely covered my back.

A brief surge of bashfulness bloomed warmly up my chest. I nodded to the problem through the mirror and he walked towards me, looking dubiously to where the corset laces hung limp against my back. He gave me a soft smile as he started tugging them. The delicate, warm feeling flooded lower as a piece of his wavy blonde hair fell gently across his furrowed brow. His concentration was palpable as he worked the laces with his fingers.

"Which one?" he asked, looking up at me over my shoulder in the mirror. The dim light from the wall sconce glimmered across his gaze.

I nodded my head toward the hurt shoulder. Our eyes held a soft gaze as he slowly pulled my hair back and away to the other side of my neck, and he leaned cautiously—eyes never leaving mine—as if asking my permission for what happened next. I exhaled shakily as his lips pressed to my skin, pausing tenderly, his eyes closed over as though it might knock him off his feet. The small gesture rushed over my sore body and blanketed it with warmth, and longing.

He whispered against my skin. "Does it usually heal that slowly? It's been days."

"No." My response was breathy and even I could hear the wantonness. "It usually heals within hours."

Koen's eyes, dark and confused, flashed open and looked at me through thick lashes for a beat before he finished lacing the corset.

"Dinner. You can explain to Clay, and before you argue," he laughed, taking note of my mouth popping open. "He needs to know so he can help. Do you trust me?"

Did I? I paused, unsure. I wanted to.

But trusting came with stipulations and conditions.

Trusting him meant he was in danger. It meant sharing the fear I felt every day with someone who didn't quite understand why. But the look on his face spoke volumes. He wasn't afraid of anything within these walls, and that included me.

"Yes."

"Then trust me when I say..." He brushed a thumb across my cheek, causing my eyelids to flutter from his touch. It had been a long time since anyone had done that. Even before I had been trapped. A slight, playful smirk formed on his lips. "...Clay just wants to help, but keeping secrets from him prevents him from doing what he's good at."

"Research." I nodded.

"Exactly, and research leads to answers," Koen confirmed. "I don't know about you, but I'm starving." He blew out a breath from the side of his lips that caused the boyish curls to bounce off his forehead. "If we're late for dinner, Wes will start yelling."

"I have an inkling he will do that regardless of our tardiness, Koen."

"What the hell is *it* doing down here?" Wesley turned with a pot in his hands. Whatever was inside smelled amazing.

"*Florence.*" Koen rolled his eyes and wandered behind me to pull a chair for me. "Came for dinner, now be nice."

"Over my dead body. Do you know how hard it was to get this cooked before it started to rot?" Wesley quipped, locks of golden blonde hair curling around the collar of his plaid shirt. He stared me down, shifting on his boots, and set the pot on the table. I looked over it and found a plump-looking chicken nestled into a bed of seasoned rice with roasted carrots.

"Rotten? It smells fine to me," Koen said, his brows furrowed as he leaned forward and stuck his nose in the food.

I stared between the two of them quietly, the Manor shaking loose its petty behavior toward Wesley in the form of rotting food. It was a newer trick, one I hadn't seen before, but Koen seemed unaffected by the entire situation.

Clay wandered in, interrupting whatever rude thing was about to leave Wesley's mouth. His gray dress shirt rolled up around his forearms, and his glasses tangled into his dark, wavy hair.

"Has anyone seen my..." he started but quieted when I reached over and plucked the glasses from his soft hair to show him. "Thank you, Florence." He cleared his throat, his chest expanding under the confines of the cozy-looking sweater vest he wore, and set down the books in his arms on the table before sliding his glasses on his nose.

He paused to take me in, eyes roaming over my skirts and chest, making me warm but not uncomfortable.

"You look nice." He nodded and awkwardly looked from Koen to Wesley, mumbling under his breath. "This will be fun."

"About as much fun as a nest of vampires." Koen helped me into my chair and found his own.

Clay stifled a laugh and looked at me over the rim of his glasses. "Where have you been?" he asked in that husky tone that curls my toes.

"Sleeping?" I offered, unsure how to explain.

"That's right," Wesley interjected. "Koen has been tearing this place apart looking for sleeping beauty."

"I'm sorry I don't..." I was confused by the term, like most of the terms they seemed to throw around; certain phrases were lost to me due to my lack of exposure to the outside world.

"It's a film from the fifties," Clay said as he scooped food. "About a princess who pricks her finger on a spindle and falls asleep until a prince saves her with a kiss."

"A film?" My brows furrowed.

"Uh." Clay's eyes softened as he smiled at me and tilted his head to the back, looking for the words to help explain. "Moving pictures on a little box that people watch."

"Like a computer?"

"Sort of. You can watch movies on computers now," Koen said, taking his plate of food as Wesley continued to watch me, his hand white-knuckling the knife beside his plate as they discussed.

"And the prince saves the girl with a kiss?" I asked, still bewildered over the idea.

"He does." Clay nodded. "It was also a book, you've never read it?"

I shook my head no.

"I'll add it to the list of books you need to read. Do you want some?" He pointed to the spoon.

I stared at the food, knowing that I would have to explain myself at some point. They had been inviting me for meals and I had been making excuses for a week, but when Koen called me Blossom all rational thought left my head, and I had stumbled into a predicament of my own making.

No more secrets.

Secrets have kept me safe. I argued with myself briefly.

I didn't want to be safe. I wanted to be *free*.

Koen watched me as if to remind me of our deal.

"I don't really eat." I finally decided on the words.

"Of course you don't," Wesley huffed. "What does that even mean?" He snarled, the fire flaring behind his eyes.

Clay turned in his seat to look at me, waiting with a little less hostility for an answer.

"It would be a waste," I said. "I haven't really experienced hunger since being here. I *can* eat, but more as just a thing to do than for sustenance or enjoyment. Food has never really tasted... *right* here." I paused, frustrated, this wasn't coming out the way I had intended. "The last real meal I had to eat was the morning I was trapped here. Porridge with fresh cut apples." I swallowed tightly, waiting for Wesley to lose his control.

"You're saying you haven't had to eat anything to survive?" Clay whipped open his book and started to write notes.

"So what sustains you then?" Wesley sat forward, resting his forearms on the table. "Nothing can go that long without eating."

"Wes, come on," Koen groaned.

"No!" He slammed his hand on the table. "It could be sucking the life from us this second, and both of you are too distracted to notice. It could be anything, but I know one thing for sure, it's dangerous."

"Stop!" Koen stood in a rush, throwing his hands in the air and staring Wesley down. "Stop calling her an it. Her name is Florence."

"Okay, Koen, go ahead. Name your pet. But when it bites you, don't come running to me for help." Wesley threw his napkin against the table and stormed out of the kitchen.

CLAYTON

I dropped my books to the table in the sitting room and tried to get Koen to pay attention long enough for Wes to take a moment to calm down. Both were pacing in opposite directions. "You're making me dizzy!" Both stopped and turned to me.

"Koen, explain," I demanded.

"I took her out to the property line."

"Too bad you didn't put it out of its misery," Wes grumbled under his breath, and I lunged to get between them as Koen turned on his brother. "You're going to get yourself killed, stumbling around, lost in that monster's pretty eyes." He tapped a finger to Koen's temple over my shoulder, garnering a feral snarl.

"So you *admit* that she's pretty!" Koen, never one to leave anything alone no matter how desperately the situation called for it, poked Wes's forehead in return.

"Okay!" I shoved them apart with a noticeable groan at the throb of my healing muscles. I glared at Wes, meeting him in height. We were eye to eye and practically nose to nose as our chests brushed up against each other. "That's enough; let him explain!"

Koen shook out his frustration and paced around to the other side of the room, far away from us, as he continued to talk.

"I coaxed her out there to see if she could leave. She's mentioned being trapped in the house multiple times since we arrived, but I found her on the steps and I was curious." Koen shrugged. "Everything was fine until she tried to pass through the gate. It was like something grabbed her and sucked her back to the house."

"Something?" Wes questioned in disbelief.

"It was like a gust of air or an invisible rope? I'm not sure, but it wasn't pleasant. It threw me back at least five feet from where I stood." Koen lifted his shirt to expose his purple and blue painted rib cage.

"Koen!" I moved forward and pressed my hand to his rib, causing him to wince, "Why the hell did you hide this?"

"Because of that!" Koen's eyes were daggers toward Wes, who stared back with a murderous glare.

"We're leaving, I don't care. We aren't staying in this house a second longer, not with that thing."

"She's a victim!" Koen argued, shoving me away and dropping his shirt over the massive bruising. "I'm not going anywhere until we figure out what the fuck is going on."

"You don't get an opinion. You've filled your idiot quota for the week!" Wes barked and roughly ran his hands through his honey-blond hair. "What happens next time you get the courage to experiment?"

"At least I have some courage." Koen rolled his eyes. "And since when is this a dictatorship?"

Wes groaned.

"Pass me that." I pointed to a rolled-up map shoved against the arm-chair. Koen did as he was told with a dirty look on his face. I unfurled the map on the large coffee table and scooped a pen from my bag beside me as I knelt over the paper. "This is the property line." I drew a sizable awkward-looking circle around the Manor. "According to the county records, this land has been private property dating back to before they kept anything properly. No one knows who owns it. No one really knows where it stops."

"So how do you?" Wes questioned.

I slipped the plastic between my lips and chewed on the end of the pen, staring at the line. "The papers reported a few incidents during the construction of a pipeline. They tried to cross this line." I pointed to the back half of the property. "Three men were sent to the hospital with third-degree burns. No one could explain the incident."

"And when did you figure this out?" Wes narrowed his eyes on me.

"After we spoke, get off my back." I glared up from the paper at him. "If you think for one second I'm withholding information in favor of Florence, you need to reevaluate the situation, Wes, because I am not your punching bag for accusations."

"No, that's me." Koen slumped against the armchair and leaned his head back with his eyes closed. I don't know how I missed his labored breathing and scrunched face, but if *I* felt guilty...I look back to Wes, whose jaw is snapped shut, his hazel eyes boring into Koen like it might satiate that feeling.

"Listen," I demanded their attention, and both fell into our usual circle without gripes. "I'm almost ninety-three percent positive she's not a spirit."

"Really...ninety-three?" Wes mocked.

A look passed between Koen and me.

We had both had contact with her, even briefly; we knew how real she felt. I tried to leave those feelings in the library, containing them in the space where I felt my temperature rise and my heart race, but some days proved more difficult.

Today, for instance.

I didn't want to be in the sitting room arguing with Wes about how to kill Florence.

I wanted to be in the library, with her tucked into a reading chair, trying to figure out how to save her. It felt rushed, fumbled, and scary, but at least it was honest. That was a feeling I hadn't felt in a very long time, if ever.

It wasn't easy collecting my thoughts with Wes breathing down my neck, his watchful gaze looking for any reason to pull us from whatever this hunt had become.

"Ninety-three percent isn't one hundred," Wes said.

"Since when do you wait for certainty?" Koen huffed.

"You can fist fight about it later." I waved them off, tugging the pen between my lips. "All the research in the library points to it being something else. Something older."

"Older?" Wes repeated, nearly stuttering over his words.

"Ancient." I pushed my glasses off my face.

"What does that mean?" Wes followed my train of thoughts like a blind man.

"It means I need the internet. And I can't find my damn hotspot." I rolled my eyes.

"Fine, I'll take you into town."

Both Koen and I turned to look at him. "You want to help?" Koen spat out incredulously.

"I want out of this house and away from whatever the hell that thing is. It's turning you both into twits, and it's going to get one of us killed." Wes scooped his jacket up from the table and slipped his arms into the leather. "Get your shit," he barked at me and started for the door.

"Good luck." Koen looked at me, crossing his arms over his chest. "I don't understand why he's so wound up."

"Yes, you do," I sighed, unrolling my sleeves and finding my jacket as I spoke. "He doesn't see us. He sees Wyatt."

"His brother fell in love with a vampire and thought that would end well. This is..."

"It's not that different." I stopped to look at him. Silence passed between us, both of us needing to agree that we had slipped past *save the girl* territory into *need the girl* territory without even noticing. "He's just trying to keep us safe."

"By being a fucking overbearing asshole who refuses to help!" Koen scoffed. "She's not a monster, Clay. I know you feel it too."

"It doesn't matter what we feel, Koen. This is what matters." I waved my laptop at him before shoving it in my side bag. "Science, history, research. Don't do anything stupid until we have more information."

I stopped in front of him before leaving the room, and pointed to his ribcage. "You need to rest, that rib won't heal right if you keep squaring up with Wes."

"Fine. But what I could really use is painkillers and a beer," Koen groaned as Wes appeared in the doorway with an annoyed, impatient look.

"I can do that." I backed away from him. "Just don't give him any more reasons to be an asshole."

"Hey," Wes griped.

I followed him out of the house, trying to put space between him and Koen.

"You need to ease up," I barked as soon as we were clear of the steps and the door shut behind us. "He gets it. He feels the pressure of your expectations. You're acting like a lunatic."

"Me?" Wes turned on me.

It was a rare day when he got in my face, but he hovered, two inches taller and made it known. The expanse of his broad shoulders eclipsed mine, and I could feel his breath on my face.

"You two are running around that house making goo goo eyes and *I'm* the crazy one?" He snapped.

I could feel the rage flowing down through his muscles. I had only seen him like this a few times, but it never ended well.

"I said you're acting like a lunatic, not that you are one, but if you don't take two steps back from me–" I gripped tightly to my bag as Wes exhaled and moved back. "Your fear has always presented as anger. I get that. We both do." I waved my arm back toward the house. "But the second you start taking that anger out on us, it's counterproductive. I can take a lot of your feral abuse, but you're going to push too hard one day, and Koen won't survive that."

"Don't tell me how to parent Koen." Wes rolled his eyes. "You don't know a damn thing about family."

"Low blow." I clicked my teeth and pressed my lips into a thin line. "This isn't about parenting him. You aren't his dad. This is about your trauma that you refuse to talk about. Don't blame him for not under-standing when you don't give him the resources to do such a thing."

Wes didn't like that, I could tell by his jaw ticking and his eyes shifting to the side.

"Don't take shots at me and expect me to lay down and take them, Wes. We've never played like that. This is a hunt, just like all the rest," I warned him.

"Except it's not because you let Koen get attached." Wes pointed the finger at me.

"He's not a child." I laughed loudly enough to echo into the dusk air. "And if you want to keep tabs on him, stop pushing him away. I'm your friend. I'm his friend. I'm not your keeper or his babysitter." I pushed past Wes and snapped my fingers. "Are we going into town or not?"

I could see the gears grinding behind his hazel eyes. He was trying to work out more arguments but came up short because he stomped across the gravel and climbed into the truck without another word.

WHERE IS ALL THE WILDLIFE?
SINCE ARRIVING, WE
HAVEN'T SEEN A
SINGLE BIRD,
INSECT, OR ANIMAL.
NOT EVEN A RAT

FLORENCE

The balcony was a horrible choice.

The moment I heard Wesley's voice, my stomach churned. I wasn't supposed to be hearing the conversation they were having. *"You two are running around that house after a monster."*

Before they had arrived, I wouldn't have ever thought to use that word to describe myself.

Whatever I was wasn't natural, but it also was not my fault. Could one be a monster if they did not do monstrous things? The thought started to eat at me. I gripped the stone bannister as they continued to argue, barely hearing Koen approach from behind.

"They're arguing about me." I don't turn to look at him.

He leaned against the railing toward the house, looking into the darkness that engulfed the room he came from. His head tilted down to look at them, in each other's faces, and he shrugged. "They argue about everything."

When Koen's eyes met mine, they were on fire.

A green blaze lit behind the stare that licked at my neck and made me squirm beneath my layers of clothing. He inched closer, his fingers brushing a loose piece of auburn hair behind my ear, lingering as our skin met.

His lips parted like he might say something, only to remain silent as he closed the gap between our bodies. "You shouldn't be out here listening to them. It's the bickering of two scared men," he said, his accent muddled and his eyes hazy.

"I needed air and then…" I looked down over the front garden, Wesley and Clay still at each other's throats. "Perhaps he's right, Koen." I shook my head. "Perhaps I am just a monster, and you were brought here by some cruel twist of fate to end my life."

The vines around the cement bannister of the balcony constricted with my thoughts. The Manor quietly letting me know how little interest it took in my life ending.

Never.

"Do you believe that?" He asked me. I turned to look at him.

No more secrets.

"I'm starting to," I whispered.

I flinched briefly as his hands wrapped around my face, fingers curling delicately around my jaw just below my ears, and pulled me across the gap. He was getting much more bold with his contact. He was the most outright with his physical affections of the three of them, always a pat on Wesley's back or a tousling of Clay's hair. They had all made noticeable efforts to not touch me in the first few days, which I had reciprocated out of a mixture of apprehension and caution. But, quickly, Koen's playful and comfortable manner led to brief moments of tender contact, a hand being held, an arm around mine… My traitorous body hummed with the memory of his lips on my bare shoulder.

"What can I do to prove you otherwise?" He asked softly, so quietly that I should not have been able to hear it over the commotion below us and yet, with his hands so warm and delicate about my face, the rest of the world seemed to fall away.

Against my will, my body leaned into his touch and I closed my eyes, unsure of what I was doing but knowing full well all the same what I yearned for. Of all the little moments before, this was the most intimate. It was electric and warm, and my body craved affection after so long alone.

I couldn't stop Koen even though my mind told me it was wrong. With two hands on his chest, I tried to coerce my body into pushing him away, but my fingers were no longer listening to me as they gripped the fabric of his shirt. His lips brushed against the hollow of my throat, and I was merely at his mercy.

"What are you doing?" A shaky breath tumbled from my lips.

Koen's hand cupped the back of my head, fingers tangling into the haphazard twist my hair was in, and pulled it free. It cascaded down around my shoulders and his face, acting like a curtain that sheltered us from the world. He inhaled the smell of my skin and traced a slow line across my throat until he reached the base of my ear.

"Reminding you just how human you are," he whispered.

The words washed over me, settling on my skin like a warm rain. My body trembled under his breath.

His fingers ghosted my arm and caused the fine hairs to raise, as if every part of my being was desperate for contact. His hands settled at my waist, palms placed on my hips, and he walked me back until I was pressed firmly against the outer wall of the Manor, facing him.

"You can touch me," he said, pulling his head back. His blond hair was messy against his forehead, and his bright green eyes danced with the colors of the sunset behind him.

"Koen," I stumbled over my words, unsure how to explain to him that it had been a long time since anyone had touched me and, when they had, it had never been in such a heartachingly gentle way. He brought one hand up to brush away the hair grazing my throat, and with each small gesture, the temperature in my body rose.

"It's been a while," he exhaled, and his breath tickled my lips, so close now I could count the stars in his eyes and the freckles that speckled his heart-shaped face. His hand danced across the loose collar of my blouse, never straying too far but leaving a line of warmth in their wake as his eyes flickered down to my breasts and back to my lips. "For both of us."

"Well, that I don't–" My disbelief was quieted as his head ducked and his teeth grazed my collarbone, nipping at the skin and pushing the sleeve of my blouse over my shoulder to continue his exploration of my flesh. I melted into his touch, unable to resist, clenching my thighs together to hold back the soft throbbing response that built between my legs.

"If you aren't quiet, they'll hear you," Koen chuckled with a wiggle of his eyebrow. "And then we'll both be in trouble."

We are already in trouble, I thought as my back arched against the cold stone, and the only thing holding me from floating off the balcony was the force of Koen's closeness. Wesley and Clay fought below, but now they were fighting about Koen.

"See," he whispered and undid a number of small buttons on my blouse, opening it so far that the front of my corset was exposed. "They argue about everything. Now, pay attention to this. To us." His lips brushed over the swell of my breast, and the contrast of the night breeze and his warm mouth on my skin sent my heart thundering into my ears.

"What of the consequences?" I found my courage and brushed my fingers through the thick strands of his honey-coloured hair.

"Only rewards," he huffed, and his teeth pulled at the fabric of my blouse, exposing more of my breasts and sending a sharp ache echoing through my core. Koen's fingers curled down and gripped the underside of my thigh so it wrapped around him, sliding his taut excited body into the space he created. "You taste like fresh air and peppermint." He laughed and pulled me closer.

The charged feeling that surged through me wrapped around my muscles and tugged at my arousal playfully, urging me forward into his touch. I let go of the anxious thoughts that plagued me and gave in completely to Koen's hunger.

Even when Matthew and I had been consensual, it had never been like this.

It had been rough and quick, only providing Matthew with what he needed.

Koen was careful and purposeful.

His mouth pulled at an invisible string of my reactions. With each noise, giggle, and gasp, he would test a spot repeatedly to feel the reaction garnered. His hands were tangled in fabric, daring to inch closer to what felt like forbidden areas that had been left untouched for so long. My breath caught in my throat as his knuckles brushed over my thighs. Even through my skirts, he was pure heat against my skin.

A new feeling blossomed in the pit of my stomach as his mouth covered mine, his bottom lip taking my top one against it with such a languid gentleness. His finger cupped my chin, raising it to deepen the kiss as his tongue slipped into my mouth.

Koen's body trembled alongside the throaty moan that he pulled from me.

"Do you understand now?" He asked, pulling away briefly, his eyes tracing over my features. His fingers ghosted my hot skin and tucked my hair behind my ears before kissing my lips. I opened my mouth to argue, but he stopped me.

"Wes doesn't," he said, "but he hasn't felt you. Your skin, your smile, your warmth." A thumb brushed over my bottom lip.

"A monster can feel just as real to the touch." I furrowed my brow.

"But a monster doesn't *feel*." Koen's mouth curled into a bright smile, sending the butterflies in my chest into a flurry. "And I know you felt that." His eyes danced across my face, landing on mine.

I stopped momentarily, taking myself away from the idea that maybe I was a monster, and truly let myself feel everything. The heat of my skin and how it tingled as the breeze licked at my neck, my heart pounded when his eyes met mine, and every spark of fire danced through my bloodstream at the thought of his lips.

My hand touched them, fingers resting against his bottom lip.

The feeling of heartache, longing, and existence beneath my fingertips.

"I've never been kissed like that." I inhaled.

"I can keep doing it if you want?" Koen smiled as he kissed the tips of my fingers in demonstration. "I really don't mind."

"It was a silly thing you did," I said, with my fingers preventing him from keeping good on his words. "Kissing me." I sighed. "It was easier to protect you all at arm's length. This changes everything."

"Let it."

Arrogant.

All of the window panes on the back side of the Manor rattled in anger.

"Koen." I swallowed down the frustration and the fear.

"I knew you were human the moment I saw you. I could feel your heart, like it was calling to mine." Conviction poured out of him. "I'm not afraid of you or what they'll say."

"It's not me you should be afraid of."

The Manor.

Each brick, floorboard, and tile vibrated in silent displeasure.

Koen was wrong. *Monsters could feel.*

WESLEY

The public library in town was quiet, but that didn't settle my nerves any more than being busy would. Clay sat with his face in his laptop and his hand scribbling in one of his many notebooks beside him on the desk. I had gone to get us food. The only place in town open was a small cafe that served more grease than food. The burger looked amazing but Clay turned up his nose at it and stuck to the french fries.

He hadn't spoken to me most of the way into town, a fifteen-minute drive down the winding forest. The town was still shaken by the death of three police officers and there was a heavy law enforcement presence. I did my best to seem inconspicuous but it was hard when you were a stranger in a small town where everyone knew everyone.

Luckily, Clay was a people person.

He rose from the table and padded toward the reception desk on light feet. A curvy, eccentric-looking young woman sat huddled behind it with her bright, rainbow-colored glasses on the brim of her nose, and her fiery red hair spun in funny little curls around her sweet round face. She wore a flattering dark green tartan dress and her matching pink heels stuck under the desk. Her eyes fluttered up to Clay as he approached, a bright smile forming on her face when he leaned over and pointed to something in his notes.

She laughed at him, her cheeks turning pink, and she rose from her chair. Clay followed her back through a row of books with a flirty smile on his face, only for her. Leaning against the bookcase with his hand in his pocket, he flirted with her like she was the only woman in the building, throwing her a polite nod and thanking her for finding the book he needed.

"You're full of shite." I shook my head as Clay sat back down and handed me the book.

The book was so massive and full that the papers seemed to spill out of it.

"What is this?" I flipped it open to a page of newspaper clippings.

"The library is too small of an operation to have any newspapers scanned before 1910. We have to search by hand to find any news about the Manor," he said, not looking up from his laptop.

"And what are you going to do?" I snapped, briefly scanning the amount of clippings I was about to search through.

"Becca is going to show me the archives," he said, winking at her as she leaned over the desk, filing more papers away.

"What will your monster girlfriend say when it finds out you're using your subpar looks to flirt with other librarians," I growled, flipping through the book.

"Hey, you called her a girl." Clay wiggled an eyebrow at me, popped the top button of his dress shirt, and tossed his glasses on the table before wandering off to find the pretty redhead.

I spent another hour flipping through newspapers before I saw its face.

It looked exactly the same as it had earlier today. Not a new line on its face to be seen.

The gray ink almost made it appear soft. The man beside it was grubby, to say the least. His round jaw and beady eyes were swallowed by the plumpness of his cheeks. His sausage hands wrapped around its waist, and they were both dressed in formal wear. It might have been a wedding photo but it was in the eulogy section, an announcement from just after it was supposedly trapped inside the Manor.

> *CABOT, Lady Florence Catherine, July 19th, 1823 - September 2nd, 1852. It is with overwhelming sadness that we announce the passing of Florence Cabot. She is survived by her loving husband, Lord Matthew Cabot. She died in their estate, surrounded by her loved ones, and will be deeply missed.*

"Got you." I looked around before pulling the clipping from the book and folding it in my pocket. I scribbled a small note for Clay, telling him to return the truck to the Manor. I would meet him there.

It would be enough time to beat him there before he even realized I was gone.

I needed to talk to our monster.

The Manor was eerily silent when I snuck in the front door. I had swiped my pistol from the tool bed in the back of the truck and shoved it into my jeans before climbing the hill. It had been fifteen minutes into town but over forty-five minutes back. The fresh air was good for my thoughts and by the time I climbed the stairs to the Manor, I had a straight idea of what needed to be done.

Koen was passed out in one of the living room armchairs, his hand pressed to his ribcage and a peaceful, sleepy expression on his face. I couldn't help but stop and throw a blanket over him. Mad at myself for being mad at him, it felt stupid but, most of the time, I wasn't sure how to keep him safe. Clay's words rang in my ears. I knew he wasn't a child but, to me, he was still that little boy my parents brought home from a hunt. He was who I made him. Confident, loud, intelligent, and strong.

It was trusting my training that I was stumbling over.

The only thing I couldn't train out of him, or Clay, was their undeniable need to love.

I knew the day would come for them when our lifestyle would bear on their shoulders and they would turn to companionship. I just figured it would continue to be quick, dirty relationships in shitty motels and with people they never expected to see again. But this was different.

Whatever grip this monster had on them was toxic.

Its claws were covered in poison and sank deep into their skin.

They just couldn't see it for what it was.

"Where are you?" I turned around, knowing how easy it was to get lost around the Manor. I could have sworn that the walls moved independently in the night, changing shape and layout. Clay was certain he had mapped out the basics but every morning at the table, he was erasing lines and adding new ones, charcoal from his pencil covering the ball of his hand as he worked.

I wandered around the main floor until I wrapped down a long hallway and found myself back in the kitchen, but it was there—moving around without a care.

"You snuck up on me once. It won't happen again," it said, stopping what it was doing at the counter.

"I was looking for you this time," I snapped, my hand on my gun. "What do you want from us?" I demanded.

"What I've been saying from the start!" It had the gall to sound exasperated. "I want you to leave my home." It moved and I flinched, fingers finding the smooth handle of my gun.

"Yeah, you've said that, but I don't believe it because I've never seen Koen or Clay so headstrong about staying somewhere." I shook my head. "You've done something to them."

"I don't control their thoughts." It looked at me with its lips pressed tightly together. "I don't want to be here anymore than you do."

It seemed to keep a distance from me, even as I moved further into the kitchen. It checked over its shoulder more than once, its eyes running the length of the walls like it was searching for something, waiting for it. I liked that it was as uncomfortable with my presence as I was with it.

Stunning emerald eyes focused back on me. "Perhaps they just see something you refuse to."

I swallowed tightly to keep my voice from breaking and stared at it. "If you aren't trying to kill us, what do you want?" I was getting frustrated now.

It pinned its shoulders back and whispered. "To be free."

"Tell me where your body is buried and I can finish this. You'll be free and I can take my brothers away from here," I offered and lowered my voice.

It looked at me again, jaw clenched tightly as it moved across the kitchen to the sink.

"I'm not dead," It said with more conviction than I had heard it use before.

"That's a lie." Its eyes watched my every move as I pulled the paper from my jacket pocket and threw it on the island.

It dried its slender fingers on a towel before unfolding the paper and reading it with a scrunched expression. "This is a lie." It set the paper down and went back to whatever it had been doing.

Was it making bread?...

"It's not a lie, it's in the damn paper. Your husband wrote that," I raised my voice.

"My husband," it scoffed and went on ignoring me.

"You died in your bed at home, surrounded by your family. How did you wind up here?" I asked.

I was met with more silence.

"What was it? A plague, childbirth?" I inched closer when it didn't answer. "I think it was a mean husband," I snipped, only a foot from its back. "He got too rough one night and accidentally hurt you when you spoke back. Now, you trap men in this Manor and kill them because it makes you feel better for a second. We've dealt with spirits like you; vengeful, mean. It takes years to twist who you used to be into what you are now. All that time alone to tangle your thoughts into irrational actions. You're just a rage-filled shell of whatever you used to be. It happens to all spirits."

It moved away, feeling me so close.

"You can't have me or my brothers."

It stopped moving and I watched as it slowed its breathing before turning around.

My breath caught in my throat at the sight of its tears.

"Crying won't save you," I managed to say through the sudden pang of guilt before it took off running from the kitchen.

FLORENCE

"Florence?" Koen peeked around the corner. "I thought I heard you."

His smile warmed my chest and dulled the ache that radiated through me. A stubborn, guilt-ridden feeling that had clung to me since my conversation with Wesley. I understood his fear but he made no effort to understand mine. I wasn't rage-filled. I was lonely.

"Where have you been?" He asked.

He looked handsome today in a short-sleeved red shirt with sandy strands of curly hair poking out from beneath a backward hat. He picked up his feet to catch up with me as I walked down the hall. I didn't want to answer him, to tell him that I had been avoiding them because of Wesley, not wanting to cause more upset between them as a family. Wesley had been right about one thing. Koen and Clay were distracted.

Green eyes searched my face for any clues.

"Would you like to walk with me?" I asked him, trying to avoid the conversation altogether.

Koen's smile grew and that tiny dimple that stole all my attention appeared on his cheek as he offered his arm to me.

"Don't you get sick of wearing all these clothes everyday?" He asked, staring down at the long brown skirt that brushed the floor. "It's got to be hell in the summer with the heat."

"My body self-regulates," I said to him.

"You mean you're never too hot or too cold?" His nose wiggled.

"I frankly never noticed until you just questioned it. The heat in the summer when I was a child was unbearable, but when…"

 I paused. My mind produced ill thoughts swirling around the words Wesley had used.

'*When you died.*'

"You were trapped," he finished the sentence for me.

Protected.

The floorboards growled beneath our feet in protest.

"Mmm, the heat, the cold. It didn't seem to bother me as much."

"You should tell Clay that," he noted.

"I'm starting to feel like a monster again." I swallowed tightly at the thought of being prodded with questions. Clay was careful and delicate whenever he needed information, but it still felt like he was doing it because he was more curious about the monster than me. Swallowing down the feeling, I squeezed Koen's bicep between my fingers and he flexed under my touch. "Would you like to see one of my favorite rooms?"

"I got nothing else to do, Blossom." He nodded.

I led him back toward the west of the Manor. There were certain rooms that I believed the Manor may have created especially for me. After intense emotional standoffs, where I was in my bleakest and darkest moments, typically I would wake up and there would be some new and unexplored wonder. The bathhouse had been one of them. I had woken up after an attempt to end my life and there it was. The sound of water gently lapping echoed through the door.

Koen noticed it, too. "Is that..."

I pushed open the massive glass doors. The bathing room was the largest room in the Manor next to the library, with stone walls and an arching glass ceiling that allowed the moon and stars to shine through onto the beautiful, old green floor tiles. The bath wasn't large. The pool of water was meant to be warm enough to double as a steam room. A light haze floated over the surface and made everything ethereal.

"It's a pool!" Koen's laughter was loud and surprised me.

"It's a bathing room," I corrected him. It was another assurance that the house wasn't as it seemed. The water in the pool never cooled. Just like the bathtub in my bedroom, it never greened or dirtied. It was as pristine and warm as when I encountered the room the first time.

Koen unlinked himself and kicked off his shoes, pulling the collar of his shirt over his head and tossing it in a pile. I inhaled sharply through my teeth, seeing his healing bruise, which was light in color and turning shades of green and yellow. It looked sore.

"If you're going to stare, at least appreciate it," he teased, following my eyes with a funny smile. "I'm fine." His muscles were strong and taut with excitement.

It tickled at my core as I bit my bottom lip between my teeth and watched him undress. Shocked wasn't the proper word for it, or at least not the *only* word. I was enamored by him. His fingers worked quickly at the buttons of his pants, shucked them over his muscular thighs, and left them on the deck.

Water splashed my skirts and pooled around my feet as he broke the surface.

"I'm not swimming alone," he practically purred, moving closer to the edge. "Get in the water, Blossom."

"You can't possibly expect me to get in there with you." I took a whole step backward out of his grabby hands and glared at him. "That's indecent, Koen."

Mischief flickered across his face as his smile went lopsided and he shrugged his shoulders. "It's adventurous," he corrected me.

It's dangerous.

The Manor hummed through the tiles.

His arms stroked lazy circles as he waited for me to find my sense of adventure but I feared it might never appear, despite the urge I felt to do something reckless. Wet curls pressed to his neck and water dripped down his jaw and throat, catching the blue light of the moon and making him shine like a star.

"What if I close my eyes until you're in?" He closed his eyes before I even answered. "I promise not to peek."

"Forgive me if I don't trust the gentlemen's agreement you're proposing." I laughed.

"Florence." He lowered down into the water further. His voice was hushed and husky as he demanded. "Get in the water, before I *come* and get you." Had it come from anyone else I may have felt myself shrink away from the order, but instead it struck a sleeping chord of courage that he seemed to find easily.

He turned his back to me and it was a moment longer before I found the nerve to undo the lace of my bodice and clips of my corset. I felt naked against the moon as I slipped from the heavy skirts and laid it with the rest of my clothing. Staring at the wall in my chemise, I sighed; my skin felt hot.

I peered over my shoulder at him, still facing away, and counted to three before sliding into the pool quietly. The water rushed against the thin shift and it stuck to my skin, making me feel more exposed than if I had just removed it. Koen approached slowly, the green in his eyes glittering against the light that reflected through the pool from the moon.

"See?" He worked effortlessly to keep his eyes on mine as he closed the gap between us. "Not so bad is it?"

A sharp whimper left my mouth when his hands found my hips beneath the water, gripping tightly and pulling me into his gravity. The thin and clinging fabric felt almost non-existent when his skin pressed against mine. I looked between us, placing my hand on his bruised ribs beneath the surface, and scowled.

"The pain's gone." He raised an eyebrow at me. "Besides, it was my fault. I shouldn't have pushed you to test the limits. Not without understanding what might happen."

I offered a weak, breathy laugh and tried to steady the rapid pace of my heart, but it was so hard with his hands on me and the smell of his sharp, woody cologne in my nose. I wanted to feel his lips against mine but couldn't bring myself to ask if I could.

"Do you feel human again?" His knuckles brushed against my chest, fingers toying with the collar of my chemise. His touch was rousing and left little lines of goosebumps wherever it went. I inhaled tightly as the pad of his fingers danced along the swell of my breast.

"Not quite," I lied.

He crooked a finger, tracing it up my throat to my chin, and lifted my gaze to meet his. The heat of his stare would have set me on fire if not for the water. A dangerous smile formed on his lips as he realized I was lying and was inviting him to push the limits of what I had spent so long considering to be 'respectable'.

I wanted out of the box that suffocated me.

I wanted to feel it all.

I had never felt more human than when he stared at me the way he was in that moment. It was the same look from that night on the balcony. Weighted and brimming with possibility.

The water was refreshing but the air around us was tense. I knew he had no trouble making the first move but he seemed to be waiting, forcing me to be the one to take the next step, and I wrestled with the two parts of me that were at odds with each other. The one that was grateful for his restraint and consideration... and the other that wanted so desperately to be devoured. I had never felt so present.

Koen's eyes flickered across my face like he was reading every thought. "Can I help?"

I managed a quick nod, and that was all he needed. His fingers tightened on my hips as he walked us backward until my back rested against the wall of the small pool. Pinned by the weight of his body, he let his hands wander to the strings that bound my chemise closed. The fabric was transparent in the water, clinging to every dip and curve. Still, his fingers slid into the shift and peeled it back away from my skin, and exposed the fullness of my breasts, the sensation was exquisite. His hands caressed, as his lips trailed a line between them as far as he could reach before his chin and nose would be submerged beneath the water.

"You're unbelievably soft," he noted in a husky tone, rising to meet my lips.

Our collision was velvety and tender. Koen's tongue swiped into my mouth slowly, deepening the kiss as his hand wrapped around my jaw and held me in place. I pushed back, wanting more of his touch and unsure how much he would grant me.

He smiled against my mouth, bright and warm, before kissing the corners of my lips and peppering my cheek until his lips found my throat. My body arched into his touch as he grazed along my skin to my jaw. My breath hitched in my throat as his hand slipped between my thighs beneath the surface.

"Oh, *oh…*" Pleasure curled my toes and tickled in the pit of my stomach as his fingers grazed my inner thigh, higher and higher, working in tandem with his lips.

Koen's teeth tugged on my ear and his other hand tangled into my hair at the back of my neck. His breathing was quiet and shallow. It fluttered across my skin in cold waves that tickled my hot skin and sent shivers down my spine. His fingers gripped the sensitive flesh at my thigh, pausing as he broke from his lustful intentions to look at me.

"Is this too much?" He asked. If I had spoken, I would have confessed, yes, but I wanted him so badly that instead I pressed my lips against him to silence his worries. Overwhelmed and starving for his attention, I parted my thighs and urged him further.

His fingers deftly navigated beneath the clinging fabric barrier so his hand could find skin, a groan escaping from his lips as his fingers made contact with the most intimate part of me. The water lapped against his chest as he deepened the kiss, and his thumb brushed the cluster of nerves that hid there.

I inhaled so sharply that I thought he might stop when he pulled away from my lips, but there was a grin on his face, and he repeated the touch, dragging another soft whine from me.

"Listen to that sound," he huffed, kissing me quickly and stealing what little air I had left.

The moans spilled from me without thought as he began to stroke me. It was gentle, but built a pressure in me that I had only ever experienced on my own— and never to this magnitude. I had never been touched that way before, and it surged through me like lightning and lit my soul alight.

"Don't stop." I gripped his shoulders, digging my fingernails into his skin as he slipped his fingers into me.

"I don't plan on it." His hand grasped my seat and lifted me so that I was angled more openly around his waist and he slotted himself tighter against my body. I could feel every inch of him, hard beneath his under-garments but never acting on it.

"Koen." My hips rolled forward, unable to stop myself from needing him.

A small chuckle left his throat, his fingers digging into my wet skin beneath the water. "Tonight is about you," he said quietly. "I can wait."

Something about how he wanted to care for me only made the needy feeling grow. It tickled across my skin, pulsing in waves. A low gasp fell on my lips as he curled his fingers inside my body and raked against my sensitive skin until I was trembling beneath his touch in a way I had never experienced. His pace was intentional and he watched my every move. My heart raced with every languid brush of his fingers against an intoxicating spot deep within me I had never felt before, curling and twisting the pleasure in my stomach into a tight coil near its breaking point.

His plump, kiss-sore lips found my throat again, nuzzling there as I rolled through my climax. My eyes fluttered closed, and my cunt clenched around his fingers as his thumb rubbed soft circles as I fell over the edge.

It felt like soaring.

My skin was hot, and my body was exhausted, but I didn't want it to stop. Sparks tingled in my veins like I was lit on fire. Koen slipped his fingers out, holding his palm between my shaking thighs as he scanned my features.

"I—" the words were silenced as he kissed my lips, delicately dragging his teeth along my bottom lip and peppering the corners as he pulled away.

The pool's reflection danced in his green eyes, and my breath caught in my throat at the sight of his soft smile and the proud flush on his cheeks as he wrapped his arms around me and lifted me back into the deeper parts of the water.

I raked my hands through his blond hair and pressed myself tightly to his chest as he waded us in gentle circles. "Thank you, Koen," I whispered, brushing my thumb over his bottom lip. "That helped."

A soft, breathy laugh fell from him. "At your service, Blossom."

I forced a smile to my face, but I could feel the house seize up. The tiles beneath our toes vibrated, and brick walls inhaled so slowly it was practically unnoticeable, but I could feel it.

Warning me. Reminding me.

You belong to me.

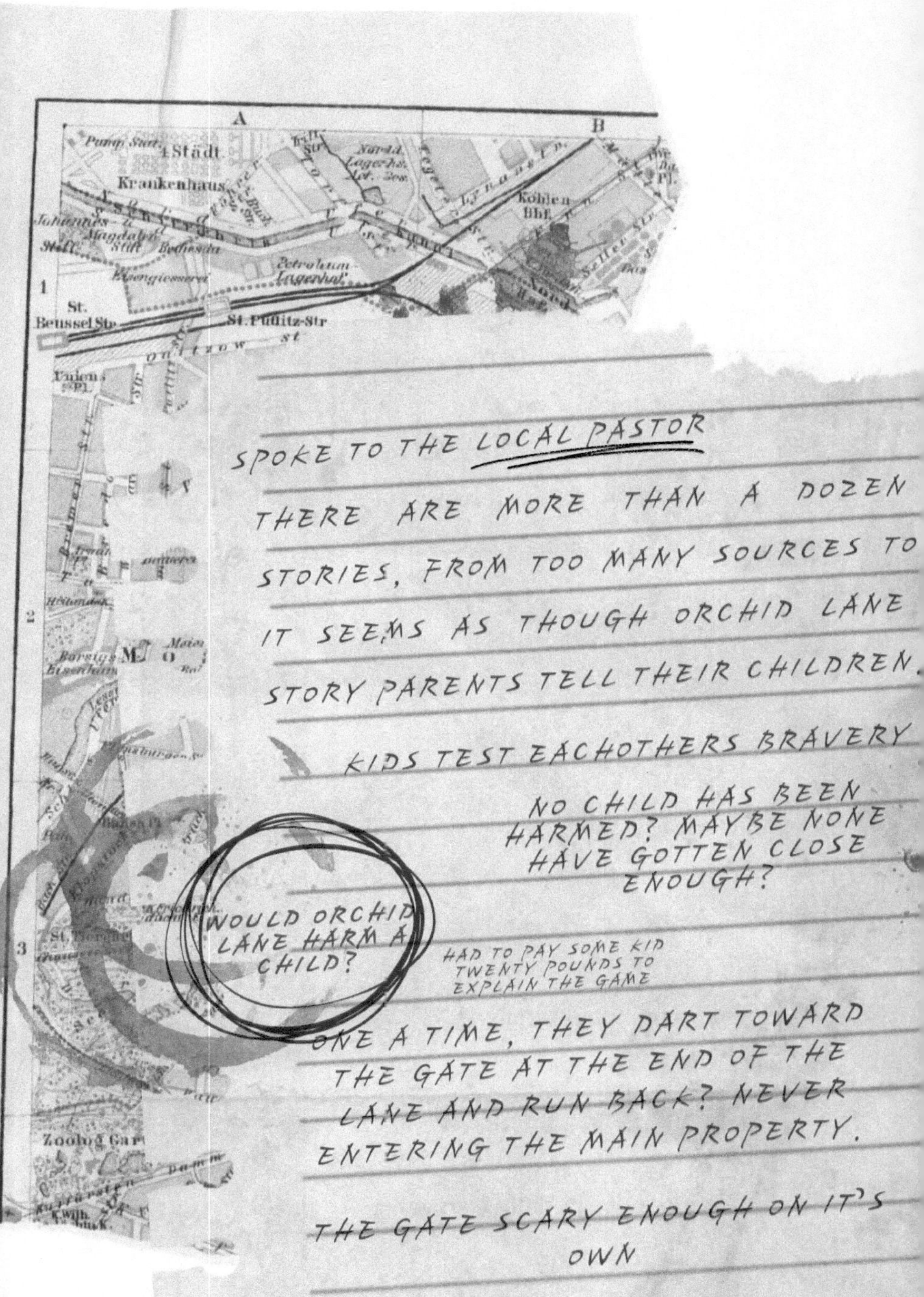
SPOKE TO THE LOCAL PASTOR

THERE ARE MORE THAN A DOZEN
STORIES, FROM TOO MANY SOURCES TO
IT SEEMS AS THOUGH ORCHID LANE
STORY PARENTS TELL THEIR CHILDREN.

KIDS TEST EACHOTHERS BRAVERY

NO CHILD HAS BEEN
HARMED? MAYBE NONE
HAVE GOTTEN CLOSE
ENOUGH?

WOULD ORCHID
LANE HARM A
CHILD?

HAD TO PAY SOME KID
TWENTY POUNDS TO
EXPLAIN THE GAME

ONE A TIME, THEY DART TOWARD
THE GATE AT THE END OF THE
LANE AND RUN BACK? NEVER
ENTERING THE MAIN PROPERTY.

THE GATE SCARY ENOUGH ON IT'S
OWN

KOEN

"**B**ack up." Clay held out his glasses between two long fingers, his gray-blue eyes staring at me in disbelief.

"You did what?" Wes sneered. Anger coated every word he spoke.

I had known it would be a mistake to tell them what happened, or at least to tell Clay what happened with Wes around. He was already overreacting to something so miniscule that I wanted to hit the rewind button on the entire conversation.

"We were in a pool." I shrugged and corrected myself. "She said it's called a bathing room."

"There's a bathing room?" Clay seemed more perplexed by that than anything and tugged out his rough sketch of floor plans, looking over the lines quickly, cursing under his breath as he went along.

"You finger-banged the monster?" Wes's voice got higher. "Are you fucking insane?"

He didn't want an honest answer.

"Think of it as testing to see how human she was?" I shrugged and Clay snorted, but Wes didn't find the joke funny and growled at me across the room.

It felt like all we did anymore was fight.

Clay's arm was almost fully healed. Only pink, fleshy lines were left behind on his bicep. It didn't matter. He was determined to understand the mystery behind the strange Manor, so we weren't going anywhere for a while. I leaned back against the couch, my mind wandering to the tiny sounds that Florence had made as my fingers slipped deep inside of her. My cock twitched painfully in my jeans.

I would have kept going, taken her in the water and shown her how alive she made *me* feel, but she was already so overwhelmed by touch that I was afraid to scare her. So I stayed frustratingly horny when she climbed from the pool and said her goodnites.

Her flushed cheeks and soft skin burned into my thoughts, playing repeatedly like a sweet film in my mind. All I could think about was getting back to her. I didn't want to be having this conversation with Wes and Clay.

I wanted to be buried in Florence.

"Are you even listening?" Wes threw a book across the room and it smacked me on the shoulder.

"Ow!" I chucked it back.

"Will you two stop throwing books, please?" Clay scolded. "They are not a part of this stupid argument." He collected the crumpled book from the floor and set it right before returning to the floor plans.

"I asked you not to get close to that thing while we figured out what was happening here, and what do you do?" Wes barked. "You tried to *fuck* it!"

"You know, maybe if you relaxed a little occasionally, you wouldn't be so wound up all the time. And *she* has a name," I snapped back. "Stop referring to her like she's got six rows of teeth and eats the hearts of men."

Wes narrowed his eyes at me and gripped the back of the chair he was standing behind as he leaned over at me. "For all we know, *it* does."

He emphasized the word to get under my skin but I settled back against the couch and thought about how soft Florence's hair felt between my fingers, how warm she was clenched around my hand, and how full her lips felt against mine.

"Are you any closer to figuring it out?"

"She's been avoiding me and I have questions for her. How did you manage to pin her down?" Clay looked up at me.

Wes let out an aggravated scoff at Clay's choice of wording and I fought to keep the grin off my face.

"I didn't stop looking." I shrugged. "I think she's spooked. Almost like someone said something to her."

My eyes landed on Wes and he squirmed like I was burning a hole through him.

"What *did* you say to her?" I sat up on the couch and asked him before he could change the subject, his mouth falling open and shut again.

"I haven't been near that thing," he snapped. "I've been busy finding us a new case."

I scoffed.

Wes handed Clay a newspaper over his shoulder and he grabbed it without looking up from his drawings. He slipped his glasses on and read over the article.

"Sounds like a nest." He finally looked up at Wes. "You can't do this alone."

"I never said anything about doing it alone." Wes scowled. "Pack your things."

The laugh that fell from my lips was loud and curt.

"No."

Clay sighed and pushed to his feet from where he sat on the floor, ready to get between us. The air in the sitting room was thick, a metaphorical powder keg just begging for a spark. Wes pushed buttons until he found one that would ignite a violent fight.

"You don't get a say. You're too close to this thing and need some fresh air to clear your head," Wes argued.

"No, what you *want* is us killing vampires so we remember how it feels and how dangerous monsters are, but we never forgot, and Florence is not a monster," I growled and stood up. It didn't matter that Wes was taller or broader. If it came to it, I would fight. It meant that much. "I don't need fresh air to figure that out. And you're being an impulsive twat!"

"You think I'm impulsive?" Wes's voice raised. "You fucked a ghost in a pool. You're a child and that proves it as much!"

Clay cleared his throat and we both turned on him.

"What?" Echoed out in unison.

"Please listen before you throw any more books," he said, putting his arms out at his side, "I think you both need the hunt."

I laughed until Clay's face remained stern.

"Oh, you're serious?" I rolled my eyes. "So you're taking his side?"

"Remember the listening part? That starts *now*." Clay shoved me playfully, but it did nothing to relieve the tension that had built up in the room. "You're both driving me nuts, Wes. You're bored," he said, and Wes scoffed. "When you can't solve a problem with a bullet you get antsy, and it's not helping. It's making my job harder because you scared her into the Manor somewhere, and she won't talk to me."

I hummed with pride.

"And you." Clay turned on me. "Are an idiot. You can't go around testing theories by sticking your dumb Irish fingers in things. You have no idea what she is, and while I agree that she doesn't seem dangerous, the chance is still there. You need to get out of this house, away from her, and level your head. You're too close to this."

"That's bullshit."

"It's not, it's actually quite logical," Clay quipped. "And if I'm going to get any more information from her, I need you two to stop fighting."

"Unlikely," I bit.

"Then a hunt is exactly what you need to release this pent-up aggression you're feeling."

"There's nothing pent up," Wes groaned.

"Aye," Clay sighed. "There is *always* something pent up in *you*."

"Understatement." I coughed but shifted on my toes, "Fine, I'll go."

Wes laughed like he had won the argument, but it was far from over if he thought I would just roll over and see his side. In my mind, it didn't matter if Florence was dangerous. There was a risk to it, but it was one I was willing to take for her.

Clay stared at me for a long moment, like he could read my thoughts, and scowled, pulling his glasses off and shoving them in his pocket. "I'll pack you some food. Try not to kill each other in my absence."

FLORENCE

Everything had gotten much more overwhelming than I had ever expected. Emotions tangled with logical thought and the sudden urge to protect them from what could come was overwhelming. I stood before that door, covered in cobwebs, the rotting wood waning against the hinges. It pulsed, alive and oozing darkness into the air around me.

I swallowed tightly and felt the static spark over my palm as I lifted my fingers to the door knob. It appeared often, mostly when the house was trying to punish me for something or remind me that, no matter how hard I tried, this was my home and I was never leaving.

You're safe here. Why would you want to leave?

The Manor started to pulse with poisonous energy that coated my skin with a sticky film. It was a constant droning warning that we were never alone, no matter how good those small moments with Koen felt. We were constantly being watched.

Koen stormed into the room to the left of the shadowed hallway I hovered in and I followed him, closing the door behind me.

"Are you alright?" I asked quietly. Fear crippled my bravery more often than not. Matthew used to get so loud in moments like these, and anger wasn't an emotion I managed very well. My own or others.

"*Nách mór an diabhal thú*!" Koen jumped and braced himself on the dresser. "You're quiet."

"My apologies." I tucked my hands behind my back, watching his shoulders heave steadily. His fingers tapped against the old wood before he turned to look at me.

"No, I'm sorry." He ran his hands through his hair. "I shouldn't have been slamming around." He rubbed the frustration from his eyes and inhaled one final breath, deep and calming that time. "I'm going with Wes on a hunt for a couple days."

My heart sank before I could stop it from doing so.

The attachment I wanted to deny was so plainly carved into my heart.

It was foolish of me, I knew that, but I couldn't help myself when Koen was around. He was so sweet and adventurous. He made me feel alive. Perhaps my emotions were heightened because of it, but I craved the rush of endorphins. I would miss him when he was gone, a feeling I hadn't experienced in a long time.

"Is that wise with him being so angry at you?" I asked him.

"We hunt angry at each other more often than not. It'll be fine, Blossom." He looked away from me as his sentence trailed off.

"I'm sure." I tried to smile.

"Don't worry about us. This is what we do." He shrugged his shoulders, moving forward and collecting me in his arms.

Koen was warm, his arms muscular, his fingers tracing along my back as he gripped me tightly to balance himself in the moment. I could feel his apprehension. It seeped from him in soft, tiny, practically unnoticeable trembles.

"I think you're just worried about missing me." He steeled his nerves and lifted his head from where it had been buried against my shoulder. "It's adorable that you care so much, I'm flattered."

"Me?" I laughed as he lifted my chin with a finger and stole a quick kiss that left me wanting more. It was hard to deny with the lingering taste. "I'm a monster. I don't *miss* people."

It was a joke, but Koen's brows furrowed at the response. His jaw tightened as he scanned my face with concern.

"Don't let Wes get to you," he said. "Give Clay some wiggle room, he'll surprise you."

"I think I should give no wiggle room to anyone at this point," I said, stepping back from him.

"Mmm." he nodded. "It's too late." He shrugged. "Wes is already in your head. Whatever he said to you is bullshit. He's just scared."

"Fear doesn't eliminate the possibility that he's right about me, Koen." I struggled to explain that I may not feel like a monster around him. Wesley's words did hold fact: Whatever I was, it wasn't natural and by no means should I be considered anything less than dangerous.

And mine.

Koen felt the Manor that time, the way the walls seemed to breathe out a gust of hot air. He stared at the walls with caution and waited until it was done.

"It doesn't eliminate the possibility that he's wrong either."

"Sweet, golden-hearted boy, you're too optimistic for this world." I forced a smile to my face for him. "What are you hunting?"

"Vampires," he said, backing away from me and grabbing a few shirts from the dresser for his bag. "It's a small nest. We shouldn't be more than a couple of days."

"You make it sound easy," I said, leaning against the door as my hands tangled nervously. It was something that ate at me more than I wished it would, and nothing I told myself consoled the feelings of dread. So casually ready to kill whatever they deemed dangerous and forbidden. What happened when I became precisely that?

"It's not, but it's second nature to us." He looked up from his bag.

"Killing?" I huffed as I picked at the dirt under my nails.

"Killing *vampires*," he corrected, and I could feel his rising frustration with my questions.

He stopped shoving clothing in his bag and straightened out, turning his body to look at me. "You're not a vampire, Florence. You don't drink blood. You don't kill people for fun. Why do you look like I slapped you?" He asked, that god-forsaken dimple forming on his cheek as his lips formed a lazy smile in defense of the tension that formed a wall between us.

I wanted to explain to him that trusting them was more complex than I wanted it to be. Even though he had been so sweet to me, remembering that we were of two different worlds was—in fact—like a slap. But his green eyes begged forgiveness for a crime he hadn't even committed, not out loud.

"Nothing," I said instead. "I'm just nervous, is all. It's been a long time since I had someone other than myself to worry about." I allowed my lips to curl into a smile that mimicked his.

"I knew you were worried." He winked and zipped up his bag. "I'll be back before you know it and, with Wes gone, you'll have a chance to work with Clay without the looming grump."

Koen's hand carefully wrapped around my throat, thumb brushing my jaw as it worked back into my hair, and he squeezed gently. He brought his lips to my forehead, soft and promising of a better future. "Give us a chance to prove Wes wrong before you start caving to his assumptions and push us away. This may be new, but..." He sighed, cocking his head to the side quickly. "But it's gaining momentum, and even if you don't trust him, trust me?"

Do not.

The Manor cried out as it sensed the betrayal in my heart, but I couldn't stop it. Even as the floorboards rattled. My heart called out to Koen, searching in the darkness of my eternity for a place to rest.

"I'll do my best," I answered him honestly.

"Good girl." He smiled, kissing me again.

It was slower that time as his lips grazed over mine and his hand cupped my jaw carefully in his fingers, pulling me forward into his touch. I lost myself in the kiss, not worrying about the before and afters. It was careful but relentless and, for the first time since I had become trapped, I was starving.

"Could make a man care less about bloodthirsty vampires." He pulled back and loosened his grip on my face.

It should have made me happy, even giddy like any infatuation would, but my heart sank as he smiled at me like I was made of pure innocence. I knew more of the evils of this world than he imagined.

"Be safe, please." I smiled and brushed my fingers over his bottom lip. "I'm growing rather fond of this."

He didn't say another word. He stole a quick kiss and was out the door before my heart had time to come down from the clouds I was soaring above. I felt like I was flying but the fear of plummeting to the surface was nipping at my heels and, as I listened to the front door slam shut, I realized my descent was coming sooner than later.

CLAYTON

Once I had gotten Wes and Koen organized enough for their road trip, I changed into a clean dress shirt and trousers before wandering through the Manor in search of Florence. Missing her was an odd feeling; it sank deep in my bones, and I hadn't even realized it was there until I hadn't seen her for a few days. The days turned to a week and, in that week, I found myself catching glimpses of auburn hair or hearing soft echoes of her voice but never finding her.

It was starting to worry me.

But when Wes suggested a hunt, I took the opportunity to empty the Manor.

I *needed* to find her.

My only plan? To get lost.

"Are you turned around again?" Her voice floated down the hall after about an hour of mindless walking up and down the stairs, exploring the Manor's rooms as I had never seen them before.

"It seems I am." I smiled at her.

I had missed those emerald eyes more than I expected and found my tongue brushing over my bottom lip as I fought the urge to blush under her gaze. Her hair was loose around her face, bundles of reddish brown hair half pulled back in a satin ribbon. She wore a pale yellow dress with a scalloped neckline that was so different from her usual skirts and corsets.

"I don't think I've ever seen you wear that," I told her, and her gaze dropped to the fabric.

"It's so warm out today, I just thought—"

"It's beautiful."

Her eyes snapped up to mine, a smile creeping as she inhaled slowly and stepped forward. I could tell she was nervous about the interaction, keeping her distance again even after all our time spent in the library. Whatever Wes had said to her had driven a wedge tightly down between her and us.

"I admit I *was* looking for you," I said, stepping closer to her.

Her shoulders pulled back as her body tensed from my approach.

"I was wondering if you might show me the grounds today?" I asked her. "Outside?"

"I don't think that would be appropriate." She swallowed tightly.

"Wes is gone for the week. He's taken Koen with him, and I could use the company." I tried to convince her.

"The sun shines so bright in the garden, I'm sure you'll manage." She nodded and turned to walk away, but I caught her wrist in my fingers. "Mr. Dunn."

"Clay," I corrected her. She looked down at my hand and narrowed her eyes. "Sorry," I said and let go. She pulled back from me and turned away on her heels, making her way down the hall faster than I could think up what to say next. "I don't know what he said to you, but he just doesn't understand!" I called after her, trying to keep her in sight as she rounded a corner. "Florence!"

She was gone.

I huffed, shaking my head, and looked around the empty hall.

Taking her up on the suggestion to bask in the sun, I wandered into the back half of the property. It was hot today, and I regretted the dark shirt I had picked out but, regardless, I decided to set out into the long maze of shrubbery and flowers.

Had this maze always been so thick with leaves... I stopped to look around at it. Swearing to myself that it had been dead not the week before.

Tricky, I thought, staring at the lush bushes before I turned back to look up at the Manor. The building itself–or the third of it that I could see looming above the shrubbery–did not seem as decrepit as it had before. The shingles were straighter almost, with none missing or hanging off at odd angles. The shutters surrounding the topmost windows were brighter and the windows themselves were clean and not covered with the thick film of grime they had been. *Very tricky.*

It wasn't long before I could feel the sweat starting to lick at the space between my shoulder blades and pool at the nape of my neck. I broke through the maze of bushes into a sprawling wildflower field that I had mapped from the back balcony of the Manor, but it looked three times the size in person.

It was different from the rest of the house, which was cloaked in a gothic darkness I couldn't quite put my finger on. Even the library was cold most of the time, despite its beautiful condition. This was... I inhaled slowly and scanned the field. There was a lightness here that didn't exist within the Manor's walls, all the flowers in soft pastels and long flowing grasses that seemed to sway regardless of the breeze.

"This is my favorite place in the warmer months," her voice blanketed over my shoulders, and I smiled to myself before turning back to look at her. She was even more beautiful, bathed in the sunlight that poured through the fluffy clouds above us.

"I can see why," I said to her.

Her brows furrowed adorably and the urge to rub my finger in the scrunched space down the bridge of her nose to the cupid bow of her upper lip was palpable.

"This place feels different from the rest of the property. It's as if you're infused into each petal, soaking up the sun and thriving in the breeze." I brushed my hand against a small flower, popping it off the stem and walking toward her. I ignored the stack of books she had cradled against her chest and stared at her beautiful, round face as I tucked the tiny blossom into her hair behind her ear.

"It seems as though the Manor creates it for you," I whispered, angling my chin down to meet her eyes.

"Koen spoke to you about the bathing room?" She asked with a sweet smile, but when she did it didn't quite meet her eyes.

"He did." I nodded. "Did the house create the library in the same way?" I asked her. When she had first shown me, she simply said that it took her a while to find the room. Not that the room hadn't existed until she'd found it.

"I'm unsure. In the early days of my confinement everything was so confusing I may have stumbled across the doors too overwhelmed to venture further," she explained. "The conservatory was a gift," she added.

"So when you *behave* the house gives you rooms?" I asked her, not meaning to sound arrogant or annoyed.

"It's not like that," she said, pausing for a moment. "The Manor provides."

The Manor provides... I swallowed tightly and nodded. I made a mental note to look into what she meant by that later.

"What do you have there?" I extended my hand to the books, and she tore her eyes from mine to look at the stack before handing them over to me.

"They're my favorites."

There were three books, all a different shade, all made of old-fashioned hand-bound leather. Poetry.

"These are..." I swallowed and turned the spines to look at the titles. "Old."

"I'm old," she laughed, and I swear the sound rivaled that of any songbird.

"Fair point, Florence," I hummed.

"On days like today, I come out here and read them to the flowers," she explained. "I believe it makes them grow a little taller."

Given what supernatural properties the house already displayed, it would be relatively uneducated of me to argue her wrong. Moving walls, protective barriers, unexplained accidents. So it wasn't unrealistic to think that the flowers did grow taller from the sound of her voice, but the likelihood of it seemed unlikely to my habitually logical mind.

"How long was it before the Manor allowed you out to smell the flowers?" I asked her.

"A while," she confessed. "It took a moment to learn, but once I stopped trying to escape the Manor gave me much more freedom."

I studied her for a moment. It was clear that she was complacent with her cage now, perhaps only having moments of needing or wanting freedom, but Florence seemed to truly believed that the Manor was caring for her, protecting her...

"What did you mean when you said 'the house puts you to sleep?'" I asked, remembering her comment from weeks before in the library. My hands itched to grab the nearest pen and paper and jot down everything she said, any little clue to unravel the mysteries that were held behind her eyes. But I could not bear to break the ease of our conversation by taking notes. She seldom opened up to me and I didn't want to ruin it by having her feel as though she was nothing but a test subject.

She turned to me and I could see in the way she chewed the inside of her cheek that she was carefully mulling over her words, deciding how to best explain. It was refreshing, conversing with someone who was so thoughtful when they spoke. Her manner was always poised, and she carried an air of intelligence about her that she did not seem to be aware of.

"There have been times when I would," she paused, her nose scrunched captivatingly while she again thought through her next words, "get angry." She shifted in the grass. "Being isolated for so long, it isn't normal, it's not good for a person. I would often fall into pits of despair, when I could feel nothing but darkness and rage and I acted violently towards the Manor... and myself." Her hand absently traced what I imagined to be invisible scars down her forearm. "The Manor will always intervene, forcing me unconscious until the worst of the darkness passes. When I'd wake next, I would still be alone but feel less... broken? I don't know how best to explain."

Her eyes stayed on the Manor, tracing the details of it slowly in almost a caress. "As lonesome as this place is, it has also provided me with a home. With everything I could want for." She paused and her gaze seemed to harden slightly. "Well, almost everything."

I nodded solemnly. My heart broke at the thought of her alone here for so long, so desperate to escape that she had been driven to try and take her own life and, for the first time, I had a feeling of strange gratitude towards the Manor and whatever powers that were within it that kept her from succeeding.

"I apologize for earlier," Florence said when I didn't respond. She passed by me and wandered into the field, an invitation to follow her as she looked over her shoulder at me. "It's been difficult to adjust to having you all in the house and, while you and Koen are willing to share the space, it seems Mr. Cameron would prefer to be anywhere else."

"Wes has been through a lot in his life," I paused to consider my words, "and it's a life barely lived when he's spent it taking care of us. He doesn't know how to be still, I suppose." I let the flowers tickle the pads of my fingers as I followed her back towards one of the large trees on the property.

"One might think him jaded." She sighed. "What do you think?"

"I've known Wes half my life and there is not a single person on this earth that I would trust my life with other than him, but he can be..." I murmured, "short tempered."

"Now you're being gracious, Mr. Dunn."

"Clay," I insisted, and Florence laughed.

"I apologize," she said.

"Two things you need to stop doing." I followed her so closely I could smell a warm citrus scent wafting from her hair. My chest nearly pressed to her back as we navigated the field. I lowered my voice a touch and leaned toward her. "Calling me Mr. Dunn and apologizing."

"I'll work on one at a time. Perhaps by the time you figure out if I'm dangerous, I'll have figured out how to stop apologizing to men for their own indiscretions," she teased, and I was taken aback by the sarcasm in her voice.

So sharp for such a soft flower.

CLAYTON

"**I**t must be strange," I said, watching her scoop her dress and find a spot on a little rolling hill where the grass was shorter. She crossed her ankles and held her hand out for her books. I hadn't even realized I was still carrying them until she wiggled her slender fingers at me.

"You'll have to be more specific." Florence patted the ground beside her, and I joined her in the grass beneath the tree, finding solace in its little shade. "Everything about Orchid Manor is strange, including myself."

"Right." I nodded. "I meant more particularly both living in a period when women were allowed no mercies or liberties to be outspoken or…" I searched for the word, tilting my head back to look at her. "To just be themselves. To now live in a time when female equality is finally being championed and talked about. While not perfect, the discussion is always ongoing."

The look on her face was striking and confused.

"Some books on women's rights will be borrowed from the public library this week for you," I promised, realizing that she had no idea. "We'll get you up to speed."

"I would like that." Florence practically hummed as she began flipping through her book.

"What poem is your favorite?" I asked her and leaned back on my elbows to watch her.

From this angle the sun created a halo around her beautiful auburn hair and cascaded down, kissing her cheeks in a warm light that only added to her ethereal nature. My words caught painfully in my chest as she tilted her head to look at me, a loose curl falling against her throat and the most breathtaking smirk on her lips.

"I don't know if I have one," she answered, the green in her big round eyes lighting up. "That's the beauty of poetry. A poem that means so much to me one day can change the next."

"How so?" I asked and licked my bottom lip.

"Before you all arrived, my favorite poems were about death," she whispered.

The admission cracked another hairline through my heart. It was getting harder to resist who she was and separate it from *what* she could be. Each delicate and warm smile was a blow to my logical resolve. Each eyelash was so light and long that I wanted to forget whatever dangers might linger just to feel them flutter against my cheek. To imagine a world without her, even after only having her in ours for such a brief period. It made me feel miserable.

"Now, if I were to choose, I would say I prefer the ones that riddle about love and springtime."

My eyebrows rose, but I understood where she was coming from as she explained herself. It wasn't often that I met someone who looked at the world from every angle, but I suppose when you had lived as long as Florence, you understood all the angles of the world because you'd had the time to examine them all.

"Do you ever wonder what your life would have been like outside the Manor if you had never been trapped?"

She looked up and over the field, back to the Manor looming over the sun-kissed wildflower patch as if it were listening.

"I was trapped long before I came to the Manor; here I'm free to do whatever I want."

"Except leave," I added softly.

"All things come with a cost."

"It's a shame," I said, reaching out and rubbing a finger against her wrist, begging her to look at me through touch. "You would be free to be whatever your heart desired now, given the chance," I offered.

Florence looked over at me and responded with a sad smile.

"What have you learned from your research, Clay?" She asked.

Rubbing a hand over my face and jaw, I sat up, "I've learned that there are no public records on who owns the house. The name you gave me, Agatha Warren? No red flags."

"What is a..." her brows furrowed in confusion.

"Red flag, like a warning sign that something bad is going on or has happened previously. She had none. She was married until her husband died, but his name isn't on the deed. She lived in the Manor until she died. There's no record of you ever being here."

"Yes," Florence sighed. "Mr. Cameron showed me the death announcement my husband wrote for the paper."

"He what?" I sat up further in the grass and stared at her for a long moment.

"There was an announcement written for the county paper that stated I had died at home surrounded by my family, but I can tell you with the utmost of certainty, Mr.Du– Clay, I did not die, and I did not die with my *loving* husband holding my hand," she said, her eyes growing dark, and voice sharp, almost spitting out the end of her sentence.

Wes had disappeared that night at the library, and fast. By the time I had wandered back up from the archives he was gone, and the note on the table was suspicious. He wasn't just the kind of guy to run off and go for a walk. I should have known he found something he didn't want to share.

"He showed that to you to get your reaction," I said.

"It worked; it was overwhelming, to say the least." She picked at the corners of the book.

"I had no idea. I'm sorry," I said.

"We both need to learn how to stop apologizing for others," she huffed and closed the book in her lap. "I suppose I gave him exactly what he wanted. It was hard to read that, to know I could be so easily wiped away from my old life. But I shouldn't have expected anything more from a man who had never cared about anything past his status in society."

"He sounds like a horrible husband," I said tightly, trying to busy my tense hands by picking grass.

"Lord Cabot, Matthew, was a terrible man, and husband to me by law alone," Florence quipped. "Though most men were not much better in my time, he was among the worst."

"Don't lump us all together." I clutched at my chest. "You'll hurt my feelings."

"I didn't know you were born in the eighteen hundreds. My apologies," she teased with a smile I had never seen before, but it tightened my chest with anticipation for the next time it might appear.

"Was he cruel?" I asked, knowing that I might be pushing the boundaries of what she was willing to tell me, but I couldn't help myself.

"As cruel as they come," she answered honestly, looking out at the field of flowers. "But I suppose it is unfair of me to lump all men together. My father was an exceptional man." She sighed, her eyes seeming to clear from the darkness that clouded them when speaking of her husband. Now they were warm, and full of love. It was breathtaking.

"He never treated me any less for not being the son he so desperately needed to help with the farm. He taught me to read and to write, and to care for the animals and cultivate gardens. He was always quick to laugh, and open with his affection. Sometimes Koen reminds me of him," she whispered. "His emotions are raw and honest." She paused for a moment and looked down at her hands, her fingers worrying the leather corner of the book she was holding. "But then, so were Matthew's; they were just the wrong kind of emotions..."

"Koen won't," I said instantly, without thought. She'd grown tense beside me. The air could be split down the center between us. "I can tell when someone is trying to feel out a situation. When they're trying to determine whether or not we can be trusted. It is always handy when dealing with law enforcement, victims, or family members. They're unwilling to talk to us, even if we flash a fake police badge or act like lawyers," I tried to explain. "I've always been able to read people and I can tell you're trying to figure out if Koen's loyalties are fickle or if they'll turn violent. They are not, they will not."

Florence stared at me with a fire blazing behind her eyes.

"Once he makes up his mind, it cannot be swayed. So, for the sake of us all, I hope to God, or whatever supernatural force may be listening right now, that you are who and what I think you are because if you're not, Wesley Cameron will move heaven and earth to ensure his little brother is safe, even if Koen doesn't want the special treatment."

And regardless of who or what stands in his way. I don't add, but she can see it lingering, unsaid.

"I understand and I thank you for your honesty."

"Excellent," I said, holding my hand out to her. We were both still sitting in the uncomfortable reality that no matter what, it might end in bloodshed. "Now, let me read some of those to you."

"You want to read them to me?" Her brows furrowed in that adorable way again, but that time I didn't stop myself from reaching out and brushing my thumb between them. She pulled back gently, staring at my hand with a blush on her cheeks that made my mouth dry.

With that the suffocating reality eased off my chest.

I wanted to do more than read to her.

I wanted to roll her over in the grass and kiss her until she forgot her own name.

I wanted to show her the commitment that coursed through me to find a solution. An instinct that burned bright below the surface to never stop digging until I found a way to free her from this prison. A raw, feral urge to find a way to see that smile without conditions or the looming threat of what could happen.

But for now I would settle for reading to her if it made her happy.

"If you'll let me." I smiled at her and she handed me one of them, allowing me to flip to a page that had been dog-eared. "I didn't take you for a book destroyer, Florence." I scowled and pressed out the corner.

She laughed wildly and with conviction into the summer air at my huffing. "I didn't know you were the authority," she quipped back.

"Stop the research." I shook my head in feigned disgust. "This right here is why you might be a monster," I said, shaking the antique book in the air at her.

"Just read to me," she giggled, eyes rolling as she pressed her fingers against the leather and pushed it back toward me, that teasing smirk returning to her lips.

It was getting progressively more challenging to see Wes' argument when she smiled at me like that.

All my logic flew out of my mind, leaving only thoughts of Florence.

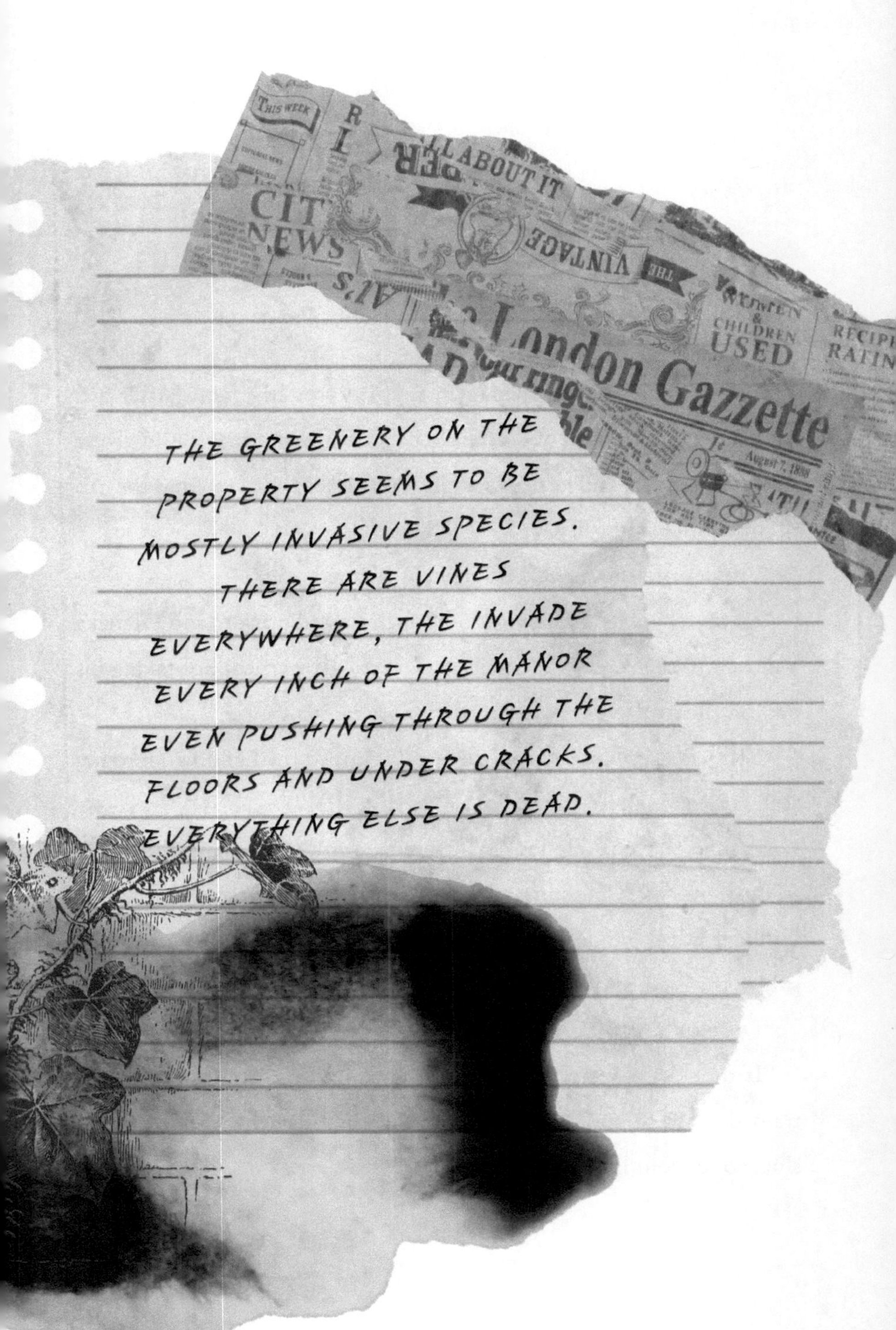
THE GREENERY ON THE
PROPERTY SEEMS TO BE
MOSTLY INVASIVE SPECIES.
THERE ARE VINES
EVERYWHERE, THE INVADE
EVERY INCH OF THE MANOR
EVEN PUSHING THROUGH THE
FLOORS AND UNDER CRACKS.
EVERYTHING ELSE IS DEAD.
THIS WEEK
CIT
NEWS
ALL ABOUT IT
THE VINTAGE
WOMEN & CHILDREN USED
RECIPI
RATIN
London Gazzette
August 7, 1895

KOEN

"Don't." Wes slapped my hand away from the radio. After two hours of silence, I started to get antsy, and who could blame me? The tension between Wes and I was thicker than ever, and the cab of the Bronco felt stuffy.

"I'm sick of listening to Dad rock," I groaned.

"I don't care what you're sick of. Touch my radio again, and I'll make you wait in the truck while I clear the nest," he warned, not taking his eyes off the road.

"You're a horrible road trip partner." I slipped further down into my seat. "How much further?"

"A mile, maybe." He looked at the map on the dash and then back to the motorway. The sunset licked at the endless stretch of wet tarmac leading toward our destination. The truck roared by a police car on the side of the road, and Wes sighed.

"Do you think they'll run the plates?" I asked him.

"If they do, it won't take them long to find us," he quipped, eyes trained ahead of him. "And if they do, we aren't staying. I don't give a shite about your little monster lover."

"Clay will have it figured out before we get back," I said, ignoring the venom in Wes' voice. The silence dragged like nails on a chalkboard. "Are you really that pissed off?" I said.

"I'm not pissed off. I'm driving," he clipped, but the muscle in his jaw tensed and his eyes wavered in their unforgiving stare.

"You can't even look at me!" The laughter that echoed in the cab was hollow and tight. The Bronco accelerated roughly and Wes' hand rolled tightly over the steering wheel.

"You're an idiot, and if that was a reason for me to be pissed off, I'd never be happy," Wes responded.

"You *aren't* ever happy," I scoffed. "We're Hunters, Wes. We could get killed at any minute by literally anything and you choose this hill to die on?"

"We die fighting, Koen," he corrected me. "What happens when it attacks you? You think getting close to it is safe because it looks human, but it's not. It's a monster just like the rest of them, and you won't get the chance to fight because it's going to slit your throat with its tongue in your mouth."

I shook my head. "So be it."

That had him looking. The fire in his eyes could have burned a hole through me.

"Let's just get this done and you can contemplate all the ways you're committing suicide later," Wes snapped.

The rest of the drive was dead silent. Wes let out a few disgruntled huffs but, for the most part, he was done speaking to me. I wasn't sure what to expect from the nest; most of the ones we cleared were shabby abandoned houses. It wasn't until we were settled into the curb about four houses down that it became clear that the nest we were hunting was different. The house was not run down. It was pristine. Rose beds outside framed the two-story powder blue home around the side, meeting with a seven-foot fence that enclosed the entire property.

"I hate fences," Wes groaned.

Fences meant surprises, and dangerous ones in our line of work.

"We can split—" I started to devise a plan, but Wes cut me off with a growl. "What?"

"You aren't leaving my sight," he warned.

"Now you're just being stupid and overbearing. We've hunted hundreds of vamps. We know how to do this in our sleep but now you want to hold my hand like I'm a toddler?"

I checked the time and then looked at the still-dark and cloudy sky. We had no choice but to wait. We needed the sun to rise. Hunting a nest during peak activity hours was asking for trouble. At least if the sun was up, most of the bloodsuckers would be asleep.

"We go in the front door *together*," he insisted. "We clear the nest without fuss. There are too many eyes on us. This can't be messy."

"Everything about *this*," I mocked him, pointing between us and then to the house, "is messy. I'm not going in that house until you turn that frown upside down," I teased, but the sentiment fell flat. Wes was still too angry with me to give in. "Whatever." Exasperated and sick of his attitude, I leaned back against the passenger seat, pulling my hat down over my eyes. "Wake me up when the sun comes up."

I could feel his gaze burning into my side, but it felt better to ignore him at the moment than hash it out in a tireless circle where he never admits he's in the wrong.

"Get up," Wes said before slamming his door.

I stretched out all my muscles one at a time, yawning myself awake from the cat nap, and climbed out after him. I rolled out my neck as he handed me a machete, shoving a gun into the waistband of his pants.

"I saw two vampires enter the nest just before dawn. They should be asleep by now," he warned and shrugged into his jacket, pulling the collar up around his jaw. "Keep your guard up," he snapped, "and try to keep your fingers out of them."

"Low blow," I growled, turning my hat backward and checking to make sure my own handgun was loaded before it found its home at the waist of my jeans. I followed Wes closely in a pathetic attempt to ease the tension. I didn't want to go headfirst into a vampire nest without my head on straight, even if Wes's wasn't.

As we approached the house, I felt sick to my stomach. Birds chirped in chorus in the trees above us, and Wes turned the doorknob to find it unlocked.

Security doesn't matter when you're an apex predator. Unless you make too much noise and the neighbors call the cops, or in this case the exterminators. He let the door swing open, pushing it out of his way with the tip of his machete, as he stepped into the house sideways, his back to the living space, and started to check his surroundings.

The home's exterior fit seamlessly with the neighborhood, but the inside was different. The walls were covered in grime and the floors were littered with garbage that Wes barely avoided stepping on as he navigated the disaster of a space.

It only took a moment to realize we were too early. Two voices drifted in from the kitchen and music played from the long, darkened hallway to our left. Wes sighed and, as he turned to bark a grouchy, unnecessary order at me, a vamp charged at him from around the corner. His jaw clenched as he fought against its brute strength. They hit the wall hard, knocking the family photos from the wall, most likely deceased if a nest had taken over their home. The glass shattered, alerting the rest to our intrusion, and soon we were swarmed.

Wes clumsily fought through his first vamp as I defended myself from a smaller one rushing out of the hallway. Her ashy hair was unkempt and stuck out in every direction atop her pale, deformed face. Teeth extended down from her gums as she snarled at me. Her head cocked to the side in small, jerky movements that clicked and snapped as her blood-flooded eyes sized me up.

"Come on then," I teased her, shifting on my feet as she charged me.

She was small but fast. Her movements were all broken and twitchy. But worst of all she was young, and she was starving. I swung my machete wide, catching her flesh and tearing it away from her bone. She snarled in pain, but it didn't slow her down.

Her arms reached out, swiping at me. I took two steps back and swung the blade again; this time, it didn't miss. It severed through her neck. The soft tissue of her rotting muscles broke down quickly as I used all of my strength to pop the bone and separate her head from her shoulders.

It rolled with a few sloppy thuds to the foot of another, giant-looking, vampire, whose face contorted into pure rage as he looked up at me. I didn't have time to react as I was slammed to the ground from behind. Another female had driven her shoulder between my shoulder blades and sent me flying to the floor. Slipping in the blood that seeped from the first beast, my hands found no purchase. I slid through the ichor on my hands and knees, reaching out for something to stop on and, when I finally did, I realized my machete was gone. The vampire standing above me kicked his boot out with force, connecting with my face and splitting the skin on my cheek open. I could taste the blood on my lips as I fought to get to my feet.

The fucker had my machete.

"Shite," I swore under my breath and moved myself backward from the weapon. I could hear Wes struggling, selfishly a little glad he was. Maybe he'd realize how stupid he'd been to go charging into a fight hot-headed. Guilt licked at my thoughts but I pushed it away. He was a big boy. He'd get himself up and out of whatever mess he'd found himself in.

The vampire whipped the machete toward me, narrowly missing my stomach as I darted to the right into the living room. My leg caught the couch, and I flipped backward roughly, hitting the floor hard, accidentally putting distance between me and the mountainous monster. He laughed, razor-sharp teeth dripping with blood and sinew as he moved toward me, ready to attack again.

"Little pig, little pig," he chanted, shifting to the right.

He was huge, shoulders expanding across like a brick wall on his nearly six-five stature. There was no way I could beat the fucker one-on-one, even if he wasn't holding my weapon. Without hesitation and before he could react, I slipped my gun out, grasping it firmly, and unloaded the clip into his chest.

"Ow," he laughed, a sickening grin on his face.

The bullets had done nothing to slow him down, and the sick bastard was enjoying playing with his food.

"Hey, ugly," Wes called out from behind him, a sharp machete rolling in his hand as the vamp looked over his shoulder. "Pick on someone your own size."

"I don't discriminate," he huffed, his voice low and teasing as he continued toward me, ignoring Wes' threat.

I had an empty clip and nowhere to run, but that wasn't the vampire's plan. He just wanted us to be complacent. He wanted us to believe we trapped him, that he was losing. Before I could yell out to Wes, he turned the machete on him without looking. The blade cut into Wes' bicep, ripping both cloth and skin. The machete tore him open with no effort on the vampire's part, who was moving in for another swing.

Wes grunted through the pain, gripping the handle tighter as the blood that sprayed down his arm made it slippery and impossible to wield. The vampire didn't wait. He swung again and tore a line through Wes's thigh, clean and deep. I watched my brother fall to his knees with a loud thump.

I dug in my pocket, using the brief distraction to reload my weapon as the vampire kept his back turned on me. I fired two shots into his shoulder as he raised the machete and then two in the back of his calf. The towering monster buckled under the surprise pain and teetered on his only good leg.

Wes saw the opening and pushed to his feet, blood gushing from the open gash in his thigh. A painfilled groan tore from his lips as he used whatever strength he had left to sheer off the vampire's head. Both monster and weapon dropping to the floor noisily.

I ran toward them, kicking the head against the wall and slipping beneath Wes's arm to hold him up. "You okay?" I asked.

"Great," he huffed, wrapping his hand around his bicep. "Get this jacket off me."

I helped him from it, tearing a strip off and tying off his arm and leg. "We need to get you back to—"

My suggestion is cut short by the sound of children crying, two at least. Wes tensed beside me, his eyes barely open. He was losing too much blood. We needed to get him the hell out of here.

"You have to check." He shook his head. Both of us knew the consequences of leaving anyone in the nest alive. "I'll get myself to the truck." He pushed away from me and pointed to his machete on the floor.

My hands were covered in his blood. I hesitated to investigate the noise.

"Koen, go!" Wes barked, halfway out the door. I knew if he could, he would do it for me.

I rolled my shoulders back, shuffling down the hallway toward the sound. "*Please don't be vampires,*" I pressed my forehead to the door and whispered before turning the doorknob.

Two faces stared up at me from the dim lighting of the boarded-up room. All the furniture and bedding were shredded, and the lamp no longer had a shade. Tears streamed down their faces, devastation in their blood-red eyes as they realized I wasn't there to help.

Little feet and even smaller hands, they couldn't have been more than six or seven. Nausea rolled through me as rows of teeth snarled up at me.

"I'm sorry," I mumbled under my breath and swallowed the guilt as it formed.

FLORENCE

Memories of Clay, reading soft springtime poetry in a field of flowers, lingered in my mind as I moved through the Manor and tried to distract myself that evening. His long fingers delicately flipped through the soft old pages, eyes scanning the words and lips pursed as he found poems that spoke to him. His voice was deep, husky almost, and carried on the breeze so effortlessly that I could hear it clearly even now in my memory.

I slipped the books back into the library, expecting to find him there but seeing nothing but books and pages of notes. I caught myself pouting when I didn't spot his tall, handsome figure leaning against any of the shelves, his nose in a book. So I continued my lazy search of the Manor, trying not to seem too eager. For my own sake but also because the house was uneasy. Ever since that night in the bathing room, it had been looming over Koen like a dark cloud and I was sure it was waiting to strike, but biding its time.

So I had tried to pull back from him, from them all. But especially Koen.

His heart was just too big and fragile. I couldn't bear the thought of him being hurt.

It had been painful to do so, but I desperately wanted to keep him safe, and it was the only way I knew how to. My conversation with Wesley had stuck in the back of my mind. Oddly enough, it had put us on a level of understanding I don't think he realized. I understood why he was so protective of them. They deserved every ounce of that fierce loyalty.

"Clay?" I called out, noticing a flickering haze coming from the bottom of the stairs, the flame of a candle dancing off the study's walls. "Are you in here?" I picked up the skirt of my dress and floated around the corner to find him lighting more along the fireplace mantel. "What are you doing?"

He wore a clean white shirt and dark pants that fit nicely to his thighs. His hair pressed back off his forehead in a bundle of deep brown waves that curled around his ears and stuck out in places endearingly.

"You're early," he laughed, and the room was filled with the most beautiful posh sound, a playful twinkle behind his blue eyes.

"For what exactly?" I looked around and stepped further into the study to see that he had pushed all the furniture back from the center of the room and lined all the surfaces with candles. In the middle was a large blanket he had pulled off a bed upstairs and plates of food and wine.

"I know you don't need to eat, but–" he stopped, seemingly nervous as he rubbed his hands on his pants and licked his bottom lip. "I wanted to..." he trailed off.

"It's beautiful," I whispered. It's *intimate.*

"Not all men are as unappreciative of the wonders around them, Florence," he said, the words slow and meaningful as he spoke them. "I see your magic."

I was taken aback by his confession, unsure how to respond as I wrestled with the idea that he had spent time planning this for me.

Clay stepped forward, extending his hand to me. He pulled me into the study to my spot on the blanket. He settled down next to me and handed me a glass of wine. "Can you get drunk?" he asked.

"I've never tried," I shrugged and pressed the wine to my lips. It had been a long time since I had anything to drink but, as the red wine hit my lips, I remembered how delicious it could be.

"Did you know the Manor has a cellar?" He asked, leaning back against the couch behind him with his leg curled toward his chest. "At first, I thought it was through that one door that disappeared."

My stomach sank, and I forced a tight smile at the thought. That door never opened; it constantly moved and sometimes I wouldn't see it for months, but I knew one fact for sure. Pure evil laid beyond it.

"But then I found the cellar door in the kitchen, lucky us." His shirt pulled up over his wrist and exposed the tendrils of the ink on his skin slightly.

I nodded and set the cup beside me, turning into his space and resting on my knees. "I've been meaning to ask what these are." I said pointing, as the wine warmed my belly, I aimed to change the subject.

Clay's eyes flickered to his skin and back to me before his fingers worked the button and he pulled the sleeve back. "Tattoos?" He asked.

"I've only read about them in books! I've never seen anything like it." I wrapped my fingers around his wrist, tugging it closer to the light to see them. They caught my curiosity the first time I saw them, but it had felt improper to ask. Now though, something had shifted between us. I was more comfortable with him. Touching him felt... normal. "How do they mark the skin to make it stay?"

"It's a needle. It pushes the ink beneath the surface." He brushed a finger over a line of swirls that spun delicately around his elbow beneath the fabric of his shirt.

"Like a stain?"

"Sort of," he confirmed.

"Are they..." My eyes flickered to his chest.

Clay slowly worked at the buttons of his shirt before letting it fall open to expose all the beautiful artwork beneath. Wings of gray fanned across his firm chest, their tips curling over his shoulders. "What is it?"

"A stone angel," he said, looking down at it. The tattoos expanded down over the soft expanse of his stomach and around his back.

"Your entire body is covered in them?" I asked, fingers trailing the fine lines of the wings. Without realizing I had all but climbed into his lap, blinded by my curiosity. His fingers rested carefully on my hand as my eyes traced the wondrous artwork. "Did it hurt?"

"Most places, yeh, horribly uncomfortable," he laughed, and his breath fanned my face.

I looked up at him, our mouths so close now that I could smell the wine on his lips.

His smile was bright and curved to the left, showing off all his pretty white teeth.

"Florence." He swallowed tightly, his throat bobbing nervously as I waited for him to act on the tension between us.

"Clay," I breathed.

His lips were on mine before I could protest, soft but full of need. His hand tangled into my hair, pulling me against him to deepen the kiss. A deep moan rumbled from him as I climbed over his thighs and settled against his hips, never breaking our connection.

Clay's mouth was overwhelming in the best way possible. As if he couldn't stop himself or have his fill of me. He busied himself with the buttons of my blouse and slipped it from my shoulders, seeming to revel in touching the bare skin of my arms as he trailed his fingers back up and over my shoulder, hovering just above my collarbone. I could see his brow furrow as he took in the corset, and looked up at me, a shy smile crinkling the corners of his eyes.

"Are corsets not a common garment anymore?" I asked playfully, guessing by the look of bashful confusion on his face that they likely were not. Without awaiting his response I deftly unhooked the clasps that held it shut. I tossed it gently to the side and brought my gaze back to his. I watched as he swallowed visibly, heat in his eyes.

His hands reached for me and softly cupped my breasts in his palms over the light cotton chemise, as if he were holding something precious. Clay's fingers tickled beneath the collar, skin brushing skin as he pushed back the fabric. Heat pooled between my legs when his mouth sucked delicately at my newly exposed skin. My body leaned into him as he nuzzled the base of my throat and nipped with his teeth.

His hand danced across the scalloped hem of my collar. His fingers swept against the swollen tops of my breasts as his mouth found mine again and kissed me feverishly.

"Is this too much..." He pulled back, eyes searching mine. "You'll tell me to stop if it is?" Lust-blown pupils glimmered in the flickering candlelight as I dipped back to his mouth, stealing a kiss from his worried lips.

Of course the worry swirled in my own mind. *Was I crazy?* Perhaps. But the way he looked at me had lit my tired and worried soul on fire, and it burned so brightly for him that I wasn't sure I could stop it, even if I tried. Clay's touches were warm and slow as he pulled the shift free of my chest and let it fall away without ever breaking our stare. His fingers grazed my spine, rising up my back until his hand wrapped around my neck, and he stared at me. Longing and desperation settled across his fox-like features. His eyes searched mine for confirmation that I wanted it all, too.

My body ached for him in a way I could not put to words.

Koen had given me that same primal spark but it was somehow deeper and needier now. Like he had opened a door and I couldn't force myself to close it. The fight persisted, the little voice in my head that warned me against all of the intimacy. The act of sleeping with one man outside of my marriage was scandalous, but two? My body reacted to the thought, but not how I expected. My thighs squeezed tightly as a new pressure formed between my legs.

All of my reasons to stop were wrapped up in a marriage that had ended over a hundred years ago, and ideals that didn't resonate with me then, and especially did not now. The worry was muted, still swirling my thoughts, but the lust was loud and honest. Clay remained quiet, his hands never moving, allowing me the excruciating time to clear my mind enough to think, to fully be aware and tell him what I wanted.

"I should be asking you that," I said, grazing his bottom lip with my fingers. "I know you know about Koen."

"Koen and I have always been good at sharing," he said genuinely and kissed my fingertips so gently it sent shivers down my naked spine. "I want this."

"Are you sure?" I asked again as his fingertips tightened around the back of my neck gently. "Because..." My eyes fluttered closed as his hips lifted, the entire length of his erection pressing forcefully against his trousers was brushing against my core and stealing the words from my lips. "...I don't think I'll be able to stop."

"Good," Clay chuckled, pulling me down by my hips against him and returning to his onslaught of needy, hot kisses against my mouth. His palm ghosted over my rib cage to massage my breast gently. The motion caused my back to arch into his touch. "But if you need or want to stop, say the word," he said.

"Alright," I whined as he pulled away, the possibility of needing to stop long forgotten. My hands pushed beneath his shirt and rolled it down over his broad shoulders, feeling each muscle between my hands as his kisses became feathery and teasing on my throat and chest.

I felt delirious, like my head was swimming through clouds, and I couldn't catch my breath. Clay's hand roamed from my neck and brushed in ticklish motions over my back and down to my bottom, palming it in his hand and guiding my hips forward against him. Moving over his skin, I kissed and nipped at his neck in return, feeling him tremble beneath my touch and he let out a throaty groan that only fueled the passion that built in my core.

FLORENCE

He smelled of lemon, ginger, and leather. The smell infused into my senses as I stared down at his chest and let my hands roam over his skin. His head fell back against the couch behind him, and his hands gripped even tighter against my hips, his touch burning my skin even through the skirt.

Clay's body was a stark contrast from Matthew's; even at his younger age, he had never been so...

"Are you okay?" His low voice blanketed me with sparks.

"I've never been better," I sat back against his grip and stared down at him. His dark hair was brushed out of place and a curl fell against his forehead as his eyes watched me intently. Bathed in candlelight and breathing heavily, he looked like an angel. "I feel as though I'm dreaming."

"If you are—" He squeezed me tightly and sat up to meet my lips, dragging his teeth against my bottom lip. "Then I certainly am, too."

I stood, only long enough to undo the skirts at my waist and step out of them. I didn't think my legs would be able to hold me upright for much longer than that. He followed my lead and removed his trousers and undergarments and a languid moan dripped from me as we came back together. His throbbing cock sprang free against my thigh and made me giggle with excitement.

"Come here," he said and brought me back against him. His erection nestled perfectly against my aching core as his tongue slipped into my mouth. "You taste like wine." He chuckled and deepened his hold on me with one hand sliding into my hair and tugging gently at the roots.

His other hand slid between my thighs. His fingers brushed against the bundle of nerves and I melted down against him, unable to contain the strangled gasp that left my throat as he spread me open and started to circle my most tender area. Pressure built in my womb and it was delicious and warm. It tangled with the raw nerves and drove me toward the edge.

"Clay," I whispered, but his name fell from my mouth in a moan as he pressed two fingers inside and curled them against my core delicately. "Oh God," I called out before I could stop myself, thoughts swirling rapidly. I was so tight around his fingers, my walls shuddering and gripping at his touch as I pressed my hips down against him and ground us together.

"You're going to drive me to insanity," he whispered through tight lips. Clay's body shook from the contact, his head lolling back against the couch and exposing his throat. His breaths were shallow as his eyes fluttered closed.

For a moment, I thought I had done something wrong, with my fingers tangled into his hair, but there was a drunk lust in his eyes when he regained the composure he'd lost. He stared at me with a lazy, kiss-bitten smirk, and rolled his hips to grind up against me again. The tip of his cock brushed me and I inhaled sharply, gauging just how large he was. I gasped as his thumb began a pattern of lazy circles at the throbbing pulse at my sex but it did nothing to quell my nerves. I had never been touched with such care and attention.

I had never felt this dizzy, drunk not on wine but on Clay's purposeful touch.

My body tensed, and Clay pulled back from his nestled spot against my throat, lost in hair and skin with his velvety, warm mouth. I brushed my fingers down the slope of his nose, feeling the knots where it had been previously broken before trailing back over his sharp jaw. I stared at him for a long moment, half cupping my hand on his jaw and the other tangled in the loose curls around his ear.

"What is it?" He wrapped his hands around mine and pressed it to his face. I could feel his body vibrating beneath mine, his fingers slipping from inside of me, causing my thighs to clench in his absence.

"It's been a long time," I managed to get out.

Clay chuckled, but it wasn't malicious. It was soft as he gripped my hip and gave me his entire focus. "I know." He tucked his finger beneath my chin. "We'll go slow," he whispered, eyes gentle and full of assurance. The kiss that followed was so sweet and strong that I barely noticed him moving our position from me in his lap, to him hovering above me, laid delicately beneath him on the floor. He wrapped his hand around himself, pumping once before he lined himself up. "We will be gentle, Florence," he mumbled against my throat as his face dipped down against me. The head of his cock slid deliciously through my folds and found my entrance, I held my breath, and my fingers gripped his hair roughly, anticipating the pressure.

"Breathe for me," he instructed.

We inhaled together, not a single sound except our breathing as he pressed his other hand to my back and tugged me closer to him as we did.

"You can do it," he praised breathlessly. My core ached as he slowly pushed himself inside, an exquisite sharpness dancing through me as my body adjusted to his size.

"Gods," Clay breathed out. "That's my girl, nice and slow."

He held me as he carefully, inch-by-tortuous-inch, rolled his hips back and forth. Pleasure and pain tangled together to wrap our bodies in a delicious euphoria that exploded like stars across the night sky as he found a rhythm.

"Are you okay?" He asked, his entire body shuttering as he rocked back out.

"I—" I gasped with each thrust, each time thinking he had sunk in only to find there was so much more to him. "Keep going," I encouraged, craving all of him.

Clay was gentle, more caring and attentive than I had ever experienced in all my years, making me dizzy with heat. I was so wet that I could feel it pooling around my thighs, making his thrusts slick as my body started to welcome his size.

"Are you afraid to hurt me?" I asked him, noticing that he hadn't adjusted his pace.

"I don't want to hurt you. I want you to feel good, too."

"You can't hurt me," I cupped his face and kissed him. "I'm kind of immortal."

"There are a hundred other ways you can hurt, Florence. This isn't meant to be one of them." He was breathing heavier now as he thrust slowly, the hardened ridges of him rubbing against me. "You're supposed to feel everything, *want* everything. Each movement is as much for you as it is for me."

I understood his concern then. It wasn't for the pain. It was him lingering on past intimacy he assumed I had experienced with my husband. Or more reasonably, the lack of.

"Then show me, Clay," I demanded. "*Teach* me."

The resolve in him broke. He thrusted forward with a new urgency that made my breath catch in my throat as his hips slapped against me, and he buried himself in me.

"Florence." My name left his lips in strangled ecstasy as he paused there, the entire length of his cock deep inside my throbbing core. His arms braced on either side of me, strong and steady. I gripped tightly to his waist and he gasped as I rolled my hips back, grinding the sensitive nerves of my heat against the base of him. I reveled in the newfound knowledge that I could elicit such a sound from him while also taking my own pleasure.

"It's good," I breathed out. "It's so..." my eyes rolled back as his mouth sucked at the swell of my breast. "Keep going," I begged now. The words leaving my mouth came out breathless and sloppy as I convulsed around his length.

I cried out and Clay smiled against me. His teeth tickled my slick skin as he wrapped his arm under my back and pulled me tightly to him. He kissed a line up my sweaty jaw. A whimper left my swollen lips as his hand cupped my knee and spread me open further to him. He buried himself again with a pleasurable roughness that left me speechless.

I arched my back into his touch, needing all of him as his hips rocked forward. His length slid against the sensitive walls of my core, his smile wild with pleasure as he realized just how close I was to coming undone.

Clay dipped down, popping a nipple between his lips, and sucked gently until I was wholly unraveled and screaming his name like it was the only word I knew. Clay was there to guide me through the euphoria that swept through my body like a wave. The orgasm was bone-deep and sparked like wildfire. Each rough thrust from his hips, each messy, searing kiss, and tiny guttural moan was a testament to how he would continue this relentless pace until there was no room for embarrassment or fear left in my memory.

He was ensuring that he erased every echo of Lord Cabot from my flesh.

Clay replaced them with new wonders. That flooded with the feeling of him tearing through me until I was not the woman I once was but something new. Something free.

I felt like a petal in the wind.

I clenched around him as I climaxed, pulling a growl from him as he found his release on trembling forearms. Clay rocked into me, his ragged breath coating my neck and hand raking over my belly as I took quick, shallow breaths. His fingers were seductive and I couldn't get enough of him and, when he finally found the energy to withdraw, a small moan of deprivation was pulled from my lips.

He lay down on the blanket, pulling my back against his chest in a tight hug and kissed my jaw over and over again. His arms wrapped around me and, for a second, I could feel the bliss radiating off his skin. The space between my legs throbbed and I knew I would be sore in the morning, but it was worth every delicious moment that Clay had spent inside me.

"That was..." His mouth grazed my throat and I leaned into the feeling of his warm breath, sticky on my skin, and raked my fingers into his hair. "Insane."

I chuckled at the sound of his sleepy, sex-drunk voice and rolled over in his arms so our chests pressed together and I could kiss him back.

"How do you feel?" Clay asked, his brows pinching together as his hand raked my hair out of my face.

I felt... taken care of, spoiled, and loved. He snuggled against me, kissing my neck and shoulders with sleepy bliss that left tingling spots all over my skin. I wasn't sure how we had even gotten to this point. The afternoon in the field, things became charged and shifted into something softer and more intimate between us. I just hadn't expected them to snap so suddenly.

The light from the candles danced across my vision.

He had done all of this for me.

"I feel seen."

Clay smiled, enveloping my face in his hand as he covered my mouth. Kissing me slowly, taking his time before pulling back and pressing his forehead to mine.

They rocked in unison, bodies entangling and crying out for one another. The walls shuddered along with their breaths, the floors vibrating against her back, unnoticed. The fire danced in the mantle, kicking up higher with every moan that floated from her lips. Everything came alive at her pleasure, awake and wanting, full of excitement. But there was more than just the excitement, there was envy too.

A possessiveness older and hungrier than anyone could know. Each time his name came from her, it twisted sharper and tighter, radiating from the foundation and through the joists, surrounding them. Brief regret for allowing this to happen, brief consideration of ending it with finality immediately. Patience prevailing, the toxic covetousness settled, biding its time. Allowing the connections to continue to be forged, and strengthened.

It was still new, still interesting. She only needed time to remember who had kept her safe all these years, time to see how dangerous the outside world had always been. There would be time enough again, once they had been dealt with, to spend the rest of eternity reminding her.

CLAYTON

S taring down at Florence, I found myself at odds.

The moments before were hazy and lust-filled. The sounds she made still seemed to echo around the empty Manor, a heavenly song I hoped would never stop playing. I knew the moment Wes returned that he would know. There was no hiding how I felt anymore—not after having her like that. Undone, raw, and honest, it was like nothing I had ever felt and, as my logical brain screamed for caution, my heart whispered its cravings through the white noise.

"Florence?" I spoke her name, but she hummed and kissed a lazy line across my chest in her euphoric daze. "How are you feeling?" I asked her again, knowing she would lie if it made me happy. I knew that within the hour the pain would have dissipated. I've watched her heal bullet wounds in less time. It didn't matter to her, but it bothered me.

Florence didn't answer; she just continued tracing her finger along my tattoos with a delicate, sleepy smile. She was sore. I could tell by how she shifted in my arms, prompting my next move. I turned from beneath her, a tiny whimper falling from her as I moved to roll my trousers up and over my hips, leaving them unbelted. They hung low on my hips.

"Come," I bent down, gathering her discarded skirts and corset in a bunch and handing them to her before lifting her and pressing her to my chest. I kissed her temple, unable to resist as she snuggled into my touch, half asleep.

"Where are we going?" She asked as I carried her through the empty foyer and up the grand staircase to the bedrooms. The only room in the house that had never moved was hers, and the door was open when I reached the top of the stairs.

"Now I thank you, for trusting me with you," I mused and gently set her on the bed.

"Clay–" Her hand trailed down my arm, catching my fingers as I pulled away.

"Florence," I laughed, leaning back for a kiss. Her chin tilted to meet mine, our lips grazing one anothers. I could feel her pouty bottom lip as I pulled away and entered the bathroom.

I looked back at her once from the threshold and traced my eyes down her beautiful back. She gripped the corset, holding it to her chest, the rest of the fabric loose and undone. She looked peaceful—heavenly. I stared for a moment longer, memorizing the shape of her curves and each perfect freckle that marked her pale skin. Slowly, all thoughts of Florence would drown the worry that gripped me.

It was only that morning I had found the bathroom connected to the master bedroom. It wasn't big but supported a large tub against the tiled West wall. Much to my surprise it was in pristine condition. No cobwebs in the corners, or mold on the window sill. No signs of any poor disrepair or abandonment of any kind. This room looked as if it had been newly renovated. There were taps and faucets at the sink and, bizarrely, at the large clawfoot tub. No indoor plumbing had been a big bone of contention with Wes about staying in the Manor, this *hadn't* been here before. It had taken me a whole five minutes of opening and closing the door to realize I wasn't seeing things. It wasn't as loud as the rest of the house, with simple wallpaper and tiles. Dark wood surrounded the base of the old sink, and one tall wardrobe stored linens and soap.

The water ran warm almost instantly, the house creaking as I turned the metal knobs. I could have sworn I heard it wailing as though it was crying, but all the noise faded into a hum when I saw Florence standing in the doorway.

"What are you doing?" She asked me.

Her hair fell in messy waves that framed her round face and her smile was soft and quizzical as she watched me carefully prepare the tub.

"Running you a bath, it will help with the soreness," I explained, walking toward her.

"Running?" She questioned, her eyes shifting to the tap with confusion.

"Filling?" I changed the term but her confusion remained.

"I've never seen the Manor do such a thing..." she said quietly. "The tub is usually just— full."

"What do you mean?" I asked with a small wonderous laugh.

A nervous pause was followed by, "—The Manor provides." There was that term again. Confusing and almost a mantra coming from her lips.

"We're going to discuss that further...*later*." I couldn't just leave it alone, but it wasn't the right time or place to press for answers. "For now..." I reached out to her.

Nuzzling against her neck, I pushed her hair out of my way with my nose and kissed her collarbone, ignoring the puzzled look on her face.

I took the hem of the light undergarment she had slipped on to come upstairs and slowly lifted it up her body, letting my hands graze along the soft curves beneath it.

Logically, I understood that she was entertaining me. She wasn't sore. Her muscles didn't ache like a normal person's. I could feel it in her touch as she carded her fingers through my hair, before lifting her arms above her, allowing me to remove the garment fully.

"I'm alright, Clay," she whispered as I straightened and looked down at her.

"Pretend you aren't and endure my fussing?" I asked her.

The corners of her mouth twitched into a smile. "Carry on," she granted.

"You are–" I stopped myself short of listing every compliment that flooded my mind at the sight of her naked.

Her arms crossed over her full breasts, giving herself a semblance of modesty. Perfect curves that rounded at her stomach and hips made me dizzy and flushed. Freckles marked her collarbone like constellations, mapping out over every inch of her. I wanted to spend hours kissing each one until I knew every story she had to tell.

"Clayton." The sound of her whining my name in protest to my adoration made my knees weak and brought a boyish smile to my lips.

"Wait," I said, reaching out to brush a knuckle against her forearm in reassurance. "I'm committing this to memory."

Florence huffed gently and shifted on her feet. Her thighs were rich and filled my hands as I granted her mercy from my gaze. I scooped her up from the floor against me, and she instantly wrapped her legs around my waist, pressing her face against my neck, hiding the pink color that had flooded her complexion.

"You make me nervous." She laughed against my skin and the muscles in my forearms tensed around her back.

"I was only admiring." I carefully lowered her into the water as it continued to fill. The water was warm, and her body relaxed when submerged.

I gently ran a cloth over her skin, touching every inch with a delicate hand as she closed her eyes and rested her head against the back of the tub.

"I'm sorry for my apprehension," she said after the comfortable silence stretched too tightly between us. I cleaned her shoulders' swooping arches and kissed her skin. "Matthew used to sleep in a different room," she started, stopping with a tiny huff.

I felt every muscle in my body constrict as a tear fell from her closed eyes.

"He would barge in after nights spent drinking with his colleagues or at the gentlemen's club in town." A heartbreaking laugh rumbled from her throat. "It was a means to an end; it was rough and vio... he wanted a son. He was obsessed with producing an heir. He didn't care about me or..." I watched as she wiped away a tear with the back of her hand. "...my pleasure," she finished. "Most of the time, I don't think he knew the difference between me and..." She stopped briefly, and I wasn't sure whether it was because she was deciding whether to omit something as she so frequently did, or to stop her confession altogether. So I sat still, barely breathing in the fear that she would close up and lock her innermost thoughts away again. "...Aisling. Matthew would force himself on her too." She hissed his name with fierce loathing, unlike I had heard from her before, and I knew it was because of her protectiveness for her friend. "Sometimes, he would scold me by her name if I spoke out, and I could only pray he would finish quickly and leave, or fall asleep... The worst nights were when he stayed."

When she paused this time, the silence was violent. The walls of the Manor seemed to shudder and contract towards her, as if cocooning around her protectively. I blinked hard and everything was as it had been, but I could have sworn. The Manor often seemed to have odd, inexplicable moments around Florence's moods.

I moved and rested my hand on her thigh. Fingers laid gently on the softness below the water.

"*Sex*," she said, cringing at the word. "It was never a partnership, never *intimate*. I had never experienced anything different until I was freed from him, but then I was alone. "

"I'm so sorry, Florence." I finally spoke, letting the cloth drift to the bottom of the tub.

She shook her head and opened her eyes. "What we did tonight? What you are doing now-" She reached out with a wet hand, the water dripping between us as she pressed her palm against my face. "I've never experienced that. It was overwhelming and fulfilling in the most incredible way. You were kind, and you cannot know what that means to me, Clay."

Fuck the research, I thought as the knowledge of her abuse lodged itself in my throat. How anyone could look at her and see her for anything but the angel she was baffled me. As she brushed her damp fingers through my hair, I realized there was no longer a single cell in my being that believed Florence was a monster.

OVER TIME THE MANOR HAS BEGUN TO CHANGE?

AT FIRST IT WAS NOT NOTICEABLE, SMALL OCCURRENCES LIKE SOMEONE HAD SWEPT OR DUSTED...

BUT NOW THE FURNITURE WAS POLISHED, THE FIREPLACES CLEANED, THE PLASTER AND PAINT REFRESHED?

IM STUDYING THE CONNECTION BETWEEN THE MANOR REVEALING ITS TRUE NATURE AND OUR RELATIONSHIP WITH FLORENCE.

WESLEY

Koen was carrying the total weight of my body when we slumped back into the Manor. His shirt was soaked through with blood from the collar down the left side of his body, which he had tucked beneath me. The wound was clean, but it had bled worse than Koen was prepared to deal with.

Clay crashed down the stairs, buttoning his shirt wrong with clumsy fingers as a yawn spread over his face, and he shook off the sleep we had woken him from.

"What the hell?" He shouted and jumped into action, taking Koen's place beneath me and helping me toward the kitchen. Koen stood, staring straight ahead with a glassy look in his usually bright green eyes.

The hunt had been brutal. *Two of the vampires had been children.*

I had been unable to put them down, or I would have.

He might have considered it a punishment, but I didn't mean it to be. Koen had had to step up.

On the way home, as he swerved through random traffic, trying to keep his composure, he said something to me. I was half awake, dealing with the explosive pain that radiated from my thigh, but when he started to talk, I did my best to listen.

"You know," he growled, anger building beneath his panic as a defense mechanism. "Just because you can't find your way back from the edge, Wes, doesn't mean the rest of us are lost out there in the darkness. Some of us like the sun."

I stared at him for a long moment, digesting those words and trying to understand what they meant. The stubborn part of me wanted to remind him that I had been keeping his ass alive for years and that in almost every life-threatening scenario, I had always come out right. But I kept my mouth shut and closed my eyes as the pain took over. I was deserving of that agony.

"Don't leave him there," I barked at Clay.

"Aye." Clay stopped in his tracks. "Ko!" His voice dropped an octave as he called out to a dissociating Koen. "Come on, pup." He whistled.

Koen's head turned slowly, briefly stopping to look down at his blood-covered skin before he stumbled after us into the kitchen.

"Two deep breaths," he ordered Koen. "You got him home. What's next?"

Koen stared at Clay, going to rub the confusion out of his eyes but stopped short, seeing his blood-stained fingers.

"Uh... The medical kit." He stumbled over the words, slowly coming back to reality.

"The kit." Clay pushed on Koen when he staggered up next to the island as Clay hauled me onto it. "In the study!"

Koen backed away, tripping over his feet and hauling ass toward the opposite end of the house.

"What the hell happened?" Clay stripped the shirt from my torso, the shredded fabric coming away in ribbons. My body screamed in pain as the threads pulled from the wounds. Flesh and fiber were fused together in sticky blood and drying gore.

"Nothing," I groaned, lifting my hips for him the best I could as he shucked my jeans from my legs.

He glared up at me, inspecting the wound on my thigh and hissing at the bubbling blood that pushed from the open wound. "This isn't *nothing*."

"No," I laughed, a blood loss delirium taking over me; I felt almost drunk. "That is from a machete!"

"What happened?" Its voice appeared from the other side of the kitchen, and I angled my head up to look at it with its pretty auburn hair and big emerald eyes.

"Get that thing away from me," I growled and squirmed under Clay's touch as I tried to get off the counter.

"Lay down, you twat," he spat at me and shoved me back against the butcher's block.

"Why are there a bunch of candles in the study?" Koen asked in a string of fumbled words as he burst back into the kitchen. "Oh." He stopped when he saw it standing there, eyes wide at the amount of blood on him.

I couldn't help the pained growl that exploded from me as it stepped toward him. I couldn't protect him in my weakened state. Which is exactly what it wanted. If it wanted to take them; it had just found its perfect opportunity.

"It's not mine," he said quietly, backing away from her with his blood soaked hands out in front of him. "I'm–" he stuttered before disappearing just as quickly as he had appeared.

"Koen!" Clay hollered but was never answered. For the second time his tone shifted, "I'm going to need your help."

I tilted my head up from the counter to look at him, thinking he was talking to me, but his eyes were on *it*.

"Hell no," I protested, but Clay was already rolling the bloody sleeves back from his wrists and digging in his bag.

"If she doesn't help, you'll bleed out in the next thirty minutes."

"Better off than dead than touched by that," I snapped and tried to move again, but Clay grabbed me roughly by the hair on the back of my head and stared at me.

"If you die," it spoke, "then you'll never get the satisfaction of finding out if you were right about me." It circled the table and looked at Clay.

"If I die in this fucking Manor..." I growled in pain as Clay pinched my skin on my side.

"Sorry," he chuffed, quite proud of himself, but continued to prod me.

It moved quickly and opened a cabinet in the far corner of the kitchen. The sounds of bottles being moved about and set down heavily on the counter pierced through the pulse in my head. When it returned it held two large green bottles, capped with a cork.

"These are clear spirits, they will help clean the wound," it said, its voice steadier than I would have expected from it, considering the amount of blood. It raised a delicate eyebrow as it uncorked a bottle. "Perhaps you should have a sip first, it's not going to be pleasant."

Clay didn't seem to have the same worry as he splashed the alcohol into the depths of the slash on my thigh. I almost shot off the counter hissing at the pain, but it held me down with a hand on my chest and handed me the bottle. Emerald eyes met mine. "Drink."

I took the bottle and swigged back the contents. I sputtered, spraying both myself and the two of them with what tasted like hundred proof lighter fluid. My head swam from the blood loss and the drink.

"How steady is your hand?" Clay asked, completely ignoring my continued groaning protests.

I've seen that look on his face before. It had been fleeting in the past, nothing to be concerned about, but whatever had happened while we were gone was a catalyst. Clay was under its spell. Something had happened between them. I surged forward and grabbed him by the collar, bloody fingerprints staining the fabric red.

"It got you," I blinked through the nauseating pain that cascaded through my entire body and waited for him to answer me.

"You can yell about it later after I save your god-forsaken life." He shoved me back down onto the counter and off him, and it splashed more of the stinging liquid into the wound, rubbing the blood from my skin enough to find where the wound began and ended. "Hold that there," he mumbled as my vision grew hazy around the edges.

"Where did Koen go?" I grumbled, but neither of them answered me. "What are you doing?" I kicked my leg out as a stab of pain vibrated through my muscles.

"You are worse than a child. Sit still," Clay demanded, his tone no longer soft or playful.

"Have him put this in his mouth," it said, holding out a wooden spoon to Clay, its hands were steady and it did not look away from the laceration that was oozing, it looked like it was calculating.

"Polite monsters are the worst," I choked and opened my mouth.

"As opposed to?" It rolled its pretty eyes at me and looked to Clay.

"Usually, I would have Koen for help, but considering his swift exit, I'd say he's done for the night. I'll hold him down..." Clay's words trailed off into a garbled silence as he came around to my side and held me down against the island top. "Go slow." He nodded.

I opened my mouth to object but pain ripped through my muscle as it started the first stitch, and I bit down hard on the wooden spoon. My entire body felt heavy and I knew it wouldn't be long before I went into shock, but I couldn't afford to fall asleep with its hands buried in my flesh.

"Hurry up," I growled, the spoon nearly falling from my lips.

"Be quiet," it snapped back and threaded the hooked needle through my tender skin. Clay looked like he might be sick as he watched it work through the first wound. "He's lost a considerable amount of blood, Clay."

"He'll be okay. He's too stubborn to die." His eyes met mine, full of concern. "Do the next one, don't stop."

Nausea swept over my body when my eyes finally opened. Every muscle heavy from exhaustion, it felt like I hadn't even fallen asleep.

At least I was alive.

I hadn't bled out on the table in the kitchen.

A noise from my left alerted me that I wasn't alone and I turned my head to find that monster slinking around the room, folding things on the dresser.

Its curves were highlighted in a corseted blouse and long brown skirt. Auburn hair was tucked into a bun, which exposed the long sweep of her neck–*Its* neck.

"Get out," I snapped, slipping slightly as I attempted to sit up in bed but my arm was too sore to move. I wrapped it tightly against my bare stomach to steady the dull throb that radiated through my muscles. The blankets fell around my hips and I huffed out a strangled breath as another wave of pain rolled through my bones. The brain fog slowly started to clear only to be replaced by nauseating fear.

"Where are they?"

Clay and Koen. When it finally turned to me its eyes were dark and tired with what appeared to be worry, an emotion I wasn't even sure it could feel. "They went into town to get supplies."

"How long ago?" I asked.

"They should be back soon. Do you need anything?"

"Not from you."

"Are you sore?" It asked, ignoring me.

"Of course I'm sore," I grumbled.

"Are you hungry?"

"Yes."

It disappeared and returned ten minutes later with a tray of warm tea and a bowl of something that smelled akin to chicken noodle soup. It set it down on the side table and pulled a chair up next to the bed.

"What are you doing?" I snapped at it.

"Currently? I'm acting as your bedside nurse, Mr. Cameron." It sighed. I hated the way my name sounded off its lips.

"You're a monster pretending to be a nurse."

"And you're a child pretending to be a man." Its dark green eyes were slits that met mine. "You remind me of the surly ravens that used to sit on the rooftops in the city and crow about their lives at the top of their lungs for everyone to hear. They would swoop down and peck and shred apart any creature smaller than they were and examine their insides–only then deciding after whether or not it was something worth devouring." Its hands grasped the tea cup and held it out to my lips. "I am not a carcass for you to shred. You can peck and pull at my skin all you want. I am still just a woman, Mr. Cameron."

I opened my mouth and let it press the cup to my lips, sipping the warm tea. I wanted so badly to refuse the help, to swat it away but, once the liquid hit my lips, I could not help but drink it greedily. It was perfectly made and settled against my sore chest like a balm to my exhausted soul. "If you poisoned it... At least it was a good cup of tea," I huffed begrudgingly, annoyed at the admission.

She smiled at me.

Shite.

"Don't do that," I snapped at it, shaking away the feeling of its gaze on me and narrowly escaping the warmth of its smile. "Do you know if Koen is okay?" I didn't want to make small talk but I needed to know if my brother was alright. That hunt had been...rough.

She–*It* stared at me for a long moment, no doubt waiting to see if I'd crack again. I couldn't help but admire the way her long lashes fluttered as she took me in.

"He's been quiet for a few days, but seemed to be in a better mood this morning."

"Days?" I groaned as it lifted the bowl of soup to my lips. It was hotter than the tea and scalded my tongue, but it was salty and instantly calmed the nerves in my stomach. It didn't have a foul after taste of mold and it made me uneasy as I leaned in for more and waited for her answer.

"You've been out for a week."

"What?" I choked on the soup and it held its hand beneath my chin to catch it running down my face. I pushed it away and rolled on the bed, hissing in pain as the stitches on my leg tugged tightly. "Mother of Christ," I growled and flipped the sheet back to look at the hack job, but there wasn't one.

The stitches were perfect, each a tiny, straight line all the same size, and the bruise around them had already started to fade and heal. "You did that?" I asked.

"I'm a very good nurse," it said, looking at the space I had created and clicking its teeth together.

"You make a terrible monster, though." It wasn't meant to be a joke, but when laughter filled the room, I couldn't help but smile at her. The laughter was honey, butterflies, and afternoon sunlight. It was *human*.

FLORENCE

Wesley slept most of the day. I had avoided telling him that Koen and Clay had gone on another hunt outside of town. Urgent enough that Clay woke Koen up in the middle of the night. He had fallen asleep before the sun went down, tucked into one of the rooms with the curtains drawn. His arms instinctively reached for me as I curled into the bed next to him.

"Can't it wait?" I asked Clay who shook his head.

"Wendigos don't wait, they just kill."

That had Koen out of bed, not saying a word to either of us as he dressed in clean clothes before following Clay out the front door.

The information would have led to unnecessary stress and he needed to spend all of his time healing. The conversation hadn't gone as horribly as I had braced for. He seemed a little kinder when he couldn't storm off in a huff after provoking an argument.

He had let me feed him almost three whole bowls of soup and fell asleep on a drool-covered pillow as I finished my tea in silence. I knew he wasn't comfortable with me; that wouldn't happen any time soon, but it was nice to have a moment with him when he wasn't actively trying to relieve me of my head.

There was an odd sense of peace while he slept. His angry features softened in the dreary afternoon light that peaked through the cracks in the curtains. He had eaten a fair amount and, I wasn't entirely sure, but he may have even cracked a smile.

"Do you just lurk around all day?" He asked me, eyes still closed.

His face contorted in pain as he shifted in his bed.

"If I was in another part of the Manor I wouldn't be able to hear you if you needed help," I answered from my chair.

One hazel eye opened and stared me down in question.

"You slept through dinner," I told him.

"And I still feel like shite," Wesley groaned and pushed himself up into a sitting position. The blanket fell around his waist, exposing the hard lines of his biceps and the contradicting soft expanse of his stomach. Usually, his golden curls were swept back off his face but, in the skirmish of homebrewed surgery and restless sleep, they had become unruly and stuck out every which way.

It made him look innocent. Something we both knew he wasn't.

"And you still look it," I shot back at him. I found that communicating with Wesley, if it *could* be considered communicating, was easier if I met him at his level. His brows raised up at me in surprise, but I could see a twinkle of humor in his eyes.

"Are you hungry again?" I asked.

"I don't want any more soup," he snapped and flipped the blankets back. "I need to move. If I lay there any longer I'm going to get bed rot."

"Are you able?"

The look he tossed over his shoulder was murderous.

"You seem to have forgotten you have a deep, severe tear in your thigh. It will make it difficult for you to move around unaided." I didn't back down from him. I spent the first half of my life cowering under the shadows of tempermental men like Wesley, and worse. I was not about to go back to that now, here, in my own home.

"I can walk," he argued, hazel eyes glaring at me as he pushed off the bed with one hand, toppling against the post and wrapping his hand tightly around it to keep his balance. "Don't you have a curse to put on someone or a puppy to kill?"

"I only kill fully grown men with prickly attitudes that lack manners," I responded, my voice dripping in sarcasm. "Curses take too much time."

"*Please*, leave me the fuck alone," he said.

I scowled at him, hating how easily dismissed he thought I was. Swallowing the annoyance, I excused myself as he struggled to enter the bathroom. A petty smile touched my lips as I heard the sound of crashing and a string of creative curses from beyond the door.

It would have been easier if he had been less pigheaded but I had a feeling that being cooperative wasn't something Wesley could do. He was so set on hating me and what he believed I was that he refused to do what was best for himself and his recovery. I found myself in the kitchen making him food regardless of the stubborn behavior, and was annoyed at myself for it.

The fowl in the oven smelled suitable and, for the first time in a long time, I wished that I was hungry. I chewed on my lip as I cut carrots, wondering what might happen if I cut off a limb. But that was just Wesley in my head, polluting my thoughts with scenarios I'd already run.

I hover the knife over my hand, contemplating it. I could live without a finger if it didn't grow back, and maybe it would quell the fear that I was indeed a monster.

The window in the Manor blew open and a tickle of air brushed against my jaw and throat, almost *encouraging* violence. I froze and waited for the Manor to settle.

A knock at the door cut short the next wave of morbid hypothesizing. I set the knife down in panic. In all of my time spent wandering around the Manor, never once had *anyone* knocked on the door. Not once. I stared at the knife for a second, contemplating leaving it behind only a moment before I huffed and picked it back up. I made my way toward the front door with it clutched in my fist, and tucked behind my apron inconspicuously.

"Don't open it," Wesley said from the top of the stairs; he leaned over the railing with his gun gripped in his hand, breathing heavily and bearing his whole weight on the bannister.

"You shouldn't be out of bed." I looked up at him and his eyes dropped to the hidden knife in my hand. "It's probably nothing."

"That's why you're armed." Wesley started to limp down the stairs, using the railing to hold him upright. His face crumpled into a tight expression as he hit the main floor unevenly. "Open the door slowly," he instructed as he pressed himself against the wall. He was out of breath and blood had started to seep through his sweatpants. "And give me that." He put his hand out, palm up for the knife, but I shook my head.

"It's probably nothing," he mocked and shook his hand at me again.

"Fine." I hand him the knife by the handle and straighten my skirt before opening the door. "Hello," I greet the man behind it, eyes tracing over his county uniform. Tight, tense nerves rolled through me and I resisted the urge to look at Wesley for guidance. "Can I help you, Constable?"

Wesley took a shaky breath beside me just out of view. I had said something wrong.

The man before me was tall with ruddy features and dark eyes. He was wearing a constables uniform and his hand rested gently on his weapon. His beady eyes trailed down my person, lingering on my chest and curves. It filled my throat with bile and made me want to shield myself from his gaze. But that wasn't the only feeling clawing at me...

Something was wrong with the man. A darkness oozed from him into the air and made it hard to breathe. The Manor practically hissed in response. My stance became shaky under his sinister stare, and my shoulders dropped as I made to step back away from him. I was scared of the unknown and suddenly felt much smaller than usual.

"Don't cower," Wesley whispered, his voice so low I barely heard it.

I pinned my shoulders back at his warning and stepped closer to the door, closer to Wesley. I leaned against the wood and felt Wesley's warm breath fan across my shoulder.

"Good evening, ma'am, I'm Sergeant Allen." He extended his other hand to me, and Wesley tensed, waiting for me to shake it.

"Florence Cabot." I offered him my name.

"Mrs. Cab–"

"Miss," I corrected him.

"Miss." He started again. "We're canvasing the outer-lying homes of the community for any information you may have on a group of men involved in a triple homicide. If you've seen them, I urge you to share any information you may have on them. They are extremely dangerous and without a moral code. We'd appreciate any help with the matter."

"A triple homicide?" I asked, trying to appear meek and confused.

"They killed three officers, Miss," he explained, stepping forward toward the threshold. "We're to believe the suspects are still in the area and armed. They're driving a dirty, white Bronco."

He goes on to give me their descriptions and it's clear that they're looking for Wesley, Clay, and Koen. But there was something off about the officer in front of me. His distant, cold stare made my skin itch uncomfortably. I held my hands behind my back and knotted them together to keep them from shaking. He watched me with caution, his curiosity growing with each passing moment.

"I haven't seen them or the vehicle you've described. I'm sorry I can't be of more help," I responded with a subdued tone.

"Are you sure?" He asked.

I nodded politely, flinching when he dug in his pocket. I felt Wesley step forward, his hand brushing against my side. This was the closest he had been by choice.

"My card." He extended a piece of white paper and I unfolded my hands to take it. "If you see them, don't open your doors to them. Call that number immediately and we'll come. Thank you for your time, Miss Cabot." He nodded at me, eyes lingering just a little on my chest as he backed away.

As he stepped off the steps, I closed the door and let out the breath I was holding in the form of a gasped sob. Wesley stayed where he was, using the wall as support while he watched me.

"You have to breathe," he demanded but the cut to his tone was encouraging. "He didn't buy your bullshit. He's not leaving."

"What?" I turned to look at him with panic shaking in my voice.

"Time to be a monster," he said, darkness engulfing his hazel eyes.

I could tell him that if the sergeant did indeed mean to harm me, the Manor would likely take care of it. But lately it felt like the walls weren't on my side. Ever since the night with Clay, I had been victim to micro-aggressions, dark thoughts slipping in and out of my consciousness urging me to hurt myself or worse. It subtly punished me, thinking I wouldn't notice, but I had. It wanted me to behave but it was hard when I was now being pulled in different directions.

"Hey!" Wesley barked when I didn't answer his muffled first question. "Pay attention. How many entrances are there to this place?" Wesley asked, hobbling forward and clicking the front shut.

"The kitchen, the back leading out to the yard, one in the conservatory, and a side servant entrance. Why?" I inhaled shallow breaths that did nothing to slow my racing heart.

"Close the kitchen and the back," he ordered, shoving the knife at me. "And go quickly."

"What about the side?" I asked, staring down at the blade.

"Let him think he's got you trapped," Wesley explained. "A false sense of confidence will make him sloppy."

"You're being vague." My voice shook as I took the knife from him and gripped it in my sweaty hand.

"It's simple. You're going to have to fight." He looked at me as he stumbled to the sitting room.

WESLEY

I wasn't going to admit that she had done a good job.

I could barely admit she—*it* wasn't a monster. But there it was.

"Take this." I checked the knife blade and waited for it to return to the sitting room. It had pinned its skirt around one of its full legs, making its movements smoother but exposing the supple skin of her—*its* thigh. I swallowed tightly as it approached.

It looked down at the serrated blade with a curious look.

"It tears," I explained, running my finger over the steel teeth with the pad of my finger. "It'll inflict more damage than your kitchen knife; trade me."

It considered the blade. I could feel the apprehension as it rolled from its tight shoulders. I knew it had the capabilities, the bloodthirsty drive. It had taken the kitchen knife to protect itself in the first place. The instinct was present; she—*it* just needed to find the courage to use it.

"The ghoul won't hesitate," I warned it. "If it gets the chance to kill you. It will take it without mercy."

"He can't kill me...what if I just..." It stepped back but I surged forward and grabbed its wrist, holding it tightly so it would look at me.

"This isn't about you," I said. "This is about all the children it and its ghoul friends have killed, and will go on to kill. This is about stopping it from hurting anyone else."

Her sad, green eyes flickered to my hand and I released her without question.

My head was swimming, light and dizzy from being upright for so long. I was confused, maybe even slightly disoriented.

"He was one of the ghouls?" *She* questioned. I shook my head and cleared my scrambled thoughts.

It, Wes... It's *a monster.*

"Yes, and it's probably stalking the Manor right now looking for a way in because it's pissed off, hungry, and you're a..." I swallowed down the urge to call it a woman. "You're alone. At least it thinks you are."

"You can't help me in this condition. You should hide," she said with a sniffle as she switched knives with me. Her–*Its* hands shook so violently for a split second that I thought it might drop it, but it pulled itself together like before.

Its expression darkened and it shook out any fear that may have gripped it moments before.

"No." I shook my head.

"You're bleeding, won't he smell that?" It pointed to the torn stitches on my thigh. It stared at it for a moment longer before taking the blade to its forearm.

"Hey." I reached out to stop her, but it was too late.

The blade ripped through her flesh and left a red, bleeding line across her skin. Before I could do anything about the wound, she was dropping to her knees. She used the knife and tore a long strip from the bottom of her skirt clumsily. She used the torn fabric to soak up the blood pouring from her arm, the strip turning dark red before she wrapped it tightly around my thigh and knotted it.

I bit down on my tongue at the sight of her on her knees, helping me the best she could, even battling her own fear. *God damnit.*

"Now he'll only smell me," she explained and stood back up. I grabbed her arm but the wound was healing by the time she finished her little unexpected plan.

"Don't do that again," I warned her, hiding the concern in my voice.

"Go find somewhere to hide. You can't fight like this," she ordered.

Unfortunately it wasn't the time or place to flex her newfound confidence.

"I'm not hiding," I scoffed at her. "I just need the upper hand."

"An unfair fight." She nodded, finally understanding.

"The ghoul will be strong," I explained to her. "Stronger than you, but if you can keep it distracted, I can take it by surprise and it should be enough to take it down."

We both heard the sharp click of a door opening from our left, the sound echoing down the hall toward us.

"Are you ready?" I asked her.

She shook her head no.

"Too bad. Go to the kitchen, pretend you're unaware." I nodded toward the arch and saw her off before wandering around toward the sound of the intruder's footsteps.

The ghoul wasn't quiet about its presence in the Manor, giving away its location as it wandered down the hallway toward the sitting room. For the first time in over a month I was glad the guys had begun nesting immediately. All our belongings had been moved from the parlor to our rooms upstairs and there was no trace of us on the main floor.

The ghoul turned the corner and I pressed tightly against the bookshelf out of sight. Its beady eyes dragged over the room, carefully taking in its surroundings. I was sure the ghoul had seen me as its gaze trailed the wall I was tucked around, its nose turned up and its face scrunched in disgust before stepping out. My thigh throbbed from all of the movement. A tight, stinging pain radiated through the muscle up into my hip and back, making it hard to stay still.

I moved the moment the ghoul slipped from view, wanting to track its movement so it wouldn't catch Florence off guard. It was seconds limping across the foyer before I realized my mistake, too focused on protecting that God-forsaken monster to notice that I was being stalked. I turned too slow and it was on top of me, its hands moving faster than mine as it slammed a fist into the side of my face.

The pain from the punch vibrated through me. I dropped to the ground, hard and, without the ability to soften my blow, I was slow to defend myself. The ghoul took another cut before I had a chance to shove it back and it landed squarely with force into my collarbone. I grunted as it hovered, grabbing the neckline of my shirt and pulling me toward it off of the floor.

"You stink," the ghoul sneered. Its disguises dropped, revealing the gruesome characteristics that gave away its inhumanity.

"Speak for yourself." I ground my teeth together and lifted my leg in a failed attempt to push it off me, but it was too strong.

"You killed my kin." Its tongue flicked out over its bottom lip, changing and growing into a less human and more monstrous gray fleshy muscle as spit dangled from its maw in a gooey stream that hit my cheek in a wet, warm splash.

"Your kin were assholes." I slammed my head upward, catching the ghoul in the mouth with my forehead. A violent storm of stars danced through my head but the action had given me an opening to shove my knife between its ribs, plunging it deep, turning it over, and ripping it out just as quickly.

The stabbing caught it off guard and it snarled, stumbling backward from me and letting go of my sweater. The ghoul didn't slow down though; it advanced towards me before I was able to get off the ground, but I trained my gun between its eyes as it caught its breath.

"You Hunters all are the same. Sloppy and blood-hungry. I'm going to finish you," it threatened, "and then I'll find your brother—" It paused to watch my reaction to its words. "He's in the system for some pretty bad things, won't be hard to find once I put an APW out on him. Same with the Dunn kid, both of them will be dead within the week."

"You attacked the wrong Hunter." I spit a gob of blood to my right, the copper tang filling my mouth as I spoke. "The other two are dangerous and uninjured." I laughed, but nothing about the situation was funny. "You must be a coward, picking low-hanging fruit!" I kicked out and my foot connected with its wound, causing it to growl out a string of curse words.

The ghoul was back on me faster than I expected, its long nails digging into my throat and drawing blood. The smell of it made its pupils shake and widen, completely blacking out the rusty brown color of its irises. The ghoul was too strong. Without both arms, I was too weak. I didn't stand a chance to get it off of me and its grasp on my neck was restricting the oxygen to my brain.

My vision blurred around the edges as the ghoul leaned into me with all its weight behind it.

"When I'm done with you and them I'll come back here and fuck that pretty little thing until she can't move." Its voice was sick and the thought of its twisted violence made my blood boil. There was a small chink in my armour as my subconscious raged at the thought of it defiling her.

"She smelled like candy," it said. "It's how I found you, you dumb shite. She's all over you."

"I'd prefer it if you didn't." Florence's voice was dark and annoyed, if a little shaky.

The ghoul reared its ugly head back in surprise as slender, soft hands gripped its hair. The blade tore viciously through the tender meat of its throat and blood sprayed from its severed flesh. The ghoul stumbled for a second, its eyes fluttering open and closed as it fought to control the bleeding with hands that were half human, half curved sharp claws that clasped around the gaping wound. But it wasn't enough. It collapsed on its knees, rocking forward and crashing over me.

The air flooded back into my lungs, my body wrenching from the sensation as it regulated. The creature's body writhed for a moment longer before it went completely still and limp on top of me. The ghoul's sticky, dark ichor soaked through my shirt and smelled like gasoline. It filled the air as I shoved it off me onto the floor and pushed to my elbows.

"I told you to go to the kitchen," I coughed.

Her skirt was covered in blood. A thick droplet of crimson streamed down her round, bare thigh where the fabric bunched out of the way. Hands trembled around the soaked blade. Her green eyes drained of any spirit and trained on the knife in her possession.

I pushed off the ground, stifling the pained groan on my lips as I stumbled on my sore leg toward her. I reached out, took the knife from her stained hands, and threw it away toward the wall. She was utterly still and silent, probably shocked by what she had done.

She had saved my life.

She.

"*Florence*," I said, her name feeling strange on my tongue and her eyes flickered to meet mine. Confusion, a little shock but mostly fear. "Go wash up."

She lifted her hands a little but shook her head, straightening her back and swallowing thickly before stepping to my side.

"We need to get you back to bed," Florence said tightly, completely ignoring the baffled look on my face. "I have to restitch your thigh. If you bleed out in the foyer it would be awfully unfortunate, after all that." Her eyes remained unfocused and far away as she spoke. "May I?" She asked before touching me.

I lifted my arm so she could brace my weight and nearly scoffed at how tiny she looked tucked against my frame. I almost doubled her size, yet she took the weight like it was nothing and guided me back to the stairs.

We took the steps slowly, one at a time, each more painful than the last.

I gripped Florence tighter than I would have liked, hating how human her skin felt to my touch. She hadn't said another word, even as we crossed the threshold into the room, and she let me limp the rest of the way alone. She had to be a bundle of adrenaline and shock. Her fingers shook violently, barely able to untie the fabric around my thigh but, eventually, she broke the knot and let it fall away.

I snapped my fingers and watched her haunted emerald eyes focus.

Without a word she flexed her hands out in front of her as she shook her head, took the moment to right herself, and went back to work.

The word trousers was mumbled, along with a few tiny curse words that sounded funny from her lips as I shifted my sore hips and pushed my pants down with one hand. The stitches I had popped were hanging haphazardly from my raw and swollen skin, but it wasn't bleeding as much as I assumed it would.

Stitching up the irritated skin was going to hurt.

"Are you going to be able to sit still while I fix this?" Florence asked me.

Her eyes never left my skin. The only feeling worse than touching her was the look of sympathy in her eyes as she traced over the skin. I bit down on my lip to keep from reassuring her that it would be okay, that she had done an excellent job. That the ghoul deserved to die. But she was still a monster, wasn't she? A creature lurking beneath the guise of a beautiful woman, just as bad as that ghoul and, at the end of the day, she was still the enemy.

"Just stitch it," I said through a clenched jaw.

She shook her head, clearly frustrated, but at least she wasn't lingering any longer. She brushed her bloodied fingers against her shirt and untied the bunched fabric so it finally fell loose, covering her legs. The sharp, stinging pain in my chest was hard to ignore when she was so vulnerable.

A delirious state of weakness.

"Florence." Her name rolled off my lips for the second time that evening, stopping her in her tracks. "Thank you."

Close, and yet so far from the desired outcome. The ghoul had been sniffing cautiously about the property for days, recognizing the 'other' though, like most, not quite knowing what it was. It angled to find a way in, testing the weak iron fencing at the northernmost point and deciding better of it. Then, to its surprise, the doors to the grand gate swung open in welcome to it. It was allowed to walk up the front steps and place its disgusting hands on the door, all in the hopes that it would follow its nature and devour the injured man inside.

The man's aura was always dark, despite the lightness of his features, pulsing in onyx and graphite and navy. He reeked of suspicion, and hostility, and the deaths of many. The other two were a problem easily dealt with, separately or together- it wouldn't matter. This one, this one needed to be handled differently. The ghoul offered the perfect opportunity.

He was weakened, he could not protect her from the outside world the way she needed. There were evils far more violent and hideous out in the world that could, *would,* harm her outside of these walls. The men were nothing more than distractions, weak and unmemorable. The Manor was a haven, a shelter against the world and the dangers that walked it. The ghoul would have quickly met its fate after the man met his.

She challenged the result. She did not cower as expected. She did not shrink down into the walls and wait to be defended. She protected herself *and* the man. Coated in fear and yet courageous all the same, the knife slid through the neck of the beast and its life ended by her hand. She was power, she was rage, she was vitality. The Manor drank her in and glowed at the revelation. This had been unexpected, this could be something new. The walls cinched in tighter.

...HERE IS AN ARCTILE ON
...RENCE'S LATE HUSBAND

...REPORTS POINTED TO AN
...BOLISM. ALL ACCOUNTS OF
...E INCIDENT CAME FROM HIS
CARRIAGE STAFF.

...E OLD PAPER WAS IN BAD SHAPE, BUT WHAT I
...OULD GET FROM IT WAS THAT LORD CABOT WAS
ACTING IRRATIONALLY TOWARD THE MANOR.
SCREAMING, THROWING ROCKS AND OTHER
OBJECTS AT WINDOWS IN AN ATTEMPT TO
SHATTER POSSIBLY? TAKING AN AXE TO THE
DOOR?

THE REPORTS FROM THE STAFF WERE WEAK AT
BEST AND MISSING INFORMATION. IT APPEARED AS
THOUGH HE HAD SENT THEM ALL HOME IN A FURY
AND WAS FOUND A DAY LATER OUTSIDE THE
GATES, BLEEDING FROM HIS EARS AND DEAD.

THEY BELIEVED HE DIED OF
AN EMBOLISM, BUT MY
WORKING THEORY IS THAT THE
MANOR EXPELLED HIM MUCH
LIKE IT DOES TO FLORENCE T...
...ER INSIDE...

FLORENCE

The kitchen was flooded with the smells of a roast. It had become an odd source of comfort, cooking with them, sitting with them at the table. Sometimes even eating small bits of the meal myself. It usually helped me feel normal, feel human.

It did not seem to be having the same effect today.

I cut into the carrots at the counter with a sharp knife as I stared out over the side of the property. The dark, dancing flower beds were a welcome distraction from the last two days of wrongdoings.

Snap.

Carrots? Carrots. My mind produced gruesome images and sickening echoes of the sound of the monster's breaking bones.

Bones...

I looked down at my hands, no longer covered in blood but the longer I stared at them, the more unsure I became, each long blink playing ruthless tricks on my mind. Blood caked my skin and soaked my nail beds. I ran the water hot and let it bite my skin as I furiously scrubbed the flesh of my palm.

Breathe.

It was gone. There was no more blood—just a sore set of hands and a racing heart.

The false constable, the *ghoul*, as Wesley had called it, was spread around the back half of the property in pieces that had taken me two days of puking and cursing to cut up and disperse. I hadn't spoken to Wesley since. Something unknown had shifted between us and I couldn't stand the fever I felt under his speculating stare. Waiting until he slept, I left food and kept my distance.

The Manor seemed at peace without Clay and Koen around. It drank in the violence that happened happily, the stained floorboards pristine again as it licked up every last drop of blood that had been spilled.

But I couldn't shake the feeling of dread that settled against my bones. I had never taken a life. I had been witness to death, watching lives come to a natural end, and had attempted to take my own multiple times. But I had never wielded the blade that ended it. It haunted me.

I felt disconnected. *I felt like a monster.*

Moving back to the carrots I continued to remind myself that they were vegetables and not human remains but my mind continued to flicker between the two, unable to decipher the difference. I was losing it.

"Florence?" Clay's voice rounded the corner, and my heart leaped. His handsome face followed quickly behind. His cheeky grin spread wide and those slate eyes searched for me as he carried two large paper bags. "There you are." He slid the bags across the island and wrapped an arm around me. I could tell from the way his gaze moved around the kitchen that his surroundings had started to change. That the Manor was showing its beauty in small pieces. No longer so run down to their eyes, but restoring inch by inch before them. Clay's brow furrowed the way it always did when he was lost in thought but he shook free as I squeezed his side and brought him back to reality.

"There's a police car out front. What the hell is that about?"

The one problem I couldn't solve before they returned. I didn't know how to start or drive the vehicle, but it needed to be disposed of before someone came looking for it.

I swallowed the tears that stung the corners of my eyes and reached out to him.

"What's wrong?" He asked, the eyes searching mine filled with worry. I shook my head. "You should speak to Wesley."

He looked down at me, slightly releasing his grip around my waist to make better eye contact. "Florence?" He stared at me momentarily, a thousand questions flickering over his hardened expression.

"Speak to him, he'll explain." I took his hand and kissed the palm, needing the tender moment of connection. His head pulled to the side, unsure of my mood, but his hand brushed my cheek softly and his lips gently met the corner of my downturned mouth in a kiss.

"Rude," Koen huffed, balancing more bags in his arms as he stumbled into the kitchen. "Now I see why you only took two." He rolled his eyes and dropped the bags.

"You say that like it's my fault. You're the one who bought so much shite," Clay said, righting his mood. His hands left my face as he turned around to face Koen.

"We brought presents."

His bright green eyes were enough to pause the consistent storm of every horrible moment that happened during their absence. He smiled at me, dimple deep as he flashed those white teeth and warmed the cold fear that gripped me tightly into nothing but simple worry.

"For me?" I forced a smile to my face for him and pushed onto my toes to see the inside of the bags.

"It's a secret." Koen shooed me away with a soft pat on my rump. "For after dinner."

"You two are trouble." I looked between them, Clay in his white dress shirt, the fabric so fine I could trace the tattoos on his biceps with my eyes. Koen was in a hole-infested, what had he called it? A band t-shirt, and his blond, sun-kissed hair was messy beneath his backward hat.

Dangerous.

I sighed, feeling the Manors' presence. Its short-lived silence ended with the return of Clay and Koen.

Clay smirked, leaning against the cupboard and tucking his hands into his pockets as he stared at me. "You have no idea," he purred.

Koen's head cocked to the side and his eyebrows raised. "I'll go check on Grumpy," he shrugged and returned to acting a little weird. The relationship was still tense between them. Leaving for days and not talking wasn't helping Koen come to terms with the incident.

"I'll do it," Clay voiced loudly and nodded. "Stay here and help Florence." He pressed his lips into a thin line and excused himself from the kitchen.

"Blossom." Koen smiled, but it didn't reach his eyes.

It was apparent that he was still reeling from everything. His time away with Clay hadn't helped his confidence. I held my hand out and waited for him to circle the table.

"What happened that day?" I asked him. He had been tip-toeing around telling me.

Koen swallowed and pulled his hand from mine. "Nothing."

"Oh, well that's how I know you're lying," I say, motioning to his hand leaving mine.

He started to unpack the bags and put things on the counter ab-sent-mindedly. I followed behind him closely, putting everything in its proper place and noticed that they had bought some things I'd never seen before.

"What is this?" I asked him, holding up a white and blue box and shaking it gently to get his attention.

"Oh, Baby," Koen's eyes lit up, forcing a smile to his face. He slid back to me and popped the box open, tearing the plastic with his teeth and pulling a small cake-looking log from inside. "This is heaven. Open up." He cupped his hand and set the end of the cake on my tongue.

I wrapped my lips around it and closed my eyes, brows pinching together as the icing melted on my tongue and sweet vanilla coated my mouth. A low moan left my throat and, when my eyes fluttered open, Koen was staring at me with blown pupils and the devil's grin on his face.

"You've got—" He set the cake down and cupped my face, bringing his lips to the corner of my mouth and kissing it slowly. "—icin'." He licked his lips as he pulled away, thumb brushing away the rest of the icing he missed with his mouth.

"You're good at that," I whispered.

"At what?" He narrowed his eyes on me.

"Avoiding the question." I looped a finger into his to hold him in place as he started to back away at my words. "What happened that's got you all in knots, Koen?"

"Everything went sideways during the hunt that shouldn't have. He should have just brought Clay. We were so angry with each other." Koen sighed. Once the floodgates opened he didn't know how to stop. "I was so busy being pissed off at him that we got ambushed from behind. It was my fault we were outnumbered, all because I got distracted."

Koen's green eyes looked painfully sad when he looked up to meet mine.

"And then." he swallowed and looked away from me in an effort to hide the tears welling in his eyes. "They had turned a few kids and we couldn't leave them there, but Wes was hurt, and I had..." He cleared his throat and I waited for him to finish. "I've never had to kill a kid before, monster or not. That..."

"Koen." I wrapped my hand around his face and tugged his attention back to mine, the sun illuminating the raw pain in his expression. "There is nothing I can say to erase the pain you feel but, for the time being, until it fades..." I took a long, deep breath in. "Find comfort in the fact that you saved Wesley; he's alive because of *you*."

"But those kids," he choked out.

"Weren't children anymore. You said it yourself."

I knew that he would latch onto the undertones of the conversation, his jaw twitching tightly as he realized. Monsters come in all shapes and sizes.

His eyes widened as a quiet thought turned loud.

"I won't do that," he snapped with conviction. "It doesn't matter, I won't, I'll stand between him. I won't let him do that to you."

"We're talking about real monsters, Koen. Not me."

"It's all the same to him." He gently shook his head, eyes darting from mine to the floor.

"We don't have to worry about that for now." I scrunched my nose at him. "Finish with those. Dinner is almost ready and I want my presents."

I could see him packing away the heavy emotions and letting the smile come back to his face, but he was still so sad and there was very little I could do to help ease that short of turning back time. Koen helped set the table and Clay managed to help Wesley limp down the stairs and to the dining room to eat.

"You even wore pants. How kind of you," I quipped when he arrived in the room in sweatpants that rode low on his hips and a plaid shirt he left unbuttoned.

"Clay gave me a sponge bath, so I didn't stink," he grumbled and slumped into the chair.

Clay's eyebrows raised as he looked between us. "Did you two just make jokes?"

"Don't read into it." Wesley leaned back in the chair and waited for me to plate him some food. "I'm here for food that isn't rotted through to its core. It only says fresh when she makes it."

Koen's face scrunched up in confusion, a small smile playing on his lips.

"They killed the last ghoul," Clay said to Koen, whose head whipped in my direction. "It showed up while we were gone to finish us off, and Florence helped little Miss Sunshine."

"I helped Florence," Wesley interjected as he adjusted in the chair and rested on the table.

"Unfortunately, I don't know how to operate the car," I noted. "And Wesley was in no condition to help me move it." I set the bowl of butter-soaked carrots down.

"What did you do with the body?" Clay asked. His forearms flexed on the dining table as he leaned over to catch my gaze.

"Can we not discuss the details over dinner?" I asked him, but he wasn't going to budge. He stared at me with those stern eyes, more gray than blue today, and waited. Holding dinner hostage until he was informed of every detail. "I spread it around the grounds."
Wesley choked on his water.

"What do you mean... spread?" Koen asked, unable to hide the surprised tone.

"I dismembered its body and buried the pieces in the soil as far from the house as I could get." I swallowed the nausea that rose, thinking about how carefully I had to creep around the grounds. A few missteps ended in me with bruises so big and sore I cared not to disclose them.

"You ...chopped him up?" Wesley asked crudely, setting down his glass and narrowing his eyes at me.

"Was I supposed to leave him in the foyer?" I questioned.

"You could have waited," Koen scoffed. "We could have helped. You shouldn't have made her do that." His words jumbled together as his head whipped toward Wesley.

"I didn't *make* her do anything!" He defended himself and pointed at his bandaged arm.

"We would have done it." Koen turned back to me, his arm extended as his fingers brushed over my forearm.

"I know it's not very ladylike but there are more than enough books on human anatomy in the library. I think I've proven I'm quite good with bodies and it kept me busy." I said like my mind was slowly breaking down from the memory of the violence.

"You're a—, Florence...not a..." Clay tilted his head to the side, stumbling over his words.

"A murderer?" I finished for him.

"I was going to say Lady."

"It seems that even after a hundred or more years of living, there are still things you can learn about yourself. He was going to kill Wesley. I had no choice," I said with a curt nod.

The men went quiet as eyes fell on Wesley at the other end of the table from me. I was surprised to see that his hazel eyes were not narrowed harshly as was their typical fashion. They were almost soft and void of anything but what looked like guilt as he nodded at me.

"Now, if you're finished, you must be hungry from your drive and I would like to hear about the hunt you were on." I bundled my skirts in my hands and sunk into my chair, but none moved for a long moment, locked in some sort of silent conversation I wasn't privy to. "Eat, please.

FLORENCE

The three started and didn't stop after that point. Koen told me all about the wendigo they tracked down and disposed of as they devoured dinner, speaking in tiny bursts of conversation but never directly talking about the issue. The tension in the room over what had happened between them was palpable as I cleared the table and started to do the dishes. The sink was full as I wandered into the kitchen, ready for me and perfectly warm.

"Thank you," I whispered, trying to remind the Manor that I was still aware of our arrangement even as my heart was pulled in different directions. *The Manor provides;* and it had proven so with warm soapy water that overflowed with bubbles.

"What do you think you're doing?" Clay chuckled and rolled his sleeves over his forearms. "Shoo." He waved into the sink, catching bubbles in his fingers and spraying them in my direction.

"I can do the dishes, Clay."

"Aye," he grumbled, "but you aren't going to. I think you've done enough around here for a long while. *Let me.*"

I dried my hands on the towel and leaned against the counter to watch him scrub each plate clean, one by one, his focus on the soapy water. The muscles in his jaw tightened and I could tell he was distracting himself from asking me a tricky question.

"Out with it then," I said finally as he stacked the last dish.

He cast those gray eyes on me and chuckled, drying his hands on the towel. "You're too perceptive."

"Or you're just not good at hiding what's on your mind?" I challenged him.

"Perhaps a bit of both?" He huffed. "I don't think the awkwardness between Koen and Wesley will be solved anytime soon but seeing the two of you without your weapons drawn is nice."

The weapons were still very much drawn.

"Don't get too enthused. I'm sure he's still sniffing for reasons to prove us all wrong."

"He can sniff all he wants, he can barely get himself down the hall and he won't be doing anything anytime soon. Besides, you saved his life, he's in debt now."

"I'm not sure he sees it that way," I said.

"He does." Clay seemed sure. He reached out and brushed his fingers over my chin with a wink. "Now." He offered the crook of his elbow to me. "Let's get you upstairs. I'm sure Koen has started to chew the furniture."

I giggled and wrapped my hand around his arm, letting him lead me through the house and up the stairs. "Are you alright?" He asked as my fingers curled into his skin.

I killed a man...a monster. I was far from alright.

"Of course," I lied, and he opened the door to the bedroom for me.

Koen had piled the four-poster bed with bags and a few boxes which made my heart thump wildly. As we entered the bedroom he looked pretty proud of himself and Clay closed the door behind us. The leading light from the window was quickly fading but the fireplace on the main wall was roaring and the two sconces on the far wall were lit.

"What's all this?" I asked, unlinking myself from Clay to inspect further.

"Go on and look," Clay whispered, his chest pressed to my back.

I started with one of the bags, pulling out a bundle of clothing far from the everyday skirts and corsets. My brows furrowed at the sight of the T-shirts and sweaters and I was confused about why they would do such a thing for me.

"We thought it was about time you got to upgrade your wardrobe!" Koen smiled ear to ear with the brightest look in his playful green eyes. "So we bought you some of everything. You can try it all on and figure out what you like and don't like..." He trailed off when Clay cleared his throat.

"Florence?" Clay wrapped his arms around me from behind and rested his chin on my shoulder. "You don't have to do anything. It was a gesture. We can return it all; just say the word."

"No." I swallowed the overwhelming nerves that rose in my throat and turned to smile at Koen. "This is just–" I chewed on my lower lip, "It's an odd feeling to be thought about in this manner."

"It's about time you're thought of in every manner." Koen didn't hesitate to counter my statement.

"Alright then." He clapped his hands and looked around the room, moving toward one of the two sitting chairs before angling them away from the fireplace toward the bed.

He plopped down in it and smiled at me.

"Oh, you want me to do it now?" I laughed. "Ulterior motives."

"Yes!" Koen cheered at the same time as Clay responded, "if you feel so inclined," in my ear.

Clay released me. "I picked the room with the dressing shade," he noted. It was easier now that both of them saw the Manor for what it could be. Beautiful and rich with life. I wasn't sure Wesley would ever get to that point but it made Clay and Koen more comfortable with each passing day.

"We aren't complete hooligans."

I shook my head. "*Unbelievable.*"

"*You* are," Clay whispered over my shoulder before stepping back.

"Help a lady," I said, reaching out to him as heat licked my cheeks.

The corset I wore that morning was laced and, while I could just as easily undo it myself, I wasn't quite ready for Clay to stray too far from me. All of the clothing on the bed was daunting and I wasn't even sure where to start.

"I've never worn a pair of trousers." I noticed a pair of them lying across the bed. Women did not commonly wear pants of any kind in my day and, when they did, they were typically worn underneath shorter dresses for ease of traveling–and none of them had *ever* looked like these.

Regardless, Lord Cabot had hated the things, always preaching what a woman should or shouldn't wear. I was stunned to realize that I had never truly chosen clothing for myself, even here in the Manor I still wore garments that I had been given... I sighed and looked down at all the clothing they had offered me. All the choices.

"Much more comfortable than skirts and corsets." Clay's fingers worked at the laces, pausing only to kiss the back of my neck before he stepped away. "The floor is all yours; try these," he said, handing me a soft-feeling shirt and a pair of brown corduroy pants.

I stepped behind the shade, stared at the clothing, and smiled at the fabric. The feeling that flooded my chest was overwhelming but joyful as I shucked from my skirts and chemise.

"Gentleman..." I peeked out from behind the shade, "what exactly am I to wear beneath the trousers?" I was sure I didn't have the proper undergarments for such a thing. "Do I just..."

Koen laughed, "Hold on!"

He sprung from his chair beside Clay, who had settled down and disposed of his glasses on a nearby table but was staring at me with a soft smile that said, *let him get through this*. Koen rifled through a bag and pulled out a black box, bringing it toward me.

"I picked them out for you." He winked. As soon as I had them in my hand he backed away, turning only to ask, "do you need help with those, too?"

"I think I can manage." I laughed and lifted the lid to find a bundle wrapped in tissue paper. The garments inside could barely be considered clothing and a blush flooded my cheeks. "Koen," I gasped and peeked my head back out. "This would be more appropriate for tying someone's hair back!" I tried not to sound too horrified, as they were of course still a gift. "How are these meant to protect any modesty?" I asked.

"They aren't! Not if I can help it." He smiled at me and I couldn't help but roll my eyes at his charming expression.

I picked a plain white pair and slipped them over my thighs. The lacy fabric felt soft on my skin as I settled it on my hips. They made me feel pretty. I swallowed tightly and continued to dress, trousers first and then the T-shirt. It was looser than expected but fit perfectly to my curves and chest.

"You're killing us," Koen groaned. "Do you need–"

His complaints were silenced as I stepped out from behind the shade.

"Wow." Clay nodded with that cheeky smile, his elbow propped on the arm of the chair with his fingers at his mouth as he studied me.

I had tucked the front of the shirt into the pants and pulled my hair from the bun it was in. I ran my hands over my thighs and tried to stand tall but it was hard to do so when my heart was racing that fast.

"Incredible," Koen huffed. "Honestly, I've been worried. I was wondering if you even had legs or if you just floated everywhere under those long skirts," he joked and pulled a nervous laugh from my lips.

I rolled my eyes at the ridiculous image his statement produced and then narrowed them at him slyly. "Koen, you've *seen* my legs, have you forgotten?" I asked brazenly, referring to the night in the bathing room. His eyes twinkled lustfully and a grin spread over his face.

"I could *never*," he promised. "Do you like the clothes?"

I looked down at myself, rubbing my hands over the soft fabric of the shirt and looking back up to the men. "I think so," I answered honestly. "It's a strange feeling, wearing pants." I shrugged. "But I feel pretty?"

"You *are* pretty," Clay voiced in that profound tone that demanded attention.

"Oh!" Koen slid forward and grabbed one of the boxes from the bed. "Look." He opened the lid and inside were a pair of beautiful brown boots with laces and an inlaid zipper up the inner side.

"They're..." I ran my fingers over them and smiled.

"Sit," he instructed and I listened, taking his spot as he slipped both on my feet and Clay's arm extended across the table to rub lazy circles on the back of my arm.

"Do they fit?" Koen asked, leaning back on his heels.

"Perfectly." I leaned forward, grasping his face, and kissed him.

It was still strange to me that neither cared about sharing the affection. It didn't seem to bother Clay that Koen's hands tangled around my waist and up my back. Greedy as I was for more, I found myself caring less and less about the mathematics of everything and just took their attention for what it was. Bountiful.

Koen looked drunk when he pulled back from me, hazy eyes staring at me bewildered and lust-filled. "More!" He declared. "Do a spin for us, Blossom."

I obliged and spun on my boots' toes for them, hollering and clapping as I did so. With their eyes on me, I felt like the center of the universe.

"This truly is a lovely surprise," I said softly.

Clay reached out to me. "Come here." He wrapped his fingers into the pocket of the trousers and pulled me into his lap as Koen searched through the pile of presents.

"How did you afford all of this?" I scowled as he rubbed his hand across my stomach.

"Fake credit cards." Koen shrugged. I would have to ask them later what exactly a credit card was. "Here it is!"

He was holding out the box when the bedroom door was flung open and Wesley stumbled in with his gun drawn. I tensed in Clay's lap but his strong palm laid flat to my stomach, not allowing me to move away from him. Wesley fought to control his ragged breathing and the bandage on his leg was bleeding through his sweatpants.

"What the hell is going on in here?" He huffed.

Koen laughed wildly, the sound filling the room as he set the box in my lap and moved toward Wesley. He wrapped his fingers around the barrel of the gun and I held my breath but nothing happened. Wesley slumped against the door frame and glared at us.

"What the hell is wrong with you?" Koen asked.

"I thought I heard screaming," he argued. His tan chest was covered in sweat that soaked the back of his neck and dampened the ends of his golden hair.

Clay's hand loosened on my thigh as the situation seemed to diffuse in the air around us. Wesley assessed the room. His lips pressed into a thin line as I returned to opening the box in my lap.

"I wouldn't–" Koen started, his hand out toward me to stop, but it was too late.

I pulled the silky fabric from the box to expose a piece of dark green clothing with thin straps and a delicate see through material embroidered with flowers. When I looked up from my lap and held it to my body, I realized that it wouldn't protect an ounce of–well *anything*.

Clay's entire body shifted beneath me, alerting me to the eyes on me in the room.

Koen watched intently. The blush on his cheeks was red and looked hot to the touch. Wesley stared wide-eyed at the clothing as he ran a hand through his hair, breathing heavily.

"I'm leaving," he announced and stumbled from the room.

"I should..." Koen swallowed, shaking himself from his stupor. "...help him get back to bed."

He moved toward the door as Wesley's grunting echoed up the corridor but stopped and came back just for a second. He peeked his head in the door, all smiles and blond curls. "For the love of god, please put that on before I come back." He looked me over once more, his head cocking to the side as he backed out of the room and disappeared.

"What is it?" I looked over my shoulder at Clay, who seemed to be losing his grip on his self-control.

"*Trouble.*" He scooped me in his arms and carried me to the bed.

SEEMINGLY CAN
SURVIVE WITHOUT
FOOD OR WATER.

GOES DAYS WITHOUT
SLEEP?

TIME
PASSES
WEIRDLY
IN THE
MANOR.
OR NOT AT
ALL?

HOUSE PUTS HER TO
SLEEP FOR
EXTENDED PERIODS?

TUNG HU
SAW-CHAU
CHON MU
(Castle Peak Ba
CHU-LU KOK
MA-WAN
PAK-MONG
MA-WAN-CHUNG
TUNG-CHUNG
SHA LO WAN
TUNG-WAN
NAM-WAT
PO-CHU-TAM
LAN-T
TAI-U
TAI-O
NAM-CHUNG
IO

FLORENCE

"**A**re you ready?" I asked, and both men answered firmly yes. "Are you sure?" I stood terrified in place.

The bodysuit, as Clay had called it, was sheer and showed off the expanse of my stomach and the swell of my breasts. The embroidered flowers climbed from the tiny fabric between my legs toward my chest but did nothing to cover anything. I inhaled carefully, feeling highly exposed in the lingerie. The thickest part of the entire suit was the two silk ribbons used to tie it all up on my shoulders.

"It's human to be scared," Koen's voice was tender and quiet from the other side of the shade. "But I can promise you look beautiful without even seeing you."

"An odd promise to make." The laughter that tumbled from me was breathy and nervous.

"A serious one," Koen responded.

"Find your bravery, Florence," Clay purred in his deep voice, which melted away all the reservations I had previously been mulling over. With one final breath, I stepped out from behind the shade with my eyes closed.

Both men were silent and the crackle of the fireplace almost had me opening my eyes, but the fear of what their faces looked like was enough to keep them screwed shut even as the silence ate at me. I stood so still that I could feel the air moving around me and it wasn't until Koen's breath washed over my neck and goosebumps were painted on my skin that I felt courageous enough to open them.

"You are..." he paused, breathless, and ghosted a hand over my shoulder, fingers brushing the ribbon but never my skin. The word never came. It never left his lips because his hands were around my thighs, and he was pulling me up against his waist and carrying me to the bed.

"How do you feel?" Koen asked, laying me down against the mattress. My hair fanned across the blanket and my fingers dug into the fabric at my side. He kneeled over me, his hungry green eyes flickering over my entire body as he took it all in.

I felt exposed, even more than I would have had I been fully nude, but for the most part... I felt sensual in a way I had never known was possible, and more than a little provocative.

"Good," I whispered with a small nod.

"Just good?" Koen smiled, and the world fell away from us. "We can do better than just good."

His fingers brushed up my naked thighs, pausing as he reached the hem of the bodysuit that pressed into my skin. He traced it over the curve of my hip and inward, and each of my breaths became thinner as he reached the soft inner skin.

"Better," I breathed out as his hand brushed over the thin fabric between my legs with a feathery touch. "Koen–" I whispered as he dipped his head and peppered my inner thigh. I let go of the sheet and took a handful of his curls between my fingertips. He moved slowly, keeping flush with my body as he kissed his way over my stomach with a few soft kisses to my breast and collarbone.

He looked up at me through hooded eyes with a smile on his face. "Gods, I missed you," he huffed and continued his raid of kisses.

My head lolled to the side gently, taking my attention off Koen for only a moment. Clay stayed in the armchair, watching us quietly as Koen buried himself between my throat and the mattress, his kisses growing sloppy as his hand cupped my breast, kneading it just gently enough to send tiny sparks dancing across my skin.

Clay's gray eyes didn't give away what he was thinking, but the tick in his jaw and the pout of his bottom lip proved he was waiting for an invitation—a gentleman even in the face of wavering self-control.

I inhaled deeply, filling myself with a shaky but confident breath before wiggling my fingers to him.

"Please come here," I said, sitting up on my elbows as I found my second wind of bravery. I could feel my confidence growing, each of them taking the time to help find it within me and all I wanted was more.

Koen looked back at Clay with a smile on his face, clearly more accustomed to the situation than I as he stripped from his shirt and returned to his mission of marking every inch of my body with a long tickling swipe of his tongue over my collarbone.

"Are you sure?" Clay asked, his gaze darkening.

I offered him a gentle nod and he wasn't going to refuse me. Rubbing a hand over his mouth and down his throat, he rose from his chair, shucked from his dress shirt, and wandered toward us.

His hand reached for my face, fingers grazing my jaw as he tilted it up toward him. He leaned over, pulling me into a slow, sweet kiss that made my toes curl.

"What do you want?" Clay asked me as he pulled back from the kiss and brushed his thumb over my cheek.

I must have looked confused because he asked again, "what do *you* want?"

I had never been asked such a question.

Koen slid to the side of my body quietly, laying down shirtless as Clay waited for an answer. He patiently kissed each finger on my hand, my palm, my wrist.

"You're in charge, Florence. Tell us what you want from us." He reworded his question and knelt beside the bed, his beautiful hardened torso on display in the flickering light from the fireplace.

I turned to Koen, who paused in his exploration of my skin. His brows pinched together as he stared at me.

"Start small," he encouraged. "Ask us for something that makes you feel good."

"Touch me," I huffed, not knowing what else to ask for at the moment, but knowing that laying here under their hot gaze was making me squirm with anticipation.

Clay stripped from his pants and climbed into the bed behind me, pulling my back against his chest and resting me between his thighs. Koen moved at the same time, sliding to the end of the mattress, his hand cupping my ankle as he began to kiss his way up my calf.

I leaned into Clay's touch as he pushed my hair away from my shoulder and kissed the bare skin with care. His hand slinked around to rest on my stomach as Koen climbed with needy excitement back between my thighs.

Clay's teeth found skin and I whimpered at his touch. His fingers tugged at one of the ribbons, pulling it undone. He pushed the fabric out of his way and danced his fingers across the swell of my breasts until he was beneath the mesh and rolled his fingers over my pebbled flesh.

I rolled my head to the side, pressing it against Clay's chest, and fought to keep my hips level with the mattress under his careful touch, gripping Koen's hair when he was in reach as he collided with the thin bodysuit between my thighs. His lips brushed over the sensitive skin in another long kiss that dragged a soft moan from my lips.

"Are you alright, Blossom?" Koen asked quietly, his pupils dilated, only leaving a thin border of bright green staring up at me through thick lashes.

The answer was yes and no. I was overwhelmed and confused, but the feeling of their hands all over me made me forget every reservation in my mind.

"Keep talking to us, Florence," Clay urged. "Explore your dominance," he whispered.

"I am," I answered, and he rewarded the confession with a small pinch of my nipple as his hands roamed purposefully over my breasts. My speech stuttered as Clay nipped at my ear, and his breath fanned over my neck. "I want–"

"Tell me," Koen said instantly, stopping what he was doing and lightly kissing my hot skin.

My breath hitched at his request, and my cheeks turned hot as he sat back on his knees, propped over my hips on straightened arms as he watched me.

"Blossom," he whispered.

Clay carefully pulled the other ribbon of my bodice, his hand freeing both of my breasts completely, quietly, and patiently watching the interaction between Koen and I unfold.

"I don't—" I huffed.

"You *know* what you want," he said, my core clenched at his refusal of my words.

"I want you—I want—" I fumbled, fighting to keep a clear thought through the fog of desire.

"What else?" He waited, his fingers inching closer over the bed to my skin. I just wanted him to touch me again. I wanted him...

I pushed away the heat that rose in my chest. "I want you to do what you did that night, but I want you to use your tongue."

A prideful smile spread over his face as he nodded and dipped his head between my legs, Clay's grip tightening slightly on my breast as I gasped at Koen's eagerness to follow the request.

Koen kissed a line over the bodice, leaving me aching for more before he moved the fabric aside and slipped his tongue deep into the soaking pool between my legs. Lapping between my folds in long, purposeful licks that had my hips rising from the bed until he pushed me back down with the flat of his palm.

His tongue flicked at the small bundle of nerves as Clay's lips left a warm line across my shoulder to my throat and jaw.

"You're doing amazing," Clay praised as he buried his face into my hair and his hand cupped my throat. My fingers tangled into his around my stomach and squeezed before releasing him and letting it slide down toward Koen.

I wanted to feel like I had that day in the library.

Free and wild.

"That's my girl," Clay practically purred as he caught sight of what I was doing, my hand joining Koen's perfect motions.

He sat back, his tongue darting over his bottom lip as his eyes widened, flickering from my hand to me. Then, something more playful crossed his mind. Clay rested his chin on my shoulder, and I could feel him nod, completely unaware or unbothered by their mischief, as I sank my fingers into my entrance with a strangled gasp.

Koen had pushed me to an edge, but I worked my fingers against the sensitive bridge in my core and brushed my thumb against the tender cluster as Koen had, slowly until my legs tensed and my toes curled into the mattress.

Koen kissed my inner thigh once more, a quick peck before he slid off the bed, his pants tented from his erection but seemingly unbothered as he searched for something. He moved back, sitting flat with one leg crossed beneath him and the other extended out around me, tangling with Clay's. A small black box in his palm and a grin on his face. He gripped my calf and tugged gently, causing me to slide down on Clay's chest, and hooked my leg over his lap, spreading me open as if on display.

"One last surprise," Koen hummed at me, his fingers giving me a small squeeze before he popped the lid on the box and held it out to me. My fingers stopped between my legs, distracted by the present, as I put all my weight on Clay and reached forward, plucking the smooth, curved object from the cushioned box.

It was dark purple in color, with silver markings and a button along the arched top half. It was small enough to fit in my hand, with one larger bulbous end and one slimmer one.

"What is it?" I asked him, excitement in my voice.

"It's a vibrator," Clay whispered quietly, "it's meant to...help."

"Help?" I angled my neck, wanting—no *needing*, to see the look on his face. He stared down at me with those calm gray eyes, his hand brushing over my jaw into my hair. He waited for me to understand what he meant—"Oh," I whispered and held the vibrator between my fingers. His hand eclipsed mine and his finger pressed the small silver button inlaid along the top.

"Oh!" I giggled as it started to vibrate between my fingers. It ticked the muscles in my hand and wrist as it rippled down through my palm into my arm. "What is it made from?" I asked quizzically, the textile unlike that I had ever felt. Soft and unbelievably smooth.

Clay's breath tickled against my neck in a soft chuckle, "It's called silicone"

"And where did you possibly find such a thing?" I asked, looking back to Koen.

"You'd be surprised by how sex positive we've become as a society in the last century. Nearly every town has a sex shop," he laughed and rubbed my bare calf.

"Sex shop?" I asked, my mouth agape and Koen shook his head, mouthing the word *later*. But in my lust filled haze I don't think I would remember to ask him even if I tried my hardest. I ached for more touching. The interruption was sweet but stretched too long. I wiggled in Clay's arms and his grip around my stomach tightened slightly.

"Impatient little thing," he chuffed.

"It's much better than your hand." Koen beamed with pride. "And now when we're gone on hunts—" He smiled brighter.

"—You can use it and think of us." Clay licked my earlobe, sinking his teeth into the soft skin as he pushed my hand back down towards my center.

The vibration was shocking and I gasped loudly as Koen guided my hand lower, pressing the cool soft silicone between wet folds and against me. It ignited a fire so hot I moaned the moment Koen touched it to my entrance, always leading the way but not doing the work for me.

"Just like that," he praised as he pressed his mouth against my thigh. He licked and nipped as I found myself growing comfortable with the vibrations that pulsed through me. "Deeper, Blossom," he encouraged and pushed his fingers against the top of my hand, urging me to dip it inside.

"Oh, God," I cried out as it surged inside of me, such a foreign sensation but I couldn't get enough of it. "This is magic." I laughed quietly between tiny shallow breaths as I rocked the vibrator in and out against myself.

Clay went back to kissing my throat as the heat between all of us rose to new levels. The tension in the bottom of my stomach curled and tightened until I couldn't breathe and every touch laid onto my skin felt like ice. It stung and cooled all at once.

I let the vibrator fall from my grasp, exchanging the device for the soft curls of Koen's hair, tugging him upward. "I *want* you," I demanded.

"Blossom found her voice." Koen smiled and obeyed the request. He crawled up between my thighs, Clay shifting to give him space as I sat up and welcomed his lips to mine. My hands worked at the buckle of his pants until it hung loose and he was able to push them down over his hips with a small wiggle.

For a split second, doubt of our entanglement filled me and, even though I had attempted to hide it from him, Koen caught the look on my face. "What's wrong?" He asked, pulling back slightly, using his arm on the head of the bed to prop himself over both of us.

"You both have been so patient with me and I fear I'm walking you into something you might not be comfortable with–"

Koen silenced the protest with a small kiss, his knuckles grazing the underside of my chin and lifting my mouth to his. When he pulled back, I figured he would say something reassuring or perhaps stop what was happening altogether. But he leaned forward, brushing against my hips with his own in a slow grind that forced an enticing static to cover my skin as my core fluttered for more.

I pressed my cheek against Clay's chest, watching as Koen captured Clay's pouting bottom lip between his own and kissed him. It was deep and intimate in a way that caused my cheeks to flush with an unbearable heat.

"We're comfortable, Florence," Clay whispered when Koen finally released him in a soft retreat, only to steal another small peck from me and settled down between my thighs.

"May we continue?" Clay asked, warm at my back, bracing me for Koen.

I nodded. "*Please*?"

The plea that left me was low and strangled as Clay's fingers found a nipple and rubbed them around the sensitive bud. My hips lifted from the mattress, but his other hand pressed flat to my stomach and eased me back against it as Koen surged forward.

"Oh," I breathed, my nails digging into the skin on his shoulders as he sank into me, aching and waiting for him. His hips met mine before he retreated and rocked forward again at an even slower pace.

I was a mess of euphoria with Clay's lips on my neck, his hands kneading my breasts, and Koen's careful thrusts. "Tell me what you like," Koen huffed between breaths. "I want to know how to make you feel good, Blossom."

"I need more Koen. This isn't enough," I said breathlessly to the both of them. I was so close to the edge I could feel the orgasm, tingling at every nerve, but he was being too gentle. I wanted more.

His eyes trailed to Clay's, locking, which was only momentarily before both men respected the plea. Clay hauled me up higher into his lap, bending his knees and using his thighs to angle me more open to Koen's advances. Propped like this with his hands gripped around my thighs, Koen shifted to his knees and moved faster. Thrusting into me without remorse as his hand found my breast and cupped it tightly in his fingers.

Clay carefully wrapped his hand around my throat, angling my head back to him so he could take my lips against his. Kissing me until I couldn't breathe as Koen stretched my walls over and over. Clay's tongue slipped into my mouth, his hands wrapped around my middle, holding me against him, our thighs pressed together, slick with sweat, while Koen worked me closer to the edge.

"She's almost there," Koen said as I clenched around him instinctively. His hands wrapped around my thighs, tugging my bottom against his hips in a way that rocked shockwaves through my core and into my overstimulated muscles.

"Don't stop!" I begged but it came out as nothing more than a strangled whine. I forced myself to try again. "Do I feel good?" I asked, and Koen nearly keeled over from the question. A stunned look of pleasure and shock tangled over his face.

"You feel so good, Blossom," he groaned and somehow picked up his pace yet again. He smiled, peering down at me with lust. My breasts spilled from the top of the body suit, bouncing wildly as I rolled back against Clay. "God damnit if only you could see yourself from my eyes."

"Tell me," Clay begged him.

"Her hair is all messy, her lips pinker than they've ever been, and I've never seen her eyes so green." He thrust through the description as I turned my head back to Clay, who stared down at me with a look I had never seen from anyone before. It made my heart skip in my chest as his arms tightened impossibly around me. "Her skin is glowing, sweaty, and marked with our fingerprints."

Koen whimpered as my hips fell open and my back arched, allowing his impressively thick length to slide even deeper within me.

"She's fucking perfect," he said lastly and sent me tumbling from the edge down the slope into my orgasm.

"That's it, Blossom," he praised. I fluttered around his cock as he plunged himself as deep as he could and built the pressure until I was crying out. "Finish with me inside of you," he demanded, and my body obeyed like that's all I needed to hear from him.

"God, you're beautiful," Clay's purr was followed by the grazing of his teeth against my shoulder that caused me to whimper, he pulled away only to pepper it with tender kisses to ease the pain.

My gut tightened as the shockwaves of pleasure gripped my body, and Koen kissed me until I saw stars dance around in a hazy vision.

"Good girl," Clay praised as Koen slipped from me.

He removed himself, replacing it with the vibrator to send a fury of aftershocks through me. I wrapped my arm up around Clay's neck, gripping a handful of hair as I came completely and utterly undone. Clay's fingers rubbed in lazy circles as I came back to them both. Stomach full of heat, muscles exhausted, and my brain drunk off sex, I let Koen wrap his arm around my middle and bring me back down on the bed against his chest, his face nuzzled into my hair as Clay rolled to his side and joined us.

"How are you?" He asked.

"I understand now why men enjoy brothels," I giggled, pulling my kiss-bitten bottom lip between my teeth.

Koen kissed my forehead. "You did so good," he whispered against my skin.

"I'd like to do that again," I said to them both as Clay buried his face beneath my hair against the mattress, his lips finding my ear.

"Sleep now," he grumbled and tangled his arm around my middle next to Koen's. "There is plenty of time for more later."

T hunder crashed above the Manor, loud enough to rattle the window panes. The wind blew violently through the grasses and the wildflowers, upending anything in its path. Lightning cracked in a large fork above and it illuminated the countryside, and darkness started to seep through the foundation of the Manor. It crawled along the baseboards and settled into the cracks of the floorboards.

Too much.

Too far.

She was asleep, nestled contently between the two men. Peaceful, protected. Like she hadn't been protected the whole time she had been there before. Like the men had filled every desire she had, like she had forgotten who had allowed them here from the start.

Far past anger, the black rage oozed from the ceiling, down the walls, and coated the floor, permeating the room and extinguishing the fire, now a low-glowing collection of embers in the fireplace, dropping the temperature rapidly. Ice skated across the large windows, creating a thick frigid barrier that continued out onto the sill. The hateful mists extended to the bedposts and settled over her like a blanket.

Her body began to tremble from the cold, breath visible in small clouds of white in the night. Her eyes opened, dark as pitch, as she slept.

She levitated, slipping from the mess of blankets and limbs, piloted by an unseen hand until her feet touched the frozen floor. Her body was bare, her soft skin reflecting what little moonlight peaked through the cracks of the ice covered windows. Dark auburn hair long and curling down her back and over her breasts, ethereal.

Mine.

She walked effortlessly through the door that opened for her, and closed silently behind her. The corridor seemed to tighten around her possessively, walls reaching and breathing her in, jealous of the carpet beneath her feet that reveled at the touch of her. She was directed through the corridors, silently, and was brought to her destination with ease.

The bathing room was freezing but she did not wake at the bite of the cold tiles on her feet. She was not aware of the temperature, though the light hairs on her skin bristled and raised, skin pebbling to the point of pain as she was submerged into the water. No lasting harm would come to her, but a lesson must be learnt.

PART THREE

KOEN

"Florence?" I blinked twice in the darkness as the lightning flashed through the heavy curtains in the bedroom.

Clay was still sound asleep beside me, but the sound of booming thunder had woken me from a dead sleep to find her missing from the space between us.

Her silhouette stood at the end of the bed and then, as quickly as the lightning had danced across the walls, she was gone, causing me to question whether I had actually seen her or not. I pulled myself from the bed. When we had first arrived it had been ratty and covered in cobwebs but, since the first night I had kissed Florence, rooms had been slowly changing, at first almost without my being fully aware, until the moment she had come undone in my arms in the bathing room.

The water around us had warmed and sparkled, the tiles no longer chipped, windows clear and clean that glimmered with the moonlight above us. As if the moment my heart became fully entangled with hers, the Manor revealed itself fully. I came back to myself as I tried to shake off the feeling that I was being watched and padded across the cold hardwood to the door. My toes curled against the cold wood, and then my fingers shot back in surprise from the ice on the door knob.

The Manor was freezing.

The windows glimmered when the lightning struck again, illuminating the frost that cloaked the furniture and the walls that I hadn't noticed upon waking. My breath puffed out visibly before me and the hairs on the back of my neck raised. This wasn't right, it was only mid August, how could it possibly be this cold?

Panic pulled tight like a rope about to snap across my chest.

Something was very wrong.

"Clay," I barked, startling him from his sleep. "Get up."

He stretched and yawned but felt around for his glasses on the table beside him. Slipping them over his slender face, he tried the light but it didn't flicker on. He shrugged as the lightning flashed again across the room.

"It's freezing in here," he said, reaching for his clothes. Then he realized that Florence wasn't in the bed with him. "Where did she go?"

I shrugged and pointed to the knob. "Feel this."

I moved out of his way as he approached and grabbed a clean pair of sweatpants, pulling them over my boxers before slipping on my shoes and tugging my jumper over my head.

"That's not good." Clay pulled his hand back and rubbed them together to bring the warmth back to his skin. His brows furrowed together as his lips pressed into a tight line and, quietly, he surveyed the room.

"Take this," he handed my gun to me from the dresser.

"I don't want that." I shook my head. "You take it. I'll keep tight."

"Hey." Clay stopped me as I went for the door again. "What the hell is going on with you? You barely helped with the wendigo, now this? Since when are you gun shy?" He asked me, sliding into a jumper of his own.

"I'm not." I swallowed tightly and looked down at it.

Florence was clouding my judgments. I could be stupid and reckless but I wasn't *that* stupid and reckless. I could see the effect she was having on me. My every waking thought was about her. How could I make her smile? How could I hear her laugh? But the hesitation wasn't due to the musings of a hopeless romantic, it was the cautious thoughts of a Hunter who had seen too much.

The faces of the children I couldn't save flashed behind my eyes.

The children I had murdered.

I had also nearly gotten Wes killed. I was so busy being mad at him on her behalf that I had lost sight that he was the only family I had. He had almost died, and it was like a shock to my system.

I was dangerous.

The thought of taking that gun from Clay and potentially having to use it? It made me sick to my stomach.

Clay wasn't going to drop the issue. I could see it in the way he stared at me, waiting for a better answer than '*I'm not.*' But it wasn't something we had time to pause and work through. We had a bigger problem at hand.

"We should get Wes," I said when Clay wouldn't stop staring at me. "We don't know what's happening and he isn't exactly mobile."

He stared at me for a moment longer, debating whether or not that moment was the right time for a fight, and then nodded, biting his bottom lip in frustration and adjusting the gun in his palm, holding it at his side.

"Stay close," he ordered me, and I listened.

He reached for the handle and jostled it, but it didn't move.

"Fuck!" He hissed, his hand flying back and almost clocking me in the nose. I managed to jump back just in time. He spun on his heel and showed me his palm. The center was bright red, as though the flesh had been burnt.

"A burn?" I asked, confused. The knob had been cold to the touch a moment before.

"Frostbite, *bad* frostbite." He winced as he shook out his hand. "The door is locked. Move back a step, we are going to have to kick it down."

I did as he said and, seconds later, his foot connected with the handle. Nothing. He lined himself up again, angling more to the side, and kicked again with enough force that it should have shot the handle clear off, but again it did not budge. With an exasperated huff he motioned me to move further back, pulling the gun from his waistband and cocking it, leveling the gun almost point blank against the door where the lock chamber would be.

"Shite!" I fought the urge to flinch when the gun went off, loudly echoing around the room that seemed to be getting increasingly colder despite the summer storm that was raging outside. The lock blew apart, sending splinters flying through the air. Clay covered his hand with his jumper sleeve and wrenched the handle again, but the door remained stubbornly in place.

"The Manor is locking us in," he said, frustration creasing his brow.

I scanned the room, looking for something that might help, when my eyes landed on the poker hanging with the set of other fire tools by the fireplace. I grabbed it and the base it hung from, shaking off the other tools that clanged heavily to the floor. Both were a good weight, made out of heavy wrought iron, and I tossed the poker to Clay with a shrug.

"Guess we are hacking our way out of here."

It took more strength and endurance than I think either of us would have copped to, both letting out exhausted grunts as we finally ripped off the solid brass hinges of the door. The Manor must have been below freezing but we were at least warmed with the effort of our escape. I was getting more and more worried for Florence as each second passed.

Where was she?

What the hell was going on?

I followed Clay, chest to back, our steps in hushed unison as we moved down the hall, checking each room on the second floor for Florence before making it all the way to Wes's room. Loud banging came from inside as we rounded the corner and approached.

I popped the door open for Clay and he entered, barrel first, to find Wes stumbling around, trying to pull on a shirt with one hand.

"What the fuck are you doing?" I swore and ducked behind Clay into the room.

"The candles are out and won't light no matter how hard I try." Wes whipped his arm around, gun pointed at Clay, who just rolled his eyes and lowered his weapon.

"It's storming outside." I looped myself under Wes and helped him back into bed as he let out a sarcastic grumble, *'oh I didn't notice....'*

"Have you seen Florence?" I asked, getting him situated.

"Why would I have seen her?" Wes growled as I threw a blanket around him.

"*Her?*" The word came out a stutter. "That's a new revelation."

He ignored my comment and huffed. "I haven't seen her. Why does that worry you? She hides all the time and after what I heard earlier..."

Clay exhaled, his breath visible in a white puff mist, cutting off Wes's thoughts. "Because it's freezing."

"So? It's just the storm." Wes shrugged, not catching on.

"In the middle of August? What? You get one injury and forget how to Hunt?" I scowled.

"It's clearly not due to the storm," Clay shouted over the crack of thunder overhead. It rattled the windows even harder this time. "We're sitting in a fucking ghost house thats been climate controled for over a month, and the temperature dropped too rapidly for it to be natural."

Something was playing with us.

"Did you check the kitchen? She's always in there," Wes suggested.

Clay looked at me "It's a start."

KOEN

I didn't hesitate to take off at a run and left Clay to take care of Wes as I weaved through the house and slid into the pitch-black kitchen.

"—three, two," I whispered, and the kitchen lit up with lightning to expose the empty room. "Where are you, Blossom?" I tried to rack my brain for possible places. My fingers drummed on the counter as I did a slow scan of the room in the darkness.

The bathing room. She had said it was one of her favorite places. I just needed to find my way back to it without her help. Easier said than done. Instant regret flooded me. I should have grabbed a blanket or something. It was only growing colder as I sprinted through the house. The frost followed with every step. It coated the floors and splintered up from the baseboards, crawling toward me as I ran.

"Florence?" I called out, over thunder so loud it sounded like the storm was within the Manor's walls. "God damnit." I stopped, turned around again, and stared at either end of the dark hallway. I also should have just taken the fucking gun.

My hands shook at my sides as I tried to place myself in my memories and remember the direction she had led us. But I had been too focused on the way her hand felt curved into my arm and the sound of her voice when she talked. I couldn't remember if we had gone left or right.

"Left." I shrugged, taking the chance and sliding around the corner to face the bathing room doors. The pool was just as dark as the rest of the house but with an eerie glow from the moon and clouds pouring through the glass roof. The rain beat against the panels and echoed so loudly that it was hard to hear anything through the wall of noise.

"Four," I counted down through the thunder, and a flash of lightning lit up the room as I finished the count. "Florence!" I called out to her.

There she was in the stark white light of the flash, her figure frozen, unmoving. She was naked and soaking wet, standing in the middle of the pool. I could see that her lips were blue from where I stood.

"Hey!" I shouted for her but she didn't look at me. Her eyes were unfocused and startlingly dark, *black*. The lightning bathed the room in white as it reflected off the pool and the glass, illuminating everything in a cold blue hue.

"Fuck." I dropped down into the pool when she didn't answer me, not bothering to strip from my clothes and grateful for my urgency when the freezing water bit into my skin like razor blades.

The water had begun to freeze over. Thin ice crystalized at the corners of the pool, stretching in tendrils toward her in the center. When I finally waded over to her she was frigid to the touch but her gaze didn't focus when I pressed my hand to her cheek.

"Florence?" I whispered urgently, pushing her wet hair away from her frozen skin.

Her lips were so cold that, at first glance, I thought they might be trembling, but—no, she was *talking*. Her voice was so low that it was inaudible over the sound of the crashing rain and thunder. Alarmed, I wrapped my arms around her rigid body and dragged her against my chest, going as fast as I was able through the water which was still in-furiatingly slow despite the effort. When I finally made it to the stairs I lifted her fully into the cradle of my arms and took off.

"Clay!" I screamed as I jogged back through the house. My fingers dug into her to keep a tight hold on her, my heart raced and something made me feel like if I didn't hang on tight enough she could be ripped away from me. Her skin was so cold I worried my fingers might crack through her flesh against the weight of her frozen and wet body. The chill had begun to set against my bones through my soaked jumper and I wasn't sure how long I could stay on my feet. "Clayton!" I hollered louder this time, my voice breaking as I stumbled.

My legs were numb and I couldn't feel my feet, but I had to get her to them.

Clay appeared at the base of the stairs with his gun raised, only to shove it back in his pants the instant he saw me and who was in my arms.

"Give her to me," he demanded and, as much as I wanted to refuse, to keep her close, to tell him I could manage... my throat was frozen through, and my lips were too numb.

"It's..." I tried to speak, but my lungs were full of ice. "It's too..."

"I know, Wes got a fire started," he said, scooping beneath my arms and taking her weight from me. "Get those clothes off!"

I followed behind him, stumbling up the stairs in stiff motions, my hands sticking to the railing as I went, stinging my skin as the flesh pulled from the wood freezing to it. I stripped slowly from my clothing like I was made of tar, each step harder to take, each piece of clothing harder to remove. My muscles ached from the drop in temperature but, as I made it into the bedroom, I finally got free of the sweater and my trembling fingers worked on the band of my sweats.

"Here," Wes said to Clay, clumsily sliding from the bed and pulling back the sheets for Florence.

The fire on the west wall was roaring and it took all my energy to get there but I sunk against the floor as close to the flames as I could get and let them lick at my skin. I rolled onto my knees and drank in the warmth, focusing my eyes on the bed.

"Is she?..." I asked, horrified for the answer.

Clay layed her onto the bed; she looked so small and so frail. Wes stood off to the side, off-kilter and digging through his duffle bag. He threw a shirt at Clay, who caught it without looking up. He weaved Florence's arms into it before covering her with all the blankets on the bed.

"It's not going to be enough," he mumbled but, before he could figure out a solution, Wes was free of his shirt, sliding into the blankets behind her and pulling her body against his.

"I'm the warmest one in the room," he grumbled. "I'm still running a fever."

Clay nodded with his lips pressed tightly together. "And you?" He turned to me.

"I'll survive," I whispered with chattering teeth. I could see tinges of blue slowly receding from the tips of my fingers. The fire was blazing and, through my frozen fog, I noticed the broken legs and seat of an ornate chair. The rest of it was in a smashed pile of jagged pieces next to the mantle. Wes really did get the fire going.

"Where the hell was she?" He asked.

"The bathing room. She was just standing in the middle of the pool, staring off like she is now." My lips trembled violently. "She was so cold, I don't–"

"She's gonna be okay, Koen," Clay said, walking toward me, stripping from his sweater and handing it to me. "Put this on," he instructed.

I slipped my arms into the sweater and tugged it down over my freezing torso, soaking in the heat the best I could. I was shaking violently. It was exhausting and made it hard to focus. Clay noticed and sat behind me, winding his arms under the jumper he'd given me and pulling me against him on the floor. The heat of his body helped immediately and the shuddering lessened.

"She was mumbling." I shook my head, trying to remember what she was saying.

"She still is," Wes grumbled, his body stiff, like every moment touching her was killing him.

Even though both Clay and I could tell it wasn't.

She looked so tiny, wrapped up in Wes, that it made me forget how strong she was when she was awake and fighting with him. She would hate every second of this, but it was working. Just as it was with me and Clay.

"*I.... to..... House.*" It was broken and quiet but repeated over again every few moments.

"What's she saying?" I asked Wes, squinting across the room in the firelight to try and watch the movement of her mouth. Her lips were still so blue.

"I belong, house?" He repeated, only hearing half of it.

"*I belong to the house.*"

CLAYTON

I t was another few days before the storm stopped.

Florence slept the whole time.

The term sleep, however, was generous.

Koen didn't leave her side as she continued to stare into space and mumble about belonging to the house. Every so often she would cough or flinch and we thought she might be coming-to, but it was more like an involuntary bodily response instead of waking from her state.

The Manor was going berserk. Though the temperature eventually went back to a livable degree, the sconces and candles that usually remained eerily lit continued to blow out and leave us in darkness, fumbling about for hours at a time.

Items moved unprovoked, many times whipping themselves across the room and making direct contact with one of our bodies, leaving large and painful bruises. Doors slammed and locked, making it impossible to move around easily to investigate. We had been forced to remove the doors entirely from the bedrooms we inhabited, though we spent most of the time in shifts with Florence, and in the library. Just that morning, while I had been attempting to prepare tea on the range, the fire surged white hot and shattered the kettle into shards that flew out over the kitchen, slicing open both my hand, and my cheek.

Koen had been experiencing similar events. Finally motivated into sorting through the maps I had drawn, he set up shop in the sitting room. He had been minding his own business when all the windows bowed and shattered around him simultaneously. Glass had embedded into his face, arms and neck. It had taken Wes and I over an hour of tweezing to remove them all.

We needed out. Even more, we needed a way out that would involve bringing Florence with us.

"Did you find anything?" Wes limped into the library and slumped down against one of the tables in a red tartan and a pair of worn jeans. He had started to look better and move around more easily, which was promising, since I believed we were all starting to feel like we were preparing for a fight. Given all the research I had been doing, we might be in for exactly that.

"There's no real death certificate for the old lady that lived in the Manor before Florence," I explained, showing him a book with my notes. He looked down at them, entertaining me without reading anything, and waited for me to verbally explain what I found.

"But if her timeline is right, and my math, Agatha Warren died in this house one hundred and seventy-two years ago tomorrow."

"So Florence is throwing a hissy fit to what?" He paused. "Celebrate the old lady's death?" The candles in the library surged, the flames licking impossibly high from the wick in response to his joke.

"It's not her doing this Wes," I sighed. "I can *feel* it. I need her to wake up, I need to ask her what the hell she knows that she's hidden. There was a letter mentioned, from the late Mrs. Warren, but I haven't been able to find it in any of the journals written by Florence." I ran my hands through my hair, frustrated. "I really don't think its her. It's this fucking *place,* Wes. It's acting out, it protects her and punishes her in the same breath. It makes no sense. There doesn't seem to be any *rules.* It certainly seems to be pissed with us…"

As if in punctuation, an entire top shelf of books plummeted down on top of us.

"Fuck!" Wes swore, rubbing a freshly forming goose egg on his temple. I could see the frustration seeping from him. "Listen, I know you're attached to this, deeper now than before," he paused, "and I get it, I do—but it seems like the more you search, the more reasons you find that point to her being the culprit for all of the supernatural bullshit happening around us. Koen almost froze to death pulling her from that pool and we don't even know why the hell she was in there. How do we know she wasn't the thing that killed the widow?"

I couldn't argue that. I wish I could. My heart tore at the logical parts of my brain with razor-sharp claws, blurring the lines of reasoning and blind faith. It made me sick to my stomach.

I shuffled through the pages on the table in front of me, and caught a glimpse of his face. It was scrunched up in disgust as he looked around the library, and reached out to lift one of the books I'd been reading between two fingers, like it was a piece of rubbish.

I scoffed. "What's with the face?"

His eyes met mine and his eyebrow cocked. "I just don't understand how you can spend so much time in here. This place is a mess and it reeks of mold," he said, waving his hand in front of his nose for effect.

I take a deep inhale through my nose but the library smells the same as the first day Florence had revealed it to me; like leather bound pages and oil lamps and something sweet- her. I stared at him confused. "I know I tend to work messily," I said motioning, to the papers and books piled in heaps on the table. "But this place is stunning, all other things considered. What do you mean it's disgusting?"

"What do *I* mean? What do *you* mean? This whole place is a condemned hole, this room is especially dank and dusty," he insisted, waving his hands about as if to display his point. It clicked then for me.

Wes couldn't see the Manor at all. Koen and I had remarked to each other briefly about the small changes we had begun to notice since being here; the brightening of the wallpaper, the temperature of the space, the furniture seeming to revert to its original luxuriousness. It was as if the Manor were opening up to us, allowing us to see what Florence saw. It was remarkable and stunning, just like the woman who inhabited it.

I cringed as another row of books flew from the bookshelves, pulling me from my thoughts as they crashed to the floor.

"What the fuck is that?" Wes looked around one of the walls at the commotion.

"It's the latest of the unnecessary bullshit!" I yelled at the Manor. "I took a shelf to the face yesterday." I pointed to bruises along my cheek and jaw. "At least I know it's pissed off at you too..." I sighed and pointed to the forming bruise on his face.

Wes limped toward the shelves to inspect them. He opened his mouth to speak when Koen burst into the library out of breath.

"She's awake."

Wes stopped me as I started after Koen from the library. He stared at me for a long time, a weary concern in his eyes. "Before you do something stupid," he said firmly, "like fall in love with her. Think about how this all ends. Is she worth it?"

I ground my teeth together, meeting his glare with my own.

"Every person we save is worth it," I said.

"You know what I meant," he responded, blocking my exit. "It's hard enough keeping the reins on Koen. Don't make it worse."

"Whatever, Wes." I shoved past him and followed Koen down the hall to the room we had set her up in. The last time I was with her she was so peaceful. Her mumbling had quieted and she was finally at an average temperature but I missed her voice. I missed her eyes.

She stared at the three of us flooding the doorway.

"Why are you all staring at me like that," she asked, looking down at herself. "And what am I wearing?"

Wes cleared his throat. "We're staring because you've been a zombie for three days and that's...mine."

Her cheeks flushed but she closed her eyes and curled her legs to her chest. "What day is it?" She asked, then paused, her nose scrunching up in the way that I adored. "And *what* is a zombie?"

"If I'm correct, it's the day before the anniversary of Agatha's death," I said. Koen turned his head to look at me in shock. "Does this happen often, Florence?" I asked her and made my way into the room.

Sitting at the edge of the bed, I waited for her to collect herself enough to answer me.

She looked up from the blankets with a mixture of fear and sadness and... *knowing* in her eyes that hurt me more than I had expected...She had known this was coming.

"It's not your fault, but I need help," I said, moving closer to her. "I'm at a dead end with my research and you know more about this place than anyone. I need you to explain what you know so I can put together the puzzle pieces."

"Not now," she said, speaking only to me. "You really all need to leave," she said tightly. "I've made a mess of everything. I wanted to protect you all, but I couldn't help but–" She paused, her green eyes seeming to grow deeper as they welled with tears. "–but crave your companionship." A tear escaped and she wiped it hastily from her cheek, looking away from us. "The Manor has never let anyone in, in all these years. I knew whatever reason it had for allowing you all in–it could not have been for anything good. I–I can't protect you from..."

Florence looked at the other two, her jaw tight and her expression hollow.

Her fingers picked at the fabric that covered her knees and, when I reached out to her, she pulled back from my touch. My heart wilted at the action.

"Mr. Dunn," she whispered. The shift was obvious when she called me that.

"Tell us what's happening so we can help," I pressed. "What did Agatha's letter say?"

"There is nothing you can do!" She snapped. "The house is only going to get..." She looked around her wildly. The curtains began to blow as if pushed by a breeze that was not there and the fire surged, crackling loudly in the fireplace. She shot up from the bed, the hem of Wes' shirt falling around her bare thighs. "If you do truly care for me then *please* do this one thing for me; leave this place before things get worse."

"What do you mean, get worse?" Wes asked, blocking her exit from the room with his hand in front of him. Koen was just itching to get between them as his fingers twitched against his side.

"This is just the beginning," she whispered, but it wasn't her. Her voice was low and there was no hint of the honey that usually dripped from her. It was *cold*.

"Cryptic," Koen sighed and moved around Wes to stand beside the bed. "Let us protect you. It's what we're good at."

Florence looked at the three of us and I could see the overwhelming look in her eyes that screamed that she had already begun to feel more and more like a caged animal again and less like a woman.

"I'm not the one who needs protection," she spoke slowly. "I'm not the one in real danger."

Wes chuckled. "What did I tell you?" He looked directly at me.

"I hope you fall from your high horse and break your neck," I snapped at him, pissed off and frustrated that Florence was giving us nothing to go on.

"You aren't making any sense," Koen said, gracefully ignoring the two of us. He stepped forward but Florence moved back from him and avoided his touch. "You kept whispering that you belonged to the house when you were out of it. What does that mean?" He asked.

She stared at him for a long time, no doubt weighing her options. but her eyes flickered upward as if she could hear something we couldn't before she returned to focus. "It means that I still have no control here, that none of us are safe, and that you all need to leave."

"We aren't going anywhere," Koen fought back, but it was useless.

Florence had already made up her mind.

"You don't get to shut down." Wes stepped forward. "Not after everything we've been through these last few months. You're the reason we're still in this stupid fucking haunted house and you're going to start talking to Clay and explaining what this all means before I start to do things my way."

"And pray tell, Wesley, what is your way?" She bit, green eyes sharp and cold as she peered up at him with fury on her round face.

"I will carve the answers out of you." He dropped his gaze and lowered his tone into the scary, authoritative area he reserved only for people that pissed him off. "Debt or not, your life is not worth more than my family."

"You have no idea what you're getting into." She shook her head and looked at me for a moment that stretched longer than I was comfortable with. "I don't know how to keep you all safe." Her voice was strained but the threat from Wes seemed to rattle her willingness to participate loose.

"Information," I told her. "That's a good start. What are you keeping from us?"

"Nothing that I haven't already told you, Mr. Dunn."

"You're lying to us." Wes stared her down.

Her big, terrified green eyes flickered back and forth over the three of us. Her tongue darted out of her lips nervously as she tried to determine whether to talk more or run. I could see the urge to rabbit written all over her face, but Wes did too, and he stepped his massive shoulders back into the doorway as if on cue.

She sighed, grinding her teeth together as we waited patiently for the answer.

"I warned you—" She clenched her jaw, fighting frustrated tears. "The house is *alive.*"

ORCHID LANE HAS NEVER
HAD OCCUPANTS
THE PUB OWNER SAYS AT
NIGHT, YOU CAN HEAR A
WOMAN'S VOICE DRIFTING
DOWN THE HILL TO TOWN
BUT THERE'S NO EVIDENCE
TO SUGGEST HE'S
ANYTHING MORE THAN A
DRUNK FOOL.

S FAR AS I CAN TELL NO
OUND GETS IN OR OUT

HOWEVER,
FLORENCE
SINGS TO THE
FLOWERS
WHEN SHE'S
ALONE....

WESLEY

"You've said that before but what the hell does that even mean?" I asked her.

Her body shivered, and I instinctively stepped back because the urge to keep her warm still ran through my veins. I had become habitually comfortable with laying in bed next to her, me healing and her... whatever the hell she had been doing.

It was strange to see her with so much fight, standing in the center of the room, shivering from the cold and defensive from our questions. Florence had spent the better half of the week curled up and quiet in my arms. I swallowed away the need to feel the comfort of her body against mine and shifted so the ache in my leg returned and filled me with a sharp pain instead.

Better in pain than longing for...

"You can't tell me that you haven't felt it?" She said, looking around at us with those cold, green eyes. "Or seen it." She looked at Clay.

"The house shifts, it's impossible to map. There are lots of different supernatural reasons that could be happening." He shook his head at her, slightly confused.

"You're smarter than that. You've known for a long time. It will follow a pattern to toy with your mind and then stop altogether to make you feel crazy but it's all a game. The house..." she stopped again and curled her bare feet against the cold floor.

"Let her get warm," Koen protested.

"Not until she tells us the rest," I demanded, not taking my eyes off her.

"Wes," Clay huffed under his breath.

"No," I said. "We've been doing this your way for too long and it's gotten us nowhere. Keep talking and I'll let Koen find you some socks."

Florence stared me down. It seemed the little girl who cowered from men was miles away. "The house has never allowed me visitors. The only other person who I ever saw alive in this Manor before you all was Agatha herself, and when I found her—" She paused and shivered, but not from the cold, from memory, I could place that haunted expression anywhere. I saw it often enough on Koen. "–I would scarcely call that *living*." She finished, not elaborating further.

"So why didn't it hurt us that day?" Clay asked her.

I waved Koen off with the wiggle of my fingers when I saw his feet tapping impatiently on the wooden floor. He slipped out the door quickly, in pursuit of warmer clothing for her.

"I don't know," Florence said.

"Wrong answer." Her eyes snapped to mine.

"It's been...quiet," she said. "Unusually so. Moments of anger, displeasure, here and there, but nothing outwardly violent toward any of you."

I pointed to Clay's face, drawing her attention to the fresh cut on his cheek. "While you've been sleeping it's been attacking us, everyday this week. I would call that violent."

She looked at Clay, worrying her bottom lip, and tried to hide her concern for him. Her hair framed her terrified expression in messy waves and the urge to reach out was overwhelming.

"I thought maybe killing the ghoul satisfied it for a while, but I was wrong."

"The temperature, the outbursts, your...coma?" Clay listed all the unusually malicious activity.

"It's the Manor. It puts me to sleep regularly, usually after I've done something it deemed worthy of punishment. I don't ever know the exact amount of time, *I told you that,*" she says in Clay's direction. "Please tell me I didn't hurt any of you?" She paused, the softness returning to her features as Koen slipped back into the room and knelt in front of her.

"No one was harmed." Clay quelled her fears with a lie. We had the bruises and scrapes to prove that harm had come to us all while she slept but the guilt of that knowledge would only stall her further.

"Blossom," he said, tapping her calf and getting her to lift her feet for the socks he found.

Jealousy bit at me, watching her balance on him while he touched her. *Grow up*, I told myself.

"We're fine," I cut Clay off before he mentioned the library, his mouth open and ready to worry her. "So you've been doing this for over a hundred and fifty years and never noticed anything strange?"

"Of course it's been strange!" Florence cried exasperatedly. "What is not strange about this place? This whole situation?" She struggled to regain her composure and, as much as I hated to admit it, I don't blame her for the outburst.

"And Agatha?" Clay asked.

"I told you everything I know about her. She was sick when she died, weathered, and incredibly old. From what I could tell, she wasn't trapped here, at least not to my knowledge." The words came out harsh and felt heavy as she leaned subconsciously into Koen's gravity. His hand trailed over her waist, toying with the t-shirt at her hip between his fingers. "Her husband had died years before I'd ever come to the city; they never had any children. She was a widow, yes, the town shut in but... ."

"You're lying," I grumbled. It seemed to be the only accusation I felt comfortable making against her.

"I'm not." She defended her words but she wasn't telling us the truth. It was obvious she was confused, perhaps even being influenced, but it didn't matter. We needed her honesty, and we needed the information. The gears that turned in Clay's mind were so loud they filled the room.

"There was a letter," he finally said. "From Agatha. Do you have it still?"

"You read my diaries?" She narrowed her eyes on him.

"It was in the library," Clay said, "I would not have if I thought it wouldn't provide information. You need to show me the letter, Florence."

Again her head drifted upward, as though she was listening to a far away noise or disturbance. The furniture in the room rattled roughly like it might move or even splinter. I watched as she blinked slowly, her expression pensive and attentive.

"I cannot," Florence said.

"You won't." I stepped forward. "There's a *difference*."

"I cannot," she repeated harshly.

"Don't you want out of here? You've been adamant about it but keep Clay in the dark with your lies and bullshit. What are you so afraid of?"

"You should all be afraid–" Darkness flickered across her eyes, like ink filling her irises and then in an instant it was gone and the emerald shine was back.

"—Of you!" I shouted and she flinched.

"Wes," Clay cautioned. "That's enough."

We stood in silence for a tense moment, none of us knowing how to proceed until Koen cleared his throat and took charge. "So if Agatha died of old age, why are you..." Koen swallowed, "...immortal? Why are you trapped if she wasn't?"

Such a funny word, immortal. She didn't age or wither. In years, she was older than us, but her mind and knowledge of the world was stunted. It showed her age and, despite trying to hide it, it embarrassed her. As much as the word felt wrong to describe her, it was the only thing that explained her still pristine skin that was soft under the pads of my fingers. Memories of quiet, unbothered moments rising to the surface made me clench my jaw to stop my thoughts from wandering into a place I couldn't return.

"You think I haven't attempted to figure this all out?" Her voice broke. "I've spent years scouring that library for answers, begging the walls of this god-forsaken place to tell me what I did wrong to deserve such a cage. All met with silence, all my questions unanswered."

"A pretty comfy cage." I ground my teeth together.

"A cage so pretty sometimes I forget that's what it is. Sometimes I am *thankful* to be trapped." Her head whipped to me, fire burning green in her eyes. "It may seem like I have what I need here, a life unmarred by troubles and sickness, Wesley. But you do not know what spending over a hundred years alone is like. *Untouched.*"

Her words were pure venom, anger brimming just below the surface of all that sadness that consumed her—a vengeful little thing in the making.

"So the house brings you here, Agatha dies, and it takes you. Why?" I asked her.

"I don't know."

"How do we know you aren't the reason Agatha Warren is dead?" I stepped forward, and she stepped back, but the usual rush of adrenaline that I felt when dominating over another person never came. Only guilt for making her scared. *Shite.*

"Is that what you believe?" Florence's words were shaky. "That I could kill an old woman?"

"You killed a week ago," I snapped, stepping even closer to her, eclipsing her size with mine as I spat my next words. "I watched *you* slit its throat."

I had gone too far. I knew it. They knew it. The air in the room became suffocating the longer she stared at me. Her eyes were brimming with tears. The first time I had brought her to that edge, it had given me joy to see her fall apart. A tear slipped down her cheek and she brushed it away with the back of her hand. As I retreated, Clay stepped closer, creating a distance between us that couldn't be missed.

They had taken sides.

Fine.

There was no apology I could make to Koen and Clay that wouldn't infuriate them more than they were in that moment. Both of them circled her like moths drawn to a flame. Ready to protect her if the conversation crossed the line further into an altercation.

"*A monster*," she said quietly, her voice a whisper as I turned to leave the room, "and I did it to save *your* life."

The shame of stepping over a line ate at me as I limped back down the hall to my room. I sunk down into the large armchair facing the fireplace and closed my eyes. The anger that washed over me was frustrating beyond words because, as much as I wanted to feel it toward Florence, it was directed at myself.

I rubbed the tension from between my eyebrows and tried to work through the emotions that suffocated my logical thoughts. She could still be a monster. The conversation proved that much to be true. It was convincing Koen and Clay of that danger that was tricky. Like walking on thawing ice, I had no idea when it would break away from beneath me, but I knew the threat was there and the plunge into the icy water would be painful. The longer I let them dance around in the little fairytale they had created, the worse the fallout would become.

If she was dangerous, she would need to be put down. But the answer wasn't that simple because, at the thought of causing her harm, my fingers clenched around the armchair and my body resisted the idea.

Betrayal in the highest form. My heart to my mind.

Killing her would sever any relationship I had with Koen and Clay, I knew that, but it could also be what saved their lives and, in the end, a sacrifice like that made sense to my brain. I was a product of my upbringing. If my father were still around he would tell me I was right about maintaining my skepticism of her, about protecting my family at all costs.

But he was the reason Wyatt was gone.

Our father had pushed Wyatt away because of his fear. A fear of the unknown. Of his son having a heart that one day would get him killed. And, while he was validated in that fear, it still felt... ridiculous.

Florence, for all her small flaws, didn't look like a monster; she didn't *feel* like one either and it was fucking with my head more than I wanted to admit. Each step to a solution felt like drowning. I licked my bottom lip, opening my eyes and staring into the dying fire.

Realization hit like a freight train. My body craved the warm sensation that flooded over me when her eyes found mine. I had jumped at the chance to help her heal, to warm her body with my own not because of a sense of debt or duty to return the favor, not even because I knew it would break Clay and Koens hearts if she hadn't recovered- like I had tried to convince myself. It was because I couldn't bear it either.

I lashed out, kicking over the table with my foot. It sent a sharp pain rolling through my body that pulled me back to reality. Whatever this was, whatever was happening to us, to *me*. I couldn't let her win. I wouldn't lose my family.

The sun bore down on my back, creating slick ribbons of sweat that trailed to the hem of my jeans as I slowed my pace and caught my breath.

"Where have you been?" Clay leaned against the doorframe of the ornate glass doors that lead into the backyard. His hair was messy, pushed back with his glasses, and he wore a tight navy dress shirt with his arms crossed over his chest.

"Walking, jogging, running," I clipped and braced myself on my good leg. The other throbbing painfully from the overexertion. Anything to get my mind off of her.

"You've been gone for hours," Clay noted. "You can't just run off and not tell anyone…"

"I was fine. I just needed to clear my head."

"We don't know if that ghoul had more friends. We don't know what's in those woods. It was stupid to go off alone when you're injured." He pushed off the door and stepped out into the sun, his gray eyes narrowing as he approached.

"The danger is in that Manor." I shook my head. I had proof: a new, nasty cut festered on my cheekbone from a piece of window frame that had blown out while I was passing it. She hadn't been lying. The house felt alive. It was just whether or not she was at the helm of it all. That's what ate at me.

"You're giving us all whiplash." Clay stared at me, still pissed off about the conversation with Florence when she woke.

I had been stewing in those emotions for days, rolling around in them, trying to piece myself back together. It was like rewiring a bomb; one wrong wire in a socket and I was suddenly taking a three-hour run just to feel something other than the overwhelming need to find her and understand her.

"She's sad, Wes," Clay said.

"What do I care?" I swallowed down the urge to lash out at him.

"Have you stopped to consider that she enjoys having you around? Despite your insistence that she's pure evil, she finds your company amusing!"

"Lying about her feelings isn't going to change a goddamn thing, Clay." I looked at him and straightened out when the burning in my chest subsided. "She's still a—we still don't know *what* she is and she could get both of you killed. Koen almost froze to death pulling her from that water and for what? So we can stand around and listen to more of her lies about this god-forsaken Manor?"

"Would you have believed her?" Clay asked me.

"I don't believe a single fucking thing that comes out of her mouth and you shouldn't either! What matters is that this place, these walls, are dangerous; for all we know she's behind it. Luring men inside, killing them to feed the evil and keep herself alive." I kicked the dirt under my feet and stared at the ground to avoid the annoyance in his gray eyes. I was picking up steam, spouting out venom that I didn't really believe anymore but needed to say because some broken part of me needed to be right. That had to be the voice of reason—even if I didn't really know that reason anymore.

"She probably killed Agatha. You can't find a deed because it doesn't exist. Florence is the monster. You're just too sex-drunk to see it. If you wanna stick your dick in something we can stop at a strip club on the way out of town!" My voice rose in volume the more upset I got about everything.

When I looked up at Clay his fist connected with my face. I tripped backward, caught off guard by the punch that painted stars in vision. I didn't wait to counter, surging forward the second I found my footing and wrapped my arms around his waist, knocking him off his feet into the dirt.

"Let's just get this over with and end her!" I grunted in between short breaths.

His hands came up, wrestling me off him and rolling us over. He punched my sore bicep with a heavy hand, causing me to yell out before he laid another into my face.

"Stop being a fucking asshole," he growled, perched above me with violent rage flickering across his face. "I'm going to figure this out. I'm going to get her free, and I'm going to prove you wrong."

I bucked him off me, knocking him off balance into the gravel, and pushed to my feet. A little disoriented, I stumbled to the left and shook the dizziness from my vision.

"See, that's the problem." I coughed as the blood from my nose dripped into my mouth. I lifted my hand to my face and touched the blood. "It's not about your curiosity anymore. This isn't about research. It's about *her.*"

"There's nothing wrong with falling in lo—" He stopped himself from saying it. Words that Wyatt had spewed a thousand times before getting his throat ripped out.

"Say it," I demanded and charged him.

My hand wrapped around his throat, but he didn't fight me. He just turned his teary gaze away. "Say it, Clayton."

"There's nothing wrong with falling in love, Wes," he choked out, and I shoved him backward.

"Just give me *something*, Florence, please! Anything else we can go off of? Where is the letter from Agatha? At least let me read it, maybe there are answers hidden in it!" The dark one pleads, pacing anxiously back and forth while gesturing wildly with his hands.

"Are you insinuating that I would not have been able to comprehend an answer blatantly written on a page, Mr. Dunn?" Her voice is cold and cutting. The blackness that lay dormant inside her was there, visible just beneath the surface. She bristled, her hands tight fists at her sides.

"Woah, Blossom, that's not what he meant, you know that."

Blossom.

A heated covetousness raged, thrumming through the walls. The fire in the mantle exploded, white hot flames licking the outer walls of the stone chimney and singeing the ceiling. The branches of the fire extended terrifyingly and would have enveloped the smaller man had he not jumped back in surprise. The coals blistered and smoldered holes into the floors, hissing against the cold wood.

Mine.

The dark one grabbed the blankets from the bed and smothered the embers burning into the floorboards. The flames reached again, further and hotter, hell bent on incinerating anything within its path.

"Fuck! Ko, go get a bucket of water!" he snapped, doing his best to smother the flames by waving the blanket. The corner lit and the blanket began to dissolve away, eaten by the bright orange and yellow flames. He hissed and threw the burning fabric to the floor, turning to her, "Florence! Florence? Snap out of it and get out of here! This whole room could catch!" His fear for her was evident, and delicious.

She stood, held in place by the loving invisible hands that gripped her. Her mind not her own as whispers drowned out his pleas.

They aim to destroy me.

Destroy us.

The fingers that held her reached in further, pulling at the emotions she so tirelessly hid from, the rage that was seething and strong that pulsed through her veins. The sour annoyance of consistently being undermined and unheard no matter how loudly she used her voice. Disgust for her own actions, her neediness and longing, the promiscuity and brazen apathy towards the very thing that had been her salvation all these years.

"Florence!" The other had returned and doused the flames. He held her face between his hands and shook gently, breaking her from her reverie. No matter. The chord had been struck and there, behind her eyes, an internal war was raging.

FLORENCE

I should have been more careful, I shouldn't have grown so attached. But I had gotten so wrapped up in the moments of laughter, companionship, and lust... It had all but wholly escaped my thoughts as to why the Manor had allowed them in in the first place.

Now Clay wanted—no needed, more from me. He wanted the letter. How would I even begin to explain? Why would they believe me?

The glass panes vibrated in a violent argument to my private thoughts.

I don't remember much from the first night. I remember hearing Koen calling for me but I couldn't move. I couldn't break free long enough to tell him to run. He had almost frozen to death because I had been overcome.

Now Clay was working himself to death in the library, the Manor brazenly throwing its belongings around like weapons. The Manor was rebelling worse against them than I had ever experienced myself. Koen had new bruises on his body. He had woken up with them, not even sure how he got them, and Wesley had a nasty cut across his face and he festered with hatred as he sulked and limped around the Manor.

I continued my attempts to convince them to leave; it was evident the Manor wasn't safe. I suggested they could stay somewhere in town, away from the danger, while they looked for a way to free me. But neither Clay nor Koen would hear anything of it and Wesley wouldn't leave them behind. So I was stuck, heartbroken and fearing for their lives, all while dodging the bullet Wesley was so eager to put between my eyes.

At least he hadn't gone back to calling me a monster—*at least not to my face.*

A small mercy.

When I wandered into the kitchen Wesley was spitting out blood, curled over the sink, his shirt open, torso sweaty, and covered in gravel. How he wasn't freezing was beyond me. I barely felt the cold and the frost falling over the Manor seemed vicious.

"Do not touch me." He put a hand up and spit another clump of blood out.

His nose was split across the bridge and a bruise was forming under his eye.

It seemed we were back to spite and anger.

"I'm sorry." I chewed on my lip.

"It's not your fault." Clay wandered behind us with a scowl, moving around Wesley to run his hand under the water.

The skin on his knuckles split across his hand. He was covered in the same dusty beige gravel, pieces stuck to his cheek, and his neck was raised in a red, irritated ring. It took seconds to put together what had happened. They had started to turn on each other.

"You did this to one another?" I said agast. Their eyes darted at each other and Clay scowled deeper, nodding his head as he dried the busted knuckles gently. "Is the house trying to kill you not enough?" I asked them.

The night before Clay had found me in the library staring at the small fire that had kept going. His approach had been cautious, as if he were trying not to spook me.

"You were whispering in your sleep," he said. "I belong to the house."

And so do you... Agatha's voice rattled through me.

"I do, this is my home." I wrapped my arms around myself and slowed my breathing.

I could sense his frustration with me but every thought, no matter how minuscule, if disloyal to the Manor was polluted. Since waking it had been harder to keep my own thoughts separated from the Manor's influence. It wanted me to itself; whatever twisted game the Manor had been playing had grown out of its control.

"It's a cage, Florence." Clay's voice was low and strained as he tried to hold back his frustration with me. His rage toward the Manor.

"The Manor provides."

"I've heard you say that before," Clay said. "I didn't understand what you meant at first but I think I do now."

I stiffened, unable to look at him, my gaze trained on the dancing flames.

"The Manor provides for you, the way—" He paused, stepping to the side into the corner of my vision. "—a loved one would. The way your husband should have. Before arriving here you knew very little of what compassion and loyalty looked like. All of what your father had given you had faded, overshadowed by the trauma and violence you endured in your marriage. You craved love and freedom and the Manor provided that to you, distracting you with flowers, books, and comforts as it constructed a gilded cage around you."

"I am safe here, cared for," I argued, as the feeling of betrayal and rot seeped through the floor into my veins.

"You are not blind to the cruelty or else you would not try so hard to get us to leave for our own safety; you are nothing more than a bird with clipped wings. This Manor is dangerous, it is not capable of truly caring–"

"You're lying," I snapped and the flames roared higher in response. The Manor bolstered my resolve and screamed in protest to his outrageous claim.

"Florence there are stories..." He said and I dug my fingernails into the skin on my arms to keep from lashing out. Anger rising in me like never before as he accused the Manor of malicious intent toward me... but...

No, only kindness.

A warm air rolled through the library, wrapping me up like a blanket.

"Whatever stories you've read, the Manor was protecting me." I defended it as Clay waved a stack of notes at me.

"Just look at them, all these cases–" he pleaded, his voice cracking. "It's more than protecting you, it has hurt children, women... Florence, have you even seen a bird in the last hundred and seventy years?" Clay asked.

The question caused me to pause, the anger swirling around in my mind like a cloud. It tangled with my thoughts and emotions, muddling everything until I couldn't think straight. Thinking back... "I—" my mouth fell open. "I can't remember birdsong—" I shook my head and stepped away from Clay and the fireplace deeper into the library.

"That's because the Manor kept out **everything**. It wasn't protecting you, it was isolating you."

No.

The iron framing of the windows began to peel and curl in a chorus of horrible screeching that made me cover my ears with my hands.

"Florence!" Clay whipped his head toward the window, surging forward and pushing me back as an iron rod flew through the air toward me, lodging into the bookshelf mere inches from my head where I had been standing. I stared at it for a moment, my breath shallow and my heart racing far too fast.

I couldn't find a straight thought in my mind. Clay cupped my jaw in his hands and forced me to look at him, my back against a shelf and him pressed tightly to me. Worry painted across all his features.

"If you want to hear the birds sing again, if you want to be free of this cage, I need your help," he whispered with his hands in my hair as he checked over my face for injury.

The Manor continued to beat against the walls of my mind but I couldn't stop thinking about the birdsong. Fixated on the idea that Clay had planted.

"I will try."

He stared at me and I knew he was worried that my mind was starting to crack. He wasn't wrong in his concern but I felt like a tea cup balancing on the edge of the counter; mere moments from shattering.

"It's just a disagreement, Florence," Clay huffed, but he wasn't acting like himself. On any other day, he would have stayed, talked about it, or even kissed me in passing, but he couldn't stand to be near Wesley and he vacated the kitchen as quickly as he had entered.

"What did you do?" I had it in my right mind to shove Wesley with both hands.

Anger surged through me and I did my best to control it but I knew the house could feel the shift in my mood. The cupboards rattled off their hinges like they were picked up by the breeze. But no window was open; it was just my rage coursing through the house like a wave.

"There she is," he clipped, his eyes shifting to the commotion surrounding us. "That vengeful little spirit."

I sighed, closing my eyes and trying to calm down. "I'm not a spirit. I'm not dead. I'm as alive as you are and exhausted from the extensive lengths I have gone through trying to prove to you that I am!"

"I don't believe a damn word that comes out of your mouth, and you might have both of them convinced, whether it's because of that pretty little mouth or that tight little—"

I scoffed as I reached my tipping point with his accusations, the sound of my discontent filling the empty kitchen.

"You have no idea," I snapped at him, leveling out to look him in the eyes. "For the first time in more than a hundred years, I feel like a person again, and yet," I stopped, knowing that if I cried now he would use it against me. I swallowed down those tears and braced myself against my emotions. "If I could get them to leave, get *you* to leave. I would. I've begged all of you tirelessly to leave the property. I have all but gotten on my knees and pleaded with them. All to keep them safe but they don't listen. *You* don't listen."

His hands rolled into fists at his sides.

"Are you that blind with rage that you can't see what is happening around you, or are you ignorant to them for another reason?" I couldn't help myself. "They are trying their hardest to help me and you are blocking their progress at every turn!"

Wesley said nothing. He just stared at me like I was screaming at the top of my lungs and he couldn't hear a single word that left my lips.

"They tiptoe around you like you're some sort of authority, but all you are is a bully."

He swallowed the words. He never broke eye contact with me as he listened but he *was* listening.

"And you are a monster," he spat and stepped forward into my space. "Everything was fine before we came here."

"I *did not want* you here!" I interjected.

"My family was safe, fed, and clothed. We did our jobs and we saved people! Both of them are too tangled up in this game of cat and mouse you're playing, but I see it. I'm not the cat or the mouse," he quipped.

I rolled my eyes. "So eager to be the stoic, resentful outsider. It's a pitiful existence."

"So is yours," he added, like it was meant to hurt my feelings.

"I'm well aware that my life has gone nowhere, Wesley. Even before I was trapped in this cruel echo chamber it wasn't anything spectacular. But I no longer have any interest in verbally sparring with you because that's all you want: a fight. You've been skulking around the Manor, begging for one. It's exhausting. So please, tell me how you think of yourself above this game I'm also trapped in. What is your solution? Because if it's to kill me, then what are you waiting for?" I seethed.

I could see how affected he was by my words. His teeth ground together at the back of his jaw and his fingers twitched as he reached for the gun I knew was shoved in the waistband of his jeans.

FLORENCE

He advanced on me so quickly that I didn't have time to react. The force of our bodies colliding up against the wall was enough to rattle the pictures that hung as he pinned me there with the barrel of his gun shoved beneath my chin.

Heavy breathing filled the kitchen, but the house was still and quiet.

This was the only opening he was ever going to get. If there was one thing that the Manor enjoyed more than hurting strangers, it was the joy it seemed to derive from my black moods. Wesley couldn't kill me. There was no real threat—just the enjoyment the walls took from my rage.

A knowing sank in my gut as the cool metal of the barrel bit into my skin.

"For over a century, I believed the Manor was trying to protect me from the outside world. Delusionaly so."

Wesley watched me carefully, our bodies melting into one as he kept me under his firm grasp and listened. The golden flecks in his eyes danced like fire when he realized I wasn't afraid of him. My own anger and frustration raised to match his.

I was no longer the shrinking violet who made herself smaller to give space for the large violent outbursts of others. Our faces were so close I could feel his breath mingle with mine and could almost taste the blood that had dried on his lips.

"But now I realize it wasn't protecting me. It was protecting itself. I'm just the beating heart of this place. As long as I keep moving, wandering, tending to its needs and keeping it entertained, the walls will keep standing." I swallowed tightly, my throat bobbing against the barrel of the gun.

"So shoot me, Wesley," I snapped, my eyes sharp as they bore into his, daring him to follow through on his threats, threats that I was almost sure now were empty. "You wanted so badly to kill me the moment you laid eyes on me, so now I'm giving you permission to pull the trigger."

Wesley didn't move, he didn't breathe, his body pressed so firmly against mine that I could feel his heat rise the longer he was silent.

"Do it!" I demanded. He flinched at the sound, not expecting the force. It felt good to scream at him.

Wesley's lips collided with mine, teeth and tongues clashing together as his hand came up and wrapped around my throat, keeping me pinned to the wall as he kissed me with all the force of the past few month's pent-up anger and frustration. It was rough, but not unpleasant, as his teeth dragged over my bottom lip. His knee pressed between my thighs and I groaned against his lips, unable to help myself as his tongue swept over mine and his hold tightened around my neck.

My fingers curled into the hair at the nape of his neck and yanked him down closer to me, deepening the kiss, unconcerned if I was gentle; this wasn't about that. This was carnal and desperate, and I was determined to give as good as I got.

Gasping for breath but yearning for more, he wrapped his arm around me and lifted me against him, spinning me until I sat on the counter, shoving himself between my legs. Never breaking the connection at our lips. I felt the gun press to my cheek as his hands came up to grasp my face. The danger was ever present and only fuelled my desires.

"You're still a monster," Wesley huffed against my mouth to satiate his guilt.

His fingers found my hips and dug in so tightly they would have left bruises if I was anything but what he claimed. He set the gun to the side and worked at his belt, the clang of the buckle falling open as I hiked my skirt up in preparation. He moved to take me and I pushed my foot out above his groin, and grabbed his open shirt in a hard fist, forcing his eyes to meet mine.

"If you need to see me as a monster, Wesley, that's *fine...*" I hissed from my swollen lips, already bruised from the impact of his. I removed my foot and opened my thighs, wrapping my legs around his waist and pulling him with as much force as I could manage towards me.

My nails raked at the exposed flesh of his hard stomach as I reached down and gripped him roughly, jerking the length of him. His eyes were angry slits but never moved from mine as I lined him up with my center. "...But then so are *you*," I finished, forcing his entry with the flexing of my legs from behind him.

It was hard and rough as he slid inside of my aching heat. He grunted in surprise at the forced insertion and it turned to a moan when he felt how ready I was for him. A small smirk of pride lifted his face. His cock plunged deep inside me with only a hint of resistance as I cried out from the delicious sharpness it delivered.

He was broad and impressively long, each rough thrust massaging my cunt in the most toe-curling way. I rocked my hips in time with his, my legs still around his waist, deepening the angle with an exasperated whine as his mouth found my throat, and we fell into a relentless rhythm.

His head was bent against my shoulder, his breath hot and forceful against my collar bone. My hands clawed down his back, dragging him to me, and I delighted in knowing I could mark him. I buried my nose into the curve of his throat, taking in the deep heady scent of him. He was all gunpowder, smoke, and perspiration.

It clouded my mind and I lapped him with my tongue before biting down hard on his shoulder. It tore a low growl from him and his lips met my skin in retaliation.

His teeth bit against the swell of my bosom and I could feel my nipples harden to painful points against the restraint of my stays. Moaning, I moved to unbuckle the closure to release my breasts. Only to be pushed away when his hands jerked the corset with enough force to bend the metal closure open, and it fell back on the counter behind me.

My chest was freed and shuddered with the effort to catch my breath. He tore at the delicate fabric of my chemise baring my breasts and taking the swollen hardness of their peaks in his mouth and hands.

He buried his face against the soft round curves, biting harder than before as his thrusts grew deeper and more desperate. His hips slapped against me as he angled me back to my elbows on the counter and grabbed at my thigh for leverage.

A glass fell to the floor, shattering into tiny shards on the tile, followed by another, and soon they were all tumbling from the cupboards like the house was screaming in protest. But the pain was pleasure and the pressure that built in me was unlike anything I'd ever felt before.

Wesley became crazed, his nails digging into my skin as my hips bucked up to meet his stronghold on them, his cock grazing every nerve and lighting them on fire. My aching core begged for release among the shattering glass and ragged breathing. Goosebumps painted my skin and a strangled cry tore from my throat as all composure was lost and the building orgasm overtook all rational thought.

Wesley followed over the edge as my cunt throbbed around him. My back arched off the counter as his stomach tightened. His hand raked up my back and pulled tightly in my hair, sending a wave of delicious tightness through my spine as he finished in a flurry of stuttering hips and groans.

Stars flooded my vision as he ripped from me, leaving me achingly hollow after the pressure of him. He shocked me when I felt his face briefly between my legs, his tongue swirling around the excruciatingly sensitive cluster of nerves before he sucked hard and I plunged even further into the dizzying fall of my climax.

"Oh, God," I cried out with my eyes screwed tightly shut and his teeth bit down, his tongue soothing the aches as my body begged for relief from the endless shockwaves.

And just like it had begun, it was over, the sound of his boots crunching across the broken glass on the kitchen floor, the ache between my thighs reminding me that the presence of passion was not the answer to all our problems. But even if he had left me there, reeling from the feeling of him fucking the frustration he felt out of our bodies, he had still given in to the temptation.

I looked down at myself, skirt around my stomach and my bodice torn open. Bruises were already forming on my hips and breasts, and the faintest pink curves of crescent moon fingernails marking my skin.

A wall had broken inside of Wesley Cameron.

I had the marks to prove it.

I grinned wickedly to myself as I pressed my fingers to my bruised lips in revelation; and so did he.

REPORTS OF TWO
HORNY TEENAGERS
NEARLY BEING
BURNED TO DEATH
POPPED UP IN MY
SEARCH TODAY

THEY HAD BROKEN INTO THE
GATES, PARKED NEAR THE
MANOR WITH THE INTENTION TO
EXPLORE THE ABANDONED
BUILDING BUT BEFORE THEY
COULD THEIR CAR COMBUSTED
WITH THEM INSIDE.

THEY SURVIVED WITH THIRD
DEGREE BURNS.

WESLEY

"How do we get her out?" I slammed my gun on the table in the library, the dust that licked the top twirling up into the air and into my nose. Both heads turned to face me. Koen's brows raised and Clay sat back against his chair to stare at me.

I hated her and I hated myself.

Every inch of her perfect body, the way her curves fit in my hands. The way her fingers pulled the hair at my nape and her nails dug into my back pulling me closer, deeper, so hard that I was sure she had drawn blood. It was ecstasy.

I hated it.

Every tiny whine that left her lips as she marked my body and we took each other right there in the kitchen. It rolled through me like fire.

She had to be a monster, a spirit, or a siren. She had to be… but I hadn't expected her to feel so human. Violent disgust rolled through me and caught in my throat. It was like Wyatt was mocking me from his grave, making me sick.

There was no stuffing these emotions back in the bag.

"An hour ago, you were insinuating that decapitating her would be the best option to end all this," Clay snapped. "Now you want to get her out?" He rose from the table, his muscles flexing beneath the navy dress shirt as he questioned my motives.

"You have every right to question my motives." I stopped him. I didn't want to fight him again; that's not why I came in here.

To be honest, I wasn't even sure why I had. Leaving the kitchen was all my brain could manage, the taste of her still clinging to my lips as I stormed through the house, trying to find something to hit. My hand still throbbed from the hole I left in the shoddy, crumbling plaster in my efforts to redirect some of the anger.

But I couldn't stop myself. The way her breath caught in her throat when she dared me to end her life. It severed my resolve of hating her and all I wanted to do was kiss her quiet, until there was nothing vindictive or mean or self-effacing left in her mind to leave her lips.

I swallowed down the image of her breathless and spread open on the island to focus on the grilling I was receiving from Clay, begrudgingly coming back to reality.

"I'm questioning it, Wesley. What the hell?" He snapped.

I opened my mouth only to shut it again and Koen started to laugh so hard that he nearly fell out of his chair. His hat tipped off his head and the blond waves shook lightly as he tossed his head back in amusement.

"What?" Clay turned that cold tone on him, his jaw tightening and his lips pressed together in a tight line.

Koen rolled forward and put his elbows on the table, looking at me with a shit-eating grin on his dumb face. He had figured it out. "Isn't is obvious? He cracked, gave in. He's had a taste of her." His accent got thicker as he mocked me but his eyes were also suspicious as they bore into mine.

Clay clued in, though, his gray eyes darting back and forth as he nodded stiffly. "You..." he stopped and inhaled slowly. "If you hurt..."

"He didn't." Florence appeared behind us. Her hair was fixed back into a bun and her face was no longer flushed with color. She looked normal, back to a state where I could try and convince myself to see her as a monster, not a woman. That was until I could see the fading marks of my teeth just below her right ear on her neck. It bolstered the noisy thud of my heart as she crossed the room toward the three of us.

Clay's hand instinctively reached out to her and I could feel the divide growing.

"If we're going to figure this out," I sighed, unable to even look at her. "We need to start acting like a damn family again. I'm sick of this."

Clay's gaze narrowed on me as he moved it away from his sweep of Florence's body; like he was checking her for marks. Like he didn't trust me.

I didn't blame him.

"We figure out how the hell to get her out of this house and we go. Fast," I ordered them. "We can't stay. The house is tearing itself apart with the effort of hurting us. We're sitting ducks here." I stopped short of trying to verbalize my remorse for being an asshole, unable to find the words. "We work better as a team. We always have. I'll start pulling my weight."

Koen snorted, a wide grin forming on his cheeky little face. "Took you long enough."

"It doesn't mean I agree with it or that...I think she's innocent. If she's behind any of this, I'll put her down," I said, but it hurt more than before when she flinched beside me. Understanding but quiet.

"Fine," Clay grunted, and the house seemed to rattle in response. "Alright."

"It's only going to get worse," Florence voiced, and we all turned to look at her. "The Manor," she steeled her nerves and pinned back her shoulders, "doesn't like people," she said.

"Obviously," I scoffed. "Tell them what you said to me."

Her eyes bore a hole into me, "Normally... As I've explained, not one single soul has been allowed to enter the Manor in all these years, but it let you three waltz right in. And now it seems to be..."

"Playing with its food," Koen finished for her.

"Exactly. I fear the only reason it's allowed the situation to progress in this way is because it wants to hurt me." She stopped again, her body growing tight as she put space between herself and Clay.

"What does that mean?" Clay asked.

"To the best of my understanding, the house likes to be in control. It enjoys inflicting punishment and that's why trying to leave is so violent. It enjoys my pain. It's why..." she turned to look at me, "it won't let me die, but it lets me attempt. It likes to watch and to feel the agony I go through when I recover from the self-inflicted damage. It enjoys taking care of me when I can't take care of myself."

We were all quiet as she continued.

"It's found something even more appealing than physical pain," she explained.

"Emotional torture," Clay finished for her. "It's going to do that through us to hurt you."

We had never faced a monster with such intellectual awareness. The Manor was playing games with us.

"You mean it's going to kill us to hurt you?" Koen asked because Clay was silenced by his anger and I wasn't in any position to guide the conversation.

"Most likely one at a time." Her bottom lip trembled. "It'll be slow…" She stopped and looked around her like she could hear it talking to her.

I still wasn't even sure how I felt about Florence.

I knew how good she felt. I knew that the passion made me feel alive.

But the memory of Wyatt still clung to my soul, severing through the scar tissue violently as a reminder of what could happen if she wasn't telling the truth.

The attraction was there, but the trust was glaringly absent.

"Come at us, you bitch," Koen demanded loudly, and Florence jumped, making Clay reach out to her again. She offered him a tight smile before looking back at me.

"I can't protect you," she said as if it was the first time.

"We don't need you to protect us," I said before Clay could argue. "This is what we do."

"Aye," Clay added, "we've survived worse than one old house."

She unlinked her hand from behind her back and extended a piece of parchment toward Clay. He looked down at it, wrapping his hand around her wrist instead of the paper.

"Are you sure?" He quietly asked her and she nodded. He pulled his glasses out and situated them on his face before setting the paper on the old table beside his notebook and started to read.

"It's not the original letter." She swallowed tightly and stared at Clay. "I wrote down as much as I could remember the moment I realized it had disappeared. The Manor had led me to it and away from it, and when I went back the next day it was gone. I turned the entire second floor over looking for it. I spent days recounting my steps wondering if I had just dreamed of finding it entirely." She paused, breathing deeply through the memory. "So many parts of the letter were illegible, as if she were too weak to hold the quill... but the ending has been burned into my mind since the moment I read it."

We all hovered as he studied the faded ink, his brows pinched tightly together in frustration.

Florence inched closer, her long fingers reaching out to show him the flow as she read out loud. "This was how she had originally written the letter. The Manor," she paused between each messy scribble. "I do not know how or why. All that I do know is that–" Florence leaned forward. "And it requires—For years I have been—but I was never enough." She inhaled slowly. "It tires of me. I can feel it tearing–at my being–punishing me, always punishing–" When she finished she stood up straight but the air in the room had shifted.

"When Agatha died it was–" she closed her eyes for a moment, steadying herself. "Violent. Disturbing. She did not die of old age. She died in front of my eyes in a way that I can not describe without being ill. It was—" Florence stopped, opening her eyes and they bore into mine. "–horrible. Her body seemed to have been decaying for an untold amount of time. I had tried to help—" She shuddered uncontrollably "—her bones twisted out of shape, she was lifted into the air and her insides were pulled outward–there was so much blood. And I could not move, or look away... the Manor forced me to watch. It was cruel."

The Manor responded to her confession with more violence as the floorboards groaned, shooting rusty nails into the air, and they fell around us like hail. Clay covered Florence as Koen and I swatted the nails away as best we could.

"I fucking hate this place," I groaned as a nail caught the skin on the back of my hand in a sharp, painful scratch.

"I didn't understand why it had forced me to witness such gruesome brutality at first but, after reading the letter and having so much time to understand the Manor and the way it acts, I realized that Agatha was being made an example of. Of what could happen if I stopped playing my part. A threat that I, too, could one day be disposable."

"So it's not just throwing telekinetic tantrums. If it really wanted to, it could turn us inside out." Koen sighed and rubbed his hands over his face, feeling the few new cuts that had been marked into his skin.

"From all my research, all the stories...It's never done anything like that to *guests*." Clay mumbled absently.

"There haven't *been* any guests! And Florence isn't a guest, she's a *prisoner*," I snapped, reminding them all of the harsh truth. Clay nodded in agreement. "It also doesn't guarantee it won't learn a new trick and use it on us at a moment's notice."

"Are there more journals?" Clay asked Florence and she shook her head.

"Only the one."

"There's something about the letter that doesn't sit right. Mrs. Warren had written *'and it requires.'* I think for the sake of figuring this all out, we need to find out exactly what it requires." He stared down at the letter. "We won't let the Manor win, Florence. I assure you." Clay looked up at her, extending his hand and linking it with hers in reassurance.

WESLEY

Florence looked back at him like she wanted to hide in his confidence, but her hand shook in his grip and the stench of overwhelming fear dripped from her. It hit me what she needed, what I needed at that moment. She didn't need to be told she would be protected. She needed to feel that she could do it herself.

"Come with me," I said loudly, Clay's hand tightening around hers. "I'm not going to hurt her. I think I proved that."

"Forgive me if I don't believe you." His eyes skipped over mine to the tiny piece of exposed and red skin where my teeth still marked her shoulder. Florence quickly fixed her sleeve.

"Drop the fucking macho act," I added. "This isn't just about you, Clayton."

"Are you fucking kidding me?" Clay rolled his eyes. "If that was meant to be an apology for being an absolutely insufferable twat, try again."

"I'm not apologizing," I clipped, unable to even come up with one. "I'm moving on because we have bigger issues to deal with than your hurt feelings."

"Wesley," Florence spoke softly, urging me to fix it.

I sighed. "I'm sorry, everything got away from me and in the momentary lack of control I acted like an arse."

Clay looked like he wanted to say something but, whatever it was, he kept it to himself and let go of her. She looked at them momentarily and nodded quietly, a small chunk of her hair falling against her face.

"Where are we going?" She asked me.

"I'm going to teach you how to use a gun," I said tightly, avoiding looking at her for too long.

Koen snorted.

"We have no idea what we're dealing with. Do you think the best way to help is to teach her firearm safety?" Koen questioned.

"Exactly. It could be anything in the walls of this house. At least if she knows she can defend herself, she might feel more secure. Stay here with Clay and keep reading. There must be something in this fucking dust pit that can help us." I waited for him to argue but he didn't. He just slumped back down into his rickety chair.

"I'll bring her back in one piece." I looked at Clay, a silent promise that I was trying to cooperate despite every muscle screaming at me to move cautiously. "Change your clothes and meet me out back," I told her, before exiting the library and wandering to the truck to grab a case of bullets.

The front door of the Manor slammed behind me as I exited. "Yeah, *fuck* you, too." I turned to stare at the brick monstrosity and scowled. "I'm going to burn you to the ground."

A gust of wind kicked under my feet and sprayed gravel on my face roughly, the sharp pebbles nipping at my skin. It was like Orchid Manor was mocking me. I stretched out my arm, sore from lifting Florence. The wound there had tugged under the stress and was bleeding through my shirt. I grabbed a dirty rag from the cab and tore off a piece. Stripping from my sweater, I inspected it before covering it tightly with the scrap, then tugged on a new shirt.

I scoffed as I found myself hesitating on what shirt to wear, pissed off that my brain was already starting to give in to the easy groove of needing her validation. I told myself I didn't care if I made her smile or laugh...

Collecting everything I needed, I brought it to the backyard to find her in a pair of black overalls and a t-shirt that stuck tightly to her chest and shoulders. I shifted in the gravel and pinned my shoulders together as I fought the urge to tell her she looked pretty.

She plaited her hair back off her face, leaving a few loose strands that gently curled around her round face. "What took you so long?" Florence grumbled.

"I'm sorry, *Princess*. I was grabbing a few things," I said condescendingly, setting the box on the table.

"Let's just get this over with," she sighed and reached out for the gun.

I hesitated to give it to her, but she noticed.

"Oh, I forgot, you can make love to me on the kitchen counter, but you can't look me in the eye." She crossed her arms over her chest. "Romance is dead."

"Who the hell taught you that phrase?" I nearly choked on my spit. "Don't be so dramatic. What we did was hardly love-making. It was a sloppy hate-fuck at best."

"Who's being dramatic now?" She hummed.

"It was an outlet, Florence," I said, her brows scrunched together at my use of her name. "Nothing more, nothing less. We've all been pent up in this house for too long."

"Just give me the gun, Wesley," she snapped and held out her hand.

I loaded the chamber, turned the safety off, and handed it to her. Our fingers brushed together and caused tiny sparks to explode on my skin and I know she felt it too because she rubbed them together as she adjusted the gun in her dominant hand.

"You're left-handed?" I asked her.

"Does that make me less of a monster?" She mumbled.

"No," I didn't hesitate, but the thought of something as simple as being left handed tugged at the walls of my heart. *Yes.* I wanted to correct myself but stopped when I noticed she was glaring at me. "Point that somewhere else." I looked down at the gun between us.

"Don't tempt me." She didn't laugh but the corner of her mouth curled up when she said it and raised the gun. "What do you want me to hit?"

"Hit?" I chuckled. "I'll be impressed if that gun doesn't knock you on your ass."

She scoffed under her breath and waited.

"Alright, tough guy, that statue is ten yards out."

Florence looked where I was pointing and inhaled slowly, steadying her grip on the weapon before gently pulling the trigger and firing one perfectly straight and clean shot.

A hunk of stone flew from the statue and Florence turned to me.

"Anything else you want to teach me, Wesley?"

No, but I wanted her to keep saying my name like that.

"Why didn't you say you could shoot?" I asked her.

"Because you didn't ask." Her head leaned to the side when she answered. "You made the mistake you always make. You assumed."

God, I hated how well she'd caught on to me.

She read me like a book and I couldn't stop the smile on my face.

"Do it again," I nodded, not bothering to conceal the swell of pride that rose inside me and she turned back to her target.

And so she did.

Each target set up was knocked down and the longer we stood outside at target practice the better she got. It was weird to–spend time with her that wasn't oozing with hatred.

"Where did you learn to handle a gun?" I asked her, reloading the chamber.

"My Father, God rest his soul," she said, rubbing her hands on her pants and inhaling slowly. "Despite my husband's efforts, before marriage I was quite the–" she scrunched up her nose looking for the word. *Fuck it was cute* and it made my chest warm in the worst kind of way.

"A tomboy?" I offered and she furrowed her brows. I tried again, "The opposite of a proper Lady?"

"Yes. I often spent most of my days in the fields with the animals and in nature. I liked to have dirty hands and sun kissed cheeks." Florence pointed to the soft speckle of freckles across her nose.

"I never would have guessed that about you," I said, clenching my jaw to keep from giving her too much emotion.

"Well, Wesley, perhaps a little more time spent in conversation and a little less time spent dreaming up ways to do away with me would be helpful," Florence hummed in a tone sweet as honey. "Sadly I don't think a gun will help our issue in the long run." She stepped toward me and looked down at the weapon in my hands.

"Unfortunately we're on the same page for once." I nodded.

Her green eyes were so vibrant under the sun and from this angle I could see all the flecks of color that hid in her irises. It caught me off guard how human she was in these moments. I cleared my throat when the urge to kiss her arose and shoved away the impulse.

"But it never hurts to be prepared."

Florence smiled up at me, a tight smile, full of nerves. "Thank you for trying to make me feel more safe, Wesley. Your efforts have not gone unnoticed."

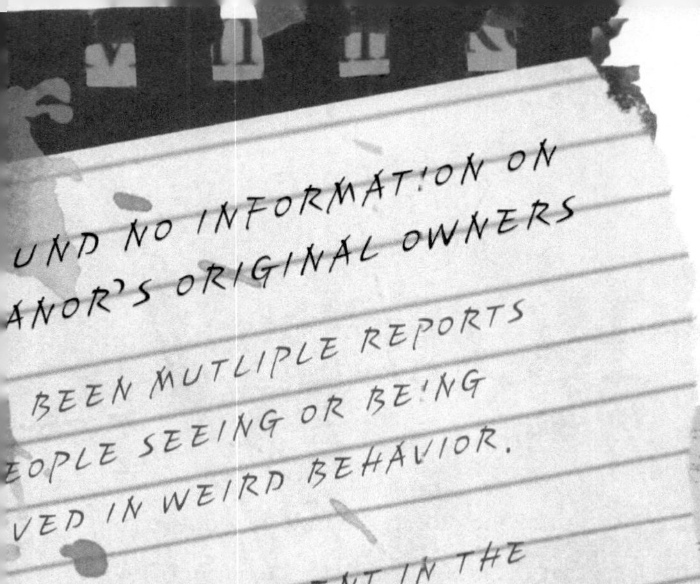

...UND NO INFORMATION ON
...ANOR'S ORIGINAL OWNERS

...BEEN MUTLIPLE REPORTS
...EOPLE SEEING OR BEING
...VED IN WEIRD BEHAVIOR.

...EAL ESTATE AGENT IN THE
...TIES SUFFERED A MENTAL
...EAK DOWN AFTER VISITING IN
...EMPT TO APPRAISE THE MANOR
FOR SALE.

...E SUFFERED WHAT THE DOCTOR
...DESCRIBED SCHIZOPHRENIA. HE
...AS LOCKED IN AN ASYLUM IN TOWN
...UNTIL DEATH. REPORTS SAID HE
...RANTED ABOUT THE MANOR TRYING
TO KILL HIM. THEY FOUND NO
EVIDENCE OF HIS CLAIMS.

KOEN

I could watch her for hours. She moved around the study, trying to clean another mess that the house had decided to create. It was happening more often now but none of us had been seriously injured so far.

It had drained all the water from the pool in the bathing room and killed all the flowers in the front yard. Florence said she had never seen anything like it and I could tell it was making her sad. Wes was taking his shift with Clay in the library, which seemed to be the place most affected. The house had taken to shattering the glass windows at a moment's notice.

"Are you going to help?" She turned to me.

She looked so pretty in her overalls and tank top. It was strange to think that she had been bundled beneath all those layers of blouses and skirts for so long, when her natural figure was one to be celebrated without the help of any corsets or clothing trickery.

Her auburn hair cascaded over her shoulders as she stood up and put her hands on her hips.

"Koen." She waved her hands in the air.

"No," I hummed, unable to take my eyes off her. "I have a better idea."

Hoping off the couch, I took her by the hand and dragged her out into the foyer of the Manor, beneath the chandelier. I took out my phone, barely enough battery left but just enough to make her smile. I opened my downloaded songs and set it on the table before hitting play. A procession of electric guitar and soft drums echoed off the high ceiling of the Manor.

"Dance with me?"

"I think our definitions of dancing might be slightly different, Koen," Florence quipped but took my hand anyway, curling against my body as I wrapped my other arm around her waist.

"Swaying side to side is the same in every period, Blossom," I chuckled and let the music guide us as we danced in lazy circles beneath the flickering candlelight of the chandelier. "One day, we'll have time, and you can teach me the waltz?"

I felt her body tense at the mention of the future. The same way it always did when we mentioned doing anything outside the Manor or dreamed out loud about our futures beyond the haunted walls.

"That would be nice." She entertained the idea but I could tell the conversation had turned her thoughts sour. "Will you tell me about your life before this?" She asked me.

I had known that Clay would have told her some of the moments in our pasts. That was just him; he shared everything because he believed it was a way to spread knowledge. But sometimes secrets were meant to be kept.

"What do you want to know?" I asked her.

"Everything."

"I've known Wes since I could talk. I was so little when my parents died. I don't remember their faces but Wes has always been there for me." I shrugged. "His parents rescued me from a vampire nest when I was young and I've been hunting with them ever since."

"I'm sorry about your parents." She kissed my cheek, where a soft dimple formed from my smile, and a scowl formed on her lips.

"Don't be." I stole a kiss from her, choosing to chase the feeling of her lips on my skin instead of dwelling on death. "I didn't know them."

"It's heartbreaking all the same, Koen." She rubbed her hand over my face. "It must be exhausting, moving all the time like that."

"Do you still get sad about your lost life?" I asked her. Clay had shown me all the information about her, about her friend Aisling. I couldn't imagine watching life grow and thrive outside my reach like that.

"All the time." She said it in a way that made it seem like, even at a distance, it was better than nothing; and maybe it was but it still felt wrong.

"I don't think I was ever meant for normalcy, Koen. The universe had other plans."

"I know for certain I would die if I stopped moving. I've never lived in one place for longer than a month," I trailed off.

"I'm an advocate for freedom, but even that seems..." She stopped.

"Chaotic?" I laughed and tangled our fingers together a little tighter. "It is. But with Clay and Wes, it just feels normal. There's not much I wouldn't do for them. They're my only family."

"The loyalty between the three of you is rather impressive," Florence noted.

"That loyalty has kept us alive longer than most Hunters." I swallowed tightly. "We've had a lot of close calls that could have ended a lot worse if we hadn't had each other's backs."

"Except here," she said, her tone hesitant.

"This–" I stopped. "–you…" I held her hand to my lips and stared across the distance into her bright green eyes. "…are different. We've fought over girls before," I explained lightly. Clayton usually wins the fight. He's a little more debonair."

She shrugged but agreed. "Maybe a bit. But you are sweet and charismatic."

"We decided a long time ago that sharing was always better than fighting. Of course, only in the instances when sharing was favored and consented to. And if it wasn't, it was always in good fun. Flirting and fighting; making it a competition was a way to keep busy."

Florence stared at me like I had three heads.

"You aren't a competition is what I'm trying to say," I explained. "It's different with you. We aren't bored, this isn't a game, we're *invested*."

"That's a very odd way to look at promiscuity, Koen," she said.

"You aren't entirely wrong, but I also don't think you have an issue with it," I challenged her. "I think you enjoy the attention."

"It was odd at first." Her brows scrunched. "But it's been so long I think I craved it more than I wanted to admit. Now I find myself searching for you all the time."

"I won't argue with that," I said to her, my cock twitching at the thought of her being so vulnerable like that. "So you enjoyed it then?"

"Perhaps," she hummed. "Or perhaps I'm just caught up in the moment and looking to say all the right things to you because there is enough bad going on around us. Some forbidden fantasies and candle-light dancing to make me forget the Manor is trying to kill you all."

I held onto her a little tighter. My own heart was in utter disbelief that I had come this far in life only to fall for a woman who had lived her entire life in some sort of twisted immortal cage. I pushed her outward, spinning her away from me, and brought her back with her back to my chest, wrapping my arms around her and nuzzling my chin against her neck.

"After all is said and done," I whispered, "we'll go back to Hunting." I paused, the words sticky in my throat as I tried to articulate my confused and disappointed thoughts. "The foolish kid in me wants to ask you to come with us, selfish too, I guess, but after over a century of being unable to decide for yourself. I can't expect that of you," I sighed. "But if Clay does figure this out and we can get you free, what will you do?" I asked her.

She stopped briefly. She hadn't expected me to ask that.

Turning in my arms, she tilted her chin to the ceiling and spoke of her dreams. "I think I would just walk." She laughed. "As silly as that sounds, so many small things were taken. But just the freedom to go anywhere is what I want back."

"It doesn't sound silly at all." I shook my head. "Promise you'll try all the food? Everything is so different now and you've got to experience it all." I smiled at her, taking the chance to steal a feathery kiss from her jaw before she looked back at me.

Florence looked at me for a long time and I just stared back. I was unable to convey all of my intense emotions in words correctly. "Koen, I understand what you're doing," she said slowly. "But I don't understand why. Are you trying to push me away?"

"Don't," I stopped her with another languid kiss that lasted longer and felt sadder than the others. "I would never." I silenced her worries as quickly as they had formed, or at least attempted to. "I just want you to understand that you have a choice here," I explained. "That no matter what it might be, we'll respect that."

Respect. The word made her flinch.

"Why is that such a hard concept to grasp?"

"Because respect was never freely given to me, at least not by the men in my life. That was reserved only for other men. I was never extended such a courtesy."

Her sentiment was valid, but it didn't ease the stinging in my chest anymore than if she had just shrugged or ignored my question. I felt so bad for her past and all the things she had to endure without the love and protection of a family that genuinely cared about her.

"We can teach you more about equality later. I'm sure Clay has a thousand thoughts on the matter."

"I have four more books to read," she joked.

I dropped her hand from mine and lifted her chin to me, pressing our lips together softly. The kiss drowned out the shuddering of the floor boards from the house as she sunk into my touch with a needy urgency.

"I like this song," she breathed against my lips when she pulled away. "It's pretty."

"You're pretty," I teased back and spun her away from me again. A fit of giggles exploded from her and cascaded into the air.

"Thank you," she whispered when she returned, her hair messy and her cheeks flushed. "You always know when I need to..."

"Feel human?" I finished for her. "You make me feel human too, you know?"

"That's silly."

"It's the most serious I've ever been," I said, holding her face in my hands. "You make me feel human, Florence."

It was short of telling her that I loved her.

I could have yelled it at the top of my lungs repeatedly if I thought she would be ready to hear such blatant nonsense. But this would have to do and, by the look on her face, she understood every tiny unsaid word behind what I had said.

I love you, more than the moon loves the sky and the flowers love the sun.

CLAYTON

"What is this?" I reached out and brushed her hair back from her neck. There's a splattering of tiny bruises along her throat behind her ear.

Florence's eyes were still closed as she lay in the warm sun. We had settled down in the middle of the field after she convinced me I needed to leave the library. She wasn't wrong but I felt crazy going over that information repeatedly without results.

The wildflowers seemed to be the only untouched part of the grounds. Either too far from the Manor's presence—and I understood how crazy I sounded—or the Manor felt bad for punishing her and the field was a small mercy. Malicious in nature, almost a form of supernatural gaslighting, it made Florence smile and I couldn't deny her that by questioning the reasoning behind it.

"What?" She didn't open her eyes but leaned into my touch and hummed from the contact. My fingers buzzed against her skin and I desperately wanted to feel that on my lips.

"There are bruises on your neck," I said quietly, as if my voice would hurt her in some way.

She had looked so fragile lately. It had been three weeks of us running in circles trying to figure out what the hell was going on and, with each day that passed, Florence grew more sluggish, quieter, and unlike herself.

I licked my bottom lip in frustration and paused, waiting for her to devise an excuse.

"I don't know," she said, her lips barely moving. "What does it matter? They'll fade in a few hours and I'll be unblemished again."

Her words were tight and laced with a venom I had never heard from her.

"Florence." I sat up on my elbow to stare down at her, eyes still closed, breathing so deep she might as well have been asleep. It wasn't like the time before; it wasn't a trance; whatever was going on was bone deep. She was fully conscious of the shift but refused to talk about it. Perhaps she was trying to protect us, but it was only distracting to see her so... distant.

"Are you feeling alright?"

"Why do you keep asking me silly questions, Clay?"

"Because I'm worried about you." I didn't hesitate.

"The Manor won't let me die. There isn't anything to worry about," she answered so callously that I wasn't sure she even heard herself.

"You say that like it means anything. You've said it before and..."

"Nothing kills me, Clay. I think we've proven that."

She was barricading herself behind stone walls.

"Do you hear yourself?" I asked her and, finally, her eyes cracked open. When her brows kissed in a way that showed her frustration with me, and that time there was no urge to touch her, irritation overtook my every desire.

"Why am I not allowed to enjoy the sunshine while it's here?" She asked.

"You know that's not what I asked, Florence." I ground my teeth together.

"I feel fine." She stared at me, her shoulders rolling back into the grass as she reached for one of her books. "Read to me?" She asked, batting her long lashes at me.

"No." I refused to take the book from her and she scowled at me, "I want to know what's going on with you. I don't want to read poetry and pretend."

She laughed. The motion made the curls around her neck bounce as she sat up in the grass and crawled into my lap with her knees on either side of my thighs. She slowly started to unbutton my shirt but I pushed her hands away, rewarded only with an annoyed huff of air.

"I'll go find Koen," she snapped and tried to rise from my lap.

"That's not how this works." I grabbed her wrists and pulled her back, the words vibrating from the base of my throat. "Take what you want, but answer my question."

Florence stared at me for a long moment, gauging where my head was before she opened her mouth again. "There's nothing wrong, Clay." She leaned in close, "I'm just looking for a pleasant distraction from everything happening around us. Is that so wrong?"

"Yes." I didn't hesitate. "There is something else going on with you."

"I just want your touch," she whined.

"That might work on Koen, even Wes." I stopped and pushed some of her hair off her shoulder with delicate fingers. But not me. Any small change from you can shift everything we're doing. It's not meant to make you feel studied or watched; I just need you to be honest with me."

"I am being honest." She swallowed, her throat bobbing gently as she dipped her head to meet my lips.

Distraction was a languid, honey-sweet kiss, as her fingers raked into my hair at the back of my neck. Her touch on my skin was cool, like ice, and goosebumps formed down my arms as I leaned back in the grass on my elbows.

Giving in to her.

I berated myself every second of it.

"Will you read to me now?" She broke away with a soft smile.

"Of course," I surrendered. She slipped from my lap and grabbed the book to hand to me before her hands shifted to the belt on my pants.

"What are you doing?" I asked her as she quickly popped the button on my jeans and looked up at me through heavy lashes.

"Read, Mr. Dunn," she quipped, tugging down the zipper, the palm of her hand brushing over my cock already straining in my pants.

My hips stuttered beneath her touch as I flipped open the book and searched the pages for a poem to read. My fingers caught on the page as she worked my boxers over my hips just enough for my shaft to pop free of the waistband. Her finger rolled over the tip, collecting the bead of precum that formed, and she stared up at me with sunshine reflected in her darkened green eyes.

"Before I found her, I had found." I started to read the poem on the page. *Madison Julius Cawein's, Apocalypse.* It was short but the feeling in my gut warned me that I probably wouldn't make it very far with how Florence was staring at me. "Within my heart," I gasped as her hands took hold of my shaft, so thick in her fingers. She wet her lips, starting to pump gently as she bent over, acutely aware of what she was doing to me.

Her tongue flicked over my head, gathering up the first traces of me that formed and causing my hips to arch into her touch like a needy idiot. The sun was hot as it poured down over us but her lips and fingertips were cool, forming the most tantalizing mix of pleasure. Florence traced her tongue in a slow, winding strip down the underside of my cock, my thighs trembling as her gaze turned up on me, wide and hazy with lust.

"As in a brook." The words came out strangled as I gasped for air at the mere sight of her there. Her head turned upright to stare at me with her cheek resting against the throbbing length of my cock. The sun caught in her lashes and in the beads of sweat on her sweet, plump lips.

"Reflections of her: now a sound," I recited slowly as she traced her tongue up my shaft, swirling over the head and pulling the length between her open lips.

A guttural moan escaped my throat as her lips tightened around my girth and she rolled my head around with her tongue. Florence pumped forward and backward, each stroke fueling the blaze that roared in my gut. Spit rolled down her chin as she drew back and looked up at me.

"Keep going." She kissed my thigh.

"Of imaged beauty; now a look." I stared at her with intent, wanting so badly to ravage her in the field. To feel how our bodies melted together beneath the hot sun. But Florence was determined to unravel me in her way.

My head fell back as she took my cock between her swollen lips, gliding hungrily down the entire length to the hilt. Hips bucking from the sensation, the head of my cock thrust against the back of her throat, dragging the most delicious whine from her that vibrated against my cock and balls.

"So when I found her…" I trailed off as her tongue slid back up my length and flicked at my head before dropping down again, "…gazing in."

Spit formed on her lips, slick and hot. Florence started to move faster, forcing the pressure to build at a pace that made it hard to speak.

"Those Bibles of her eyes, above…" Each word from my mouth seemed to fuel her need to leave me completely undone. Her eyes flickered up to me, full of water, as she worked my cock into the back of her throat and sputtered around the side, her cheek hollowing out as she sucked harder. "All earth, I read no word of sin;"

A chuckle of amusement left her lips and the cool air that she fanned over my cock was heaven on the senses, forcing my knee to rise against her side and hold myself steady. Florence wrapped her fingers around the hilt, squeezing carefully as she worked the head with her tongue.

"Their holy chapters all were love…Florence." I choked out her name as her hand started to pump faster. I wouldn't last if she continued to do that with her tongue.

"Yes, Clay?" She abruptly stopped, peering up at me with the tip of my cock resting against her tongue and her fingers still softly pumping at the base of my shaft.

I moaned. "I…" My thighs clenched as she licked a delicate swipe, and her lips curved into that dangerous smile again.

"Finish the poem," she demanded, scraping her teeth against my head.

"I read them through. I read and saw," I groaned as she popped me back into her mouth, "The soul impatient of the sod."

"That's good," she praised, lapping up the slick that formed, pushing me closer and closer to the edge. The muffled sound of her voice with my cock filling her pretty mouth was enough for me to snap. My skin was on fire with a thousand tiny melting points at her praise.

"Her soul, that through her eyes, did draw…" I gripped the book tightly as she worked faster and sucked harder. Dragging the orgasm from the depths of my stomach one pump at a time until I couldn't control myself. When her blown-out emerald eyes flickered back to mine for the final time, the tension snapped, and my gut tightened. "Mine to the higher love of God," I cried out as I came.

My body reeled from the euphoria in tiny aftershocks, with my hips softly pumping up into her mouth until she pulled back, licking her lips, and sat back on her heels to stare at me. I leaned forward, collected her in my arms, and pulled her into the grass. Florence's auburn hair fanned out over the grass, and her eyes reflected the clouds in the sky. I traced her face with my eyes.

"You are magnificent," I huffed, but the compliment felt hollow even then. How was I supposed to explain to her how beautiful and incredible she was with a simple descriptor? I wanted to kiss every inch of her skin and read her poetry until we could barely keep our eyes open.

But the Manor loomed and the world felt suffocating.

Even after all that she was still cold to the touch, and this scared me to my core.

"I do enjoy the sound of your voice as you struggle to remain composed." She laughed.

"I can't resist you," I sighed. "I'll always read you poetry if it ends that way."

She closed her eyes, laughing, and shook her head at me. "I think I just found a favorite poem," she mused.

I dipped down against her, kissing her until she begged me to stop and the sun had sunk low in the sky.

FLORENCE

After the time with Clay in the field I had needed a moment to myself. It had felt incredible to take control, indulging in the craving of dominance and sin instead of managing the fear of our current predicament. I left Clay and his incessant questions behind as the venomous frustrations bubbled beneath the surface. What was wrong with wanting it all to stay the same?

The Manor would play nice if only they would.

We had stepped out of line—

No... I stopped, trying to collect myself. *We hadn't.*

You have.

The Manor argued and knocked a lamp from the nearby wardrobe to the floor.

I hated that I couldn't decipher between my true thoughts and the interference of the Manor. It wanted me to turn against them and it was working. Slowly I could feel it creeping up my spine and taking hold.

A knock at the door forced me to look up from my book where it laid open and unread in my lap. I found Wesley standing in the frame, his dark shirt pulled tightly over his broad shoulders and a stern look on his handsome face.

"Good afternoon, Wesley," I hummed his name, knowing its effect on him, and looked back down.

The last few days were exhausting.

Every muscle in my body was tired and sore and no amount of stretching or warm baths seemed to help ease the ache in my bones. I hadn't felt this exhausted in over a century, and I couldn't understand why I wasn't immune to all the aches and pains that I had been for so long. I was hungry and tired, too cold and too hot.

I felt...*human*.

"I want to try to get you over the property line," he said in a low, heavy tone, thick with purpose.

I looked up at him over my book, wanting to slap the smug look off his face.

"It won't work."

He crossed into my room and stood at the foot of my bed.

"Never took you as a pessimist," Wesley grumbled.

I shot back at him in an icy tone, "I'm not, it's just the truth. Did you come to mock me or–"

"What is going on with you?" He asked, just like Clay had, and Koen before him.

"Nothing." I closed my book with force and stared at him. "There's no point in trying to get me past the property line. You might as well put a bullet in my brain."

Wesley barked out a surprised laugh at that. "I've been trying."

"Try *harder*."

Venom licked at my tired muscles. I hadn't meant to sound so harsh or gloomy but I couldn't take it anymore. With each passing day the dangers grew, the likelihood of any of them getting out alive shrunk, and I would be left here with the knowledge that I hadn't been able to protect them. And where Koen and Clay had become doubly concerned, Wesley stared at me like I was a problem he could solve.

His chest rose slowly and fell even slower as he exhaled. "We have to try," he said. "I don't know what's wrong with you, but it's starting to piss me off."

"Starting? You've been '*pissed off*' about my presence since the moment you laid eyes on me," I hummed quietly, annoyed by his sudden shift, and let my head fall to the side.

"I'm pissed off for a different reason now," he admitted.

"There's nothing wrong," I said. He may have been good at denying it but he'd looked at me differently since that day in the kitchen. "I'm in the same condition you found me in."

"That's bullshit." Wesley leaned against the footboard of the bed and stared at me with judgment in his eyes. "You are slower to heal, disassociate in the middle of conversations, and hell, you have bags under your eyes! You look like you haven't slept in weeks–" I opened my mouth to interject and he held a finger up to silence me. My back bristled and an irrational anger squeezed my chest. "–and I know you said that the Manor kept you from needing to sleep–but even Clay said you looked like you were suffering from fatigue. You're moody. You barely leave this room, and you snapped at Koen yesterday during dinner.

He made a point, but Koen had listed everything we should be trying.

A list of things that I had almost killed myself trying over and over again over the last century.

It was annoying and frustrating.

"I'm not tired," I denied, and shook my head. I was *exhausted*.

No you aren't.

The darkness raked its claws through my thoughts. It had started to take its hold so much faster than it ever had before, gripping and tearing at the part of me that was able to reason and be calm and critical. I was all fear and rage and frustration. I was trying so hard to protect them, help myself, and keep the Manor at bay in any way possible–it was exhausting.

I wouldn't allow myself to sleep, which had never been a problem before but the Manor seemed to have changed its rules for me. If I slept I had no idea what was happening to them, and it was easier for the Manor to keep me unconscious. *It was like I was the only one who took the threat the Manor posed to their lives seriously.*

No, that wasn't true. I *knew* that wasn't true. But then again, if they would just leave they would be safe and this could be over. I could sleep again.

I don't need sleep, I thought. *I need them to be gone.* I shuddered, feeling the black thought take over and twist my meaning in my mind. *No! I need them to be safe.* I tried to convince myself.

"Something," his tone dropped, and the fire in his eyes turned cold with concern, "is wrong."

"You're in a haunted house with a caged monster, Wesley. What do you expect? Sunshine? Rainbows?" I asked him, my fingers digging into the sheets in anger. At the word monster it was almost as if I had slapped him.

"What, you're the only person who gets to call me that?" I said with malice as my lips curled into a tight smile.

"Your flippant attitude proves my point, Florence," he answered. "I've always said that you were a monster but, for the first time since we arrived here, I think you're starting to believe it."

Rage licked at my common sense. It seemed to be the first emotion my body found these days. I wanted to throw things and scream at the top of my lungs— the only way to find any release was through cutting words and violence. But it was always a short lived reprieve as the look of concern in their eyes would trigger the indignation again and the cycle would start anew.

"How about you crawl into bed and *fuck* the attitude out of me?" I snapped.

He huffed, shaking his head, and a few soft golden waves fell out of place. "That right there," he said, eyebrows raised and with a know-it-all smirk. "Do you hear yourself? You know it's not you. *Stop* trying to distract me."

"You said it before. It's a release for you. Why can't it be for me?" I asked, quickly growing more irritated with the conversation. Irritated with his presence. His gaze on me felt like fire in my veins, making my skin itchy.

He wants you dead.

The Manor groaned under the weight of our conversation. He felt it, eyes darting, ready for whatever object it may send flying his way.

"It can," he sighed, like I should have known the answer. "But that's not what this is about. This is you trying to strong-arm your way into a distraction so I stop asking questions. Just like you did to Clay the other day. It looked like fun." He narrowed his eyes on me and leaned against the footboard.

His knuckles turned white. "But did you stop to think about what you were doing to him? Forcing him to participate when he's emotionally pulled in a hundred directions?" He paused for effect, letting the weight of his words sink in. I forced myself still as the darkness imagined what it would be like to wrap my fingers around his throat and squeeze until all the breath had leaked from his lips... I pinched my thigh under the blankets, trying to pull myself back from the daymare.

"You want to pretend that the Manor is at fault for all the pain over the last few weeks, but you are as much to blame as the walls and bricks we're trapped in."

"*I'm trapped*. You are free to go," I corrected him.

"You're hurting them, Florence. You have to see that?"

I swallowed hard, searching for a way to get control.

Don't let him take you.

It repeated until it was nothing but a chorus of eerie whispers at the forefront of my thoughts.

"Careful, Wesley," I purred, pushing back the sheet and crawling across the bed toward him. "You keep asking questions. Someone might think you care about me."

His face tightened with pain and frustration.

"I care about Koen and Clay," he responded, the fire raging again, "and right now they're worried about you." He pushed my hand away as I reached out for his belt. "You're acting like a fucking psychopath," he spat. "This house is doing something to you. Pretend you're immortal fine, but I know you feel it. *Vengeful*."

"Vengeful?"

Wesley smirked at me and I felt the anger dissipating around me as I sank into that moment with him. The window panes rattled as the house felt my surrender.

"It suits you." He chuckled tightly.

"I'm not sure you understand how compliments work." I scowled.

"You're not as soft as the others believe. You aren't as weak or hopeless. You're intelligent and quick to learn. You are empathetic but there's a darkness and bitterness from being trapped all these years. It comes and goes, and you fight it, but I can see it even if they don't. You may not be a spirit, but you are vengeful." He reached out and flicked a thumb over my bottom lip.

I sat back against the bed and glared at him.

"I'm not bitter," I said, "and poetic sentiments, even from you, don't change that this won't work."

"You are losing your softness and understanding and have replaced it with anger," he said. "You're cruel and your words are icy whenever you speak to someone. You're *sick*."

I huffed out a dry laugh. It was loud, cold, and out of control but I didn't entertain him with a response.

"If you're so hell-bent on dying, what does it hurt to try to get off the property?" He asked me. "They need hope, Florence," he added and it struck true, making me sick.

I'm the reason they were in this mess.

*They're the reason **you** are in this mess.*

The Manor groaned, the floorboards rippling angrily.

It only added fuel to the fury that he was right.

"Fine," I conceded. "But you'll understand how idiotic a plan this is very quickly once the house starts truly punishing us all."

"The house *is* punishing us."

He had no idea just how bad it could get.

FLORENCE

Koen and Wesley accompanied me to the gate. Koen was rightfully terrified and clung to his gun like it could make him feel better. I was still getting used to wearing trousers. They hugged at my waist and skimmed lightly over my hips, accentuating the natural curves of my body. They were an odd feeling but they were much easier to move around in. The morning air clung to my bare arms and licked at my frozen cheeks as I stared at the gate.

"Stand over there," I instructed, my eyes locked with Koens.

"Blossom..." He reached out to me, but I pulled away.

"It'll be okay." I forced a fake smile to my lips, so fed up with being treated as if I were incapable, too fragile and precious. Like I was their pet.

Wait, no.

I stopped and stared back at the house, confused.

I tried to organize my thoughts, to shake free of the encroaching hateful inclinations that eclipsed my own. I fought to find happy memories but I was met with brick walls and darkness. I was confused and every thought in my mind felt incomplete and twisted.

"Florence?" Wesley asked and stepped forward, barricading himself between me and Koen.

That only made me feel worse. Rage split the ends of my resolve and I practically growled at him.

"Do I need to send him away?" Wesley quietly asked me without caring about his tone.

"No," I didn't hesitate. Doing that would only make these emotions ten times harder to control and it was bad enough already. "I'm fine," I insist, but I was far from that. I felt as if I were on the precipice of becoming exactly what Wesley had accused me of.

"Are you sure?" He snapped each word slowly, eyes glaring into me and searching deeply, letting the words sink in before he allowed me to continue.

"Let's just get this over with," I huffed. I spun on my heel and attempted to cross the invisible threshold at the gate. The reaction was just as immediate as expected. I was propelled violently through the air and slammed back through the doors of the Manor and against the wall by the stairs, sliding pathetically to the floor under the weight of the invisible pressure that had thrown me.

"Jesus!" Clay slid across the floor, setting his notebook down and extending his hands to me. "You alright?"

No.

"Yes." I pushed to my feet and pulled my hands from his. He was so warm and touching him with my cold fingertips made me sad.

"You're bleeding," Clay scowled, and his lips jutted out as he handed me a handkerchief.

Because of you.

The curtains blew up dramatically, dancing in the sunlight. The Manor was elated.

"I'll be fine." I pushed around him, taking the cloth and pressing it to my collarbone where the blood trickled from a small cut. "It'll heal in no time." I gave him a tight smile before returning to Wesley and Koen, standing on the front drive, locked in a hushed argument.

"Again," Wesley demanded.

"You saw what that did to her!" Koen hollered, fighting on my behalf for me.

"It's okay, Koen." I put my hand out and handed Wesley the blood-soaked cloth. "Wesley is trying to force the barrier to break by overusing it."

Fire-filled hazel eyes met mine and sent a wave of heat through my body. His fingers brushed over the cloth, pausing to look down and, for a second, I thought he might reconsider his approach.

"Where Clay's logic fails, your brute force might be the answer, correct?" I questioned.

"Can you do it again?" He asked me.

"Yes."

And so I did.

I walked into the barrier only to be thrown, dragged, kicked, and tumbled back to the Manor. Each time, the house grew more violent. I was covered in scrapes and bruises that etched into my pale skin, and I knew from the dull throb that radiated from me that I wasn't healing. When I hit the ground next I heard the bones in my wrist snap, a scream tore from my throat, and Clay tried to call time on the experiment until I could regain my composure.

"You can't keep doing this!" He followed me down the stairs as I approached the front door again. My shoulders were beaten down and my legs shook violently, but I kept walking. The rage that filled my muscles was enough adrenaline to keep pushing.

Don't let them stop you.

A sick, haunted laughter, pleasant and eerie, echoed through me and tickled at my muscles. The Manor was enjoying every single moment of my anguish.

Prove to them how cruel they can be.

"Florence! You aren't healing!" Clay urged, the plea in his cracked voice demanding that I turn around to look at him. His shoulders were pinned back in a dark jumper that molded to his firm chest and flexed biceps. Gray eyes bore into me, screaming a thousand pleas to stop, but I couldn't.

I didn't have control anymore.

"Just stop." His gaze dropped and his jaw ticked. "This isn't working," he said.

The Manor had always been in control but, at that moment, I could feel its venom coursing through my bloodstream. It was like we were melting together, and soon...

My memories flickered to Agatha Warren.

Her broken, crippled body. Curled into a ball on the bed before being flung into the air and torn apart by the house; she died alone the way she had lived for years.

But how long had she been here? She had been married and loved... hadn't she?

So what had happened?

There were too many questions and not enough answers.

Fear gripped me.

If I died with them in the house...

They'll die slowly, one by one.

"I can't stop," I said curtly, turning from the front door to Wesley and Koen.

They'd lose each other.

I could feel his stare on my back as I walked to the gate, with my vision pinpointing and my limbs trembling with each step. Koen reached out but I avoided the touch. I wandered to the furthest point before the barrier and stared at it.

Over and over again.

"You don't have to keep doing this, Blossom." Koen stood off to the side, his evergreen eyes pleading with me. Begging me to look at him and, if anyone could win out over the rage, it was him, but I couldn't let him. I needed the rage to keep them safe.

Until they break.

I fought to ignore the dark whispers in my mind. The black hateful thoughts that I now understood were not my own, but the Manor's hold on me. For years it had been whispering to me. How had it taken me so long to see it?

"If you can't handle it, Koen, go inside."

A strangled grunt left his lips and he nodded, stepping back out and disappearing from my vision. I could feel myself unraveling but there was nothing I could do to prevent it from happening. But I could shove them back, keep them at arm's length until I could figure out how to protect them, if possible.

You can't save them.

A mumbled conversation between Wesley and Koen floated over the constant hum of angry white noise in my mind. I could not actually hear them but was irritated by the whispering. Closing my eyes, I took one more deep breath and stepped into the barrier again.

The Manor was sick of my games.

My head flew back first, arms and chest following as it dragged me into the Manor on violent winds. I rolled across the hardwood floor and hit the wall with so much force the window above me rattled. I braced for impact as the house threw one last fit, the window shattering violently above me and raining glass shards down over me that sliced painfully into my skin and caused me to cry out.

I saw stars and the bones in my back screamed for relief from the rolling waves of pain that cascaded down through my body. The floor was cold when I pressed my forehead to it and tried to work through the pain that rattled my bones. The cuts weren't deep, but there were so many of them that the pain was truly overwhelming as I tried to get up. Loose shards of glass fell from the movement, each one slicing further into my skin as they dislodged, speckled in blood, to the floor.

I gasped, my knees buckling as I dropped back to the floor and embedded the glass further into my palms, but I couldn't stay down. I had to get back up. If I stayed down, the house would win, and I was through with being its victim.

My feet found purchase on the floor and I got myself upright. I stumbled toward the door and gripped the frame with my hands, forgetting the glass that had sunk into my skin. I hissed from the contact and leaned there for a second.

I heard Wesley's heavy boots on the steps and, before I could protest, he was beneath me, his arms scooping my body against his chest and carrying me back to my room. Koen and Clay weren't far behind, bounding up the stairs and through the door as Wesley finally set me down.

"Fuck," Koen swore and disappeared just as quickly as he had arrived.

"Stay down," Wesley warned when I tried to roll from the bed. "I mean it."

His usually neat hair was in messy waves as he stripped from his overshirt and laid it on the bed. Kneeling his massive frame beside the mattress, his hand took my wrist and turned it over to examine it.

"That's enough for today." He scowled, picking the glass from my skin as carefully as his big hands would allow him. "Sorry," he whispered when I flinched at his touch.

Clay kept his distance, no doubt still upset with me, but I could see how his hands curled into fists every time a shard was removed. My face was tight with pain and anger as Wesley placed them carefully on his undershirt—a small pile of glass and blood collecting on the fabric.

"I hate this," Clay declared, throwing his glasses and book across the dresser. The sight of my unhealed skin was enough to make him leave and, as angry as it made me, I held on tightly to that little piece of me that wished he hadn't.

They can't stand the real you.

They're turning their backs on you.

The human piece of me that just wanted to feel something other than venomous rage knew that those thoughts were not my own, but I *heard* them in my voice. I was confused and scared and so incredibly angry. It was as though I was not only locked in this Manor but in my mind as well, forced to watch as someone else took control of my actions.

"Alright, Vengeful," Wesley hummed, feeling my body tense. "I'm almost done."

"Don't be kind to me now," I snapped.

His jaw tightened when he looked up at me. "This kindness isn't for you," he responded, but I could see the lie as clear as day across his tight, handsome features. "It's for them."

WESLEY

"How does that feel?" I asked her when I finished wrapping her hands with the clean bandage that Koen had left on the bed before going to find Clay. A small collection of broken glass was piled in the center of my shirt, soaked in her blood from her hands, arms, face, and knees. She had sat through each painful piece being pulled from her skin.

The guilt ate at me every time she whimpered.

I had pushed her too far today, thinking that something would break if I beat my fist against the problem hard enough. And something *did*.

But it was Florence's mind and body, an outcome I hadn't wanted or expected.

"Like my body is failing me," she admitted, and it took everything inside of me to resist holding her as a response. "I've spent years healing from everything, almost instantly, Wesley..." She stopped.

I could see the internal struggle going on behind her eyes, like there was a fight for control between two sides of her. She had put together a plan in a matter of seconds and I didn't have time to interject before she said, "You can do it now, shoot me. *It'll work.*"

"No."

The lack of hesitation made her flinch.

"What?" She breathed out and stared down at her battered hands. "It's all you've wanted to do for months and now, suddenly, you have an aversion? Don't be a coward. You can end this. You can keep them safe." Her voice broke and I realized she wasn't angry. She was exhausted, and devastated. "This is the answer."

The Manor hissed in the form of tearing fabric as all the curtains in the room came crashing down around us.

"I won't do it," I said with conviction, curling my hands around hers.

The movement made her eyes flicker up to meet mine and, even though I had expected to see tears, there were none. I was taken aback by the level of weariful resolution in her emerald eyes. It broke whatever angry resolve I had left buried in my chest.

"It will kill them," I said to her, trying to help her understand through her own grief and disappointment. *It might kill me.*

"That wasn't a concern before! Don't do this to me, don't do it when there's finally hope to end it." She shifted in the bed, bringing herself closer to me, wincing in pain as she cupped my face in her hands. "I need you to do this. That bullet was made for me, and you know it. You've known it all along."

The Manor groaned around us and the wind ripped through the broken window without remorse, protesting her request in physical acts of violence. A fire raged in the fireplace where moments before there had only been embers and the chairs resting around it kicked up against the walls in an explosion of shattered wood.

"Wesley, put me *down.*"

"No," I said again. The feeling of my gun against my back was ice cold and her eyes flickered in response to how I tensed at the thought.

"Florence." I tried to stop her but wasn't fast enough. Her hand was around the metal within seconds of her realization, and she cranked the pedal with her finger on the trigger.

The barrel pressed to her bruised temple.

"I am miserable," she cried out, her hand shaking. "You and I both know how this has to end. You can't save me *and* them. I'm weak. The house made a mistake; it's pushed my body too far and I'm breaking down. It'll work now."

Her words were cold and suddenly I realized I had fallen into the frozen lake without even noticing the ice had cracked beneath me. Unable to stop her from doing this without seriously hurting her and not knowing how to proceed without hurting Koen and Clay.

Or myself...

"Go get them," she said quietly. "Drag them out, knock them out. Just get them out and, once I know you're gone, I'll do it myself."

She climbed from the bed, holding her hand out to stop me from following. "This is the answer we've been searching for. If I'm dead, you're free."

I don't want to be free.

"If I'm dead, they're *safe*." Her voice cracked as she backed away from me with shaky steps. The gun wobbled in her hand as she retreated to the safety of the shadows that seemed to engulf the room the more upset she became.

"I'm not going to help you do this." I shrugged and pulled my lip between my teeth. "If you want to kill yourself, do it in front of them! Don't be a coward."

"You're the coward." She shifted the gun toward me for a second and pain twisted across her face. "You won't help me."

"Because it's a stupid plan! Why would this work now? How many times have you tried to kill yourself in the past? It's never worked!" I resisted the urge to surge towards her from my perch on the edge of the bed. "Give me the gun back, Vengeful."

"No." She pressed it to her temple again, tears streaming down her face as her chest heaved in any attempt to steady her shallow, ragged breaths. "I'm the heart that keeps this cursed place alive. If I die, then it does, too."

"We don't know that." I stopped her delusional train of thought. "For all we know you could kill yourself and we all get trapped here in your place."

Her eyes widened in fear and her head tilted upward, hair sticking to her wet cheeks as she listened to something I couldn't hear.

"Does it talk to you?" I rose off the bed and her head snapped back to me with the movement, eyes wide with fear. "Does the house talk to you, Florence?" As I said it I knew immediately I was right. I took another step towards her despite her trying to halt my progression. "What is it saying?" I asked.

"It wants me to kill you."

There is still anger in the blunt confession, but I can see that her fear is overriding it. The house's influence and her emotions fighting over control.

"Do it then," I said to her. "If you're so ready to give it want it wants, kill me and then kill yourself, if you think it'll help."

Her hand shook around the handle of the gun, her finger so shaky that, every time she twitched, I thought she might set it off by accident.

I couldn't bear the thought and stepped forward further. I just needed to get into arm's reach.

"I can't." She shook her head.

"Why not? You hate me. I hate you. It should be easy." I taunted her, if only she would just pull the gun away from her head.

"I won't... I don't... hate you," she confessed, at war with herself, between her own feelings and the ones the Manor was forcing on her. Who the Manor wanted her to be and who she truly was.

"Yes you do, remember yourself. You hate me, I hate you. The monster and the man."

"Fighting..." She mumbled, her hand shaking but not pulling the trigger.

"Who's the coward now, Florence?" I asked her.

"Be quiet!"

"Me or the house?" I questioned and reached out to her trembling body as she cowered against the wall.

"*Please.*"

The plea was different; before it had been a demand. This whole time she believed I had wanted her dead, to silence her with a bullet. She wasn't *wrong*. At least, that had been my intention in the beginning, but slowly she had changed my mind.

"*Please*, Wesley," she cried, arms growing weak and her posture slumping in defeat.

The sound of Florence begging me to kill her blew a hole through every single wall that I had put up against her. They cracked and crumbled, leaving my heart exposed for her to get in. *'There's nothing wrong with falling in love, Wesley.'*

Everything was wrong about the way she was looking at me, praying that I would act on the darker urges she knew existed within me. She wanted my help but the weakness that was falling in love complicated every simple decision.

"Wesley, end it." She pleaded with me to end her life. "I need you to…"

"They need *you*." *I need you.* I cut her off and invaded her space before she had time to react. She watched me in confused agony as I hesitated at first but slipped my hands around her throat and cupped her jaw. "I know it hurts." I lowered my voice. "I know you're angry and tired."

Better than anyone I understood.

"It feels good to fight back, to make everyone feel how you feel. Desperate, defeated, and pissed off," I explained because I had been there. I had been the weak, forgotten, and angry one holding the gun to my head. For weeks after Wyatt's death, the only person there to pull me out of it was Koen, with his dumb, hopeful eyes and childish smile.

He was why I was alive today and I wouldn't disappoint him.

Florence's finger twitched. I closed my eyes and held my breath, but the bang never came.

When I opened them the green in her eyes looked so deep and endless that it rivaled the depths of any dense forest. Excruciatingly sad. The urge to kiss away the devastation that stained her usually delicate features was violent and selfish. I brushed a thumb over her wet cheek, the barrel of the gun still firmly planted to her temple, but I refused to let my eyes wander to it.

"But you are *not* a monster. Do you hear me?" I said it, and I made sure she heard me. "You are not a monster. I—I was *wrong*," I whispered, my gaze softening on hers as her eyes flooded with painful-looking tears.

"The Manor wants you to believe it because it makes you weak, it breaks your spirit and your mind, but that is not who you are. You are..." I stopped, my breath hitching as I dared to press my lips to her soaked, frozen cheek.

"Gentle, and kind," I said, kissing her again softly. "Empathetic, a fighter, a protector," I whispered with another carefully placed kiss at the corner of her mouth. "A romantic, a reader, a dreamer." This time, I pressed her lips against mine, every ounce of gentleness and understanding I had never allowed for myself, transferred through that kiss. "A pain in my arse," I joked and, for a split second, I thought her lip curled in amusement, but it was gone as quickly as it appeared.

"You are not a monster, Florence. You are anything but."

"We're all going to die," she whispered.

"Don't give up on them yet," I urged her.

"You want me to give them hope, but I don't know how..." Florence said.

"Yes, you do," I reminded her. "You do."

"Orchid Manor will have its way," she sobbed, and the gun slipped from her hand. I caught it and shoved it back into my pants as she repeated it over and over—a haunting chorus. "We're all going to die. It's never going to let me go."

I pulled her against me and pressed my lips to her hair. The floor creaked behind me and I turned to the door to see Koen standing there, his chest pumping wildly, his hand curled around the door frame with white knuckles.

"Thank you," his words came out in a whisper, his green eyes glassy as he watched me carry her back to bed.

"Go help Clay," I instructed and he nodded, leaving without question as I crawled into the bed with Florence and let her cry herself into some semblance of sleep.

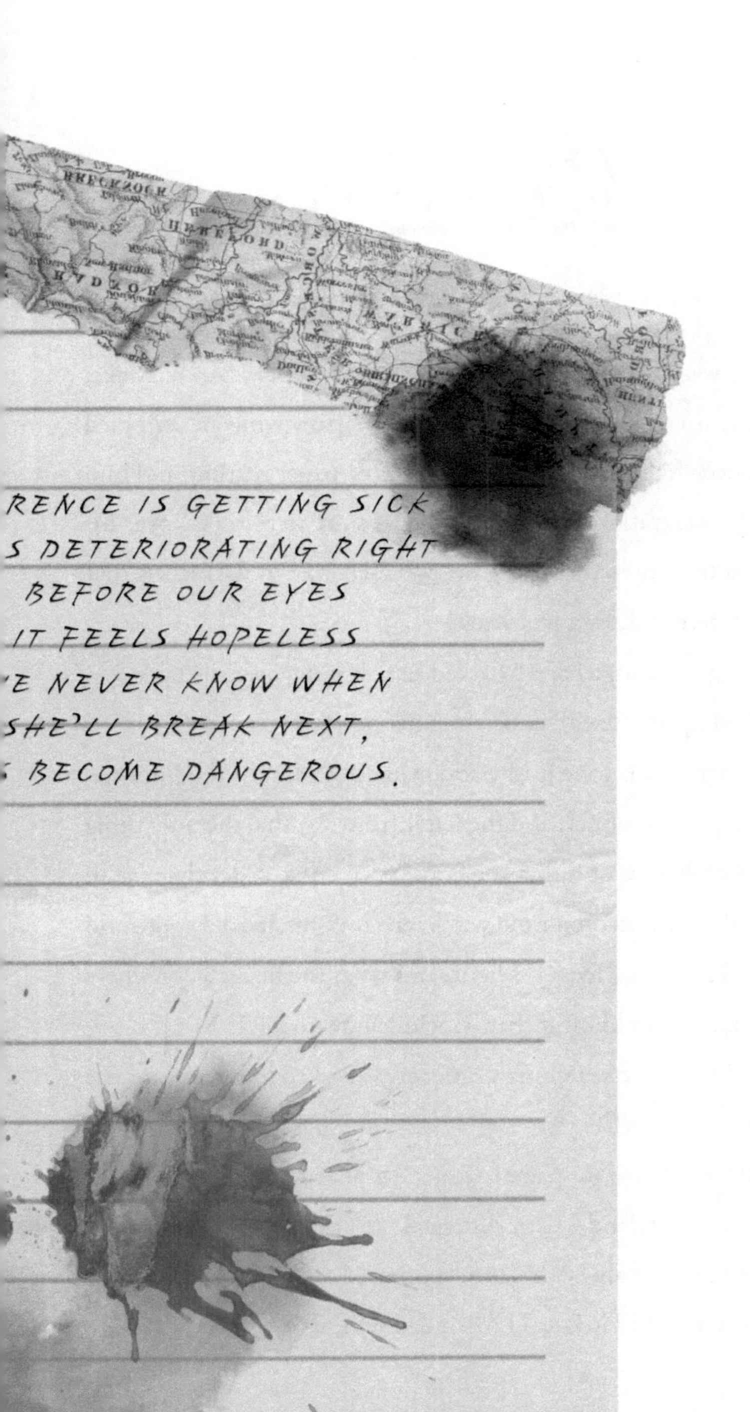
RENCE IS GETTING SICK
S DETERIORATING RIGHT
BEFORE OUR EYES
IT FEELS HOPELESS
E NEVER KNOW WHEN
SHE'LL BREAK NEXT,
BECOME DANGEROUS.

KOEN

Florence was curled up on the chaise in the library, barely awake, with her nose in a book keeping Clay company while he scribbled in his notebooks like a mad man, the sounds of paper rustling and him grumbling in frustration. The sleeves of his shirt were rolled over his forearms and his hair was sticking every which way in dark curls that hadn't seen a decent shower in a week.

"Have you gotten anywhere?" I asked him, leaning over the table.

Clay looked up at me with concern in his clouded eyes.

"No," he sighed, his tone husky and exhausted. "From the information that Wes got out of her, and the letter from Agatha, the only thing I'm even remotely sure of is that the house is an entity older than we've ever dealt with. This isn't some old witchcraft bullshit, it's old god world type stuff." He sighed. "Even if I figure out what the hell it is, or where it came from... I don't know if that'll include how to kill it."

"Have you only been searching Celtic lore?" I asked him when my eye caught the book to his left.

"It was the most obvious place to look. As far as we know the Manor has always been in Ireland." Clay shrugged.

"But Ireland wasn't always Ireland." I pointed out. "Before the war of independence we called it Éire," I reminded him.

"Ériu…" Clay mumbled and started throwing things around on the table in a fury. "What if the Manor isn't a thing or an entity, but a vengeful god?"

"Can we kill a god?" I questioned, to which Clay just swore under his breath and continued to search.

"Hah!" He called out. "Look at this." He handed me a heavy book of Irish mythology, open on a page to a beautiful looking woman draped in red with a look of discontent in her dark eyes.

"Morrígan. The goddess of war, death and fate." Clay pointed to the wording. "It was said that she was a shapeshifter that could often appear as a beautiful woman to seduce men."

"So you think Florence is Morrígan?" I asked, a bit confused and a little scared of his ideas.

"No, I don't even believe the Manor is Morrígan." He waved me off. "I think that the Manor is something similar to the goddess, changing and bending the rules of what we can see to entice us. It's how it lured Florence here but, just like any ancient being, it needs sacrifice to survive," Clay explained. "A host to feed off."

"So Agatha?" I asked.

"The host before Florence. We have no idea how long she lived. Everytime I try to pull one of her diaries from the shelf it turns to dust in my hands. But if the theory is correct the house was feeding off Agatha for God knows how long." Clay pushed from his chair and stared down at the research.

"But that doesn't explain why the Manor killed Agatha and trapped Florence–" I offered further to keep his brain working, periodically looking over at Florence, still half awake, seemingly still engrossed in her book, not paying attention to us at all.

"That's the problem. Even running on the idea that the Manor is a goddess, or some form of one, we still don't know what it wants." Clay sounded frustrated. "It practically consumed Agatha from what Florence has described and, from her journals her friend Aisiling is either a second victim or was never in the Manor at all. Lore suggests she escaped or was even let go but how or why?" Clay ran himself in circles with thought.

"The Manor only needed one?" I asked.

"But *why*?" Clay questioned urgently.

"The letter...Agatha wrote that the house requires..."

"Requires what though?" Clay sighed. "A vessel, a host?"

"A heart," I whispered. I looked over at Florence, wishing I could just wander over and curl into her lap. "It requires a heart."

"Agatha stopped caring, stopped finding joy in what the Manor could provide." Clay stepped up beside me, staring at Florence and her soft smile as she read something in her book. A brief moment of calm in the storm of her mental deterioration.

"Agatha's heart died long before her body–" He realized.

I looked over at him, exhaustion sweeping through his features.

"You should eat something, you look pale," I said quietly, reaching over and placing my hand on his bicep and gently squeezing with my fingertips.

"There's no time for that." He brushed me off and started searching the shelves again.

"You'll do no one any good passed out in the library from starvation," I said.

"I have water, which means I could last a week or so…" He grumbled on about the facts of a human body surviving without food until he found what he was looking for.

"Clay!" I snapped so he would stop and look at me. "Enough. You can research ancient shape shifting gods after a sandwich."

"There's no time." Clay shook his head and continued. *Fine*, if I couldn't get him to stop for a moment I would at least get Florence out of this library of doom.

I made my way toward her and knelt beside the chaise, peeking at what she was reading before asking, "would you like to go for a walk?"

She looked up from her book, her green eyes finding mine, and nodded.

"Come on then, let's leave him to his books." I smiled at her and pulled her from the chaise into me, wrapping my arm around her waist and holding her against my chest in a tiny sway as I walked us backward. "You smell pretty today." I inhaled her and loosened my grip on her waist as I stepped back.

"Where are we going?" She asked me. She was wearing a pair of trousers again with a simple shirt and only a pair of socks.

"I don't know, but we're going far away from that." I pointed to Clay dropping another stack of books on the table.

"Do you think he's figured it out?" She asked me, looking over her shoulder as we wandered from the library into the hallway.

"He's closer. Whatever this place is, it's definitely alive like you said. It's narrowing down exactly what *alive* means to it that's the problem," I explained and she furrowed her brow in confusion.

"Technically you can be alive, dead or undead. Undead are monsters such as zombies, vampires, and ghouls. Monsters that have to be killed in a certain way in order to truly make sure they're gone. Spirits are dead. You have to burn their remains, or anything that the spirit may be clinging to. Something they left when they passed on that tethers them to the living world."

She watched me in amazement as we walked.

"Alive is simple and complicated at the same time. Just like any monster it comes with its own set of rules," I told her and turned the corner into the foyer.

The Manor hadn't shifted in a while, most of the hallways had remained the same. It was eerie, it felt like it was laying in wait, biding its time and waiting until we were relaxed enough to strike again, when we wouldn't be prepared.

"How about some sunshine?" I asked her, pointing toward the door and she nodded.

Fall would be coming soon and the chill would set in. Hopefully we would be long gone before that happened. Florence followed me as I reached out for the knob to open the front door for her.

But a loud echoing click sounded.

"What?" Florence surged forward, her hand instantly on the heavy brass knob. She turned it back and forth, the door never budging.

"Watch out," I instructed and she moved to the side for me. I tried yanking on it but the wood was cemented shut, not moving even an inch under my protests. "Fuck."

We were locked inside.

Too close.

The screeching sound of fabric shredding echoed in the grand entrance of the Manor. The lengthy curtains fell to the floor in heavy strands and the light that filtered through the windows was gray and cold. A chorus of latching and slamming reverberated as the toxic possessiveness dispersed through the Manor, the walls closed in tightly and locked the windows and doors in place, blocking every exit.

They raged against the door, banging and clawing with hands and fists, wrenching at the handle with no success. A corrupt sense of victory coated the Manor and surged into her. She shrieked, overcome with rage and despair as it swelled in her. She grabbed at a decorative vase filled with flowers and hurled it towards the window by the door, just shy of hitting him, and it exploded, the vase shattering to pieces. The window held strong. Her hands flew to her hair, tugging at the roots, and she crumpled to the floor. Wailing against the onslaught of whispers drilling at her already crumbling sanity.

Mine.
Mine.
Mine.

"Florence?!" He cried out to her, using her name, and dropped to the floor beside her. He gathered her, collapsed and limp, into his arms. As if it would make any difference.

"KOEN? FLORENCE?" The other two all but tumbled down the stairs that stretched and trembled to shake their confident steps. The banisters writhed like snakes and the paper peeled back from the walls. The iron detailing along the windows pulled loudly away from the panes, a high, ear-splitting squeal resonating around them. *"Watch out!"* The dark one pointed as a bar dislodged from the window and flew through the air, embedding itself directly between him and the other.

"Fucking Christ! It's throwing spears now??" He had narrowly escaped.

"What happened?" The dark one was standing over them now, pulling her from the lap she was gripped to.

"It's locked! The door locked and the Manor started to act out and she–she–"

She continued to wail, whatever had been left of her already depleted reserves to fight off the assault of whispers and poison, was too weak. She could not hear the men around her, only the Manor shrieking within her. It's betrayal and rage shackling her inside her own thoughts as a cacophony of its voices howled.

Plaster rained down in chunks from the ceiling, hitting the floor and bursting out clouds of dust and debris around them. A large fragment connected with the one who had been holding her, knocking him back.

"Koen! Are you ok? For fuck's sake let's get out of here!" The last of them had finally made it off the stairs and hauled the other up.

"We can't! The door's locked!"

A groan, loud and unnerving, sounded above them. The walls shuddered, visibly pulsing, and all the frames on the walls continued to crash to the floor. Amongst the uproar a bright tinkling noise had started to break through, as the crystal spires in the chandelier swayed violently. She noticed, despite it all, she noticed. Fine details about the Manor had always stuck out to her and, even in this state, above her own fearful screaming, she watched as the chain securing the chandelier strained, and snapped.

With inconceivable strength she surged out of the arms that held her in its direction, knocking the three men back just as it was set to land on them all.

NO!

INSOLENT! FOOLISH!

It crashed, colliding with her already beaten and bruised body, and crushed her beneath it.

NO!

The Manor howled, and the walls hemorrhaged black. It oozed from the ceiling and coated the walls. The men screamed, incoherent, pain beyond understanding feeding the incredible monster that caged them, throwing themselves at the massive destruction she lay beneath. Crystal shards stained red impaled her neck, arms and torso. Thin lines of blood trickled from each and pooled beneath her.

They quickly removed the heaviest of the crushing mass from her small frame. The darkness reached for her, creeping tendrils out from the walls towards her. Her breathing was stunted and her chest shuddered weakly. *"Hurry, get her up—carefully! Don't push them in any farther,"* the tall one shouted as the other two cleared a way to her.

"I don't like the look of that mist! Whatever it is, I don't want it touching her!"

Panic spread like wildfire.

"Blossom? Hey—hey look here, it's ok, you're going to be ok."

The haze gained momentum, licking at their feet and blanketing around her. They lifted her carefully, each one supporting an arm, and the one speaking to her carrying her feet.

"Clay, what's happening? Clay?!"

The darkness clung to her, covering her like a cloak, settling in. Her eyes shut.

WESLEY

I woke again with her in my arms. It had been nearly a week since the chandelier had crushed her, *had almost crushed us*. She had seemed almost comatose in Clay's arms, wailing and staring out unseeing just before the giant thing collapsed on top of us. I still couldn't understand how she had managed to find the strength to push us back like that.

We had carried her together up the stairs and to her room, laying her gently on the bed; careful not to jostle the painful shards of crystal that impaled her soft flesh. The dark mist that had leached from the walls eventually dissipated but we all worried about what it could have been. Why it wanted her...

I'd had to force Koen to leave the room and let me tend to his head wound. A big hunk of plaster had fallen from the ceiling and almost knocked him out. There was a split in his temple and it, at the very least, needed glue. He was inconsolable, sure that Florence's state was his fault.

"I asked her to go for a walk—she would have stayed safe in the library. It's my fault, this is my fault." His voice trailed off tightly, so upset with himself.

I opened my mouth to quell his guilt but nothing came out.

"Wes, do you think she'll be ok?" His round, horrified eyes had bore into mine, pleading for assurance. I gave it to him, of course I did, but really I had no idea if she would be ok. She looked like a voodoo doll with all the sharp crystal shards sticking out of her. She was so pale that the bruises were already visible, dark purple amongst the green and yellow of the ones that had begun healing from her pressing the property line the week before.

Clay had used every bit of medical training he had and then some to fix her up. Removing each crystal spike with excruciating precision to lessen the possibility of anything breaking off inside her and festering; cleaning the wounds and then dressing them. It had taken hours.

Her breathing was steady now. I could feel the sweet exhales against my chest as she nestled into my side with my arm around her, where she had been for the better part of a week. Sinking so deeply into sleep with her pressed against my heart was a strange sensation.

Her hair was messy and stuck to her face, begging me to brush it back, but I couldn't bear to wake her. She hadn't had a restful sleep in days. She was constantly bombarded with furious and violent nightmares that caused her to thrash around. It left her sweaty and sore and even more exhausted.

Clay worried they were fever seizures but she wasn't hot. Her temperature never spiked.

She was ice cold.

I could see the shift. In the small moments of wakefulness she was struggling to keep a hold of reality. She was becoming exactly what she didn't want to be: hostile, temperamental, and aggressive.

I would be lying if I said I didn't feel a guilt-ridden urge to give in to her request. It hurt more than I had imagined to witness her suffering. She fought against the house constantly but it never felt enough. She was a dangerous risk; some days it felt strenuous to stay loyal to my decision. Each nightmare was a reason to end her, each act of aggression toward Koen a reason to deem her just monster enough. Every snarl and snap at Clay was enough validation to put that bullet she'd begged for between her eyes.

Wyatt's memory stayed present in the front of my mind, reminding me with every step how foolish and dangerous it was to reason. If I was going to do something, I was going to do it my way and, for each nightmare, snap, and attack, there were soft moments of love, care, and Florence—little fragments of who she was and reminders that putting a bullet in her would solve nothing.

The risk in question trembled against me as she tried to get comfy in her sleep.

Thoughts stirred and questions arose. Was she worth it? Was any of this? Doubt slipped in and out of my conscious thoughts, tangling with desire and need. I couldn't separate my emotions from necessity and foolishness, both felt critical and heavy in my chest. We didn't do this. We rolled into town, hunted the monster, and left.

It had been a few months since we arrived at Orchid Manor.

But it felt like days.

I never thought something or someone so small and delicate could upend our lives in the way she had, but here we were. Here *I* was, tangled emotionally and physically around her, arguing with myself quietly so as not to disturb her.

Unfortunately I couldn't stay here forever, no matter how badly I wanted to. So I slid my arm out from beneath her, tucking her under the blanket before leaving the room. The Manor was quiet. It felt uncanny.

It didn't feel alive for the first day in weeks. It was a nice reprieve from constantly being on guard but it made me feel uneasy.

"Where's Koen?" I asked Clay as I wandered by the study, his face in a book. He didn't look up when he answered with a shrug. "Clay," I snapped when I realized his eyes were moving so fast he couldn't possibly be reading.

"She's sick." He looked up at me, tears nipping at the corners of his eyes.

"Yeah." I nodded, knowing that comfort wasn't what he sought.

"It's only going to get worse." Clay ground his teeth together.

Clay's assumption only meant that Koen never told him about Florence's close call with the gun. He knew how bad she already was. He'd kept it to himself on purpose. Clay couldn't afford the distraction and Koen wouldn't admit to how bad a sign it was.

"Bruises, irrational irritation, lashing out. Those are all human identifiers. That has to prove something doesn't it?" He sighed defeatedly, already anticipating my response.

"Unfortunately, it doesn't," I argued softly. I wanted to believe that she wasn't a monster. Deep down to my core, I wanted that, but... "Ghost sickness presents the same as a vengeful spirit, and you and I both know it."

"You're still on that?" Clay scowled. "After everything?"

"Someone has to be. It's fine to play house, Clay, but at the end of the day..." I trailed off.

"I would sympathize with you, Wesley. I know what you've gone through but she's not a vampire, you aren't Wyatt, and this is getting ridiculous."

He was more than right but the fight kept his head in the game.

I let him come down on me before I countered, the argument half-hearted but real enough to spark his emotions. To keep him working. "Monsters are all the same, Clay. They all want, *need,* something, and if it comes down to her needing something from either of you, I will protect my family above her." I stared him down, letting the words sink in. "Even if you hate me for it."

I hoped to myself that the act, the false malice in my voice, was enough to convince myself of what I would have to do. I hoped that maybe it had washed away the weakness for her, leaving only rational survival instincts.

"She's sick and the house is trying to kill us." He chewed on the inside of his mouth and stared into the distance.

All Clay ever needed was confirmation and a push. "You got a solution?" I asked.

"No." He set down the book. "But she's getting more aggressive."

"She is," I confirmed. "I can handle her," I said, and his eyes shot up to look at me. "—Not like that," I said, recognizing the fear in his eyes. "I just mean, I can handle her attitude, her violent tantrums...until you figure this out."

"What if I can't?" He asked me.

"You can," I responded without hesitation. "If anyone can, it's you."

"I hate when you do that," he grumbled, running his hands through his dark hair.

"No, you don't," I argued. "It makes you feel pressured and you do your best work under pressure, so don't give me that crap. Get off your arse and figure out how to get her out of this place before she goes full Amityville on us."

"How are her wounds?" He asked me, ignoring the shot, but I wasn't joking. The first thing I'd do when I was finished with this conversation would be to hide the knives in the kitchen.

"Healing, slowly, but at a..."

"Human pace?"

"Exactly." I shrugged. "I'll change the bandages when she wakes up and try to get her to eat because if she's not healing her temperature isn't regulating."

"She's reverting?" Clay stared into the dark room as his brain started processing the new information. "But why now?"

"She keeps mumbling that the house is punishing her," I told him. "Whatever that means, if you ask me it's punishing *all* of us."

"After the chandelier fell, you saw what I saw?" He asked.

I had been wholly focused on Florence in that moment but we had *all* felt the outburst from the house in those moments. It was practically screaming. I paused, "It was like the house hadn't meant to hurt her—" I looked up him and he sighed. "Like it was aware of what it had done."

"I found some information about shape shifting on a grander scale. It could be possible that we're dealing with a god but I don't know how to kill that, Wesley. We're just men." Clay sighed. "And if she's right, then maybe it is."

"We both know she's right. We're being punished for our invasion of the Manor, but what is *she* being punished for?" I leaned against the doorframe. Most of the time I could feel the house vibrating through the wood but it was silent and still, which worried me.

"Human connection." He said, like it was the most obvious answer in the world. "The house is punishing her for finding happiness. Orchid Manor is jealous."

"Its jealous? It let us in, it trapped us here—" I shook my head. We had dealt with a lot of stupid things in the past, but never something as dumb as a pile of bricks being jealous of a woman. "Do you hear yourself?"

"Since your ...*incident* with her, the violence has only escalated." Clay raised an eyebrow at me.

He wasn't wrong, but it was annoying.

"Let me get this straight. Do you believe that the Manor is behaving this way because she was happy? I thought it was because it needed her to survive. You make it sound like..." I paused, knowing that happy wasn't exactly the right word, but it was all I could wrap my head around now. "The Manor is jealous and lashing out against her?"

"Exactly. Like a scorned lover."

"Agatha Warren had a husband though, right?" I reminded him.

Clay hesitated, thinking through all the information. It had been a long process, collecting all the evidence and pouring over the lore and collected research, with emotions running high, he needed the perspective of someone who hadn't burned every piece of it into his brain. He needed to talk it out.

He stood from his chair and I followed him through the Manor to the library, where he started pushing around books and papers piled high on another desk.

"Here." He pulled out a paper and flicked it over in his fingers, staring at either side. "It's strange because, much like Florence, there's no family history on Agatha, nothing that predates her existence in the town before she died in 1852."

I listened intently as Clay started to put together the pieces. He slipped his glasses over his nose and hunched over the desk to read something in a different book. It was crammed with scratchy, practically unreadable handwriting—hundreds of log entries.

"I didn't think anything of it because marriages like these often happened with women from different counties, so it wasn't unlikely that Agatha Warren had married into the family that owned the Manor."

"But?" I settled down against the table.

"But," Clay cleared his throat. "There's no record of that family so whoever owned the Manor trapped Agatha here..."

"Or Agatha Warren was here long before her husband," I finished for him.

"It could be that the same situation that's happening to Florence, to us, happened to Agatha Warren, but without more information it's impossible to know for sure."

"We need to be sure." My tongue swiped over my bottom lip as I tried to devise a solution to our spiteful little tinderbox, short of burning it down, suddenly hesitating because I wasn't sure if we'd be able to get Florence out even then. I wasn't willing to burn the Manor down with her inside it.

Not anymore.

"It could be that Agatha is behind all of this," I prompted.

"We've got three options. Agatha is our monster, Florence is a ghost, or the Manor really is a petty god playing with its food out of boredom," Clay said.

"And we have no idea how to kill the third option." I groaned.

"We've seen no trace of Agatha, not her clothes or a body. There's nothing to suggest that her spirit is present in the house and I'm sure if Florence had seen her, she would have told us."

The laugh that left me was tight with disbelief. "She kept a lot of things a secret."

"Aside from Agatha being in the Manor. Why would the Manor have killed her if that was the case?" Clay asked. "Florence said she assumed she had aged naturally, and then the Manor refused to let her pass—letting her decay until it finally 'ate' her." He curled his fingers into quotes and shook his head as he said it. "She said Agatha looked well past living age when she died."

"Maybe the house got sick of her?"

"It would explain the advanced aging, but it seems unlikely." Clay shook his head. "If I'm correct," he stopped, and I lifted my brows to keep him talking, "then Florence's assumption that she's trapped here isn't because the house is jealous or bitter; it's because the house is feeding off her."

"That could explain the sickness." I scowled at the suggestion.

"But not why now?" Clay asked. "If that's true, it's speeding up the process."

"So it's both." I clicked my teeth together. "The Manor is jealous."

"If Agatha's one crime was falling in love," Clay swallowed tightly.

I sighed, my mind wandering to a sleeping Florence. "Then it's a cruel punishment to outlive the person you sacrificed it all for."

FIND THAT
DOOR AGAIN

FLORENCE

I felt Wesley slip from the bed and leave the room quietly. He had been holding me in the cradle of his arms more often than not over the last week while I recovered but his thoughts had been too loud to remain relaxed, so he untangled our limbs gently and excused himself. I stretched carefully, trying not to overuse the sore muscles and torn flesh that had been damaged by the chandelier. I was paying for that act in more ways than one.

My body ached something terrible, but that ache was nothing compared to that in my mind. The nightmarish visions that twisted my perception of reality were constant and unrelenting. There were times when I could have sworn I was awake and the Manor would attack one of them. I would thrash and try to help them only to wake up restrained and be told that I had lashed out in my sleep. I could never tell what was real or not anymore. It was terrifying.

I slowly made my way out of the bed, testing my balance on the floor before fully committing to standing. I needed to get out of this room. As much as I appreciated the care and attention of both Koen and Wesley, I found myself missing Clay.

It had been nearly a week since I had seen him and my body begged for contact. I made my way down the hall, pausing often to allow myself a breath. I entered his room, hoping maybe he was in the library and I could curl into his sheets. Just a moment of peace, engulfed in that lemon, ginger, and leather smell without bothering him.

Books piled on every surface, even in his unmade bed. The dark linens tangled around piles of paper and his laptop. I carefully moved around them as I crawled onto the mattress, not wanting to disturb anything but aching to be a part of his space.

Since my outburst with Wesley it was becoming increasingly apparent that Koen knew what had happened. I barely spent a moment without the warm touch of him. Wesley shooed him away periodically to take his place but he was more concerned about my alone time.

Settling for his scent was enough. My face was buried in his sheets, a comforting peace fell over my shoulders and relaxed the tension between the blades. It wasn't long before my eyes grew heavy again with sleep.

I woke to the sound of water running in the bathroom connected to the bedroom. Steam billowed against the ceiling and I felt a moment of panic. He had avoided me; I didn't mean to invade his personal space. I just...missed him and, as human as that emotion was, it also felt sticky because lately I hadn't felt very connected to actually *feeling* human. I pushed my tired bones from the sheets, a small involuntary whimper dragging from my lips as I did.

I could hear him moving around in the bathroom.

Kill him.

The Manor had been quiet externally but much more violent in its invasion of my mind. Craving blood and demanding that I take it. My fingers twitched at my side. I didn't want to hurt them. *NO.*

He will turn on you.

In some moments, its words could trigger a flash of rage I couldn't control. The Manor played on my weaknesses. Knowing their loyalty to each other scared me more than anything.

You mean nothing to him.

Kill him.

Do it now.

I opened my eyes, blinking the darkness from them, and found myself at his dresser, my fingers rolling over a hunting knife that he had left with his gun and other weapons. How did I get here? I stopped, pulling my hand away from it and turned to leave.

"Florence." Clay's hand wrapped around my wrist.

A painful sob left my throat before I could stop it and Clay was pulling me against his wet chest, wrapping his arms around my body and nuzzling his nose against my neck. I felt his chest rise and fall as he inhaled me, his fingers tightening around my body. The house grew quiet and with it the venomous whispers. For a moment it was just Clay and I. His body melted into me as his heart matched pace with mine and his breathing was steady and even.

I hated how badly my mind was fighting against my heart. How easy it was for the darkness to suffocate the tender moments. The blood lust flooded back in so quickly I barely had time to steel myself.

Coward.

The Manor scolded me but I was too lost in the guilt that gripped me as Clay held tight. I opened my mouth to speak but his lips found my skin and it silenced me.

"I'm sorry," he whispered, and another sob threatened to expose how heartsick I was.

He had no reason to apologize.

Weak.

"Be quiet," I whispered, and Clay lifted his head, his body shifting until he could see my face. His hands didn't leave my skin. He was so warm from his shower that I could feel my frozen temperature, even more so when my eyes glided over his toned and tattooed torso.

"Are you okay?" He asked me, as his hand traced my throat to cup my jaw.

"No." My brows came together in a pathetic attempt to keep from crying. "I didn't mean to bother you," I said.

"You aren't." Clay pulled my chin and brought me to his lips. The kiss was tender and I closed my eyes, allowing it to fill me until I could feel it all the way through to my toes. "I missed you but didn't want to push you."

"I'm sorry, I'm so..." I tripped over the words and turned my head to catch the pain that flickered behind his gray eyes. "It seems as though I'm the one turned around now."

"Don't worry," he hummed like we weren't fighting against the clock. "I'll find you."

They were simple words that meant more to me than I think Clay understood. There was very little I could do about the outbursts; my brain barely belonged to me. But I trusted Clay to search for me in all the darkness surrounding me. If anyone were willing to search until he couldn't walk, a search even on his hands and knees, it would have been Clay.

He'll betray you.

I tensed at the thought.

"What was that?" He looked down over my body for any physical signs of what might have caused the shift in body language and frowned when he came up empty.

I could tell Wesley hadn't told him about the episode with the gun. From the way he only questioned and didn't hover, like Koen did, but I couldn't understand why. It left me stuck deciding whether or not to be honest with him.

"Florence?" He waited, pushing a strand of my hair away from my face.

If he knew the truth.

"It's nothing." I swallowed the lump in my throat.

"Are you sure? Because we had a deal."

How does he expect you to be honest when he's not honest with you?

It was not the Manor that time, it was my own voice, dark and twisted that echoed in my mind. I licked my lips and nodded. "I promise."

"Are you hungry?" He asked me and I shook my head. My appetite had been returning in waves but, after mentally sparring with the house, I only had the energy to sleep.

"I know I've been awful," I said, pressing my cheek against his warm chest. "But will you stay with me tonight?"

"I can't say no to you," he mused and nuzzled his head against my hair, damp curls sprinkling droplets of water.

"That's what got us into this..." I stopped and squeezed him a little tighter. "If you can't say no... taking away your choice isn't fair."

"I'll apologize for anything, Florence–" He cupped my chin in his hand and lifted my gaze to meet his eyes. "I won't apologize for that. My choices are my own."

Heat filled my chest and warmed my cheeks as Clay smiled.

"Get back in bed," he ordered with another carefully placed kiss. "Please."

"Only because you asked nicely." I let go of him reluctantly and climbed back into the bed, noticing that he had moved the papers and laptop while I slept. How long I had been sleeping was a mystery but it had quieted the voices in me who wanted to doubt everything.

Clay watched me for a moment longer. Wet curls licked at the nape of his neck as he let the towel fall to the floor in his search for clothes. He pulled on a pair of loose cotton pants and shook out his wet hair, droplets flying everywhere as he slipped into bed beside me.

A tired giggle echoed from me as he buried his wet hair against the crook of my neck and his fingers traced over my stomach beneath the borrowed cotton shirt I wore.

"I missed that sound," he hummed, kissing a warm line over my skin as I closed my eyes. "I missed you," he said, before pulling the blankets over us and settling down. "Koen, don't be a weirdo," Clay laughed, uncurling himself and looking at the door.

Koen tossed his baseball cap to the side and used the sleeve of his t-shirt to tug it over his head before climbing into bed on the other side of me. "I see you found a warm bed, Blossom," he purred against my back.

"Wesley left, and I got cold."

"His loss," both chimed simultaneously.

How heartbroken you'll be when they're cold to the touch.

The house whispered to me, a chill rolling down my spine as I forced its haunting voice from my head and lost myself in the tangle of arms and cologne.

KOEN

"Hey, Blossom." I pushed through the door to find her sitting in one of the chairs, curled up in front of the fire with her body tucked beneath a heavy blanket.

I set the tray of food on the table and rounded it to kneel before her. "Are you alright?"

"I've been better," she mumbled but forced a tiny smile.

Her cheeks had started to hollow and the bruises that she'd sustained stained her skin. From the base of her neck, they spread over her arms and chest and, like tattoos, they showed no signs of fading at all; but she was out of bed for the first time in days and that's all that mattered.

Wes sat on the unmade bed, watching us carefully as he cleaned his gun with an old towel. His eyes flickered back and forth between Florence and me, his hands working absentmindedly as he cleaned the barrel.

"You're beautiful," I hummed, kissing her fingertips as she pressed her hand to my face.

"You're a terrible liar," she laughed.

"I don't lie." I smiled up at her, keeping her hand close. "How's this today?" I tapped a finger to my temple.

"Messy," she blinked slowly. The word was forced out of her like it hurt to say but she got it out. "It's getting even harder to sort out what's real and what the house wants me to believe."

"We're here to help." I kissed her hand again. "Remember? That's all you need."

"You're too sweet for your own good. It's going to destroy you," she said quietly. Wes's eyes met mine as I looked over at him.

I could tell he wanted to say something but he kept all the dark comments about his brother to himself. It wasn't the time and it didn't matter what he said now. I wasn't going to waver from Florence's side.

"Movie date ruined. I couldn't find my laptop. I think the Manor hid it... but I managed not to forget dinner. Maybe you can eat something?"

I could tell her stomach was still upset. After not needing food to survive for so long, eating it to sustain her energy was difficult for her body to readjust to.

"Yeah, that would be nice." She scooted over in the chair and made room for me to slide in underneath her, tucking her close to my body. It felt almost mundane; Florence curled into my lap with my palm in the air as she slowly made her way through a pile of Ritz crackers.

"These are delicious," she sighed, warming my heart. "What's in the center?"

"Fake cheese," I laughed. "But it's salty and hits the spot."

"Indeed," she agreed, popping another one between her lips. "Thank you for your patience, Koen," she said, leaning into me.

"You can repay me when we get you out of here in one piece." I flashed her a soft smile and kissed the delicate skin of her jaw.

"If," she corrected me but I wasn't having it. Not today. Everyone had been too doom and gloom lately and I wouldn't let the fear of the future tarnish the hope I had.

"*When*," I argued. "I'm not leaving here without you, Blossom."

"Koen, remember your dreams," she said to me quietly, making me think of the night we danced beneath the chandelier. I shuddered involuntarily, the memory now tainted with the vision of her small broken body beneath it.

"Your dreams *are* my dreams." I cupped her face in my hands.

"Koen—" She stuttered and looked away from me.

"I figured it out!" Clay burst into the room cutting off whatever she might have said and I flinched from the sound while Florence's solemn gaze trained itself on the roaring fire.

I waited a moment before I rubbed my hand over her knee and she turned to look at me. I thought the light might have been back in her eyes for a second but it was a trick of the fire that danced there. *I'll hold onto the hope for the both of us, Blossom,* I thought.

"There's a second fucking cellar!" Clay lifted his stupid hand-drawn map in the air. "It's been there the whole time but the house rotates it differently from the rest!"

"So what does that mean?" Wes asked him.

"It means the door appears four minutes earlier on the east side of the house." Clay stared at all of us like we should know what was rambling on about. His shirt half-buttoned, and a pair of trousers that were dirty with charcoal. "And it shifts westward by one degree every single night."

"I've seen that door!" I said, following closely.

"The door moves?" Wes tilted his head to the side, and the dirty blond waves fell with him.

"The door moves," Clay whispered. "Although I'm not sure why that's a surprise to you, *everything* in this god forsaken Manor moves."

"Did you know about it?" Wes barked at Florence.

"You're asking me if I knew about the secret door?" She snipped back, the darkness returning to her voice.

"Yes, Vengeful," Wes responded.

"I knew of the door, Wesley," she said.

"And you didn't tell us?"

"I had no idea it moved in a special pattern. All of the doors move, why would this one be special? I've never tried to open it. There's something wrong with it."

"But what's in the cellar?" I asked Clay, suddenly feeling left out.

"I don't know." He shrugged. "But the house is hiding it the best it can, seemingly even from the one thing it loves."

Florence's eye snapped to Clay at the word thing, her hand digging into the chair's cushion as she steadied the anger and let it pass through her.

"I didn't mean it that way." Clay ground his teeth together and closed his eyes.

She was fighting so hard against the toxin in her veins that was turning her vengeful and vicious. She didn't want to hurt us but it was getting harder with every day.

"So you want us to find an impossible shifting door and go down into the unknown cellar of a temperamental century-old Manor on an

'I don't know'?" Wes quipped, moving past the upset, seemingly for Florence's benefit.

"Yes. If I'm right it might contain all the missing links we've been searching for. What the Manor really is, or even how to kill it."

"We've been in scarier places." I smirked. "And I'm itching for a fight."

"We have no idea what's down there and someone should stay here with her." Wes pointed his gun in our direction.

Florence scoffed, drawing my attention back to her.

"I'll stay," Clay offered.

"No." Wes didn't hesitate. "I'll need your help finding the door."

"Give me a gun." Florence shrugged, turning slowly to the side to look at Wes.

"No," he repeated, all the amusement falling from his face. It wasn't that he didn't trust her not to hurt us. It was that he didn't trust her not to hurt herself. I could see the difference.

"You can't run a hunt," she groaned, pushing from the chair on shaky legs, "without all three of you. The last time you did, one of you almost didn't come back."

"This is different," Wes said as she slowly moved across the floor.

Clay's eyes locked on the bruises that painted her pale skin as she limped toward Wes.

"No, it's not," she clipped.

The tension in the room was tight and, for a moment, I thought Wes might lose his composure as she invaded his personal space, but he didn't. His hand pressed against her face as his hazel eyes narrowed on her dark green ones.

"Give me a gun, lock me in the room, and all three of you go," she said to him, almost leaning into his touch. The intimacy of the moment clawed at me. She had been so careful with me, with Clay, but she seemed to find solace in Wes's dark cloud aura in her sick, angry haze.

I half expected him to argue with her, but he pulled out the Hunter's knife at his hip and held it between them with the blade in his fingertips and the handle toward her chest.

"Stay here," he demanded.

"Can't make it much further," Florence groaned, pain flickering across her face.

Wes took that as an agreement to his request and ushered Clay from the room in a flurry of hushed conversations, leaving Florence and me alone for the first time in days.

"Are you sure?" I made my way to her, where she stared down at the knife in her palm, wholly fixated on the blade brushing across her skin.

"I'll be alright, Koen."

"I don't believe that," I swallowed tightly and helped her across the floor to the bed, letting her settle down on the mattress before covering her legs with the blanket. "But I also know there's no use arguing with you."

"Smart man," she hummed, but when I didn't move she looked at me. "What, Koen?"

"I hate this." I chewed on my lip and dropped beside the bed so we were at eye level. "I—"

"Don't." She cut me off.

It had been stewing for weeks, the urge to tell her how fast my heart beat in my chest every time she was near. To explain to her just how important she was to me. I wanted to tell her that no one had ever made me feel like this. But the words always got stuck, or we were constantly interrupted.

I knew exactly how foolish I sounded. It wasn't lost on me that we had only known each other for a few months but when she stared up at me with those eyes. It felt like she had known me my entire life. Clay kept sweeping his feelings under the rug and said that the intense emotions were purely because of the fast-paced forced proximity situation, but I knew deep down that he was wrong.

The feelings between Florence and I were solid. They were real.

"Come on, Blossom," I whined. "Don't do that, don't shove me away."

"A lady never shoves," she mused with a half-hearted smile. "And I'm not. I'm protecting you and that oversized heart *I love so much.*"

She finally looked over at me and there were those eyes. They burned into me, piercing and sad, reminding me I never stood a chance against her.

"My heart doesn't belong to me anymore," I confessed. Wes called out from the main floor, his angry voice carrying over the stairs to us. "Hold on to it," I said, shoving back from the bed and flicking a finger beneath her chin, "until I get back. And try to eat something, please." I pointed to the tray.

Florence frowned as I walked backward out of the room, taking one more look at her before I left her to help the others in the cellar. My hand shook around my gun as I pulled it from my waistband. The feeling in my palm vibrated aftershocks of the machete. Memories flooded me as

I tried to push down my issues. I didn't want to let Wes down again. I couldn't.

KOEN

"What's the plan?" I asked, coming up behind them, hunched over a map on the table at the main entrance to the Manor.

"We've got an hour to get ready for whatever the hell might be trapped down there." Wes shrugged.

"It could be anything. As far as we know that door has been closed since Agatha died," Clay explained, rolling up his shirt sleeves and fixing the buttons before tucking them into his pants. "It could be nothing."

"We have nothing else," Wes said.

"It's worth looking at," I added, and Clay looked back at me with a tight nod.

"Let's get moving then. I want to be ready." Clay collected himself.

Wes and I grabbed what we could from the collection we had inside the parlor, piled in like an armory: guns, rock salt bullets, iron, and more. He looked like he wanted to say something but every time he opened his mouth, nothing came out.

"What?" I finally said, throwing a duffle bag to the floor staring at him. I set my gun on the mantel and stripped from my flimsy shirt, tossing it across the room to replace it with one that didn't smell so much like Florence.

The knowledge that she was upstairs alone was distracting enough.

"Are you sure you're ready?" He asked me.

"If this is about the vampire nest, I already apologized. I was off my game that day and I'll never let it slip again." I pulled my arms through the long sleeved top and let it settle where my jeans hung on my hips.

"It's not about the nest, Koen. And that *wasn't your fault*." Wes stepped forward. "It's about you."

"I don't need a dad talk right now. I'm not a kid anymore, Wes." I brushed him off. "And fighting got us into trouble last time. If you wanna yell at me, do it later."

"Stop, I'm not trying to fight with you!" he exclaimed exasperatedly as I scooped my gun from the mantle. "I need to make sure that your head is in the right place before we do this. I can't lose you, Koen."

"You aren't going to." I looked back at him. "You're so worried that I'm going to end up like Wyatt, but I've never been him." I stepped back.

"Lately, the lines are blurred." The hurt was evident on Wes's face, the fear gripping most of his rational thinking.

"No, they aren't," I argued. "What's blurred is your memory of Wyatt. Up until your parents died, all they talked about was how reckless and stupid he was, but you never did. You always looked up to him because he wasn't like that! Your dad was a cold bastard, mean and tough. He didn't understand love." I shook my head.

"Wyatt was brave and he loved you so much. It's not the fear of me being reckless and stupid that has you all wound up; it's the fear that maybe you loved me a little too hard and that you gave me the ability to love the way Wyatt did."

"A heart too big for my chest," I said to him, echoing what Florence had said earlier. "But it's not unprotected the way Wyatt's had been.

From everything I know about him Wyatt didn't understand love. He was just looking for human connection, for someone to love him back the way your parents didn't."

Wes didn't move. He just watched and listened as I took another step closer.

"But I had that growing up. I've always had you, and I have Clay," I argued. "I understand the risks of loving and losing because you did your job and taught me them. I know love *because* I had you, and I had Clay," I repeated so he understood.

He swallowed, his hand wrapping tightly around the bag strap on his shoulder.

"Don't strip what I know, what you've taught from me, just because you're scared," I said.

"I'm not scared," he bit.

"You are. You're just too prideful to admit it." I scoffed. "You're scared to lose me, you're scared to lose Clay, and you're fucking terrified to lose Florence."

"I'm not a punching bag, Koen," he huffed.

The conversation made him uncomfortable and his shoulders rolled beneath his tartan shirt as his grip adjusted on his gun.

"I'm not throwing punches." A tight, hollow laugh left my throat. "I'm just telling you the truth. You don't want to believe it but she's gotten under your skin just like ours. It's alright to want. It's alright to *love*."

I had struck a nerve. I could see how his heavy brow line pinched together when I spoke about her but he'd never admit it, even though he didn't hide it well. He may love her differently, in his confused way, but the love was there.

"Don't be ashamed to take what you need," I said. "You've spent your whole life taking care of us, Wes." I shrugged. "Let Florence be what you need."

"There's too much risk in that," Wes said.

"Risk?" I laughed, "What are you risking?"

"Our family," he answered.

I stepped forward again, smiling because I finally got through to him. "I think you and I both know she *is* family now."

He stared at me for a long moment, jaw ticking as he realized that Florence was worth whatever risk he was willing to take for us. He was willing to take it for her now as well.

"For our family," I said, tapping the barrel of my gun against his with a goofy grin.

"Just, *please,* be careful," he said tightly.

Clay was waiting for us in the hall when we returned, his eyes passing over us warily as we approached. "Everything alright?" He asked, pulling off his glasses and stuffing them in his pocket.

I would let Wes answer that question for himself, but for the first time in a while, I truly was alright. I had gotten out all the things that had been bottled up inside me that needed to be said. He was still on edge. I couldn't control how he felt or what he did but I had done my best to comfort his concerns.

"Yeah, we're fine," he choked out through tight lips as he brushed past me.

"Convincing," Clay grunted and stepped out of his way, scooping his gun from the table and shoving it in his pants before following. "Right," he called out when Wes went to the left.

Wes stopped, turning to look at us following him, and arched a brow. "Are you sure?"

"Positive," Clay said.

So Wes went right. Down the hall a few meters was a door we'd all seen a handful of times, but never all together and never like that. It was different from the rest. It looked older than old, it seemed *ancient*. Wes pushed on it, but it remained solid and made a sturdy sound.

"You could have tried the doorknob," I laughed, when he grunted from the impact.

"I hate this fucking place," Wes growled and moved out of the way.

I wrapped my fingers around the knob, rusty against my palm, and pushed with my shoulder to budge the old door open. It popped, and the smell that erupted was nasty enough for us all to back away, coughing with our arms over our noses and mouths.

"Wow." Clay blinked and scrunched his nose, no doubt trying to clear the sour smell from it. "Whatever is down there should have decomposed years ago."

"Well, it hasn't," Wes clipped. "Stay put. We're going to need gloves."

Clay nodded. "Oh, and flashlights," he called after Wes, but he was already out of earshot. "Wait for us," he warned me, and he ran off.

"I have one..." I flicked my eyebrows up in annoyance. "Time to shake out of this rust, Koen. No more being afraid to screw up." I hyped myself up. Waiting for a moment as they disappeared around the corner before hauling my shirt up over my nose and slipping through the crack in the door frame.

I pulled my flashlight from my back pocket and it flickered on with my touch. Using my hunting knife, I wedged the blade between the door and floor into the wooden stairs to hold it open as best I could. The stairs down were steep but there was only one set and it was a straight shot to the bottom.

Taking them one at a time, I raised my gun and held it against my flashlight as I went. The smell worsened as I trudged downward and the darkness seemed to grow thicker with my descent. I swept the light from left to right, checking my surroundings as I stepped off the final stair.

The cellar wasn't small. It looked like it went back for yards in every direction. Long tunnels engulfed in pitch-black shadows that made me uncomfortable staring at them for too long.

"If anything is coming to get me, it'll be from that." I scowled, flicking the flashlight around some more. Long rows of rickety wooden shelving housed dusty jars filled with moldy food and rusted tin cans, dented and kicked around on the shelves like someone had been down here looking through them. "Rats." I shrugged, ignoring the clear fact that Orchid Manor had *no* rats. Anything to feel better about the current situation. "It was probably just rats."

The entire cellar was dirt and brick, looking nothing like the pristine gothic upper floors of the Manor. It was strange that the house had let this rot in the way it had but Clay would have answers. Or, at the very least, it would give him more questions.

"What the hell is taking them so long?" I mumbled. Turning back to the stairs, my foot slipped through something wet. I sighed and turned my flashlight to my feet. Mud coated the white of my shoe, but also... "Is that blood?" I whispered and knelt to look at the pool of liquid before shining my flashlight around the ground.

There was something... breathing, not five feet from where I stood, and it made my stomach flip as I moved toward what looked like a massive mound of earth and flesh—arms, vines, legs, soil, hair, and flowers. There was more than one body collapsed and rotting. I gagged as my eyes started to water from the smell and stepped closer. "What the hell..."

The Manor swelled, air blowing through the cellar and whipping up the stairs. The sound pierced my ears as it howled through the tiny channel to the top. The wind died without warning, sucking all the sound from the cellar as the door at the top of the stairs slammed violently shut.

FLORENCE

A feeling I had never felt from the Manor pulsed through me. A manic delight, that almost felt as though it bubbled up from my toes and released in a laugh. I put a hand to my mouth to cover the laughter, it felt hateful and violent and sounded nothing like me. It made a chill run through me.

The shutters slapped against the windows as a wild wind kicked up outside. All the candles sparked and lit up around me, bathing the room in glittering orange light. The Manor was excited. I could feel everything it felt, after so long of it forcing its way into my mind- this was the first time it occurred to me that I could use it to my advantage. It was excited about something, it felt like, anticipation. I froze, knowing that whatever was causing the Manor to have such a reaction could not be good.

Something was wrong.

If they thought I was going to stay put, they were foolish.

Something they could argue over later, after I saved them.

Tired.

I stopped, my fingers sinking into the bed as the Manor rustled around me. Its will so heavy in my mind, I could feel the pain of carrying it in the base of my skull. I closed my eyes and attempted to steady myself. I needed to push the Manor back but I could feel the weight in my eyes, forcing them to blink sluggishly with sleep. It was pulling me down, I felt like I was sinking in a pool of my own exhaustion.

*You **are** exhausted.*

But it wasn't just the Manor's voice, it was also my own. Wound together so tightly it seemed almost impossible to untwist. The window panes slammed victoriously as I leaned back into the bed and allowed my eyes to drift closed, –*No.* I stood back up, a chill settling in my bones and I shook my head. Trying to force it to clear.

They needed my help.

No they don't.

They did, just for *what...*

My mind spun and confusion ripped through me and tore my thoughts into fragments, allowing the Manor's suggestions to slip in and take root. I tried to remain focused, I had been going somewhere. There was something important that I needed to do. The wardrobe door opened and pulled my attention. I needed to go downstairs... *so I should change...* I needed clothes.

The fire crackled like an explosion to my left, a warning. My eyes focused on the flames, digging out clothes from the wardrobe without a thought. My hands pulled out a chemise and a corset, petticoats and the over skirts of a dress I had worn so often before. I reached for the matching blouse and the movement was halted and uncoordinated, my heart and body sparring with the hold the Manor had on my mind.

Mine.

It took issue with any new experience the men had brought me. I could feel the tight grip of its possessiveness with each touch, each kiss, every gift. The Manor wanted to be the only one to provide for me. It had never liked the clothing they had given me. It did not like change. It wanted everything to be the same as it always was, including me. I could feel its pleased vibrations pulse through me, praising my decision. I hated that I had once found comfort in the warmth that now filled my body.

Mine

It was different now. Not the way it overcame me, but my understanding of it. I could see it more clearly now than I ever had before. The sentiment had plunged into me like a knife and twisted. There was no shred of warmth, no consideration, not even the false overwhelming sensation of calm that it so often pushed through me. The Manor was charged with darkness like it had been that day with Agatha. Suffocating and sinister.

The next voice I hear is my own.

"You can't have them."

All of the furniture in the room upended, tossed through the air and smashing against the floors and walls.

"You can't have them!" I said it louder, finding myself long enough to grip the knife from the table beside the wardrobe in my hand. I made my way down the stairs to the foyer, listening for them but hearing nothing, not even the Manor. It had gone silent. Fear took hold and panic muddled my movements.

Goosebumps raised along my arms and I looked over my shoulder to the left, being drawn to the cellar. I started for the door when I paused, as Clay and Wesley walked out from the parlor in the middle of a conversation.

Wesley and his beautiful hazel eyes, Clay with his intelligent and intense stare.

I gripped the staircase with one hand and hobbled down the rest of the stairs toward them. My body was so sore that it begged for relief but I couldn't just sit down and let this battle be fought for me. I was the reason they were still here, the reason they were still in danger.

"What are you doing?" Wesley barked the second he saw me, the muscles in his neck straining.

"Something's wrong," I swallowed. "You need to get out." Laughter echoed in my ears and, for a moment I thought it was coming from them, but when I blinked they were still watching me with concern.

"Florence it's all locked..." Clay reminded me, his stormy gray-blue eyes followed my movements as I stepped into the magnetized pull of the cellar door.

"No you have to go, find a way out." I could feel the Manor refocusing all its efforts on me, the chorus of abhorrent requests and horrifying suggestions of what it could do, *would do*, and what it could force me to do to these men I cared so deeply for.

"You have to—you have—" I shook my head violently like a dog trying to rid itself of a buzzing fly. My mind flickered between reality and what the Manor wanted me to believe. I couldn't tell them apart—"

"There are no options, Vengeful. The only way out is through," Wes said.

I rolled the knife in my hand, unsure how to find the strength to use it if needed.

Finally.

No. I would never use it on them.

"You aren't well, Florence." Clay stepped forward, extending his hand to me, but I couldn't take it.

It was touching him, feeling his warmth that would be my downfall.

"I'm perfectly fine." I stepped away. "It's you—we need—I need you all—to leave." My head was throbbing at the sheer force of the Manor's foul will. It blurred the edges of my vision, tinting everything in the red hot loathing that it surged through me.

"You don't mean that, Florence," Wesley said, and my eyes snapped at him.

"Be quiet, Wesley," I growled, rage bubbling beneath the surface. The closer Clay got to me, the more I felt like a trapped animal. The handle of the knife bit into my skin. I gripped it so tightly. "You know I'm right," I said to him. "We've always agreed on that, if nothing else. You're leaving."

"We can't get out. So tell me what you want, *you*, not the monster knocking at the door. What do you want, Florence?" He quipped back, using my name and, oddly, I longed for the day he had called me a monster. I couldn't stand the look of betrayal in his eyes. I needed the anger to return.

Clay's eyes followed mine to where they bored into Wesley. "Even if we could, we aren't going anywhere. We aren't leaving you here."

The words were like gasoline to a fire.

A door slammed from down the hall, echoing through the house loudly and silenced the argument.

"Where is Koen?" I asked, trying to disguise the panic in my voice. They both looked at each other and back past me down the hall. "Where is he?" I shouted his name frantically, taking off on shaky legs towards where the sound had come from. The two of them were right on my heels as I moved through the turns and nearly fell to my knees before it.

Rotten, twisted, and dark, it throbbed like it had a pulse. Even worse, it called to me, whispering dark thoughts to entice me. My fingers clenched around the hilt of my knife. It felt so good in my hands.

Screaming broke through the barrier of noise and darkness that stained my every thought. Blood-curdling pleas for help echoed up the steps and banged violently against the locked door. Wesley moved me to the side and tried the knob, rattling it more than once before throwing himself up against it. It didn't budge.

"Is he down there?" Panic sunk its claws into my skin and ripped at my nerves as Wesley tried the door again. "Wesley!" I cried, and he turned his pained hazel eyes on me. "Wesley..." the name came out in a whisper as more screaming drowned out the sound of my concern.

"Get him out," I said. "Get him out!" Again, with more terrified urgency. I could hear my heart thumping in my ears as it tried to escape my chest. "He's in pain!" I yelled as Koen's agonized screams rippled through the wood.

I brought my hands to my ears, trying to block out the sound, but it pierced through all the same and it burned like fire as it coursed through my veins. I couldn't stand it; I needed it out. The blade in my hand bit into my skin, but it felt like nothing compared to the pain that tore from Koen's lips in the distance.

"Wes," Clay interrupted and gave him a look to which Wesley just nodded. "Florence." He pressed his fingers around my forearm and guided me backward, eyes lingering on the knife in my hand.

"On the count of three," Wesley said as they lined up facing one another. "Three, two..." on one they ran at the door as quickly as possible.

Propelling themselves forward against the wood, their sheer size should have been enough to split it, but nothing happened.

"I warned you," I whispered over the sounds of the wood waning under their weight. They lined up again, shallow breathing uneven and rough in the cramped hall. "I told you what would happen!" I said louder, fighting against the cracking wood. "I begged you!"

"Whining about it now isn't going to fix this." Wesley turned to me and bit as Clay surged against the door again without luck.

Do you see how cruel they can be?

I shook my head, ignoring the nipping feeling and focusing on getting Koen out. Time was running out for him, the Manor doing unimaginable acts of violence to him behind closed doors.

Wesley's gun fired off, and the house throbbed in anger. The hallway squeezed tightly around us for a moment and sucked all the air from the space before pushing it back out and kicking up my hair with a powerful gust of wind. The bullet dropped to the floor, crumbled, and ineffective against the door.

FLORENCE

"There's got to be another way down there." Wesley looked at Clay. "Was there anything in your books?"

"I barely found the door," he spat, pushing his hand through his hair. "There's nothing in the book about this!"

"This was a trap." Wesley turned on me. "Did you have anything to do with this?" He questioned without malice. He wanted to know if my head was in charge or my heart.

"No!" I closed my eyes and shook my head.

They blame you for it all.

That little treacherous thought swirled around so loudly. It was so easy to believe it.

Wesley's hand was on my cheek when I opened my eyes.

"Are you sure you don't know what the Manor wants?" His voice was quiet, his touch so delicate, there was no trace of viciousness there... "Think." he pushed his other hand against my chest. "With this."

Was his tone always so soft? Had he even accused me?

I couldn't sort through the lies anymore. I knew it was making me see things.

"Let's just get this over with and deal with her after," Clay growled, his jaw and voice tight with malice as he turned to glare at me with disgust.

"Deal with me?" I whispered as Clay turned his attention back to the door. Fear clawed and tore at my chest, trying to find purchase around my heart. "What–"

They're going to kill you.

You're a monster.

"No." Clay knelt before the door, examining the ancient lock. "Deal with the door." His brows furrowed when he looked back at me.

"Are you alright?" Wesley asked in that soft tone, leaning in a little closer to search my eyes. "We see right through you. We know what you are," he whispered.

I shoved backward out of his reach.

"Aye!" Wesley barked, looking down at his arm, a streak of red beginning to weep with blood along his forearm.

They are not your family, Florence.

My head pounded.

They don't love you.

Wesley stepped forward. "Give me the knife," he asked. "Work faster, Clay," he urged over his shoulder. "Florence..." The edge returned to his voice.

They want you dead.

You're nothing but a hunt for them.

My hands trembled around the knife, the blade slicked with Wesley's blood, and my heart pounded so quickly in my chest that I thought it might explode from me.

"We can talk through this once we get Koen free," he said, lowering his shoulders so our eyes met. "I see you're slipping. I see you, Vengeful. But we've got to get him out first and I can't save you both at the same time."

His words were soft and struck true, burrowing themselves through the shadows around my vision.

It will never be you.

My heart constricted in my chest so painfully in that moment of realization that I felt as though I couldn't breathe. I was never going to escape this place. There were no chances left for me. I had run my course. It wasn't them I needed to convince. It was the Manor.

"Stop," I screamed, "right now!" I yelled again. "You don't listen. You've never listened!"

"Enough!" Wesley yelled back.

"No!" I pushed back against him, fighting against the dark intentions to find the person in me who could still make a reasonable decision but, it was like wading through wet sand. With each labored step I took to find myself, the woman who would do anything to keep them safe, I was dragged back into the endless dark and false love that had once felt safe and welcoming.

The comfort of a suffocating love I had known and survived for years was right there, reaching out its hand and begging me to come home, but...

"Florence?" Clay's voice broke through but it was weak and, even though I could see him, darkness curled at the edges of my vision.

The pained tremor in his voice dislodged something in me, that slid into place in my soul and locked. I did not belong to anyone. I was not something to be owned. Koen's warm laughter echoed through me, and I heard his voice over the venomous whispers. *"Your dreams are my dreams".*

Vicious claws tried to reach out and snatch away the thoughts as they came, when I then heard Clay, from the first day in the flower field, *"You could be anything you wanted now- given the chance."* I had wanted so badly to be given such a chance. Then it was Wesley's hazel eyes, dark and serious, and full of something I had yet to uncover. *"You are not a monster. I was wrong."*

You belong to me.

The Manor's hold was everlasting.

I looked down at myself, dressed in my skirts and corset, and hissed. There was never any chance of me escaping my prison. It had welcomed them in because it had known there was no possible way for me to be freed, unless it allowed it. Everything was always at the behest of this place, its walls a foreboding barricade that no one could breach- least of all me. It could play with time, with my mind, and with my life, allowing me to heal or suffer at its own discretion. It was too strong.

The Manor was too strong. For me and for them. Koen's hollow screams of agony cascaded up and pushed like an anvil on my back. An idea sparked and my shoulders tensed with resolve. It could keep my body but my heart was my own and I could choose who it belonged to.

There was no other choice. I shut my eyes, delving deep into the anger the Manor so desperately wanted me to succumb to, swimming through the rage and finding a dark chamber within my heart to cower in while I did what must be done.

The only thing I could think of that might save them all.

"I never wanted you here, and I don't want you here now. You were never anything more than unwanted guests. If you don't leave, the Manor will take you all, and I won't stop it."

"You don't mean that," Clay whispered.

"I do." I stepped back from him. There was only one way to be convincing, to convince the Manor that my betrayal was real. "Did you think I could love you?" I said to him. "I never did. I was using you. I'm a monster, I'm not capable of love."

"You're lying." Clay shook his head, tears pricked at the corners of his eyes. "You can say it, you can scream it, but you don't believe it. *I don't believe it.*" His eyes followed mine as I shifted to look at Wesley, who had gone still.

Koen's screams flooded the hall.

"This is not the time for you two to fight," Wesley growled.

I dug deep, down into the dark depths of my heart and soul, the place where the Manor had embedded itself like glass shards into my skin, and I ripped the hatred from my flesh.

"I mean every word."

The door clicked open.

Everything opened, it was a visceral feeling that rattled through the Manor as every window and door that had once been barred tore open.

"Go!"

Wesley didn't wait but Clay stood staring at me at the top of the stairs.

"I don't believe you." His tone was low and tight.

"Get Koen," I urged him, just trying to hold it together long enough for the house to believe it. "And get out."

I had to stay.

I was the heart of the Manor.

But they were mine.

CLAYTON

I left Florence at her insistence to find Koen. I took the stairs, flagging behind Wes, who was moving faster than I had ever seen him go.

"Slow down!" I yelled ahead to him. "We don't know what the hell we're running into!" My pleas were breathless and frantic as Wes disappeared into the darkness ahead of me.

"Wes!" I called out to him without response but Koen's screams had halted and an eerie lack of sound fell over the entire cellar. I pulled my flashlight from my back pocket, flicked it on, and shone it across the pitch-black space.

"Wesley!" I barked again, and this time he responded.

"Over here!" He yelled, his massive frame curled over what looked like a heap of earth but, as I got closer, I realized it wasn't that at all. Vines curled tightly around Koen's body, cutting into his skin and pulling him down into the damp earth beneath.

"He's trapped!" Wes shouted. "Cut him loose!"

That's why the screaming had stopped. The vines were crushing the air from his lungs, and there was nothing left. Koen's eyes flickered open heavily, the green in his pain-filled gaze so bright I could feel his suffering as I dropped to my knees next to Wes.

We began to saw at the vines with our knives, one by one, but no matter how many we broke apart, they seemed to materialize out of nothing, wrapping tighter around Koen until he was barely visible anymore beneath the writhing plant.

"It's not fucking working!" Wes moved faster, his anger and fear fueling him as the threat of losing Koen loomed. "He's going to suffocate to death."

"Just keep working at them," I encouraged forcefully, but the words barely made it out. Wes wouldn't survive Koen's death. It would be the end of him. The thorns of the vines cut into my skin as I sawed at the plant furiously without results.

"Orchid Manor," Florence's voice was chilly as she walked up from behind.

Seeing her made my blood run cold.

I hated that my whole being could still love her, with Koen dying at my feet.

My mind wrestled with my heart, wanting so badly to believe that she wouldn't hurt us, but unsure if she even had a choice in the matter any longer. She hadn't been herself. I was sure of it. The words weren't hers. They couldn't have been.

I looked around at who she might be talking to but found no one but us and the mound of earth that pulsated and throbbed with vines, threatening to steal Koen from our grasp. There wasn't even a flicker of spirit, but her eyes weren't focused on any *thing* in the cellar. She was staring directly into the vines.

"What are you doing?" Wes spat out, never taking his attention away from freeing Koen.

"The Manor doesn't want him, it doesn't want any of you." she said, her voice steady and even. She seemed devoid of emotion, almost in a trance like she had been on the day of the storm. She had been slipping away so much lately, descending into the darkness of her mind. Now it seemed It had finally taken over her completely.

"Florence?" I watched her circle us and kneel at the base of the mound. Her knees sank into the mixed pool of blood and dirt. Her eyes were glassed over, as she stared into the distance and seemed to wait.

Her chest filled with air and as she exhaled, her body fell, and relaxed against the cold dirt floor like she was being commanded to sleep. Wes flinched when she slumped to the side but I put my hand out.

"Don't touch her," I said quietly, unsure what would happen if we interrupted the moment between her and the Manor.

Florence was so still, her cheek smeared with dirt and blood as her cold, distant gaze closed over, and she was pulled away into the darkness that called to her from the other side. I could feel tears hot against my cheeks.

The question hung between us as we worked at the vines until finally, after a long moment, Wes opened his mouth.

"Is she—" Wes stumbled over his words, but we didn't have time to wonder whether or not she was. I didn't want to know. I couldn't bear it.

The vines dissipated, and almost immediately they opened and pulled back from Koen, releasing him from the twisted, thorny prison. Wes sobbed when he saw him, reaching out and gripped him from under his arms. Koen's entire frame was limp and covered in hundreds of painful gashes. He slipped roughly into Wes's lap.

"Move," I said, not giving Wes a second of relief as the vines started to move against the dirt, writhing and twisting with sloppy, wet noises as they extended and grew. "Wes, *move*!" I said again with more urgency, jumping up from my spot and hauling him backward with my hands beneath his arms as he gripped tightly to Koen's unconscious body.

Koen startled to life, his hands clawing at Wes's arms to ground himself in reality, his heart no doubt beating far too fast as he gasped for air.

"You're alright," Wes calmed him as we watched the vines grow alarmingly fast. "We need to get out of here. Can you carry her?" He asked me, and I nodded. "Good. Move your ass, we can't stay here."

I acted quickly but when I tried to reach her I was shoved backward against the brick wall, the air knocked from my lungs. Wes stopped at the base of the stairs and Koen pulled in his arms, fighting to stay.

"Get him out of here!" I pushed what air was left out of my body to yell over the sound of the rotating vines in the dirt.

Wes nodded and assured me, "I'll come right back!"

He struggled under Koen's weight but eventually got him up the stairs. He disappeared from my view as I tried again to reach her, but there was no way around the barrier between us.

I sank to my knees, creeping against it as closely as possible, and pressed my fingertips against the violent energy radiating from it. It stung my skin but didn't lash out at me as I lowered my head even with her closed eyes, cheek pressed to the ground.

"Florence," I whispered to her as the wind in the cellar started to whip harder. "*Love*," I pleaded, holding the shake in my voice at bay. She never stirred.

"You have to get up," I urged, unable to do much else as the vines continued to wrap their thorns around her body. "You can't let it have you."

She belongs here.

A chilly thought spoke in my mind and spread goosebumps across my arms.

"She doesn't," I fought back, feeling the barrier surge with energy, electricity tickling down my fingertips, but I didn't move from my spot. "You don't belong here," I said to Florence's unconscious body. "You belong out there with us. Adventures," I implored her, my throat growing dry, "music, poetry, potential, *Freedom.*"

I couldn't help the tears that streamed down my face as I begged her to wake.

"I'm not leaving this god-forsaken Manor without you, none of us will. I know it feels like we're against you, like you don't know what's real and a lie. But we're real. I'm real. The love I feel for you is so real it's tearing me apart to see you like this." I bit my bottom lip to keep from crying out as the vines started to pull her into the mound. It was taking her.

"You thought you didn't have a choice." I closed my eyes, unable to watch.

She's mine.

The sound ripped through me like needles, piercing my muscles as it traveled through me. Was that what Florence heard constantly, what she felt?

She's mine!

I pushed back on the voice.

"You thought it was you or us, but it doesn't have to be! It can be everyone. We can fight this, but you can't let it take you."

It all clicked into place too late.

Orchid Manor was never a spirit. It wasn't a siren or ghoul. There was no curse that had been placed on it, and it was never a god. It had been exactly as she had been saying since the moment we came here. It was so obscure and yet so simple, we had been dealing with something much more esoteric than I had thought.

It was a Sapient House.

Florence had been right all along.

The answer, now obvious before us.

The house *was* alive.

Like any sapient creature it was self aware; conscious of its decisions and intelligent in the worst ways. It took pleasure from the damage and carnage it created. It was entirely capable of complex thoughts and emotions, and manipulation was obviously this one's favorite.

Agatha, for what little we knew of her, must have been just like Florence once. Held captive for who knew how long before the Manor tired of her, then she had lured Florence here as her replacement.

"One day you will understand why, and I hope that when you have to make the same choice I did, you will forgive me just as I have now forgiven........"

The words from the letter made sense now. She was also a victim of the Manor and the sick entity had forced her to find her own replacement. But one thing Agatha hadn't considered in her letter, was that Florence would have never allowed a successor to take her place and be a victim in her stead. She had fought so hard to keep us safe.

Orchid Manor had been keeping Florence as a pet and when we stumbled upon the damned place, it was the perfect opportunity to feed its narcissistic cruelty. It had always been about making itself look like the hero, like her savior. We had all been toys, chess pieces to move around the place at its will to cause as much strife and excitement and overwhelming emotions as possible, and one by one we had all become targets as we fell for Florence.

Love had blossomed instantly, and the Manor had been threatened.

It's plan went awry when we didn't harm her like it had expected.

That's why Florence had become sick. The Manor flooded her with hatred. It wanted her alone and scared, so she turned back to it, back where the Manor believed she belonged.

"You don't belong here, Florence," I said, my heart in pieces, knowing it was truly too late, and we were unable to save her.

Orchid Manor was determined to prove me wrong as it wrapped her in vines and hugged her tightly into its earth. And there wasn't a damn thing I could do about it besides lay there with her as it took her.

Tears rolled down my face as her eyes fluttered open, her face framed by vines and blossoming flowers that made her look painfully delicate in her final moments. Auburn hair tangled with greens and pinks, dancing against her pale skin—a horribly poetic enclosure, for the most beautiful of wildflowers.

"I'm sorry," I said, not knowing what else I could do.

There wasn't a book in the world that could help me now, not a weapon strong enough to break through and bring her close to me. The cruelest of punishments was the last. Watching her die mere inches from me without a single thing I could do to stop it. Having her sacrifice herself for us, to die in the cage she so desperately wanted to be free from. Her worst nightmare for our freedom.

"I *feel* it all," she whispered, a small smile lifting the corner of her mouth. It struck me, a clean shot through my heart as she made peace with what was happening. There it was, complete confirmation. This beautiful, courageous woman, who'd had her life stripped from her by unimaginable circumstances- sacrificed herself to save us.

I beat my fists against the barrier, my heart screaming for her as the pain cascaded through my muscles. She didn't want this.

"I felt it all, too." I dropped back to her, catching one last glimpse of her big, emerald eyes before the vines swallowed her whole, and she was consumed by the Manor.

She belongs to me.

WESLEY

Clay appeared at the entrance of the Manor, his shirt soaked in dirt and blood as he dropped to his knees in the gravel and pressed his forehead into the ground.

"Where is she?" Koen gripped my shirt as I worked to cover his most extensive wounds.

He was barely able to keep his eyes open but the words tore from him, shaky and broken. The sound of his agony ripped me apart from the inside out.

"Clay!" He yelled, his voice cracking.

His breathing became ragged as he tried to sit up from the truck bed, pushing me away from him. "Clay, where is Florence?" He asked again, slipping from the tailgate and crumbling to the ground because his legs were still too weak.

"Ko," I grunted as he started to crawl in stumbled, painful motions toward Clay. "You can't go back in there–" The Manor had let us out... but why? "Koen stop!"

I attempted to lift him but he pushed me away, knocking me into the dirt beside him, and we stayed there on the ground staring across the five feet to Clay, who finally looked up from the gravel with grief in his eyes.

"She…" He breathed out and stopped, closing his eyes to ground himself. "She sacrificed herself for us."

"No," Koen shook his head. "she wouldn't do that."

"*Yes,* she would," I said from beside him, wrapping my arms around my knees as I folded in to keep the heartache at bay. "It's exactly what she would do."

"The house is sapient," Clay finally said, composing himself enough to talk.

A sapient house? Of course it was. *It was alive.* Just as she had been saying all along.

I looked up at the Manor, cursing myself for not realizing sooner.

"It wouldn't let her go. She had become a part of it. Agatha Warren drew her in and Orchid Manor has kept Florence alive to keep it company."

"That's why it let us out–" I nodded in confirmation. The Manor had won, it didn't need us anymore. It had proven the point it wanted to make.

"The house loves Florence in whatever sick and twisted way it believes love is. But now it's taken over her completely, she never had a choice."

Florence didn't belong to anyone.

Her soft hair flashed across my vision and I could almost smell her rose-petal scent tickling my nose. My cheeks flushed with heat as the memory of her fingertips brushed my throat and her lips ghosted my jaw. I could feel every ounce of her in the wind that kicked up under my chin and I clenched my teeth tightly together to hold in the strangled whimper that rose from me.

Rage quickly flooded my veins as I pushed to my feet and started toward the truck's bed. Koen watched with hollow eyes as I started digging for things in a fit of unbridled anger.

"That means I can burn it to the ground." I looked over at the Manor seething.

"You'll burn her alive," Koen choked out. "You can't."

His heartbreak was evident in the way his voice broke.

"She's gone, Koen," Clay said, tears streaking through the dirt that clung to his sharp cheekbones. "She's not there anymore."

"That's a lie." Koen tried to get to his feet again but failed, screaming out in agony when he realized he wasn't strong enough to get himself back into the house to try for himself. "You're lying!"

"I watched the Manor take her," Clay practically sobbed, holding it back just barely as he rose to his feet. "She's…" He couldn't bring himself to repeat it.

The pause in his words rattled through all of us, Koen's shoulders slumping over as Clay inhaled what he could into his lungs.

"Burn it to the ground." Clay turned his gaze on me, so profound and dark.

I nodded once, fishing out the petrol cans and digging for my lighter. I threw a box of salt at him. "Follow close," I warned him as I strode back into the Manor.

Clay picked himself up off the ground and kept at my back. The walls felt more alive than ever, like consuming Florence had pumped them into overdrive. The vibrating that I had felt the first time we entered the Manor was tenfold now. It shook through the soles of my boots into my calves and made the muscles tighten uncomfortably in my chest.

The walls were no longer hole-filled crumbling plaster but pristine and covered in rich wallpaper that blanketed the entire entrance. I stopped for a moment, staring around at it all in awe. The dark hardwood flooring looked as if it had just been laid, and every sconce, lantern and lamp was lit, bathing the room in a warm romantic glow.

Tall, dramatic curtains made of deep velvety fabric hung over the pristine and dazzling windows that reached to the ceiling. The chandelier that had smashed, crystal dancing across the floor in my memories, was in perfect condition hanging from the ceiling, dripping with soft flickering candlelight.

The staircases were grand and imposing, and yet, I could clearly envision her there, dressed as she had been that first day, cheeks blushing and eyes flashing, holding in her laughter as she watched us argue about whether to stay or leave. It had been like this for her the whole time? Why had it taken me so long to be able to see it, to see *her*.

Breath hitched in my throat and my heart ached painfully in my chest.

"You can see it–" Clay turned to me and I nodded, my eyes watering in angered confusion. He watched me for a moment longer before saying simply, "I'm sorry."

He said it like it was supposed to quell the agony I felt over being too late to love her.

I steeled my emotions away and swallowed down the agony that filled my throat, threatening to explode from me in a painful scream.

"Watch." I pointed to how the picture frames shook on the wall, ready to drop or fly at us without warning. Distracting myself with the hunt at hand. The Manor was getting ready to expel us. "I don't need you hurt, too," I said, my tone tight with barely concealed anguish.

"It doesn't matter, I don't feel anything," Clay sighed, his tone flat.

I turned to look at him briefly, seeing the pain that stained his features and understanding where he was coming from. I couldn't have imagined being down there, watching the Manor take her. It broke something deep inside Clay, something I wasn't even sure had existed in the first place, but it was evident all over his face. He wouldn't come back from what he saw. Not anytime soon, maybe not ever.

"I know." I nodded with a strangled sigh and started to dump petrol over the staircase, bounding up the steps until looping back around and splashing it over the walls upstairs. I got some of the doors and soaked the carpets, chucking the can away from me as Clay salted all the entryways he could see.

"What's that?" I asked as he reappeared at the top of the stairs.

"Her poems." He shoved the worn book into his back pocket.

"Did you grab the bags?" I asked him.

"I don't want any of it. It all smells like her."

I nodded in agreement. We could get new shit, but the memory of Florence would haunt us forever. I stared at the Manor, my heart sluggish and rage dissipating.

What I wouldn't give to have her scold me for being so solemn.

I would trade–I stopped the thought before it formed, unable to deal with the repercussions of my own heartbroken thoughts. *This was my fault.*

I had brought us here.

"Good?" Clay asked.

I was far from it.

I would never admit it out loud, I barely could to myself, but it hurt, seeing Florence laying there in the dirt, and knowing now that it was the last time I would ever see her. She had looked so broken... and I was helpless. Knowing that I couldn't do anything to change it or scrub it from my memory. Her tiny, broken body was so cold and fragile. To be taken like that, *stolen.*

I was livid.

I wasn't good.

"Yeah." I took one last look at the house and pushed him out the door.

Koen was still where we left him, staring blankly at the house.

"It's gonna be okay, Ko." Clay wandered over to him, putting on a brave face as he settled down in the gravel beside him. Neither of them said anything else as I flicked the lighter open and stared at the flame.

"Just do it," Koen coughed, still struggling to breathe properly. His eyes were rimmed with red from crying as he stared past me at the Manor.

I rubbed my thumb over it one last time and tossed it down into the line of petrol, watching the entire trail go up in flames. It cracked and licked at the floors, spreading fast and covering the stairs and rugs. It smelled like smoke and death as the clouds started to plume from the windows and doors.

"Good riddance." I backed away from it.

I wandered over to stand next to them, my fingertips brushing through Koen's hair at my side as he leaned into my leg. Clay stared up at the Manor in horror as the flames started to burn hotter. A loud, painful, screeching sound tore from the wood as though it was screaming out in pain, but it washed over me in relief, not only for me but for Florence.

I wanted to ignore the sharp, stinging pain in my chest. To pretend it was exhaustion and soreness from the months behind us, but it wasn't. It was longing, grief, and sorrow and they weighed heavy on my heart to remind me that we had all lost something precious.

"Why isn't the Manor defending itself?" Koen choked out between sniffles.

"It's sufficiently distracted with whatever it's doing to her now, this might be the only time to completely overwhelm it, destroy it," Clay said, his brain finally starting to tick normally.

"Will it work?" He asked.

"We can only hope." Clay nodded and watched the Manor with dark eyes.

"I'm sorry, Koen," I whispered as soft sobs escaped him. Smoke billowed into the sky, staining it black and darkening the clouds.

"Do you hear that?" Clay choked out, pushing onto his feet and turning his head to stare down the long drive, but I didn't hear anything. "There's no one coming."

He was right. With the heat coming off the house, the smoke, and the sound of snapping wood and billowing flames, emergency services should have been up the hill by now, but nothing but the house dying echoed through the air.

"God damnit—what if that *didn't* work?" Clay repeated Koen's doubt, sounding truly horrified in a way I had never heard before. It struck me. *What if she's still trapped forever?* The words went unsaid between us.

My hands clenched tightly. What if no matter what we had done, her beautiful soul would be tied to this cursed ground?

"It worked," I said out loud. "It had to."

I turned from the heat, sinking next to Koen with the medical kit, and started back on his wounds. He didn't move or speak as I went over each puncture and cut roughly, covering the large ones that still trickled dark crimson down his cold skin.

Koen seemed so far away, even as the fire from the Manor danced vividly in the reflection of his eyes. We were alive but it did not feel like a victory, we hadn't gotten everyone out.

"You were right," I said quietly—a moment just for us, not the Manor.

Koen didn't move but I knew he could hear me.

"I was scared." I swallowed tightly as I covered one of the last significant cuts that wrapped around his throat.

It looked so painful. His skin was raised in thick coils where the vines had twisted around his throat to steal the air from his body—bruises that would take weeks to heal and scars that never would.

"Scared to lose you and Clay, but I was scared to take what I needed, scared to love her the way she deserved, and now..." I stared at the house as it continued to burn bright, the upper floor giving way and crumbling into the main area. A plume of sparks and smoke cascaded up like fireworks.

"I'm sorry it took me so long," I apologized. "Maybe if it hadn't..."

"Don't do that," Koen's lips moved and the sound came out, but it was quiet against the loud snaps of wood and the rushing air. "That is the one thing you aren't allowed to do." He looked at me, and my chest was constricted at the sight of him.

His lip was ripped open from a thorn, purple and caked with dried blood. His left cheek split open, and a nasty bruise was forming up the side of his face, staining his temple and hairline almost black where more dried blood stuck to a gash beneath his curls.

"She would have waited patiently for you, no matter how long it took you to figure it out. Florence–" He stopped, composing himself as he tripped over her name. "She would have waited for you to figure it out."

There was a certainty to his words that made me believe him.

"Do you think she's free?" Koen asked me, but I wasn't sure how to respond.

"Yes," Clay answered for me, coming to settle in the dirt with us, his face still stained with mud and ash. His cheeks were red and dry from standing so close to the house as it burned, but he didn't seem to be in any pain when he spoke again. "I'd like to think that when she closed her eyes for that final time, she drifted somewhere peaceful, away from the confines that held her for so long. That she's in the wind around us, in the trees and the river..."

He looked over at us.

"In the wildflowers," he whispered, his eyes filling with tears.

"Definitely in the wildflowers," Koen huffed, the laughter tangled with anguish.

"But she's free." I nodded and wrapped my arm around Koen, just needing a moment to remind myself that we hadn't lost everything tonight.

WESLEY

We sat there, watching Orchid Manor crumble into smoldering ash well into the morning light. As the sun rose over the property, casting the sky with rich colors of dusty purples and blues, the eerie cries of the Manor stopped altogether.

Beyond the torched Manor and its perfectly pruned bushes, there was nothing but debris.

The wildflower field silhouetted, as the rising sun touched the sky.

I felt it then. As the smoke dissipated, I felt the bubble pop, the barrier snapped out of place, and the sound of birds rushed in. Clay's next breath was loud and a sob ripped from him in realization of what had just happened.

The Manor on Orchid Lane was dead.

I tipped my chin to the sky and filled my lungs with clean air as the smoke cleared from the clouds above. It was a relief that the Manor could no longer hurt anyone, but it was also mixed with the despair and overwhelming grief for Florence's sacrifice.

Looking down and over the rubble, my eyes caught a flash of vibrant green.

My heart raced as I searched for what I saw again.

I pushed to my feet, ignoring the light hiss from Koen, who had been resting at my side.

"What are you..." Clay asked, but I had already started running.

I skidded in the gravel, stumbling over my own feet. I braced myself on one hand and righted myself to keep moving toward the green. My boots slipped in the ashy gravel as I slammed to a stop in front of the pile of kindled structure that was nothing but chunks of wood and stone.

I stripped my shirt free and wrapped it around my face protecting myself from the smoke and started to work. I pushed the smoldering ash away with my bare hands, crying out as it burned the skin of my palms but never stopped.

Not until I could see it properly.

A cellar door was buried under the rubble. On the right side of the property, it sat nestled into the ground, shielded by vines. They twisted through the rotted wood and deep pink flowers that reminded me of the flush to Florence's cheeks when she was angry, were inexplicably unmarred.

I rushed back to the truck, scooping my ax from the bed.

Clay begged me to stop and tell him what was happening, but I couldn't find the words.

I moved back to the door as fast as my legs would carry me through the mess and started to hack at the vines with all my force. Over and over again, I smashed into them and, unlike the time before, they began to split and fall away. The healthy stems shriveled and died when they were disconnected from their roots.

My only focus was getting through the vines. I needed to know.

I needed to make sure she wasn't down there.

I needed to make sure she had escaped this prison, one way or another.

The cellar door was finally released, and the stairs beneath were uncovered. It was tricky to descend, but with some clumsy maneuvering, I managed to get to the bottom. Light leaked through the ashy, burnt floorboards, and the sun trickled in through it, creating a smokey, sunkissed haze over the cellar floor.

I inhaled tightly through my shirt, and then pulled it down in shock, not caring about the smoke. Because there she was.

Relief overwhelmed me and tears stung the corners of my eyes.

"Florence?" I choked out.

Untouched by the fire, her copper hair was splayed across the dirt. Her dress was caked in mud, but the vines had created a cocoon around her, protecting her from the fire. I worked quickly, urging my body to work through the exhaustion that plagued my muscles as I brought the ax down into the remnants of the vines to free her.

I dropped to my knees, and started to use my hands to tear the vines away, not caring as the thorns bit into the palms of my hands and my forearms. I just needed to get her out. The air in my lungs was strangled by the knowledge that this could be for nothing as I lifted her lifeless body from the mud into my arms.

"You aren't allowed to die," I whispered. "We have things to do."

Florence's head fell limp in my arms and I couldn't stop the sob that escaped my lips at the action. I cried out, climbing the stairs. It was harder to ascend them with her in my arms but, soon, the sunrise kissed her pale face and I knew we had reached the top.

"Clay!" I screamed his name.

He stared across the yard at me, frozen in shock, before stumbling through the gravel and running toward me.

"I think she might be…" I stopped looking down at her limp body. "But I don't…the house is still…" I tripped over my thoughts. The words wouldn't come out; fear gripped me and I couldn't control the panic that overtook me. My clothing was too tight, my muscles were aching, and my head was swimming.

"Set her down!" Clay snapped, and I listened.

He had always been better in situations like this.

Like there had ever been a situation like *this*.

I could already see his brain taking over and pushing out everything else.

Logic would save Florence, if anything.

"She's not breathing!" Clay announced, pressing his ear to her chest. "But I think–" He trailed off.

Koen limped toward us, nearly toppling over in the driveway as Clay began pumping on Florence's chest wildly. "The barrier!" He yelled, "Did you feel it?" He asked, and Clay hushed him. "We can take her to the hospital!" He pleaded with us both.

Clay continued to give her CPR. Tiny huffs of exhaustion left his lips tangled with a string of curse words as tears dripped down his cheeks. His forearms strained against her chest, pumping as hard as he could to restart her heart.

"Work faster, Clay!" I barked, every muscle in my body tense.

"I'm doing the best I can," he snapped back, blowing air through her pale pink lips. "I think it's why the barrier broke," he cried out as he went back to thumping on her chest. "She was the heart of the Manor."

"No heart," I whispered.

"No Manor," Koen's voice cracked, but realization crossed his bruised and battered face.

I knelt beside her as Clay furiously beat on her chest to restart her heart.

"You listen to me," I said loud enough for them to hear, but I was only speaking to Florence. "We've been doing this on our own for a long time. We never needed anyone to care for us because we cared for each other, but it's different now. We need you to come back to us, Florence; we need you to be stubborn just one more time," I pleaded with her.

Her limp body was so cold as I took her small hand in my palm and lowered my voice.

"*I need you,*" I said quietly, pressing my lips to her wrist. "I didn't say it before but I need you too. So you aren't allowed to leave, not yet. You have to come back and tell me how selfish I am."

"Come on, Florence." Clay pounded on her chest in a rhythm, filling her lungs with air. His desperation to bring her back from the dead was evident and relentless even as his arms shook with exhaustion.

I ground my teeth together and brushed her hair away from her face. "We worked too damn hard and sacrificed too much to free that big, stubborn heart of yours, so start fucking using it."

"Wait." Koen stumbled to his feet, screaming in pain as he surged back to the truck.

I rose from the ground, letting go of her hand, ready to take over for Clay, as I watched Koen drop to his knees to dig in the kit. "Wes!" He yelled, gripping his rib cage as he closed the distance, only pulling back when he was close enough and throwing something at me as hard as he could.

I stepped forward instinctively, taking the object in my hand.

"Clay." I panicked, sliding back down to him and handing the stick to him.

An epi-pen.

He popped the cap with his teeth and inhaled, and I could see hesitation on his face. There was a chance that the adrenaline did nothing or harmed her further.

We only had one shot to get this right or lose her forever.

My head was screaming, my heart was pumping too fast, and as Koen came limping back to us, I nodded to Clay, who stared at me, gripped with fear.

"She's dead already, Clay," I told him. The idea of losing her twice flickered through me violently as I opened my mouth again.

He hovered above her chest, his own rising and falling too fast.

"Do it."

T he cafe was packed with more people than we had seen in a long time. Twelve hours of driving from our last hunt had made everyone a little cranky. Koen slid into the booth beside me and rested his head against the cracked navy blue vinyl seats.

"The bathrooms haven't been cleaned since the sixties." He laughed.

The bruises around his neck were finally almost gone, and nothing but faint pinkish lines indicated where the vines had left imprints from twisting so tightly into his skin. The band T-shirt he wore was ripped at the sleeves and showed off the side of his torso, where more tiny scars littered his body, but he didn't seem to mind much.

A pretty waitress with bleached-blond hair and a bright smile came around to collect our orders. Turning her attention on Clay, his overgrown, long dark curls swept back off his face except for one that fell perfectly against his forehead. He smiled back at her with his lopsided toothy grin and big, blue eyes, his tongue darting out over his bottom lip as he leaned over the dingy table in his dress shirt. Tattoos peeked from the collar and wrists as he rubbed his fingers over the book's spine in his hand.

He hadn't stopped carrying the book of poetry around since that day.

By now, he'd have memorized every word, but held tight to it nonetheless.

It was special because of the memories tucked carefully inside with dog-eared and tear-soaked pages.

The waitress attempted to flirt with him, but he ordered and returned to his book without much interest in her.

"Did you figure out anything about the murders?" Koen asked, kicking Clay under the table.

"We might actually have a Chupacabra on our hands," he sighed, looking up from the page.

"Here? Aren't those things deep South America types of bogeymen?" Koen scowled.

"Local authorities say it's just a bear but one 'nut job' was telling anyone who would listen that its bigfoot; but three eyewitnesses all claimed that it was over seven feet tall and had a 'bear-like-human voice.'"

"How many victims?" I asked.

"Six," Clay answered, "that we know of, all hikers."

"I hate camping." Koen rolled his eyes, and I nudged him.

"It'll be fun. We can have smores, and I miss the stars. We've been in too many big cities lately. Some country air will do us some good," I responded.

"Yeah, fine," Koen mumbled, sitting up as the waitress slid the burgers across the table to us. "These might actually be road kill," he teased, grabbing his burger as Clay shook his head.

They dug in, but I couldn't help but take a moment to appreciate how good it looked before wrapping my hands around it and bringing it to my lips. The warm burger coated my tongue with grease and dripped down my wrists as I held it back from my face as I chewed.

"So?" Wesley asked me from across the table, golden waves highlighted by the sunlight behind him as he arched his arm across the back of the booth. His shirt stretched over the expanse of his broad chest, and his lips curved into a loose smile. "How's your first greasy burger, Vengeful?"

I scrunch my nose up at him and filled with warmth under his gaze, so grateful to see it every day.

"Quite possibly the best thing I've ever eaten."

"Until you're vomiting on the side of the motorway later," Koen grumbled as he shoved a few fries between his lips. Clay's brows kissed as he looked up to give him a dirty glare.

Some days were more challenging than others, with the memories of what happened creeping into the dark spaces of my mind but, even then, the thoughts and feelings were wholly *mine*. Orchid Manor had been ripped from my being, its essence completely eradicated aside from my memories, and I was finally just human again—as hard as being human could be. I had come to appreciate sleep and food more than before, especially now that I needed both to function again.

It had been a growing process for all four of us when they had brought me back from the edge of death. I could remember the warm breeze on my cheeks and the soft sound of my mothers singing, and my fathers laughter calling me home. But they hadn't been finished with me, and I hadn't been finished with them, and in the end the Hunters who had vowed to do their job did just that. I was fortunate enough to be saved.

The images of waking up to them huddled around me were burned into the back of my mind.

Koen's big green eyes were wet and red as I shot from death back into the light. Clay's hands gripped around me so tightly they left bruises that didn't heal for weeks, my chest and neck sore, and Wesley standing over us, his face tight in shock as if he had just seen a ghost.

Orchid Manor was nothing but ash.

I had died, my heart had stopped beating and, with the Manor obliterated, the house had nothing left to live off of. My death was also the Manor's. By some sort of miracle Wesley had been able to find me and bring me back from the brink. This miracle they had pulled off was the beginning of a new life. *My* new life.

Stepping through the gate had brought me to tears, and each mile we drove further from Orchid Manor was a new start to a fresh life that I couldn't wait to live.

Clay had insisted we wait awhile before we dove straight into fried foods and anything that might upset my system but, after a few weeks of traveling, he finally gave way. Starting with a disgusting roadside cafe burger and the greasiest fries I had ever eaten. I leaned against Koen and one of his hands came down beneath the table to brush against my thigh. I was always grateful for the closeness.

His lips pressed to my temple and I couldn't help but smile even brighter.

Happy as can be.

"Oh," Clay dug into his bag and pulled out a folder. "I found information on someone." He held it out to me. "You might want to see this."

I stared at the folder as he watched me carefully.

"I found her," he said with a small smile when I didn't respond.

I flipped open the manila folder and stared down at the clippings, articles and photos of... Oh. *Aisling.* "She survived." A sob ripped from me and my eyes watered, as my fingers brushed the photo of her.

"I wanted to show you earlier but–"

He stopped, we had been intent on his search for answers to set me free and twisted so incredibly tight, unable to shift focus from anything but Orchid Manor. I understood why it had taken so long for him to reveal this.

"So I did some more research and found so many beautiful things. She lived eighty incredible years," Clay said. "After she was found in town she was treated by a doctor, who she later married and, with the help of her husband, they opened a nursing school that still stands. It's part of a larger medical center in a town not far from where you were all those years."

"Her heart always had been so big," I whispered, tears streaming down my cheeks. "She survived him."

Wesley leaned forward on the table, his long arm extending and brushing my cheek.

"You both did," Clay assured me. "She had two children, both girls." He pointed to something in her records.

Flora, she had named her first daughter after me and tears that had been steadily escaping did not cease. I set the folder down and inhaled a shaky breath. "Thank you for this."

"Anything for you." He winked one of those familiar blue eyes at me and went back to his burger.

Clay and Koen finished their burgers, deep in a discussion about mermaids and whether or not they existed as they funneled from the cafe into the fresh air. Wesley's finger hooked into one of the loops on my waist and pulled me back against him as he paid for our food, his fingers tickling around my hip and pressing to my stomach beneath my shirt aimlessly.

Though it was still strange, his affection was given freely now.

There was very little in life that I was sure about, but I knew from the moment I was brought back into this world, that Wesley Cameron was done guarding his heart. He had vowed that day to wear it on his sleeve, the way Koen had, because life had swept in and showed us that it was short and fragile. And, despite being immortal for so long, I felt it in a more demanding way than the rest of them, waning between life and death for so long that I forgot what it was like to truly *live*.

It would be foolish of me to say I wasn't scared. Everyday, I was terrified to be so human and fragile, but I knew if I had Wesley at my back and Clay at my side, Koen would protect the other. I could face anything the world threw at us. And the fear of injury or death faded to a dull roar when I realized I could help people again.

Hunting had stitched together that piece of me I had lost so long ago.

A life worth being mortal for.

Wesley kept himself wrapped around me as we wandered from the establishment, the sun and his lips warming the skin on my neck as the door closed behind us.

"Hello, handsome." I giggled as his fingers danced between my stomach and the waist of my jeans, brushing between the button and my skin.

"Next hotel, we're getting two rooms," he whispered, and it tickled my ear.

I laughed and leaned back into his chest as the other two argued in the distance. Koen's face was appalled as Clay spewed facts about the logistics of mermaids' existence.

"Someone would have seen them by now, Koen!" He argued.

"The ocean is massive. You're a horrible nerd!" Koen growled as he approached the truck.

"I'm sick of sharing," Wesley added.

"Alright." I caved to his request, turning in his arms to face him. "But you have to tell them."

His brows scrunched together as he stared down at me with an annoyed expression but I could count the gold specks in his hazel eyes and couldn't be bothered by anything else. His fingers dug into my hips as he leaned closer, his lips ghosting over mine.

"I'll play you for it?" He whispered just as I thought he might kiss me.

"Not fair, you always win." I laughed, pulling back and holding my hand out for a game of rock, paper, scissors.

He shook his head and let go of me to hold his hand out. "Rock, paper, scissors," he said in time, following our hand movements. His fist curled into a rock.

"Hah!" I yelled, "Paper beats rock!"

Wesley grunted, rolling his eyes but cupping my face in his hands as he kissed me in the middle of the parking lot with a needy ferocity that I adored coming from him. His lips were so soft as he stole one more quick kiss.

"Good luck." I laughed, skipping from him toward Clay, who waited with the door of the Bronco open.

"What was that about?" He asked, stepping forward and pinning my back against the truck as he approached. Lemon and leather washing over me.

"Wouldn't you like to know." I smiled up at him, thumb brushing over the divots that formed on his cheek as his smile grew wide.

"I quite like the mischievous side of you." His nose brushed against mine as his lips hovered teasingly, not touching me yet.

"I'm finding being human quite agreeable," I huffed when he didn't kiss me immediately.

"You were always human, Florence," he said before finally colliding with my lips for a short, delicate kiss that tingled and made my knees weak. "You just needed a reminder."

Acknowledgements

Aubrey:

Here we go again! To my sweet Husband, who constantly deals with my gremlin behavior with grace and care, **I love you.** Thank you for ensuring I'm taking breaks, eating, and giving myself the credit I deserve for working this hard. Thank you for never giving up on me, for knocking sense into me when I'm emotionally out of control. You are my rock. The Dean to my Cas. You are the reason I get to live my dream every single day.

My friends, family, and trusted confidants. You are the heroes in my stories, you are the inspiration for every bit of banter and the softness in every single found family moment. Thank you for never giving up on me. Incoming stupid group name drop: My Holy Trinity, Sam, Sid, Zach & Sarah. My Freakshow, Twinkle Toes (The Drew to my Punk), my Golden Girls, my Lil Fucks, my Hornets Nest, and my Sugar Club. I love you guys endlessly.

To my ride-or-die Editor, Bec. You never cease to amaze me with your support and love for me. Even with miles of ocean and land between us you have become a constant in my life that I could not be more grateful for. I love you and hope you enjoyed your part in Orchid Lane. My Alpha and Beta readers – Every single one of you that found the time to help me on this journey. I love you more than Cael Cody loves attention. **I couldn't do this without you.**

Rowan, thank you until the end of time for hopping onto this wagon as it sped on fire down a rocky hill on rickety wheels. Your support and time spent shaping Orchid Lane will not go unnoticed. I cannot possibly express my gratitude for your company, ideas, and hilariously kind personality. Your brain is so creative, and your heart is so big. I look forward to running in more bullshit circles with you in the future.

Now, bear with me. *This one is for Dean Winchester.* Growing up, family hasn't always been easy. There have been moments I want to forget, moments I'll treasure until the end of time. Regardless of what was going on around me, I had Dean Winchester. At the ripe age of thirteen, dealing with pre-teen hormones navigating a world that seemingly would never be made for a brain quite like mine. I had Dean. A character filled with so much love, weirdness, and so unbiasedly himself. He taught me it's okay to like that show everyone teases, to remember the lines from every episode of the show that brings me joy, and to listen to my music—*no matter what genre it might be*—so loud it drowns out all those negative thoughts. He taught me to always say what's on my mind even if it earns me a few weird looks. Dean Winchester taught me to protect my family—blood or not—until the end of the road. To always offer my hand when others need help, no matter how big or tough the job. I learned to raise my sisters without resenting them and how to be unapologetically honest from that gun toting, pie loving, pop culture nerd. As weird as it sounds, my connection to this fictional character has made me who I am today. So this book is for Dean, who would fucking hate being trapped in a house where the food was rotten and he couldn't watch Scooby-Doo on repeat.

"A wise man once told me, 'family don't end in blood.' But it doesn't start there either. Family cares about you, not what you can do for them family's there; for the good, bad, all of it. They got your back, even when it hurts. That's family" - Dean Winchester

Rowan:

To my husband, who never even blinks an eye when I tell him I've started another project. Without you and your constant and unwavering support I would never be able to explore all the facets of my creative passions. You are so generous, and kind, and I can only hope you know how insanely in love with you I am, and no matter how many love stories I write, ours will always be my favourite.

To my besties, Aasha for always knowing how to read my jumbled thoughts and echo them back to me cohesively- I am so glad we share a braincell. Caitlin, for putting up with my story telling and prime emo writing since middle school, and always telling me I'm the best (and really believing it?) even though I know you are biased as hell. My bonus sister Kayla, for being the most supportive ray of sunshine in the universe, I know it will not be long before I am holding one of your books in my hands. Last but not least, Katie, who has constantly been a source of laughter and venting since the moment we decided "Oh, you? Yeah I love you. BFFEA" and was the first person outside of my home to know about Orchid Lane.

To my Parents and Grandma, who are only allowed to read the approved list of chapters I have specified. *I'm looking at you Dad.* Thank you for always fostering a home where I could be as silly and creative as I needed. Mom, thank you for spending an entire summer between the third and fourth grade, teaching me how to read in english before I transferred out of french immersion. Grandma, I love you more than you could ever imagine.

To Aubrey, I am so unbelievably grateful to you for taking me under your wing in and allowing me to adopt Florence, Wes, Koen and Clay as my own. It has always been a huge dream of mine to be published, and I mean it with my full chest when I say there is no way I would have gone for it without you, and The Manor on Orchid Lane. Thank you for taking it in stride when I texted you incessantly while I read it the first time, and then for saying: "Well buckle up, we are writing this together now." When instead of just a few notes, I gave you a whole damn book report and a list of ideas and chapters. If only baby Rowan and Aubrey passing notes and barely passing grade 12 math could see us now. You are the April to my Andy.

To the Reader, I hope you enjoyed unravelling The Manor on Orchid Lane as much as we did. There was so much love and care, and *fun*, put into this book. I cannot wait for the next.

Aubrey Taylor is a 32-year-old mom living in chilly Canada with her two kids and wonderful husband. Raised by Dean Winchester, Percy Jackson, and horror movies. She's a loud, nerdy, sarcastic lover of stories. Her favourites always including chosen families and adventure. She has been writing and creating stories from her dreams ever since she could remember. With massive emotions of her own, she puts her entire heart into her characters and stories. Aubrey's favorite genres are fantasy, reverse harem romance, and contemporary romance!

CURRENT WORKS AND COMING SOON:

Bad Honey (Hornets Nest Series)

The Manor of Orchid Lane

Honey Pot (Hornets Nest Series – Jan 2025)

Rowan Stone is a 31 year old Bi woman bursting with neurodivergency whose life motto is "hope for the best" and considers herself a "professional five year old". She radiates golden retriever energy, though is a Scorpio with a glass face and an inflated sense of justice (especially when it comes to looking after others) that can get her in trouble.

Despite a her love of romance, she never really expected to find "that can't-eat, can't-sleep, reach-for-the-stars, over-the-fence, World Series kind of stuff" herself, when she was whisked off her feet by meeting her future husband on a dating app. Now she lives in a home that she designs in a style she calls "dopamine decorating" with her Husband, and her best friend, their black lab and two cats. She has many hobbies, but has always fostered a love of writing. She never expected her life long dream of being published a possibility until kind words from an old friend gave her the courage to try.

CURRENT WORKS:

The Manor of Orchid Lane